HONOR

BY JAY CROWNOVER

The Breaking Point Series
Honor

The Saints of Denver Series
Charged
Built
Leveled (novella)

The Welcome to the Point Series
Better When He's Brave
Better When He's Bold
Better When He's Bad

The Marked Men Series
Asa
Rowdy
Nash
Rome
Jet
Rule

HONOR
The Breaking Point

JAY CROWNOVER

wm

WILLIAM MORROW
An Imprint of HarperCollins*Publishers*

HONOR. Copyright © 2016 by Jennifer M. Voorhees. All rights reserved. Printed in the United States of America. No part of this book may be used or reproduced in any manner whatsoever without written permission except in the case of brief quotations embodied in critical articles and reviews. For information address HarperCollins Publishers, 195 Broadway, New York, NY 10007.

HarperCollins books may be purchased for educational, business, or sales promotional use. For information please e-mail the Special Markets Department at SPsales@harpercollins.com.

FIRST EDITION

Designed by Diahann Sturge

Library of Congress Cataloging-in-Publication Data has been applied for.

ISBN 978-0-06-243556-9

16 17 18 19 20   RRD   10 9 8 7 6 5 4 3 2 1

Honestly, I want to keep this book all to myself. I'm full-on obsessed with it. I'm obsessed with the man and the myth. I'm obsessed with the romance and the spectacle. I've never had any character hound me, haunt me, and hunt me the way this unapologetic devil did. I loved every freaking minute of it. So yeah . . . I think I'm going to dedicate this one to me, myself, and I. I had an outrageous love affair with words and writing while telling this story.

Something tells me the man responsible for my fixation would wholeheartedly approve.

INTRODUCTION

I have a feeling this book is going to prove harder to read than it was to write. I wrote like a demon, which is par for the course when you're bringing the devil to life. But if you've made it this far in the world of the Point, we both know you're made of pretty tough stuff, open to adventure and willing to read a story that might hurt a little bit on the way to the last page.

As with all my books set in the Point, this one has moments of splendid exaggeration and taking things as far as they can go, but unlike the other books, this one starts in a place so much worse than the Point and gives a backstory to our devil that is, unfortunately, all too real.

When I first introduced Nassir in *Better When He's Bad*, I knew I wanted him to get his own story and that he was going to be the actual big bad in the Point. His cunning and quiet brutality were impossible to ignore the more and more the world grew with him at the center of it. I also knew the only way he could exist in the world I was creating, unfazed and unaffected by the darkness and carnage around him, was if he originated from a place that made the Point look like Disneyland. Sadly, there are so many places in our world that have been at war with each other regardless of innocence and loss of life for far too long. I knew that as cool and collected as Nassir was in all the previous books in which he appeared, he had to come from a place that was always bathed in tension and unrest, so I picked the part of the Middle East that has never known peace.

I remember reading about the West Bank when I was in middle school, and then again hearing about the turmoil in high school current events class, and then in college I met people my own age from that area of the world and felt so sad for them, sad that they were never going to know peace because their homeland would never be safe. It was tragic then and it's tragic now. That area of the world is always locked in a state of unrest that can flare up at a moment's notice. Nassir needed to be a man born into such violence so that what happens in the Point really meant nothing to him.

I wanted this book to be both current and relevant. It is both those things, but it also managed to turn out achingly romantic and surprisingly poignant. Our devil is full of surprises, and I'm so excited for everyone to finally find out what makes the man with all the plans in the Point tick.

Welcome back . . . we've knocked on the devil's door long enough . . . he's finally decided to invite us all in.

xoxo

Jay

The only difference between the saint and the sinner is that every saint has a past, and every sinner has a future
—Oscar Wilde

PROLOGUE

I was a man born into a fight for things I didn't understand, things that held no value to me even as I grew into adulthood. Money, oil, land, power, prestige, the right religion, the proper beliefs . . . they were just words. They were the battle cry that tore from my lips before I even knew how to speak in full sentences.

I was a man given life by a woman fueled by rage and anger, in a place that fed on those very things. Her cause became my own, and even though her fight was never mine, I wanted to make her proud, wanted to be a good son, so I let the things that filled her up and burst out of her bleed onto me. I lived inside her hatred and animosity for so long it was all I knew. I took her cause as my own. Only none of it led to my mother's approval or adoration. I was never nurtured or coddled. Instead I was honed and molded into a thing that barely had any scraps of humanity left inside of it. There was no childhood, only revenge and vengeance. To her, that was how I honored her and my deceased father. It was how she forced me to honor a cause that was never mine.

My mother was a widow and I was a fatherless son caught between cultures and seeking revenge for deeds that I had no concept of. I was nothing more than an instrument of destruction, and often used to obliterate things I didn't understand, things that mattered nothing to a boy, to any child. Mother knew best, and I followed blindly. I was never allowed a childhood or any semblance of a happy healthy home life. We lived in a war zone and our home was part of the battlefield. We were soldiers, not a family. I played with weapons, not with children my own age. I learned war tactics and how to handle explosives before I knew how to read and write.

Before I grew facial hair or reached my full height, I had already done and seen more than any child—any person— should. And with each new and increasingly violent and dangerous act I committed, with each new violation to my tender soul, I thought I would finally make my mother proud. In my young and untried mind, I foolishly thought that once she was proud, once her burning need for revenge was sated, I would be set free. Once the war was won, I could go back to being a normal boy. It was naive to think like this in a place that was historically unstable and soaked with the blood of the innocent.

There was no end in sight, and as I grew, as I became more skilled, my mother became more feared and ferocious. Her soul seemed to become greedier and more bloodthirsty. Soon it wasn't enough to go after the people, the men she felt had wronged her, the men and the government they represented that had taken my father away. No, she wanted the entire infrastructure to collapse. She wanted to wage war on an ancient land, which had conflict soaked into every grain of sand that filled its hostile desert landscape. It was futile, but she wouldn't listen to reason or to the pleas of her scared and scarred son. She handed me off to men who continued to use me to kill and destroy, all before I had even kissed my first girl. My mother never said good-bye or explained where I was going. She never once let me believe that I had lived up to her expectations of me or let me fool myself into believing that I had ever managed to honor the memory of my late father.

The rest of the world hears words like "holy war," "the Gaza Strip," "the promised land," "fundamentalist terrorism," "infighting," "genocide," and can turn on CNN or click on a link to see shaky footage of bombs dropping in the desert, but for me it was my day-to-day. I wasn't just part of a war . . . I *was* the war. A man with an American mother and an Arab father and no place that was mine. The men whom I was handed over to, basically a trained child solider already with bodies and blood on his hands, tried to stoke the blind rage inside of me that my mother had ignited at birth. They tried to take all of the hostile and horrific teachings I learned at my mother's side and turn me into a machine that was fueled only by the need to fight for customs and country. They tried to fill me up with the same kind of fury that my mother had inside of her because of the loss of my father, who had sacrificed his life fighting for the supposedly right side. Always the cause . . . it was everything to these people, and nothing but words to me. To me there was no right or wrong side. There was no promised land and hereditary right to the sand that blew everywhere and stung my skin. All I could see was the side with the highest body count and the side inflicting the most damage depending on what day it was. By the time I reached my midteens, I didn't want anything to do with any of it and my loyalty to my mother and her cause was fractured enough that I was starting to see the world beyond it.

I wanted to be a man, not a weapon.

I was over it all, soul-sick and exhausted from living in a war zone, depleted from years of seeking my mother's approval, and then the acceptance and praise of the men who took me, all to no avail. Right at the moment when I was ready to surrender it all, give up myself for the only kind of peace I would ever know after all the horror I had created, the government came calling.

More accurately, I fell into their hands when they stopped the loaded-down truck I was supposed to be protecting. A truck full of explosives and headed for a primary school in a UN compound. I didn't want to protect the truck. I didn't want to be where I was. I didn't want to be anything or anyone. I couldn't see any more people die in a war they had never asked to be part of. If Mossad hadn't intercepted us, the truck would have blown long before it arrived at the school grounds, taking me and the actual devotees to the cause with it. I had my hand on the trigger of a submachine gun and was beyond ready to use it. Kids were innocent in all of this and there were lines, even then, that I would not cross. I couldn't— *wouldn't*—be used anymore, and I was finally ready to make a final and drastic stand.

My plan was to die by my own hand and to take as many of the bastards that had used me, handled me, and controlled me with me on the way out. It was the only way I thought I would be free of the goddamn cause that hung around my neck like a fucking albatross, but then Mossad ambushed us, snatched me up from death's door, and offered me a chance to vanish if I stayed with the cell I was embedded in as a double agent for five more years. I took them up on the offer without much of a second thought. I had no loyalty left, except to myself. I would dig up all the intel and turn it over with no qualms as long as I was guaranteed a way out. Gaining my freedom became my only goal.

That was my new cause to fight for, my new objective, and I didn't care that it was entirely self-serving.

All I wanted was out, and dropping bodies for a different, more organized, and better funded organization made the most sense if they were going to give me an exit. They dangled the golden carrot in front of me and I couldn't say no. Anonymity. Freedom. Forgiveness for every horrific crime they could pin on me. So I chased the carrot that hung in front of my eyes until my legs gave out. I signed on to kill the "right" people for the wrong reasons, from the inside . . . anything motivated by money and political goals to me smacked of immorality, and there was about as much honor in setting up young zealots to die as there had been in killing for my mother's revenge and shattered heart.

I turned over sleeper cell after sleeper cell. I prevented bombings and bloodshed. I kept weapons out of the wrong hands and led the right people to them. I burned drug fields and turned over more money than I thought I would ever see in one lifetime to the proper authorities. I uncovered secrets and plans for attacks worldwide. I uncovered the location of terrorist camps and led more than just my government to the hidden locations in various hot spots around the globe while I played go-between for my government's special operations and whoever they were in bed with at any given time. If there was something darker than black ops, that was where I was operating, and I hadn't even grown out of my teenage years yet. I did everything that was asked of me, got in as deep as I could go, and once my time was up, the five years come and gone with more bodies and blood than I cared to think about, I fully expected the powers that be to keep up their end of the bargain.

I trusted them, like a fool. My mom had taught me better than that.

I should have known better than to blindly believe anyone with an agenda. I knew better than to think a human being ever came before a conviction or powerful people with ulterior motives and deep pockets.

The government wasn't an extremist organization fighting for a belief, even if their motives and schemes were just as corrupt as any group labeled terrorists by the media. No, they were a massive political empire with their own endgame and motives to retain power and prestige, and I knew I couldn't just walk away from them without repercussions. It was then that I realized there was more to the war than the winning side and the losing side. I realized there was my side. The side of the fighter. The side of the man going through the motions, not out of passion, but because he had no other choice. There was the side of desperation, and on that side, there were no rules. There was an army of one, and the war he fought was for survival and self-preservation.

When my five years was up, I was barely in my twenties; Mossad came back with more missions, more targets, more things they needed my special skill set to handle. They had invested too much time and energy in me to simply let me vanish into thin air. It became clear that the only way I was getting away, the only way I was leaving the desert behind, was if I did it on my own terms. Even if those terms meant that my blood would end up staining the desert sand. My mother had long since taken her own life, just one more sacrifice for a belief I couldn't force myself to fight for anymore. I had no one and nothing left to lose.

I blew my cover on purpose. I let myself get caught, and when the bad guys tried to use me as leverage, tried to get the government to barter for me, I said nothing. I let them think I had value beyond my killing hands, and when the government and the military claimed they had no clue who I was, when they denied that I had ever worked for them, I let the men who had molded me and trained me take me back to where it all had started. I knew if I went with them I could finally have a chance at the one thing I had been after since I was old enough to figure out that what I was doing was wrong. Freedom. The chance to call my own shots for my own causes for once in my life. I knew the men who had turned a child into a killer wouldn't go easy on a traitor, a man who not only double-crossed them, but who willingly went against everything they thought was worth killing for. Part of me welcomed the fury and pain because it meant an end to being nothing more than a weapon.

They tortured me and threatened all the worst kinds of

punishment. I fully expected them to go after my head . . . literally.

But I was born into hell, so everything they did to me had already been done.

They wanted a spectacle. They wanted a show. They wanted something that they could put on TV so it got worldwide attention, so that the Americans would have to see what was going on in our little sandbox. I wanted to explain it was futile, that it was a lost cause. No one would care. *No one.*

I didn't bother. I needed them to take me into the center of their camp so I could get my hands on what I needed in order to become a ghost. Terror was well funded, and if this war had taught me anything, it was that the side with the most capital had the upper hand on the playing field. Always.

Lifeless on the inside. Empty. I was already a dead man, so they didn't expect a fight, but a fight was what they got. I could fight dirty and mean like them. I could fight cold and methodical like the government. But what would always give me the advantage over any adversary I faced was the first lesson my mother ever taught me. I had been born and bred to fight and never give up. The fight was in my bones. It was in every breath I exhaled. It was in every drop of blood that poured out of me and painted the soil.

I left no man standing. I took it all—money, guns, drugs— then I hiked what felt like a thousand miles into a desert that was even worse than the one that spawned me. Money in the right hands, guns in the wrong ones, making deals and promises as I slipped across borders and got myself on a freighter to that other promised land I'd heard so much about . . . America. Land of the free . . . home of the brave. To me it was just one big, sprawling, endless landscape of noise, people, confusion, and clutter that I could lose myself in. I would be another forgettable face in the crowd, and maybe I could finally stop the fight that had been hammered into me so hard that it felt like it was the only thing I was made of.

I bounced around a lot as soon as I hit the shore. I never got comfortable anywhere. I thought it was best to keep on the move just in case my old government or my new one was looking for me. Besides nothing seemed to fit. The glamour of L.A., the glitter of Vegas, the throb of New York . . . all of it felt wrong and made me antsy. There were things in each place that felt familiar, parts of each city that allowed me to sink into oblivion and indulge in all the ways I had been denied my entire life.

So many girls. So much money. So many different vices at my fingertips. I knew if I wasn't careful, I could easily become a slave to another master. Addiction made men weak and the last fight I wanted to fight, now that things had become so quiet, was one with myself. So I drifted and listened to the people deep in the shadows. People like me.

One place was uttered over and over again.

The Point.

From what they said, the city had apparently been a booming port town, but when the recession hit and the money left, it had fallen by the wayside. Empty shells of buildings were welcome signs to squatters, arsonists, and every denizen of the darkness . . . and so they came, the people that wanted to disappear and that wanted to make their money in obscurity and on the streets. Decades passed, so did hope for rebuilding, and the city—like too many places—had been forgotten by the rest of the country. Or so people said. Forgotten was what I needed, and so I listened to that whispered name. The Point.

I made more money and managed to see that more illegal goods changed hands and soon I found myself headed there. My old home received prime airtime on the national news . . . the home I was headed toward seemed to exist only in nightmares and warnings.

I was in the Point for less than a day when I got word that the man that ran the streets wanted to see me. I liked to lay low. I liked to blend in, but here it didn't seem like that was an option. Instead of desert sand, the battleground here was asphalt and concrete, and as soon as my presence was known, it was as if this place recognized the fight lying dormant inside of me. This city called to it. I don't know why I instantly felt like I fit, but I did. So I went to see the man in charge, fully expecting to offer him the last of my cash in order to gain a foothold in the desolate kingdom. I was a survivor. I could do without money for a little bit. No man was more resourceful than I was.

I walked into a disgustingly gaudy strip club, offended by its crass ugliness. I was expecting to meet the ruler of the land, state my intentions, and let him know I would bow to no man here or anywhere else ever again. I was expecting a shakedown and maybe some strong-arming since I was obviously foreign and undocumented. I was technically legal since my mother had been an American citizen before she fell in love with an extremist, but I hadn't really existed on paper since she handed me over to killers and radicals when I was just a kid. Mossad didn't want me to be anything other than their trained attack dog, so they hadn't offered up any proof of identity for me during my time at the end of their string. What I wasn't expecting was that my cause, my reason, my purpose for living, and my something to believe in would be dancing nearly naked on a horrifically ugly stage, looking like she was going to cry at any second. She was so much more than freedom.

She was Honor.

She was beautiful, young, innocent, and so obviously resigned to her fate. It pulled at a heart I was stunned to find I still had buried somewhere deep underneath the brutal history that filled up the inside of me. It was the first time I felt it beat, and the pulse of its yearning scared and electrified me in equal measure.

I started to move toward her like all those invisible gods I spent my life killing for were leading me directly to her when suddenly a man twice her age and triple her size leaped from his seat next to the stage and hurled himself up onto the platform directly at the girl. In the blink of an eye he was on top of her, rough hands all over her naked flesh. I heard her scream. I saw her long limbs flail and thrash under him. A red haze filled my vision and I forgot all about staying quiet and laying low. I forgot all about being a ghost, and realized that I could channel the fight that had been forged into my very soul, the fight that was slumbering restlessly inside me at that moment, into protecting something so innocent. She woke the fight up and she kept it alive.

I was on the stage before my mind even registered that I had moved across the room. I pulled the hulking man off the dancer and offered her my hand. Pretty eyes the color of an overcast sky glimmered up at me. She looked at the hand I'd offered like it was her lifeline out of this place, out of this vicious world, and clutched it ferociously as I pulled her to her feet.

We stared at each other in silence and I knew in that instant that this young woman would mean more than anything in my life had ever meant.

"Are you okay?"

She blinked at me like a terrified animal and I felt all the dead things inside me roar to life with new purpose and passion.

"Yeah. I could've handled him. He just surprised me."

She was so young and her words pounded into me so hard they hurt. She shouldn't have to handle him at all. I was the opposite of innocent and suddenly all I wanted was to keep her as different from me and my life as I could.

I squeezed the hand I still held and told her, "I'm Nassir Gates."

I gave her the name of the man I had decided I was going to be, half Middle Eastern, half American, one hundred percent lie. All the things I had done, all the things I had been, were no more. I was just a man that was going to make this new place his home. I didn't know at the time it was going to require as much blood and warfare to survive here as it had in the desert.

As the guy who attacked her started to make noise on the floor behind me, I turned to regard him. I was far from done with the bastard, but I wanted a proper introduction before I did what was inevitable the instant I watched the brute put his hands on her.

She smiled at me softly and returned the squeeze like we were going to be friends or something. "Keelyn Foster." Her eyes widened and she bit her plush lower lip, and I wanted to put my own teeth there more than I wanted anything in life. She was almost completely naked but I couldn't look away from those eyes. "I mean, Honor. Around here I'm Honor."

I smiled at her, and I was pretty sure it was the first time I had smiled. *Ever.* "How about I only call you that here in this club. I'm new in town but I have a feeling we'll be bumping into each other. Keelyn is a pretty name."

She blushed. She was gyrating for the pleasure of strangers, but giving her a throwaway compliment had her turning hot pink. And at the sight of her smile, everything suddenly made sense in my world.

"Thank you," she whispered, but I heard the words as loud as a thunderclap.

I inclined my head at her and turned around to the man trying to crawl his way back off the stage. I could be civilized. I could be restrained. I could be calm. But when I thought about those meaty paws all over her, I didn't want to be anything other than what I had been born to be . . . a killer.

I was on him between heartbeats. His face disintegrated under my hands. His bones turned to dust. His breath was stamped out under my feet. His life was nothing to me until I caught sight of stormy gray eyes looking at me like I was evil incarnate. Now they were the color of charcoal, and full of fear . . . fear *of me.* I shook the blood off my knuckles and walked away from her before I inflicted more damage.

The man in charge watched the whole thing go down. Instead of asking me for money to stay in his city, he offered me papers that were fake but good enough to make me legalish. He asked me if I could get my hands on some armor-piercing rounds. I said yes to both the papers and the ammo, and my plan for laying low swelled up like a balloon and popped right over my head. I would never be able to run from who I was, or what I was, so I figured I might as well make the most of it in this place that was eager to embrace it. This place was a different kind of war zone, where every man seemed to be fighting for himself. It was familiar enough that I knew I could thrive here, could find a place where I fit. I could absolutely work with what made the Point tick, and while here, I could watch the girl. I could wait for her while she realized this was hell on earth—and when you make your home in hell, you want to have the devil in your corner.

I could fight for her even if she thought I was a monster. After all, I already knew all about chasing a lost cause.

The devil's voice is sweet.
—Stephen King

CHAPTER 1

Keelyn

Maybe if I hadn't spent the last six months slinging pancakes and greasy hash to hungover hipsters and avoiding the too-curious eyes of the cops who liked to hit up the diner for early-morning breakfast, I would have noticed the ominous shift in the air.

Before I came to Denver six months ago, my senses had been honed to pick up on the slightest threat. Before, anything that might be dangerous, that might put me in peril, had made my skin tingle, made everything inside of me vibrate with awareness. Now I had settled into a simple, dreary rhythm. Every day was the same as the one before it and there was no outside threat constantly hounding me, hunting me, haunting me. I let my guard down. I had gone soft, and as a result the biggest danger of them all managed to slip into my new normal without giving any kind of hint he was there.

My nonslip shoes—that were probably the ugliest things

ever made but absolutely necessary considering the greasy food the tiny kitchen pumped out—squeaked on the laminate floor as I made my way over to the lone patron who had taken the last available seat in my section. The massive plastic menu completely covered his face, but the Rolex on his wrist and the perfect cut of his suit jacket let me know he wasn't my typical kind of customer. There wasn't a flannel shirt or police blues in sight, and as I got closer, a whiff of something exotic and familiar engulfed my senses and stopped me in my tracks. Of all the things I had left behind, he was the one I had tried hardest to forget.

The tingling across my skin spread. My tummy tightened. Blood rushed loudly between my ears. My shaking fingers curled around the pen in my hand like it was a weapon. Before I could pull it together and walk away, the menu lowered and I was pinned to the spot, immobilized by eyes the color of spiced rum.

They were wicked eyes. Eyes that saw far too much and gave nothing away. Eyes I daydreamed about. Eyes that caused me to wake up in a cold sweat. Eyes that turned me inside out and shook me up as they made a slow perusal from the top of my head to the tips of my god-awful shoes, returning to my face and staying there as I struggled to keep my shit together.

He slowly put the menu down on the cracked tabletop and leaned back in the booth. He was strikingly out of place here and I absolutely hated how that sexy twist of his mouth, a mouth that I dreamed about almost every night, made my traitorous heart flutter and my pulse kick.

I was also strikingly out of place here, but I'd learned to

fake it. He, obviously, never bothered to fake anything. He wasn't a man with virtuous intentions and he never pretended to be.

Gone were the mile-high stilettos that I always wore. In their place I now donned work shoes that prevented me from falling on my ass as I ran food and dirty dishes to and from the kitchen. I was hiding in plain sight, knowing that the last place on earth anyone who might come looking for me would check out would be this greasy spoon. This was the opposite of me and the life I had always lived, so even though I could afford better, craved more, this was where I needed to be . . . until he showed up.

Gone was the long, flowing hair dyed the perfect shade of auburn and styled in a way meant to give men dirty ideas. In its place was a boring, brown bob that hit my chin. There was hardly enough hair left on my head to inspire men to do anything other than feel sorry for me. Gone were the short skirts that left nothing to the imagination, and the shirts cut down to my navel so that the boobs I paid a small fortune for were on obvious and prominent display. Today I wore faded skinny jeans with a hole in the knee and a plain black T-shirt that covered those spectacular boobs. I hadn't put on a full face of makeup in over six months, and since I was no longer dancing hours upon hours a night, I had put on some weight. I would never pass for a plain Jane, but I was close. Average was probably the first thing that came to mind when strangers laid eyes on me, especially if they didn't bother to look closely. I definitely wasn't the same girl that had left this man, and the world he not only came from, but ruled.

Those predatory eyes rolled over me again, and his lips twitched in amusement when they landed back on my ugly footwear. "Nice shoes, Key."

My fingers tightened instinctively on the pen I was clutching, and I heard the plastic crack under the pressure. I resisted the urge to shift in said ugly-ass shoes, and instead narrowed my eyes at him. Weakness around a killer should never be shown, and I knew this particular predator would eat me alive if he got even the slightest chance. He'd been hungry for a taste since the first day I met him, and while I had always been tempted to feed the beast, fear of losing more than my fingers to those vicious jaws always kept me from offering up myself on a platter. The only thing I ever wanted was to be my own person, to thrive and be independent, making my own rules and answering to no one. The only thing Nassir Gates wanted was for me to be his.

"What are you doing here, Nassir?"

Nassir Gates, half man and half monster. He was lethal and toxic, keeping all that sinister beauty covered up in a ridiculously expensive suit that made him look elegant and falsely civilized. To the untrained eye, Nassir was an outrageously handsome man that looked like he was on his way to a business meeting, but if you had spent any time on the streets, if you were familiar with life in the gutter, there was no missing who he really was, what he was. The top of the food chain. If you knew about what it took to make it where I came from, you could look at Nassir and see that he not only thrived in chaos, but was comfortable there. He even managed to make it look good.

I left all of that behind. I liked Denver. I liked the laid-back vibe. I liked the monotony. I liked the predictability. I liked that I could walk to my car after my shift at the diner and not have to worry about taking a knife in the ribs or getting a revolver shoved in my back. I liked that I didn't have to shake my ass or get naked to pay my bills. I liked that here, soccer dads were just that, and weren't secretly banging hookers in the back room or gambling the family's grocery money away at an illegal poker game. Most importantly I liked that I didn't have to look my biggest addiction, my worst temptation, in the eye every single day and pretend like I didn't want him. Here I didn't have to deny that I had been infatuated with him for years. I was foolishly obsessed with this particular devil in a designer suit and I knew he was absolutely detrimental not only to my safety but to the thing I valued above all else . . . my independence.

After a childhood spent evading the hands of my mother's overzealous and unhinged boyfriends and barely escaping the clutches of a sick and twisted stepfather, and too many years working my ass off—literally—to make a life for myself, I could never risk letting myself care for Nassir the way I wanted to because I knew that if I did, I would become nothing more than his, and I refused to be any man's possession or accessory.

When the opportunity arose to take off without an explanation or without looking like I was running from him and the promise and future I saw so clearly in his eyes, I grabbed it. Ran away with both my heart and my tail tucked between my legs. But now he was here in this fragile and predictable paradise and I wanted to stab him with the broken pen and jump in his lap and put my mouth on his smirking lips all at the same time.

"*You're* here, Key. Where else would I be?"

His inky-black hair was longer than I remembered, touching the collar of his shirt, and his voice was even smoother and more musical than I recalled. He spoke with just the barest hint of an accent, which no one could pin down the origins of, and Nassir wasn't the kind of guy who offered up even the tiniest sliver of personal information. He was a beautiful tawny color no matter what time of the year, so I always assumed that with his dark hair and golden complexion, he had to have come from somewhere in the Middle East. He never confirmed or denied my suspicions. All I knew was that he'd landed in the Point when I had just started stripping, and from the second he stepped into the scene, he had been at the center of all the action. He had also always been the one danger I was smart enough to steer clear of. A task that grew harder and harder the older I got, and the more aware I became of him and the pull he had over me.

"You shouldn't be here. I don't want you here." I hated that my voice dipped. I was never a very good liar and I never wanted him to know he was my greatest weakness even though he had never hidden the fact that I was his.

His dark eyebrows lowered over those golden eyes and the smirk fell off his too pretty mouth. Luckily, another table called me over and I had to run back to the kitchen. It gave me a much-needed minute to get my head back on straight. I should have known that just the sight of him after all these months would be enough to throw me totally off my stride. He was that impressive. That consuming. That hard to quit.

I was headed back toward his table with a mug and a pot of coffee when a light hand landed on my arm. I looked at the pretty redheaded cop that came in all the time. Sometimes with her partner or other cops, but more often than not with her boyfriend. They must have lived close by because she was often going to work when he was getting off. He ran a bar, or a couple of them, here in town, so their hours were opposite, but they seemed to be making it work. At first I couldn't believe someone that looked like her carried a badge on purpose or that she seemed to be genuinely interested in being my friend. She mentioned that we had a mutual acquaintance that had asked her to check up on me when I first got to town, but now she seemed to be curious about me all on her own. She was so lovely and fun, plus her man was a charmer. Blond and way too handsome for his own good, he reminded me of an old flame I had back in the Point. I was intimately acquainted with men like him, only the pretty cop's boyfriend didn't have the same kind of ruthless edge the Point bred in the men I was familiar with. But the southern charmer had his own kind of dangerous and sexy aura that led me to believe his story would be an interesting one if he bothered to share it.

"Are you okay? You look like you just saw a ghost." She was sweet but she was looking at me with cop eyes, and there weren't enough hours in a day to try to explain to her all the things that were wrong with Nassir sitting at that battered little table in this run-down diner in Colorado. He should be anywhere but here.

"Yeah, just busy." I gave her a weak smile and stopped to fill up a few more cups of coffee before going back to Nassir's table with resolve. I took the mug, set it in front of him and filled it up. I nudged it toward him with a scowl.

"Coffee's on the house. Drink it and leave. I don't have anything else to say to you."

He looked at the coffee and then back up at me. His eyebrows shot up and the smirk returned to his mouth. It was such an arrogant look. I wanted to smack it off his beautiful face.

"Well, can you sit down for a minute? I have plenty to say to you."

I shook my head before he was even done speaking. "No. My section is full. I'm working. I don't want to hear anything you have to say. The Point is dead to me. You're dead to me." My voice dropped again as I threw the words out. I really should be a better liar. I used to sell the illusion that I wanted sex, that I loved grabby hands and clawing fingers all over my body every single day, and I did it with a purpose. I could be whoever I needed to be as long as it benefited me in the long run. For a while I told myself that once I had enough money saved up, I would do something good with it, something that would help girls like myself that had no other options, but instead I took the coward's way out and ran. I was so scared of losing me that I didn't give a second thought to the good I could do or to the women that needed me back home. Convincing this man and myself that I hated him was a battle I had never been able to win. "I left Honor behind, Nassir. She's six feet under."

He leaned forward in the booth and that sexy, expensive scent that seemed to naturally be a part of him almost brought me to my knees. I wanted to inhale him, to absorb him . . . and that was the problem.

"I came here to talk to you, Keelyn, not to Honor. I know the difference."

I let out a bitter, broken-sounding laugh and pushed some of my short, basic brown hair back behind my ear. "Do you?"

Honor was the stage name I used when I'd danced at the Point's most popular strip club, Spanky's. Honor was beautiful. Sexy. Strong. I was none of those things anymore, by choice, but the reminder of the life I had left behind and the woman that flourished there still stung. Spanky's was a hive of illegal activity. It was run by mobsters. It was a den of sin and debauchery. It had been home. I refused to miss it or the girl who had grown up there, but with Nassir right here in front of me, that was much easier said than done.

"I always did." His accented voice got a little rough and I almost bolted out the front door when shivers tap-danced down my spine. "I have a business proposition for you, Key. I want you to come home."

I put my hands on the edge of the table and leaned closer to him. I felt like I was drowning in his scent and being pulled in closer and closer by his unwavering gaze. We were almost nose to nose. I was breathing hard and could see the way his Adam's apple bobbed up and down the nearer I got.

"I. Am. Never. Coming. Back." I pushed off the table, snatching up the coffee carafe, and pointed a finger at him. "Go away, Nassir. This is a nice place. This is a nice life. I've never asked you for a goddamn thing, but I'm asking you not to screw this up for me." I'd never asked him but he had always shown up and done what needed to be done regardless.

When other girls had to fight off the advances from the handsy club owner or risk losing shifts, I never worried. When other girls got so desperate for money they were willing to turn tricks and work on their backs, the thought never crossed my mind. When I got sick and had to miss work for an extended period of time, he made sure I saw a doctor and got the proper medical treatment, and I knew he was the only reason I had a job to go back to when I was better. Strippers that couldn't dance weren't of any use, and since Spanky's was one of the few clubs with a guaranteed clientele, I knew I could be easily replaced. It was smart for women to stay inside after dark in my old town, but I had never been trapped indoors and hidden undercover. Nassir pulled strings I never even knew were tied to my life, and because of him, the Point always felt like home, even when it tried to kill me.

If I hadn't been so aware of him, so attuned to his every movement, his every breath, I wouldn't have seen his hands tighten into fists on the cracked tabletop. Nassir wasn't the type to show any kind of emotion, so that tiny little movement showed me he was hearing what I was saying to him. And he didn't like it.

He uncurled his fingers and started to tap them on the table. His eyes glimmered with hellfire and his sexy mouth tightened. He wasn't happy, but he wasn't going to push me. He gave a nod that was just the barest tipping of his chin and then started to slide out of the booth toward me. I knew I should move away, that I needed to keep space between the two of us, but I stood stock-still as he got up and took a step forward so that we were toe-to-toe. He seemed even taller than he had been when I left, more imposing. I had to tilt my head back to continue meeting that amazing gaze.

He reached out and I thought he was going to run the backs of his fingers over my cheek, but the tricky bastard went right for my heart. Unerringly, his palm landed high on my chest and off to the side right where a bullet had torn through me. Right where it had flayed me open and finally shown me that the Point, and the things that I loved in it, were going to be the end of me no matter how tough I was. My heart tried to jump into his hand, and I gasped a little as he smiled at me. A real smile. One that made his sharply angled face softer, made his eyes melt like soft candy. No, my devil wasn't going to push me . . . he was going to do what devils did best. He was going to tempt me.

"I think this life is too easy for you. There's no challenge here. I waited for months because I thought you were going to get bored. You don't belong here, Key, but if you're happy here, then I won't be back. Things are changing in the Point. You should be a part of that."

His hand felt like it was searing into my chest. It seemed like the ugly scar the bullet had left behind would magically vanish and the print of his hand would mark me there in its place.

"The Point always changes, and it's never for the better. I need you to go."

I took a step back from him and it felt a million times harder than all the steps I had taken to get my ass out of the Point and away from him in the first place. Nassir looked down at his expensive watch, gave me one last smirk, and then disappeared out the front door. It should have been easier to breathe with him gone. I should have felt solid, safe, but like he always did, Nassir shifted the world around him.

The pretty cop was at my side again, and this time the concern on her face couldn't be ignored. She was looking in the direction in which Nassir had disappeared, and I would bet good money everything inside her was screaming that he was a bad guy. That she shouldn't let him walk away.

"Ex-boyfriend?"

I sighed and waved at a table of customers that were making air gestures at me for their bill.

"Not even close." My relationship with Nassir was beyond complicated, but we had never so much as held hands. I went out of my way not to touch him, not to accidentally brush up against him, and the only time he had ever had his hands on me was when he was trying to stop the bleeding when I got shot, and then today when he placed his hand on the same spot. "We used to work together. He's an unwelcome blast from the past."

She waited on me while I cashed out a few customers and refilled some drinks. I got a new table, and by the time I got the new customer's order started, she was leaning against the front door. I didn't have to keep talking to her, but she was sweet and she knew nothing of my life before, so there was no judgment in her chocolaty-brown gaze as she watched me scuttle around.

"I have to go . . . my shift starts in a few." She smiled at me and lifted one of her rusty-colored eyebrows. "I know we aren't exactly friends, but I am a trained observer and I know a thing or two about the kind of guy that oozes trouble and secrets like that one does. You can totally tell me that I'm crossing the line, but I feel obligated to tell you to be careful."

I gave her a weak smile in return. It was so funny that anyone thought they had to warn me about anything. I used to be the girl that *was* the warning. *Don't end up like Keelyn. Don't make the same choices Keelyn made. Do you want to be a stripper like Keelyn? What does Keelyn have to show for a life of hard work and fighting to survive?* I had me and I was bound and determined to hold on to her until my very last breath.

"Believe me, I've always been careful around him. He won't be back, though, so I don't think you or I have to worry about it."

As soon as the words were out of my mouth, I felt like I was going to fall over. I would never see him again. I would never hear that smoky, lilting voice again. I would never smell that spicy, mysterious scent again. It felt different when I had been the one to walk away, but now that I'd sent him away, told him in no uncertain terms that I was never coming home, it felt so final. It burned worse than the bullet that had almost killed me.

"Well, if you're ever interested in getting out and about, I know some very cute single guys."

That made me laugh. Sex and anything having to do with the opposite sex had been the last thing on my mind until the second Nassir had popped back up in my life. The last six months had been the longest I had ever gone without a companion, without boys telling me I was beautiful and giving me whatever I wanted. Being by myself had been enlightening, but it had also made the impact Nassir had on me all the more tangible and strong. My skin was still too tight and my heart was still beating too fast, proving it wasn't just any pretty boy with a wicked smile who could turn my life inside out.

"Maybe I'll take you up on that one day. Right now I need to finish my shift and pretend like I'm not totally freaking out on the inside."

"Okay. And just so you know, I am very familiar with the things that can hide in the dark. If you ever want to talk about where that beautiful man came from and why he made you turn as white as a sheet, it's a story I would be happy to hear."

I waved at her as she walked out the front door. I never had many female friends, at least not any that didn't take their clothes off and grind on laps the same way I did, and I really liked the pretty policewoman. The last thing I wanted to do was pull the curtain back and introduce her to Honor. I didn't want that crafty bitch anywhere near Denver.

I shook it all off—Nassir's surprise visit, the cop's probing questions, the reminder that I used to have a very different life—and focused on finishing up my shift. It was mindless. Take orders, get the food out, refill drinks, smile and nod a bunch. Repeat for nine hours and then drag my butt back to my tiny little studio so I could scrub out the smell of bacon and eggs from my hair and veg out until it started all over again the next day. Only today, after my shower, I couldn't stop the past from pulling at me. I couldn't get Nassir out of my mind. Couldn't get all the memories that were attached to him from buzzing around in my brain.

I started dancing at Spanky's when I was barely eighteen. A runaway with a nightmarish home life and a stepdad with wandering hands. Back then, I'd been scared out of my mind and achingly desperate to have a life and a place of my own. At that point, a callous and cold-blooded crime boss who went by the name of Novak held the club—and the city— in a choke hold. Even though there was a no-touching rule in effect when the girls were onstage, it was hardly ever enforced. I was doing a routine to some stupid pop song, trying hard to stay upright on shoes that were too tall and too ridiculous for words, when a burly, drunk patron lunged at me. I was trapped under his sweaty flab while he groped at my naked boobs and pawed at my barely-there G-string. It was terrifying and all too familiar. Just when I thought the worst was going to happen right out in the open, in front of everyone, the bulk had disappeared, and what looked like a fallen angel loomed over me, offering me a hand.

Even back then he dressed like a million bucks. His hair was nothing like the midnight locks he wore now; then it was military short and he was much leaner than the tightly muscled warrior's body he had now. His eyes glowed like hellfire, and I almost threw myself back to the ground at his feet. He was that potent. He smiled at me with that sinful mouth and asked me if I was okay. I told him I could have handled the situation myself because I really wanted to believe I could have, but it was clear in those magnetic and mysterious eyes, the first time we stared at each other, that he wanted to take

care of things for me. It scared me. That kind of possessiveness from a man I didn't know . . . a man that made my young
heart quiver and my foolish body warm and melty. I didn't
have anything of my own yet and all I wanted to do was hand
what little I did have over to him. That kind of acquiescence
terrified me. The desire to simply let him take control of a
life I hadn't yet gotten the chance to live made me throw up
every single barrier I could think of, and had started the dance
between us that we had been doing for years. He almost killed
a man in front of me with his bare hands, and yet it was the
threat he posed to my newly found freedom that had me keeping him at arm's length when I really wanted to pull him as
close as I could.

After that unforgettable introduction, the only time I saw
Nassir was after backroom deals with Novak at the strip club,
or when I made my way to the underground club he owned.
Nassir quickly became the guy in the Point that could get his
hands on anything and everything that was bad for you. If he
didn't have it on hand, he knew the people that did. Novak
was now no more than dust and bad memories, but Nassir's
power had only grown.

Last year his club—the front for all his illegal activities—
had burned down when the city found itself caught in the
middle of a war for control after Novak was killed. As a result,
Nassir had moved into Spanky's, and every single day I went
to work felt like I was dancing for an audience of one. His eyes
watched my every move, and even though I worked mostly
naked, I felt even more exposed than I was. He kept me safe
while letting me grow into the undeniably sexy and powerful

woman I was meant to become, and all the while I tiptoed around him and the fact that I knew if I ever let him have me, I would belong to him heart and soul forever. We played a tense game of advance and retreat, but I knew enough to stay out of the kill zone, and for whatever reason Nassir let me play with the fire but never let me get close enough to burn. I never understood his motivations, but since his actions let me live a full and mostly happy life in a place that destroyed most people's souls, I never questioned why he did what he did.

When the war barged through the front door of the Point and I ended up bleeding out on the floor of a strip club, I realized his motivations came from a place deeper than the undeniable attraction we had for each other. His heart was in his eyes as he tried to stop the steady stream of blood leaking out of my shoulder and I would never forget that it looked just like me.

I was never ashamed of being a stripper. I was proud of how long I lasted, more like thrived, in the Point, but it was Nassir ripping his shirt off to hold it to my bleeding shoulder and looking at me like I was the only thing in the world he cared about, that really made me feel like I had to leave. That look was enough to make me give him everything I had once and for all, and if I did that, there would be nothing left of me. I would just be some pretty girl tied to a dangerous and powerful man, and when his life turned on him like it was bound to do, I would be left alone with nothing. That wasn't something I could bear. So of course I left, and now I had sent him away, making sure he knew I would never be going back to him or that life.

It was enough to keep me up most of the night, hating the

girl who looked back at me in the mirror as I brushed my boring and nondescript hair the next morning. I groaned when I pulled out my work shoes and scowled at the drawerful of T-shirts, folded-up jeans, and yoga pants when I started to get dressed for my shift. Normally, I found all of these basic things comforting and calming; what I wore was a solid costume and the girl that wore it served me well. But for some reason, today she made me furious. Somewhat defiantly, I pulled on the frilliest, most see-through, sexiest, completely nonfunctional underwear I had brought with me from my old life, under the drab garb. Instantly the part of me that had spent so many years being Honor sparked with signs of life. I hated how good it felt, but I didn't change my outfit. No, I took it a step further and slicked on some lip gloss that was also buried in the back of a drawer. It was the closest I had come to dolling up or appealing to my own vanity in what felt like forever.

Refusing to acknowledge how deeply Nassir's visit rattled me, I headed the short distance to the diner, prepared to immerse myself back into my routine. There was absolutely nothing wrong with slinging greasy food to hipsters. It was a perfectly acceptable way to make a living until I figured out what I wanted to do with my sizable savings from my old life and the chances of catching a bullet or falling for an enigmatic and mysterious crime boss were almost nil. I was happy-ish here. I was secure here. I didn't have to fight to survive here. Nassir was right: there was no challenge and that's what I wanted. I had earned a break after all the Point and he had put me through.

Since I worked the morning shift, I got to the diner just as the sun was coming up over the mountains. It was really early and the parking lot was empty like it was every single day. But for some reason, today it seemed even emptier. I locked the car door behind me and made my way across the asphalt, my mind still stuck on my surprise visitor from yesterday. Once again I was reminded that I had lost my edge, that I had gone soft, when hard hands grabbed my arms from behind and spun me around, almost knocking me off my feet.

I gasped in surprise and jerked myself away from the grasping hands. I had seen the guy around before. He liked to hang out in front of the diner and beg for change. Usually the cops chased him off and sent him on his way, and usually, if I thought about it, I would make him a box of goodies when the kitchen switched over from the breakfast menu to lunch. He had never spoken to me, and I was stunned he put his hands on me now.

He lurched forward, his eyes a little crazy and his hands outstretched as I stumbled back another step.

"Hey, buddy. Knock that shit off. I don't have anything for you."

His eyes were wide in his dirty face and I could smell his rancid breath as he stumbled closer and closer to me. I didn't know what was wrong with him, but when he reared back and took an actual swing at me with his closed fist, I had had enough. I shoved him away from me, and when he stumbled and fell back on his butt, I put my hands on my hips and glowered down at him.

"What in the hell is your problem? You do realize that this is a restaurant filled with cops, don't you? Do you want to get hauled off to jail?"

He swore at me and the next thing I knew a rock came

flying at my head. At first I thought it was just a little pebble, but suddenly I was on the ground looking up at the early-morning sky and I could feel blood leaking down across my face. I blinked to try to get my bearings when a heavy kick thudded into my side. The homeless guy loomed over me, looked like he wanted to say something, but when I went to pick myself up off the ground, he took off running.

My head was throbbing. I could tell by the amount of blood oozing that I had a nasty gash and my ribs were scream-ing from the blow. What in the hell? This wasn't supposed to happen here. Denver was supposed to be my sanctuary. If I was going to get jumped in the parking lot walking to work, I might as well just go back home . . . where it would never happen because no one messed with the girl that Nassir Gates had claimed as his own.

I rubbed the back of my hand across my bloody forehead and frowned in the direction the homeless guy had taken off in. It was a random and completely unprovoked attack. It was almost like someone had put the guy up to it. I groaned as I climbed to my feet and dusted off the back of my jeans. I would bet a million dollars someone *had* put the homeless guy up to jumping me.

I knew my devil never played fair and that he was capable of doing anything . . . regardless of the outcome, to get his own way. Pushing didn't work. Tempting didn't work. So he had re-sorted to trying to scare me home. The prick. I was probably going to have another scar to go with the one on my chest.

Too bad he didn't know the only thing in the world I was actually afraid of was him.

CHAPTER 2

Nassir

Surprised to see you flying solo, boss. I figured that even if she told you to take a hike, you woulda hauled her back over your shoulder."

The light in the office gleamed off Chuck's bald head and made his ebony skin glimmer as he chuckled at me. I shoved my hands through my long hair and sighed.

"I thought about it. She's dug in, and right now there's no shaking her loose."

"You've been paying that PI in Colorado to keep an eye on her. He didn't tell you any of that?"

I sighed again and curled my fingers into my hair. "He did. He told me she has a routine, keeps to herself, and seems to be doing all right for herself. All I heard was that she's slipped into a predictable pattern, and that makes her an easy target. I thought seeing me would shake her up."

Chuck grunted and unfolded his massive frame from the

love seat he dwarfed. He smoothed his silk tie down the front of his shirt and tugged on its pressed cuffs. I knew for a fact the cuff links in the sleeves were sporting lots of flawless diamonds surrounded by real gold. The man was a snappy dresser, which was just another reason I had no trouble letting him represent me and my business interests.

"I think seeing you might give her nightmares, boss. The girl survived in hell for most of her life and now she's living the dream on easy street. She made it out. You should be happy for her, not trying to drag her back into the sludge."

"The dream is not waiting tables at some run-down greasy spoon and pretending to be someone she's not. Beautiful things grow in the sludge, my friend. Haven't you ever seen a lotus flower?"

Chuck grinned at me again and cuffed me on the outside of the arm. He was so big and so strong the simple gesture almost knocked me over. I scowled at him and pushed off the desk.

"Key isn't a flower. She's a girl that got put into a hard spot way too young and has always done everything she had to do in order to survive. Sound familiar?"

I didn't answer.

Not many people knew about where I had been before I called the Point home, but Chuck did. When I offered him the job as my head of security, he had agreed only as long as he knew who exactly it was he was going to work for. I gave him the same old song and dance I gave anyone when they asked about my past, but Chuck was smart. He was halfway out the door before I realized he was serious, so begrudgingly I laid it all out for him. Who I was and the things I had done . . . he hadn't run. Hadn't even blinked an eye, just told me that was a sad story but there were a million more like it in the Point, so I better stop thinking I was special and that I should quit using my past as an excuse for all my shitty actions.

"You have the fight set up for tonight?" I walked around the metal desk and took a seat behind it. In my old office, my desk was hand-carved mahogany and it took an army of strong backs to move across the floor. I missed the finer things in life, so with or without Keelyn here to take the spot I kept reserved by my side, I needed to get the ball rolling on the new club. The club had started all about her and as a way to bring her home and keep her here, but now the new club had to be all about the bottom dollar. I couldn't wait any longer on the business part. I felt like I could wait on the girl forever, was pretty sure I had been.

"Race set it up. He brought in a ringer from Vegas to take on that grease monkey that works for Bax who's been unstoppable the last few weekends."

Race was a good partner. He understood money and the lengths people would go to get it and how easily they would spend it when you offered them something they wanted. He was crafty and understood the tricky ebb and flow of the streets. He didn't trust me. It was always good to have a partner that was watching what you did like a hawk. It kept me as honest as I was ever going to get, and when I tried to cross the invisible line from shady into downright evil, he was usually the one there to pull me back from the edge. We didn't like each other very much but we made a good team, and as long as the money kept rolling in, I had no problems sharing the profit or the reins with him.

"Bax know about the ringer? He's gonna be pissed if we take his guy out." Shane Baxter, Bax to those that had watched him run the streets since he was just a punk kid, was Race's best friend and pretty much the undisputed gatekeeper of the city. He used to boost cars for the old crime boss and he was still helping Race collect debts that were owed on the side. Not much went down or happened in the Point without Bax's approval. He was also Novak's son and the half brother of the cop that was screwing the knockout I hired to manage my strip club. The big bruiser also used to be one of the top earners in the circle of blood. The boy was connected and not someone I actively tried to piss off even if the way he had of going about things was far brasher than how I liked to operate.

Chuck dipped his chin in a nod. "Race told him, and the kid still says he wants a piece of the guy. He's running high on multiple wins and all the money he's been making. His ego is making choices his skull is going to pay the price for when it hits the concrete. Bax warned the kid, but he don't wanna listen."

I looked at my watch and pressed the palm of one hand over the fingers of the other so I could crack my knuckles. "Pull the kid. I'll take the ringer on. It'll be a more evenly matched fight and Bax won't be all over my ass if one of his guys gets annihilated. The kid can have the fight next weekend."

Chuck's dark eyes widened and he blew a long breath out of his nose that made his nostrils flare out at me. "Shit, Nassir, again?"

I nodded and stilled as some of the guilt and desperation that fueled my actions to get my girl back home swirled in my gut. When I didn't get my way, when a situation was out of my control, it made everything inside of me go nuclear. I had to have an outlet for it. Most of the time I used sex. Some of the time I used violence. I had never felt the need to get in the ring before Key had left, but now it was a common occurrence. I had earned more money on the rigged fights in the last few months than Bax used to rake in back in his heyday, and I wasn't even as close to being as big and brawny as the former car thief. No, I didn't have a heavy bulk like most of the guys in the ring. What I worked with was training, cunning, and enough bodies on my hands that adding another one never caused me any kind of hesitation. I was never actually fighting the opponent in the ring with me, so size didn't matter. I was fighting myself. Fighting the things I couldn't control. Fighting the urge to simply take without asking and ruin any chance I had at forever with the one person I had ever wanted to promise that to.

That meant I never lost.

Guys three times my size went down. Guys with weapons were disarmed and snoring by the time I was done. Guys that fought professionally were taken out with a single, deadly move. Guys that were amateur brawlers didn't stand a chance and posed zero challenge, which was why I only wanted the ringers, the guys we brought in to fight mean and dirty and that took no prisoners. Tonight especially. It wasn't often that I allowed myself to dwell in old hatred and self-loathing. I accepted the man and the monster that I was. But resorting to fear tactics, to underhanded dealings with unknown entities to try to get my girl back home, was something else entirely . . . and the disgust that was boiling in my blood told me I needed to let someone hurt me for her. I deserved it and so much worse, but I wouldn't even feel the punishment because my insides were numb.

She sent me away.

I tapped my fingers on the desk and met Chuck's hard look with one of my own. "This will be the last one. We need to get the club open. I can't wait for her any longer."

He smoothed his tie again and flashed me a grin that had a hint of gold in it. "'Bout time. That beauty has been sitting there just waiting for her chance to shine."

The waiting list to be a member of the exclusive club was a mile long and was not only full of the people from the Point. Many of the upper echelon of the Hill—the ritzy, expensive part of the city whose residents had just as much money as I did but not nearly as much fun making it—wanted in too.

"Move Booker into your old spot here. I want Reeve to have someone on hand at all times in case something gets stirred up on the floor. She likes him and that'll keep him out of Race's sight."

Noah Booker was another knee breaker like Chuck, only younger and a little bit more of a wildcard. His loyalty still hadn't been proven through and through, so it was never clear if he was working for me or working for himself while I footed the bill, but the bastard was calculating, scarred, and seemingly bulletproof. Aside from the fact that there was some bad blood between him and Race that still hadn't been hashed out, he was an asset, so I always tried to utilize him where I could.

"I'll get everything situated."

"I know you will."

He moved to the door and paused for a moment after he pulled it open. Immediately loud dance music flooded the office. I rubbed my forehead. I hated the music the girls danced to. I would be happy to retreat into my own space once I had the new club up and running. Even with Reeve Black, the new club manager who was sprucing this joint up and making it less garish and revolting, it still wasn't a place I felt comfortable in. I liked the finer things. I liked the best and that was what I was surrounding myself with in my new space. It was time to live like a king. Not the black knight I'd always been.

"I know you miss your girl, but no amount of fighting or fucking is going to fix that, boss. You need to figure something else out if she really isn't coming back."

He pulled the door shut behind him with a soft click and I had to fight the urge to smash my forehead into the desk once I was alone. It was a day full of frustration and disappointment. I just couldn't fathom a world that she wasn't a part of . . . and yet we had never even kissed.

I was only after the best and Keelyn Foster was the best. She was undeniably beautiful. She was sexy. She was full of attitude and fight. She was strong. She was street savvy. She was my equal in every single way. I had wanted her from the first instant I saw her, when she was just a scared kid stuck under an abusive blob of a man, a kid who was doing everything in her power to escape, to fight for herself, while Ernie, the old club owner, looked the other way. When I pulled the asshole off of her, she had looked up at me with those clear, perfect gray eyes like I was her hero and I think I knew then she was the one I would hold above all else. We were a match made in hell.

Disgusted with myself and the unpredictable things I set in motion out of desperation, I sent Race a text letting him know I was taking over the kid's spot in the fight tonight, and wasn't surprised when all he sent back was a question mark.

We were partners, not friends, so I didn't feel like I had to explain myself to him. He was the one that handled the money on the bets, so I knew he needed to know that I was the one going into the circle to keep the spread alive with the betters. The odds would be in the other guy's favor just because he was a pro, but most of the die-hard fight fans knew we only brought in the best of the best to take on a proven winner. The way we made money was when the underdog won, shocking the entire room by pulling a win out at the last minute. I wasn't an underdog by any stretch of the imagination, but I had a reputation as a guy that pulled strings rather than got my hands dirty. Little did anyone know I had been born with filthy palms, stained with blood and devastation. No amount of scrubbing would ever get them clean.

I checked in with Reeve, stuck my head in the dressing room to see how the girls were doing, and made a few calls to check on the escorts and the guys running the card games before heading over to the gym. Maybe I should've changed out of my tailored slacks and hand-tooled, Italian leather belt, but I didn't see the point. I left on my expensive shoes and pristine white, button-up shirt as well. I did take off my Rolex and hand it off to Chuck, who was already waiting among the hungry crowd. He just shook his head at me and flashed that gold-toothed grin.

Race was across the ring with the fighter he had brought in from Vegas. The guy was huge, and very intent when he locked eyes on me, obviously ready to get down to business. Race frowned at me, which elicited a shrug in return. It wasn't like he couldn't find a new partner if I ended up a pile of broken bones after the event. I didn't mistake his annoyance for concern as I started to pull off my shirt. I was ready for the rest of me to hurt like my soul did when Keelyn told me I was dead to her.

I heard a few gasps from behind me when the tattoo that ran from the base of my neck to the base of my spine was revealed. I didn't look like the kind of guy that would be sporting a full back piece, but the black-and-gray image of the Four Horsemen of the Apocalypse had a lot of meaning to me, and the endless hours I had spent getting the ink driven into my skin were a sacrifice I was happy to make in order to sport the living tapestry. It was just one more way I tended to shock those that thought they had me all figured out. No one really knew about the horrors that had spawned me.

"You ready to do this, boss?" Chuck folded my shirt over his arm and scowled at an overly eager girl as she tried to grab for my arm while we made our way to the edge of the circle.

"I'm always ready." It was a cliché, but also achingly accurate. If you weren't ready for the inevitable shit life was going to throw at you, then you were never going to make it.

The guy across from me had a warrior's stance and the flinty gaze of a man not just fighting for a win but for his pride and name. There wouldn't be a hidden blade with this one. There wouldn't be a drug-fueled advantage that made him slippery and unpredictable. It was going to be a brutal mashing of fists and feet and we were both going to bleed—me by choice, him because he was bound to underestimate his opponent. It was exactly what I needed after my shitty day in Denver.

One defeat today was one too many.

CHAPTER 3

Keelyn

This boy was good with his mouth . . . and with his hands. He also seemed to be really sweet and invested in putting far more effort into getting me naked than he needed to. I put it right out there that if he came home with me I was pretty much a sure thing, but he was still doing his best to seduce me with kisses and woo me with kind words. None of it felt right, so I kept focusing on the pleasant way it felt when his lips touched mine and the way his corrugated abs felt as I ran my fingers across them. If I did that I could block out the fact that his hair was shaggy but not long enough, and that it was brown and not raven's-wing black. I could also ignore that he was as pale as I was, and not a beautiful tawny golden-brown color.

He was too nice, too soft, and too easy. He kept telling me how pretty I was, how nice my body was, and kept saying he couldn't believe how lucky he was that I had picked him out of all the other hipsters and locals that frequented the Bar.

He was lucky.

I didn't know his name, couldn't recall the color of his eyes if I wasn't looking at him directly, and every time he opened his mouth to give me another compliment I wanted to scream at him to be quiet. He sounded like he was from the Midwest, not like he was from another country that I would never see. He was all wrong, and I hated Nassir even more for making it feel that way.

I liked sex. Liked the way it made me feel, and often the things it could get me. I never shied away from taking what I wanted and fulfilling my own needs and desires, but as this too cute and too simple boy moved his hands up my chest and started to fumble with my very expensive bra, I knew I wasn't going to be able to block out the wrongness of this anymore. His hesitation annoyed me. His blundering hands frustrated me, and no matter how hot his body was or how fun his kisses were, there was no getting around that he wasn't who I wanted. Frankly, he couldn't handle me, even this watered-down version of me, so there was no way he could give the real me anything close to what I really wanted or needed.

That was Nassir's fault.

Damn him for showing up and reminding me about everything I left behind. I longed to hate him. He tainted everything, and now his stupid handsome face was all I could see while this guy pawed at my boobs like they were a matched set of stress-relieving balls. Granted they were as fake as a three-dollar bill, but they were still sensitive and deserved to be appreciated for the work of art they were. Now that things were heating up, the guy had lost some of his finesse and was getting grabby and anxious. I hated desperation in a man. It reminded me too much of the lonely guys that used to come into Spanky's looking for a cheap thrill. He wouldn't be here if I didn't want him here, so there was no need to rush . . . only now, with gleaming bronze-colored eyes taunting me, I was no longer in the mood.

With a sigh I put both my hands on his chest and felt his muscles tense as I pushed him off of me. I scooted out from under him and scrambled to the other end of the couch. I was glad I hadn't taken the cop up on her offer to set me up with one of her friends. I was about to kick this guy out with a serious case of blue balls and that wasn't something most men in my experience easily overlooked. I didn't need the cop on my case about that like she was on it about the gash I was still sporting in my forehead from the attack in the parking lot. The redhead saw too much.

Instead I went to the bar that her boyfriend owned part of and picked up the first cute guy that seemed like he could give me what I wanted. I thought I was after sex. I thought I needed to take a guy home to prove to myself that I was in Denver to stay, and getting some kind of social life back was part of that. I thought I needed to prove to myself that it didn't matter if Nassir wanted me, because so did other guys, and other guys were always a better choice than my devil. Any guy was . . . at least that's what I thought until this very moment.

I shoved my hand through my newly styled and freshly colored hair and looked at the horny guy who was mumbling my name in obvious confusion. I should have known when I gave in to the temptation of the fancy underwear that more of my old self was going to start knocking against the bars I had caged her in. First it was the bra and panties, followed by actually wearing makeup to work. Then it was a totally revamped hairstyle, which I told myself was simply to cover up the nasty scratch that was still above my eyebrow. It was a lie. I cut my boring locks into a drastically short bob that was significantly longer on one side than the other so that my hair partially covered my eye when it hung in my face. I dyed the sharp new do a fire-engine red so that it was bold and bright, totally eye-catching in a different way than my old stripper hair had been, but just as vampy and sexy.

After the hair, there was no way I could justify wearing those ugly-ass nonslip shoes to work anymore, and even though I almost fell and broke my backside in the kitchen every time I walked in to pick up an order, I was back to wearing four-inch heels that cost more than the rent on my apartment. The changes hadn't gone unnoticed.

"I need you to go." Funny, I had said almost the exact same thing to Nassir a week ago. The look this guy gave me was nothing like the soul-stripping, heart-crushing one those predatory eyes had leveled at me. This guy looked puzzled and then panicked.

"Did I do something wrong?" I think his voice actually squeaked and it made me cringe. I sighed again and straightened my clothes while I leaned over to grab his shirt off the floor.

I tossed it at him. "No, but I'm not into this anymore." I sounded just as cold and callous as the man I needed to forget, and that made my skin pull tight.

Wide eyes stared at me like I had lost my mind, so I got to

my feet and moved toward the door. "I'm sorry. I know I practically guaranteed you a piece of ass, but this isn't working for
me." He was what wasn't working for me and he never would
because he was the wrong guy.

He pulled his shirt on and messed up his already tousled
hair. God, he looked so innocent, so clean, and so uncomplicated. My heart twisted and my stomach pulled. He looked
boring and basic. I wanted to slap Nassir across the face for
pulling my blinders off and making me see everything that
surrounded me here in Denver without the rose-colored
glasses I had been wearing since I landed here months ago.

"Um . . . okay." He got to his feet and reached for the
hoodie I had pulled off of him in a rush. "I really hope I didn't
do anything wrong. You seemed into it."

I tucked the longer chunk of hair that covered my face
behind my ear so I could look him in the eye.

"I *was* into it, but now I'm not. I really am sorry."

His brow furrowed and his nostrils flared. "You're a goddamn cocktease is what you are."

I couldn't stop the laugh that snapped out before I could
bite it back. "You have no fucking idea." I had made a fortune
off of being a tease. I was the best at making promises to men
I never intended to keep. Kind of like my promise that I was
never going back home. I shivered at the thought.

He gave me a scathing look as he swept past me out the
door. "And that scar on your shoulder is ugly as fuck."

Man, he even made leaving him hanging uncomplicated.
With his last words, any kind of guilt I might've been feeling
fled as I slammed the door shut behind him.

I couldn't imagine the fight I would have on my hands if I tried to tell Nassir to stop in the middle of something like that, especially after years and years of the back-and-forth between us. I knew he would stop if I asked him to, he always respected the distance I insisted we keep between us, but I knew if he ever got his hands on me, he would taunt, torment, tease, torture his way right back to where he wanted to be and there would be no more stopping. He was not a man to be denied, and I had always taken great pride in being the one thing, the one person, to elude his very clever grasp even if all I wanted to do was let him hold me close and keep me safe. I was too smart to believe in the false sense of security a man like Nassir offered. Everything about him and his lifestyle was dangerous even if I knew he would treat me like I was his most prized possession.

I refused to be his anything . . . let alone his belonging.

I snorted at myself as I locked the door and headed to my bathroom. Not so clever anymore if all I could think about was him after I had purposely sent him on his way. I needed a shower to wash the feeling of defeat and wrongness off; then I was going to curl into bed and finish the book I was reading. My love life sucked, so I saw no reason not to live vicariously through a cute teenage girl that was in love with a dead sexy alien with attitude who turned into beams of light. It was fun and made me forget about my own nonsense for a minute. And the fact that the hero of the story was exotic, dark, and mysterious didn't hurt things either.

After I was curled into bed and realized I was reading the same page over and over again and not comprehending a single word, I shut the Kindle down and picked my phone up off the nightstand next to my bed. I scrolled through the contacts, purposely skipping over the *N* section, and found the number I was looking for. It was late but I knew she would answer. I didn't have anyone I really called a friend, but Reeve Black came close. She grew up in the same kind of life I did. She understood why it was hard to let anyone in and she helped me when I needed someone to spring me from the hospital after I got shot. She also promised not to tell me "told you so" when I came crawling back home with my tail tucked between my legs.

Her cell rang once before she answered. "What's up, bitch?"

I could hear the noise of the strip club in the background. I tended to try to forget she was working for Nassir. She had taken over Spanky's and made it as reputable as a strip club run by a crook could be.

"I just kicked a guy that was a really good kisser out of my apartment." It wasn't what I meant to say but the words just sort of tripped off my tongue.

I heard Reeve laugh and then she told me to hold on while the noise and music in the background faded away. When she was somewhere quieter she said, "He must not have been that good if you made him leave."

"No, he was; really, really good, but it felt so wrong and I haven't been laid in almost a year and I'm going crazy. It's all Nassir's fault."

"A year? You've only been gone for six months, Key."

I blew out a frustrated breath and looked up at the ceiling. "Yeah, but Nassir took over the club a year ago. You think anyone was going to go home with me with him looking over their shoulder? Ugh . . . I hate him."

She laughed again. "We were all surprised he came back alone. He's not familiar with the word 'no.'"

"Tell me about it. Before he left, he paid some hobo to beat me up in the parking lot."

"Are you kidding me!?" She swore. "Why would he do that?"

"Because I hurt him." The words whispered out and I hated that I could always ache for a man I was pretty sure didn't have a soul.

"He is such a dick." She sounded furious on my behalf, and that was why she was my only almost-friend.

"He is, but it was his face I was picturing while the guy from tonight touched me, it was his voice I kept hearing in my ear. I know he's mostly terrible and has no remorse for doing shady, illegal things, but I can't seem to forget him."

She clicked her tongue in a tsk. "I told you before you left that there is no accounting for what the heart wants. In your case, it sounds like you can't fool your body either. There is no substitute for a guy like Nassir."

I put a hand over my eyes and roughly rubbed my temples. "He'll destroy me, Reeve. He'll take over my life. All the choices I've made, the way I've struggled to build my life on my own terms . . . it'll all just be wasted time and effort because he'll control everything. I'll hate myself and then eventually I'll for real start to hate him." And that I couldn't bear. My heart had been twisted up over Nassir for so long that the idea of it actually turning on him for good made me sick to my stomach.

She made a sympathetic sound low in her throat and I could hear her tapping her fingers on something. "Sometimes you have to burn it all, level it all to the ground, for something new to sprout up out of the ashes."

My heart skipped a little beat at the idea of someone as formidable and impenetrable as Nassir being breakable. "Man, the cop has turned you into a big ol' pile of mushy goo, bitch."

Reeve had hooked up with a detective and was head over heels for him. Last I heard from her, she was trying to get knocked up and live the kind of life the Point usually smashed. Reeve was a fighter and a survivor, so if anyone could hold on to a dream and not let the city steal it, it was her.

She giggled, actually giggled, and I felt an answering smile twist my lips.

"Shut up. I'm just saying you never know what can happen. Even Hades loved Persephone."

I snorted. "He kept her trapped in hell and only let her loose a few times a year."

"Stop crapping all over my awesome analogies. You get my point and . . ." She paused and I could almost hear her turning over what she wanted to say next in her head. "He's been really off ever since you left. Like even scarier than normal."

A chill raced across my skin and I sat up in the bed. I wasn't aware that my fingers clutched the phone in a death grip until my knuckles cracked. "What do you mean?"

"He's been fighting."

I heard words floating around inside my head but couldn't seem to grasp on to them. "What do you mean, fighting? With you and Chuck?" Nassir didn't fight. He said his piece, made declarations of how things were going to be, stated his standards and expectations, and then waited for things to be done his way and his way only. He didn't waste his words or his time on an argument he was bound to win.

"No, Key, like fighting the way Bax used to, and it's terrifying. No one has ever seen anything like it. He goes in the circle and doesn't come out until the other guy is almost dead. He took on this ringer, a professional fighter Race brought in from Vegas during the last one." She paused then made a noise that had me wanting to climb through the phone and shake her until she kept talking. "The guy was huge. Bigger than Titus, so way bigger than Nassir. And he was a pro. Bax said it was obvious he didn't care about the money he just wanted to fight. Apparently Nassir walked into the circle still wearing his slacks and his fancy shoes and the guy laughed at him."

"Oh, that was a mistake." The words whispered out.

"A big mistake. Race told me Nassir let him get in exactly two punches, one to either side of his face, before he took the other guy to his knees with some kind of crazy martial arts move and then proceeded to pummel him into pulp. The fight lasted maybe three minutes when Chuck waded in and pulled Nassir off the guy before he killed him. Race said if Chuck hadn't stepped in, Nassir wouldn't have stopped."

I wasn't surprised by the violence or power that she was describing. What shocked me was that he had purposely let the other man hurt him, had withstood injuries to that perfect face of his without defending himself. Nassir wasn't a man that would express his remorse and guilt at his misdeeds outwardly, but I had no doubt that he was regretting his decision to set the homeless man on me without being there to make sure his plans didn't take a violent turn. I hurt him, he hurt me, and then because we hurt each other, he let a stranger hurt him physically to leach the poison out. He sought punishment for the injuries he inflicted and doled it out for the ones I had left on him.

I told her what I had known was going to be the inevitable truth since he moved the menu away and I saw that unforgettable face after six months of missing it. "I think I'm coming back."

"Thank God. Maybe that will set him back to rights and he can go back to being his normal level of frightening and ruthless."

"I'm not coming back for him, Reeve. I'm coming back for me. I thought I could make a life here but I didn't even really try."

She hummed a little. "Why didn't you try, Key?"

I looked around the small apartment and gritted my teeth. "Because as much as I wanted my own life and my independence, as much as I wanted to do something good, when I saw Nassir I realized I didn't want to do it here and I never will. Denver isn't home."

"You can keep your own life and your independence and still love someone as long as it's the right someone, you know?" Her tone was quiet but it was sure and steady. "Hey, I need to go work. One of the girls just tried to go onstage drunk off her ass and that's a big no-no. Call me when you get back to town and let me know if you're going to take Nassir up on his offer."

She was about to hang up when I screamed her name like a crazy person. "What offer?"

"What are you talking about, Key? I really have to go."

"Take Nassir up on what offer, Reeve?"

"The business offer he went to Denver to tell you about. He wasn't just asking you to come home so he could fuck you, though I'm sure that was his primary reason. He's been sinking a ton of money into a new club and he wanted you to be a partial owner. He knows you have a pretty hefty nest egg stacked away from dancing."

I was so dumbfounded I could barely speak. "A club?"

"Yeah. It's massive and super swanky. It's way too nice for the Point, but people are dying to get in already. He finally decided to open it next week. I think he realized you meant it when you said weren't coming back." She snorted. "Men are dumb."

"What kind of club?" His old club had been part dance club and part fight club. It was seedy and oily. It didn't fit him at all but it generated all kinds of cash, and he was pissed when someone burned it to the ground.

She laughed. "A sex club. What else? I gotta go for real. I miss you, bitch."

"I miss you too." I said it automatically as I hung up. I stared at the glowing screen and couldn't decide if I wanted to laugh or throw the thing across the room.

In my head I heard him as clear as if he had been in the bed next to me . . . *"I have a business proposition for you, Key."*

His voice, with its faintest hint of an accent as he looked at me with those candy-colored eyes, gave nothing away. Of course, when he offered me something other than sex and physical temptation, it was a chance to get into bed with him in a different way . . . a way that would probably be just as dirty and complicated as the traditional way. Only Nassir would take something people did anyway and charge for it. He was already making money from the strip club and from the working girls he looked out for, so why wouldn't he take that a step further and make money off of people chasing a chance to indulge in their kinky vices. It simply made good business sense.

I scrolled back up to the Ns in my contact list and stared at his name before pulling it up. It took another ten minutes before I could get my hands to stop shaking enough to type out a text message. I couldn't call him. The sound of his voice after what had happened with the guy from the bar tonight would be too much. I would be in my little Honda Civic racing back to the Point and throwing myself at him like a lunatic. I needed to keep the upper hand with him if I was going to go home, if I was going to even consider tying myself to him in any way.

I'm coming home, asshole.

I sent the message off and stared at the phone, expecting an immediate response. Expecting a "good" or an "about time." I got nothing. Zero. Zilch. The screen stared back at me, taunting me in silence for hours. When I couldn't stop hitting the message button to see if anything was there, and as dawn started to cross the sky, I finally gave in to frustration then and threw the thing across the room.

There had been good men and bad men in my past. There

had been men I wanted to stay longer than they did and ones I couldn't get rid of fast enough, but in the background there was always Nassir . . . always. I couldn't escape his pull and not even time and distance had done anything to stop the irresistible attraction I felt toward him. I told Reeve he couldn't be the center of my world, but the reality was that he had been the core of everything from the get-go, and all I was doing was orbiting around him. Forever circling and trying to get as close as I could without succumbing to his gravitational pull and colliding into him.

I fell asleep after the sun was in the sky and was so tired and stressed out from the night before that I slept through my alarm, missing my shift at the diner. I guess it was a good thing I was going back to the Point. I didn't think my ego could handle getting fired from a waitressing job I never really wanted in the first place.

I shoved the covers off and went to retrieve my phone from where it had landed. The battery was almost dead, but there was enough life left in it for me to see Nassir never texted me back. I almost threw it again but stopped when I noticed I had an e-mail. I never used the app on my phone. I had no need for an e-mail address and didn't want anything that was easily tracked, but I did like to shop on Amazon, so there was no getting around having one. When I clicked to open it, my heart started to race and I got a little light-headed. I was so surprised, mostly that I was surprised, that I sat down heavily in the center of the floor and just stared dumbly at the first-class ticket with my name on it for a flight that was scheduled to leave tomorrow morning.

His message was brief and so very Nassir:

Get your ass home. Leave your shit and I'll send someone for it later.

No "I'm so happy" or "thank God" or "hallelujah." Just the ticket and the order to get my ass home. Had I really expected anything different?

I rested my cheek on my drawn-up knees and pondered my ability to handle getting back in the game with him. He controlled everything. He was everywhere. He devoured whatever was in his path, and I didn't want to end up being nothing when he was done with me.

I must have stayed in that spot longer than I realized because when there was a knock on the door it actually hurt to unfold my body from the bent-over and curled-up position. I groaned as my spine snapped and popped when I went to open the door. The pretty redheaded cop was on the other side. I couldn't say I was that shocked to see her. She was a persistent little thing.

"I made your boss give me your address off your application when he said you didn't show for your shift. I heard you left the Bar with a guy last night, so I was worried when I heard you missed your shift."

This was my own fault for using a place where she knew everyone as a pickup spot. I let her into the apartment and offered her something to drink. She was in her uniform, so I wasn't sure if she was still on the clock or not. She must have been off because she took the beer I held out to her.

"I brought a guy back here with me and realized it was a mistake. I sent him packing and then decided it was time I went home. I like Denver, but this isn't where I belong."

She considered me thoughtfully for a second as she sipped on the microbrew. "I think I would be really interested to know where home is for you, Keelyn." Her gaze dipped to the collar of my T-shirt, which had slipped to the side, showing off my scar. "It doesn't seem like a very friendly place."

I adjusted my shirt and grinned at her. "It's not, but I'm not really a very friendly person, so it works for me. I miss it, and no matter how hard I try I can't seem to forget it."

She tapped her nails on the glass and lifted an auburn eyebrow at me knowingly. "Can't forget it, or can't forget him? You've been a different person since that guy came to see you."

I sighed and gave her a level look. "No. This is who I really am. This is who he came to bring home. The girl that was here before his visit was a fake. I thought I could be her, learn to love her, but now I know I can't."

The cop considered me thoughtfully and pointed at the still-raw mark on my forehead with her bottle. "She didn't have to worry about getting jumped in the parking lot either."

I barked out a laugh and lifted a couple of fingers to the cut. "I know it sounds crazy, but that's part of the problem. I'm leaving tomorrow morning."

Her chocolate-colored eyes popped open wide. "Wow. That's fast."

I nodded. "He doesn't mess around."

"No. He didn't look like the type that does." She finished her beer and walked over to give me a hug. It was so weird. No one hugged in the Point unless they were naked and about to get it on. "Be safe, and I hope wherever you are going and whatever you are chasing makes you happy."

I hugged her back and followed her to the door. "I don't know that I'll ever have happy, but I would settle for content and satisfied."

She tossed her long hair over her shoulder and gave me a hard look. "If you're going back to a place that puts bullets in you and to a man that you can't stay away from, then don't settle for anything."

She sounded so fierce and so determined that I found myself agreeing with her. "Okay. I won't settle, and thank you."

She frowned at me as she started to pat all her pockets, looking for what I assumed were her keys. "For what?"

I leaned on the doorjamb as she continued to search, and laughed as she did a little victory dance when she fished them out of her back pocket.

"For being normal and for showing me what a regular life with real friends could be like. It's not something I'll ever forget."

Her mouth made a little O of surprise but before she could ask me anything else I closed the door and dug a suitcase out of my closet so I could start packing. The Point might not be normal and life there might not be what a real life looked like to anyone else, but it was mine, and now that I was committed to going back, I could feel the way it called to me. I felt the dirt on my skin. Heard the call of sex and decadence in my ear. Tasted the power and the influence of bad things on my tongue. The shell I had been hiding in shattered and the real me that had been banging angrily at my insides took her place back on top. There was nothing dull or boring about me. I was made to stand out not to blend in, and I was going back to the Point ready to shine.

The city and the man that ran it in the darkness were two things I couldn't live without and I was done trying to deny myself either of them. They were both a part of me just as much as I was a part of them. Leaving was not something a woman that wrote her own rules and made her own way did when things got tough. No; the woman I was, the woman I spent my life trying to be, needed to shore up her defenses and fight for her place. A place that wasn't beneath the man in charge but by his side. I didn't want a spot on the court Nassir played on; I wanted a spot on his team.

It was time to go home . . . After all, that's where my heart was.

CHAPTER 4

Nassir

Why is the cooler open?"

I was more irritated than I needed to be, but that was because Keelyn's plane had landed over two hours ago and I had no idea if she had gotten on the flight out of Denver or not. My typical indifference had fled and I felt like all my nerves were strung too tight, and like angry bees colored with anxiety and anticipation were buzzing underneath my skin.

I went to slam the heavy door to the walk-in cooler but paused when I noticed a bunch of boxes on the floor. Since I'd pushed to get the club open by the end of the week after letting it sit stagnant for half a year, everyone was rushing around to get the gorgeous monster ready. That meant a flood of bartenders, cocktail servers, barbacks, security, dancers, and the men and women that were hired for the real purpose of the club were all running around trying to primp and polish before I threw the doors open. People were just as eager to sell sex and debauchery as they were to buy it, but even in all of the haste I didn't tolerate sloppy work. The boxes on the floor of the cooler held bottles of champagne that, combined, cost more than most midsize cars. There was a small fortune sitting carelessly on the floor of the cooler, and it was enough, in my already tense state, to make me blow a gasket.

The fact that it was on the floor where anyone could trip over it or could set something heavy on it was just unacceptable. So was the fact that the cooler was wide open, letting the temperature drop on the hundreds and thousands of dollars of product stored inside. I muttered a few ugly words in my first language and made my way inside the big metal room to sort the mess out myself. I had run security checks and done intensive digging into the backgrounds of everyone I hired to work at the club. No amount of research on a person could tell me if they had a quality work ethic, though. That was the problem with an operation this big. I had to bring so many strangers on board to help keep the business going, and all I had to keep them in line was my reputation and their knowledge that I didn't tolerate anything but perfection. The champagne on the floor didn't give me high hopes that I was off to a great start with my new lot of employees.

I shivered a little bit as the cold from the cooler snaked down the back of my collar and touched my neck. I hefted the first box up and moved it to its correct place on the wire shelving that stored all the booze and beer that was supposed to be served cold. I was still swearing in Arabic when I turned to get the second box off the floor. I had to rub my hands together for a second because of the chill. When I stopped I heard a noise. Frowning, I put my hands down and looked around the cooler. It was just a big metal square divided into rows by miles of metal and wire shelving stocked full of bottles and cases of liquor. Feeling like an idiot for being jumpy, I picked up the case and was about to muscle it into place when Chuck appeared at the doorway I left open.

"Hey, boss, you have a visitor upstairs."

I lifted an eyebrow at him. "In my office?"

Since we were closed and the employees all had specific tasks they were supposed to be attending to, I knew it could only be one person, and my heart lurched at the thought.

"Yep. I told her you were busy but she said she would wait." Chuck grinned. He had known Keelyn for as long as I had, and most of the time he treated her like she was his unruly daughter rather than my downfall. He liked to push her buttons and she always pushed back.

"Let me put the rest of this away and I'll head up. I want to know who left it on the floor."

I moved to the shelf to set the case down, and just as I let go of the box I heard another noise. The earsplitting sound of metal scraping across concrete and the sound of expensive glass shattering as it rattled against itself and rolled onto the ground as the entire row started to tip on its side toward me. At first I was dumbfounded, so I stood there numbly until the first beer bottle cracked open and got my very expensive shoes wet right at the same moment Chuck barked my name.

I might've hated my earlier life, but there was no denying that the training I received and the survival instincts that were woven into my every thought and movement still served me well. I took a flying leap toward the door just as the entire section of shelving hit the floor. My feet barely cleared the heavy rack as I landed with a grunt and scrambled upright in order to avoid drowning in the very costly river of booze that was rushing toward me.

"Jesus, boss. That was close."

I dusted off my pants and scowled when I noticed a black smear that ran across the front of my shirt that wouldn't wipe away. My palms were stinging from the impact and appeared to be torn open and raw in spots. I knew I was going to have bruises on my knees.

"This is unacceptable, Chuck. Find out who installed the racks. Find out who left the champagne on the floor and left the door open. I want to talk to both of them." And by "talk," I meant intimidate and make them understand this kind of shoddy work was unacceptable on my watch. The punishment for such laziness wasn't going to be a simple slap on the wrist.

Chuck rubbed a hand over his bald head and gave me an odd look. "I was here when they installed the rack, Nassir. They did it right. I made sure of it. The bottles shouldn't have fallen over like that. Not unless they were pushed or messed with."

I shook my throbbing hands out. "Well, no one was in the cooler but me, and no one else is in there now." It wasn't like there was anywhere to hide in the square room. "I'm going upstairs. Have the barbacks clean up this mess and make sure they understand what happens when things are not done properly. Someone needs to pay for all this lost product."

Logically, I knew I was the only person that could afford to cover the loss, but it was the principle.

"Glad you're okay."

I grunted a response and made my way to the private elevator I had had installed that led up to my office. I punched in the code and flexed my fingers. I needed to get my adrenaline in check before I came face-to-face with her. It wouldn't do me any good to rush at her, throw her on the ground, and climb all over her like I wanted to do. She was back, but I didn't know for how long, and my goal was to make her stay forever, so I needed to make sure I moved with poise and caution. It was the only outcome I was okay with. She couldn't leave again. I felt like I was missing the very thing I lived for with her halfway across the country. I needed her in my life; otherwise everything I did and everything I was had no meaning.

When the elevator doors opened, they revealed my massive, glass-topped, walnut desk and the beautiful woman sitting in my leather wingback behind it. Oh, Key was back all right and she was back with a vengeance. Her hair shone like the paint job on a fast car with all its bright red intensity, her makeup was heavy and sultry, and from what I could see of her body, she was back in clothes that were designed to make most men come to heel. Her tight black top dipped down low into her cleavage, showing off both her impressive rack and her raised-up scar. She looked like the overly sexualized villain in a superhero movie and I could hardly handle it. I wanted to rush at her, snatch her up, throw her on my desk, and bury myself so deeply inside of her she would never be able to shake me loose. I breathed out low and long through my nose and told myself to keep my baser instincts in check. I might be a monster, but I wasn't an animal.

She had her legs crossed, and her heels, which I was sure cost the same as my now ruined suit, were propped up on the edge of my desk. It was the hottest thing I had ever seen. I shoved my hands in the pockets of my slacks and willed the erection that was stirring to life to settle down. I needed to know what her agenda was before I tried to make her understand that my only agenda was her . . . and always had been. I took a few steps into the room and paused when she swung her long legs off the desk and climbed to her feet so she could start walking toward me.

I met her halfway and we stared at each other in a strained silence for a long minute. I could feel her breathing. I could see her delicate pulse fluttering in her neck. I could almost taste the tiny drop of moisture that beaded up at her hairline and dipped across her temple. I was so consumed with having her back where she belonged and being so close to her after so long that I didn't see her fingers curl into a fist. When the blow landed on my cheek, it whipped my head around with enough force to make me gasp in surprise. She had a good enough arm that the punch made my teeth clamp down on my tongue, and before I knew it, I had a mouth full of blood. I grumbled at her and took a step back as she shook her hand out and glared at me.

"That was for the bum you paid to beat me up. You're such an asshole, Nassir."

I walked around her and went to my desk to find something to spit the blood into. I fell into the chair she'd vacated and pulled a tissue out of the drawer.

"He was supposed to scare you, not put his hands on you." Anger at myself and the situation I created pricked at my skin. Her blow was a thousand times more deserved than the ones I let some stranger land on me for her. I never wanted to be responsible for causing her pain, physical or otherwise, and yet that's exactly what I had done because of my own short-sightedness.

She pushed the longer front portion of her hair off of her face and pointed at a healing red mark that blazed an obvious trail over her eyebrow. "Well, he didn't get that memo, which isn't surprising since he was clearly a tweaker. You can't ever leave well enough alone."

I spit another mouthful of red out and then stuck my tongue out so I could probe at the wound. Man she had a killer right hook.

"I couldn't." That was the truth. I couldn't leave her in Denver. I couldn't forget about her. I could never leave her alone even if that was really what she wanted. I was a desperate man doing desperate things for a woman that hated desperation in all its forms. "But I'm not going to let that waste of skin get away with putting his hands on you either." I had a guy traveling to Colorado now to get her car and the rest of her stuff. I was going to make a call and make sure he paid my homeless friend a visit. It was no wonder she hated men that were reckless in their need. I could have cost myself the one thing I wanted most, the one thing I had never been able to own or control because of my careless actions.

She sighed and moved back toward where I was sitting. I thought she would take a seat in one of the chairs on the opposite side of the desk or on the ornate chaise that sat by the opaque windows that overlooked the bar. She didn't. She walked around the corner of the desk, squeezed herself between my legs and the edge of the wood, and propped herself up right in front of me so that our legs were touching. The outside of her almost naked thighs pressing against the fine wool in the inside of mine. I felt the contact throughout my body like an electric current.

She crossed her arms over her enhanced chest and looked down her nose at me. "You can't punish someone for something you orchestrated. You are the one at fault here, Nassir, not the bum. He never bothered me. Not for six months, until you showed up and waved a big ol' juicy steak at him. Be accountable for your shitty behavior for once in your life."

I didn't respond. I couldn't. She was fooling herself if she thought I was going to let anyone put their hands on her in a violent way even if I was the one that had set the wheels in motion. I wasn't going to argue because what was done was done.

"What do you think of the club?"

Her soft gray eyes widened and then narrowed. "It's big and fancy. You can't miss it as soon as you drive into the city." There was a pause and her breath hitched. "You named it after me."

I grinned at her. She was the key to everything that mattered in my world and in this city. Of course I named it after her.

"All the members got a lock or a key when they joined and paid their membership dues. The men all have a lock, one that is either open or one that is closed. If the lock is open, it means the gentleman is attached, married, has a partner, but is still up for anything and everything. The closed lock signifies that

that particular man is off-limits and must engage with another member on his or her own terms."

She lifted an eyebrow at me. "And the keys?"

I shrugged. "The women have the keys, to the locks and to the men's hearts. Don't they always?"

She moved a little closer and our knees brushed together, and I felt it in my balls. I sucked in a quick breath as the mere touch made my dick throb.

"So the women can just go around unlocking and locking men up all night long? They have no rules?"

"Women make all the rules when it comes to sex, Key. You should know this better than anyone." I wanted to reach out and pull her off the edge of the desk so that she was sitting in my lap. "They have the key but they don't have to use it, and if a member with a closed lock doesn't want them to set them free, then that's it. There is no pressure. There is no persuasion. It should all be mutual and it is all facilitated by men and women that want to be here. I'm paying a small fortune for the people that know this industry inside and out. I built a grown-up amusement park where nothing is off-limits. People love their kink. People love their sex."

She blew out a breath and I wanted to lean forward and capture it with my own mouth.

"What about you? Do you love your sex and kink, Nassir?"

I smirked at her. "Sex is a part of life; it's necessary and here in the Point it is currency. Kink I can give or take depending on the person on the other end of it. I've seen too much torture and degradation in my lifetime for the extreme and dark side of sex to be appealing."

I saw the questions my quietly spoken words fired to life in her eyes, but instead of asking them, she was the one that decided to change the subject.

"Tell me about this business proposition you had in mind when you came to Denver. You want me to dress in latex and spank people? You want me to get on my back and spread my legs for a line of guys while people watch? What's your game plan?"

I frowned at her and couldn't stop myself from moving closer to her as she spit the harsh words out at me.

"You think I want to watch you have sex with other people, Key? You think it's been fun for me to watch you burn your way through every available and not-so-available boy in the Point because you weren't ready for me?" I narrowed my eyes at her. "Now, which one of us needs to have some accountability?"

She flushed pink and leaned closer to me. She might be scared of me and the way I wanted her, but she never backed down, and that made my desire for her burn in a way that would never be extinguished.

"What did you have in mind, Nassir?"

I reached out with the very tip of my finger and brushed it along the raised-up surface of her scar. She flinched away from me and I could still see her on the filthy floor of the strip club, her crimson life force covering my hands as her eyes fluttered closed. I refused to let her die just like I refused to let her leave. I was not a man to be denied the things he wanted most.

"I want you to buy in and be a partner just like Race did. You are what sex is about in the Point, Key. Your face. Your

body. Your heart. Your attitude. The legacy you left. Everything about you is what men dream about in this place. I want
you to lure them in, empty their pocketbooks, and then send
them on their way with a smile."

She reared back and then burst out laughing. She cackled so
hard her eyes started to water. "You want me to be a mascot."

I furrowed my eyebrows because I had no idea what she
was talking about. She must have seen my confusion because
she stopped laughing long enough to fill me in.

"Like a dancing chicken or a singing taco. Like the big
stuffed furry critters that dance around for the crowd at half-
time during a football game. You want me to be a mascot for
a sex club."

I was lost. "I don't watch football."

"Well, trust me; that's exactly what you're asking me to do,
and I have to pass. I need more out of my life than flaunting
my boobs and getting groped for a dollar." She flicked that
bloodred hair out of her eyes and stared me down.

I blinked at her slowly and lifted a hand to rub my thumb
across my lower lip. I liked the way her eyes tracked the movement. She was as affected by me as I was by her; she just hid it
better. She always had.

"The amount of money that this place has already generated without the doors being open is double what the Pit
cleared in a month. Lock & Key is poised to be the unofficial
bank of the Point, Key. Being a partial owner entitles you to a
portion of all of the revenue the club is going to generate. It's
enough money to allow you to do whatever you want, buy
anything you ever wanted, and all you have to do is be here.

You make the place tick. You give it life." Just like she gave life to me.

"It's all dirty money, Nassir. What happens when the club gets shut down? What happens when someone burns this place to the ground like the last one? You want me to put all my eggs in one basket. A basket you are holding in your hands and can drop the second you feel like it."

She didn't trust me.

She was smart.

I stood up, which made her gasp and had her leaning back so that she was almost lying flat on my desk. Her legs parted involuntarily to let me between them and her hands went to the center of my chest as I hovered over her with my hands next to her hips on the glass. The cuts burned but I didn't want her to see them. Now wasn't the time to show weakness.

"You buy in and you own it, Keelyn. You get a say in how things are run, what happens, and the role you play in it. Your buying in means you are part of the business whether it prospers or fails. We are on equal footing and the only person holding the basket is you. I'll manage the profits and the power . . . you manage the people." I didn't have it in me to pretend that the basest human behaviors were interesting or important, but she did.

Her fingers curled into the fabric of my shirt and my cock ached as it pulsed against the inside of her leg. We had never touched this intimately and this was the closest I had ever been to her. I could feel my body humming in reaction and my blood whispering at me to take her, to claim her, to make her mine after being denied for so long.

"I buy in and I have to stay?" Her voice shook.

I nodded, and some of my hair fell forward and brushed against her cheek. I felt her shiver and it made me want to trace those faint tremors with my hands.

"You have to stay." She had to stay if she bought into the club or not, and eventually she was going to realize that.

"I can do what I want, suggest changes, use the money I make however I want even if it goes against everything that makes sense to you?" She gulped as she asked the questions and her clutching hands went flat and pressed into my chest where my heart was trying to reach out for her hands. "What about us, Nassir?"

"What about us?" Even though there had always been an "us," there never really had been an *us*. I wasn't sure what she was asking me, or what kind of plans she had for the sizable profits she would make if she agreed to buy in.

"We get all tangled up in business and pleasure and then one or the other goes bad, and where does that leave us? You can destroy me without even trying. You've been doing it for years."

I could destroy her, but she was the only thing in the world that made me weak, so she could end me without a thought just as easily. I wanted her to be mine. I wanted her to let me have her in every conceivable way, but more than that, I needed her here. I needed a life with her in it, so if that meant I had to make a choice, I chose keeping her around over having her under me panting my name in erotic satisfaction hour after hour and day after day.

I pushed off the desk and threw myself back into the chair.

I pushed it back on its wheels so there was some breathing room between us and so I had space to think.

"You buy in, I'm taking that as your agreement to stay for the long haul. No more running, no pretending that the grass is greener somewhere else, and I'll agree to keep my hands off of you. We'll be business partners and nothing else."

I could see my offer shocked her. Her mouth moved like she was trying to make words, but none would come out. I understood the way her tricky mind worked, so I lifted both of my eyebrows up and told her, "You are not going to fuck me and forget about me like you think you can do, Key. We are so much a part of one another that separately we are almost unrecognizable. You are so deep down inside of me I feel like I'm missing pieces of myself when you aren't around. If keeping you here where I can see you, where I can smell you, where I can breathe the same air as you means that I know you're safe, happy, and whole, I will keep my hands and my cock to myself." It might kill me but I had endured worse torture and torment in my time.

Key blinked those stormy eyes at me as the words sank in and she must have read the resolve on my face. She wasn't going to take me to bed and try to burn me out like she did with all those other boys in her past. I wanted all of her, and once I had her, I was keeping her forever, but for that to happen she needed to give herself to me for safekeeping. She didn't have to trust me, but she did have to love me.

"No sex?"

"Oh, there will be sex. Tons and tons of sex, but none of it will be between us if that's what it takes to get you to agree."

She harrumphed and slid off the desk so she was towering over me in those killer heels. I was glad she was back in her right skin.

"Business only?"

I nodded solemnly and ran a tired hand over my face. It was a deal with the devil, but we both knew she was going to make it anyway.

"Very lucrative and profitable business only, and if for some reason the cops shut me down, I'll return your investment plus fifty percent of my own."

"How much did you sink into this place? And how much do you expect me to buy in for?"

I shrugged. "I spent enough to make it what I wanted and you can pay in the same Race did. Two hundred K. I'm the primary backer, so my word is law, but if you see something not working or a way I missed to bring more money in, we can have a discussion." Race had actually put in double that amount, but I wasn't about to tell her that, and no one had ever accused me of being honest.

She whistled. "That's a lot of money."

"You have it." She would hate to know that I knew exactly what her bank balance was. It paid to have a computer hacker on the payroll. There wasn't much about her I didn't know, both inside and out.

"I do have it. I just don't know if I want to give it to you." It sounded like she was talking about a lot more than money.

"We open this weekend, so you don't have much time to decide."

"I feel like I never had a choice. The second you showed up

in Denver, this was all bound to happen because you always get your way."

I shook my head slightly. "Not always." We both knew that.

Her eyes sparked with charcoal flecks and she took a step closer so that she could bend down and put her hands on the arms of my chair. She leaned closer and closer until her mouth was hovering a mere millimeter away from mine. When she spoke, the words danced across my lips and tasted like victory and fate.

"No, not always." Her lips pressed into mine and I had to curl my hands around the arms of the chair to keep from grabbing at her.

She teased the clamped seam of my lips with her tongue and lightly scraped her teeth across my bottom lip. I wanted to toss her backward on the desk and bury myself inside her with no finesse, just pure, animalistic lust. She brushed her lips back and forth and laughed lightly as I bit down on my already injured tongue to keep from reacting. If I mauled her now, it would undo any progress I might have made with her.

She pulled back and reached out to run her finger over each of the high arches of my eyebrows. It was the softest, gentlest touch I had ever felt from another human being and it made me focus on her pulse even more heavily than the one in my veins.

"Fine. I'm in. I'll write you a check."

I couldn't speak, and if I tried, all I would be able to say to her was that she needed to get naked so I could taste her. She was going to kill me if she didn't surrender soon. I was going to get up and move away from all the temptation she emanated when she moved her hand so that it was cupping my cheek.

"Oh, and one more thing . . ." The smile she gave me had my hard-on dying and me gulping in legitimate fear at the degree of mischief and trouble I saw in it. "I don't have a place to stay since I left Denver in such a hurry. You don't mind me coming to stay with you until I get situated, do you? If not, I can always call up one of my old friends, or one of my old customers from the club."

She practically purred the last words, and I felt my resolve to keep things professional turn into a cement block in my gut. Shit. What was I supposed to do with that? Avoiding touching her, breathing her in, dreaming about her naked at work was one thing. Trying to keep my desire in my pants while she was in my private space, my retreat away from this world, would be impossible. But she had me backed into a corner and she knew it.

"You can stay with me for as long as you need to, Key."

Both her eyebrows shot up and she licked her bottom lip. She was already launching her first salvos at me. She was a fighter just like me . . . she just used different weapons. Hers were infinitely more effective.

"Shouldn't be a problem if we're just going to be business associates, right?"

I groaned and muttered every dirty word I could think of in a language I knew she wouldn't understand.

"Right."

She gave me a fake smile that showed all her teeth and the challenge shone in her eyes. She was always fierce and ready to fight me. It shouldn't be the kind of turn-on that it was.

"It's good to be home. I have plans, Nassir, big plans."

I sighed. "It's good to have you home, Keelyn."

She flicked her wild hair and pushed off the chair as she sauntered toward the door. "Let's see how long you think that."

The elevator swallowed her up as she left the office and I didn't exhale until she was out of sight. She was going to torture me. She was going to taunt me. She was going to try to break me. I should've warned her that I was forged in fire and that the flames of torment felt like nothing more than rays of sunshine to me. I was going to let her burn herself out and then scoop up the ashes.

Then she would be mine.

CHAPTER 5

Keelyn

I wasn't sure what to do with myself after I walked out of Nasir's office. I was shaking, both from being so close to him and from the gauntlet I'd boldly thrown down. Every single time I thought I had the upper hand with him, he twisted things in a different direction that left me reeling. Business partners, my ass. I was going to make him regret even suggesting he could keep his hands off of me after all this time. There wasn't much I excelled at in this life, but making men stupid and weak with lust was sure as shit at the top of the list.

I don't know what kind of insanity had prompted me to ask him to let me stay at his place until I was settled. Walking into the devil's lair willingly wasn't the brightest plan I had ever concocted and I loathed that everything inside of me went molten and liquid when I saw the regret and anger in his eyes as his gaze landed on the healing cut on my forehead. He should feel bad—it was his fault—but there was something about the way remorse looked on such a powerful and commanding man that tugged at places deep down inside of me. And good Lord, the healing bruises high and dark on both his chiseled cheekbones made me want to grab his face in my hands and kiss each injury better. I hadn't even been back home for a day and already the man was making my mind and body go crazy.

I went where I always went when I was lost in the Point. Back to the place that had been my home and my sanctuary for so long. Plus, it was within walking distance from Nassir's new club, so I didn't have to call a cab or ask Chuck for a ride. I pushed open the doors to the newly remodeled Spanky's, the club newly christened as the Empire, and almost stumbled over my own feet.

The place looked completely different from the inside out. There was no longer eye-burning pink splashed across every surface. The dingy carpet on the floor was no longer stained with blood, and God only knew what else, on it. All the chairs had been replaced by sleek, black leather booths, and the garish neon lighting had been pulled out and replaced with a soft, vintage glow that made both the girls onstage and the customers look better. It was still very much a strip club. There was no escaping the multitude of boobs and scantily clad women that filled the place wall to wall. There was no mistaking the familiar lustful ambience and overly eager throb of the crowd who were avidly watching the talent. However, now it was a classy strip club and it looked and felt expensive. A pang of regret shot through me that I had left before I was able to see the place that had been my home for so long rise from the ashes into something so beautiful. If I'd had my way and had been able to put my money into something in the Point, it would be a place just like this. A place where girls could take their clothes off, make a living, and be proud of it.

A few regulars called out to me and I was stopped by two different cocktail servers that had been here just as long as I had. They both hugged me and told me they loved my new hairdo. I hugged them back and made chitchat as I tried to locate where Reeve might be. I had so much spinning around in my head I needed a safe place to try to lay it all out, and Reeve was the only person that was even kind of my friend.

I caught sight of her dark hair by the bar. She was leaning on the edge of it talking to a huge man that had a wicked-looking scar that bisected one half of his face. He was dressed in a dark gray suit that fit him to a T but he had on heavy and serious-looking boots. When he caught sight of me staring in their direction, he straightened, and there was no missing the black gun tucked into his side. He might look like a business-man, but I would bet anything the business he was in involved a whole lot of blood and broken bones. He inclined his head in my direction and muttered something to Reeve, which had her head jerking up so that she saw me.

The big man scowled when she nudged him out of her way so she could come around the bar. I wondered what his story was as Reeve barreled into me for a hug. She'd changed a lot since hooking up with the hot cop. She wasn't much of a hugger before, and as she pressed into me and I hugged her back I noticed what was probably the biggest change that had occurred since I had been gone. Her normally lithe and toned figure was a little bit softer and a whole lot fuller.

I pulled back and looked at her with huge eyes. "The cop knocked you up!"

She pulled back and gave me a little squeeze. Her eyes were an odd shade of dark blue that hovered on the edge of navy, and right now they were shiny with the kind of pure happiness I didn't think existed in the Point.

"He did."

I pointed at her barely-there belly and narrowed my eyes at her. "Why didn't you mention something?"

She put a protective hand over her stomach and shrugged. "I haven't really said much to anyone." She snorted and shoved some of her long, black hair behind her shoulder. "I see Nassir every single day and he hasn't even noticed. Aside from Bax, Dovie, Race, and Brysen, no one really knows. It's kind of just been in the family." She hooked a thumb toward the big guy that was still watching us with narrowed eyes from the bar. "Killer over there was actually the first person to guess, but I think that's because my hormones are all over the place and one minute I'm crying all over him and the next I'm threatening to cut his balls off if he doesn't get out of my way."

My eyebrows shot up and I snickered. "I'm surprised Nassir let a stranger watch over his club for him."

Reeve shook her head and sighed. "Booker isn't a stranger, and believe me, he's paid his dues and then some. He deserves his place at the table with the rest of the shady and sinister."

It was my turn to sigh. I shifted on my tall shoes and looked toward the back of the club, where Nassir's office, now Reeve's office, was located. "Can we go back there and talk? I really don't need the entire city to know how ridiculous I am."

She nodded and cupped her hands around her mouth to shout to the guy she called Booker that she would be back in a few. He just did that head-tilt thing guys did and turned his attention to his phone. I didn't know who he was talking to, but I bet by the time I left the club, word of my sudden reappearance would be all over the city.

Reeve took a seat behind the desk and groaned in obvious relief when she did so. She was barely showing, but growing another person was hard work, especially in a place like this.

"I can't believe you're going to have a baby. Are you planning to leave the city once it's here?"

"No. Our life is here, and if that means making sure a baby is safe in that life, then that's what we'll do. Plus, you should see Bax." She laughed. "No one believes me when I tell them that I think he's more excited about this kid than Titus is. He calls me at least twice a day to check on me."

I blinked in shock. "I thought Bax hated you." There was bad blood there because Reeve had been involved with something that threatened Bax's girlfriend, Dovie. It hadn't ended well, and Bax wasn't the kind of guy to forgive and forget.

She lifted a shoulder and let it fall. "He's not my biggest fan, but he is infatuated with this little human inside of me. I think the idea of something new, the thought of a fresh start, appeals to him. This kid couldn't have a better guardian angel looking out for him or her in this city."

I laughed. "No kidding." Bax was a brick wall when it came to protecting those he cared about. It would take an army to get through him if he was keeping his new nephew or niece within his protective circle. Not to mention the baby's dad was armed and dangerous in his own right. If any newborn had a fighting chance of having a normal life in this very abnormal place, it was this one.

"I'm happy for you, Reeve."

"Thank you. Now tell me what's up. I assume this look on your face is because you wasted no time in seeing the man behind the curtain when you got back to Oz."

I shoved my hands through the longer part of the front of my hair and tugged at the roots. "I'm losing it, you know? My mind that is."

She lifted a midnight-colored eyebrow at me and settled farther back into her chair. I tugged on my hair harder.

"I can't stop what I feel for him. I can't stop playing his stupid games. When you mentioned the club, all I could hear was him whispering that he had a business proposition for me. I thought it would be ridiculous, that it was just one more way for him to keep me close so he could silently pull the strings in my life. And it is, but it isn't. He really wants me to buy into the club, and the profit margin is huge."

"He's a brilliant businessman. The things he does with money are fascinating to watch. He's building his own infrastructure."

"He's building an empire. He wants to control all the money and commerce that happens here. He's going to be untouchable." Except from me. I was determined to touch and to get him to touch in return. I needed his hand on me in order to have the upper hand in all our dealings with each other.

Reeve rolled her eyes. "Look around, Key. He already *is* untouchable. Nothing that happens here doesn't have his fingerprints on it somewhere. He's been infecting the Point for years and now it's spread so far and wide there's no antidote."

"I know. That's exactly why I wanted to tell him to shove it, but it's too good of an opportunity to pass up. It's legitimate money without having to shake my ass and show my tits." I snorted. "Well, there will be some of that since he wants me to get people in the door."

"Like I said, he's a smart businessman. People will show up because you're there. Your sex appeal is enough to get the curious in the door, and once they're in, Nassir will rob them blind."

I nodded in agreement. "I buy in and I have to stay. I can't throw money at him and run. He won't let me."

"Of course not. He wants you here. He wants you, period."

I gritted my teeth and my hands curled into fists where they were resting on my thighs. "He told me he wouldn't touch me. He said it'll be business only and he'll keep his hands off. How in the hell am I supposed to work with him and be around him when I came back because I couldn't stay away from him? He makes everything so fucking hard."

She bit down on her lower lip and twirled a piece of dark hair around a finger.

"So what are you going to do about it?"

Wasn't that the million-dollar question? I threw my hands up in the air and let out another broken laugh. "I don't know, and because I can't stop myself from pushing back when he prods at me, I asked him to let me stay with him until I figure out where I want to live now that I'm back."

Her eyes widened and she opened her mouth then shut

it, because really there were no words to describe how truly stupid that idea was. "Wow."

"I know. I'm an idiot."

I saw her blue eyes get darker and could almost see something working in her head. Reeve hadn't lasted on the streets as long as she had by being stupid. She was a crafty young woman and had a hot cop and a baby on the way as proof. She tapped her fingers on the soft swell resting in front of her and considered me thoughtfully.

"If you want an even playing field with him, you're going to have to bring him to his knees."

"Can you picture Nassir on his knees for anyone?" The idea was laughable, but she nodded.

"For the right person, even the most formidable man can bend. I've seen it happen with my own two eyes more than once."

I swore and looked down at the shiny toes of my stilettos. "What do I do if he does bend, Reeve? I end up fucked? Literally and figuratively? What happens if who I am disappears for real this time because Nassir is enough to suck even all of this into that vortex of menace and danger that swirls around him." I gestured to my body and my painted face. Not easily missed but practically invisible compared to the natural charisma and allure of my devil.

"I guess that depends on what you do now that you're back, Key. You wanted more before you left, you were working because you wanted to do something good. If you manage to do that, then you'll never be overshadowed by any of the darkness that lives here, including Nassir."

I lifted my gaze back up at her and glared. "You are such a

bitch." It would take a pregnant former criminal and current strip-club manager to remind me that my ultimate goal had been to be my own woman, a woman of worth, a woman that would never let her light and brightness be eclipsed or undone by the man that moved between her and her world.

She smiled at me and it lit her up from the inside out. She was a pretty woman normally, but now she was remarkable. She knew exactly what winning in this place looked like. "I missed you too."

I huffed out a sigh and fished my phone out of my bag as it pinged with a text message. I couldn't stop the shiver and warm glide across my skin when I saw Nassir's name in the box. I popped the message open.

Chuck is coming to get you and bring you to my house.

It was so like him. He didn't ask if I had other plans, if I was busy, if I needed anything. He just issued commands and orders, expecting his edicts to be blindly followed. I wanted to defy him and I would have, but unfortunately all I had with me were the essentials in the bag at my feet and no other prospects for shelter for the night.

Fine. I'm at the Empire.

Not even two seconds passed before my phone dinged again.

I know where you are. I always have.

That shiver turned into a mini earthquake that raced across my soul. I wanted to feel invaded, violated, but I also didn't. Even when they scared me, having those bronze eyes on me always made me feel safe and protected. I knew the Point was my playground because Nassir made it possible for me to play unfettered and unafraid. He was most definitely my devil, but he was also my guardian angel.

I put the phone away and told Reeve that Chuck was on his way. She had me help her back to her feet and we went back into the club. The dancer that was on the stage was doing her routine to something bluesy and slow, which was a nice change of pace from the typical electronic beats that filled the space. She was also completely naked and contorted in a way that made me a little bit envious. There was a field of green bills on the stage, an obvious reward for her impressive performance.

The big guy with the scar came over and tapped Reeve on the shoulder. He muttered something about a high roller getting too close to one of the girls in one of the private back rooms, so she squeezed me hard and told me to keep her updated. I nodded my agreement and kept my eyes locked on the girl onstage until a light touch landed on my shoulder. I would've jumped but I had spent so many years with Chuck watching my back that I would never miss his woodsy and fresh scent or his own special way of handling me. He was soft with me, gentle even. Maybe the only man that had offered me that in my entire life.

"The boss sent me to snatch you up. You sure playing house with him is a good idea, little girl?"

I hooked my arm through his and let him guide me out the door.

"It's the worst idea ever, but this has been a storm brewing for too long and the clouds can't handle the weight anymore. It's time for a downpour."

He huffed out a breath and took me to a huge black SUV that had windows tinted so dark they were almost impossible to see into or out of.

"You think you can handle the flood?"

"I can't be away from him and I can't live a life where I'm nothing more than his pretty bauble. Something has to give, Chuck. There has to be more than desire and denial between the two of us."

Chuck pulled open the door, but before I could climb up into the tall vehicle, he bent his head and brushed his lips across my forehead. I closed my eyes and let my forehead fall so that it rested in the center of his beefy chest.

"I would never bet against, Nassir. I've seen what the man can do and have watched him systematically rebuild this city on the bones of what Novak left behind. In this case, all my money is on you, little girl. You have always been scrappy and determined. You have bested him like no one else ever has. You keep him in check."

I pulled back with a laugh and lifted up on my toes so that I could kiss him on his cheek. "Your faith in me is greatly appreciated and grossly inflated, old man."

I hopped up into the seat as he swung the door closed and walked around to the driver's side of the vehicle. He got in with much less effort and wheeled us out of the parking lot.

We made small talk on the way out of the city. Leave it to Nassir to build a kingdom in the gutter and not want to lay his head there. At first I thought we were headed to the affluent part of the city, simply called the Hill, but Chuck kept going past the burbs and past the Hill right out of town, toward the foothills that rested on the outskirts of the city. I asked him a few times where exactly we were headed but he just kept rambling about the new club, about what an amazing job Reeve had done with the place, and he even had heaps of praise to lay on Booker. I was shocked he wasn't sad to see his old position turned over to someone so much younger and someone obviously so much rougher than he had ever been. He kept up a steady stream of conversation until we suddenly stopped at a massive wrought-iron gate that looked like it had been carved into the side of the mountain.

I was struck speechless as a man in an all-black uniform armed with an assault rifle stepped out of someplace I didn't see and waited while Chuck rolled down the window. The guard and Chuck knocked fists like guys did and the other man's gaze flicked to me.

"Go ahead and head up. The boss just showed up a few minutes ago."

"Thanks."

The window rolled back up and Chuck looked at me out of the corner of his eye as I sputtered, "He has armed guards watching his house?" Jesus, he really *was* like a Bond villain or something.

"You're surprised? Nassir has made a lot of enemies over the years and you would be shocked how many have nothing to do with his business in the city. He's earned a lot but he's taken even more. Armed guards at the gate are the least of the security measures he has around this place."

Another one that was obvious was the long, winding drive that led up to the house. It had to be at least a couple miles long, and even out of the darkened windows all I could see was a dense grouping of trees and foliage. It looked imposing and impenetrable. Nassir had gone and built himself a castle deep within the goddamn woods. It was unbelievable.

Once we rolled to a stop in front of the house, I was again surprised at what waited for me. I was expecting something modern, some kind of fortress of glass and steel hewn into the mountainside. I was expecting a monolith that proclaimed expense and extravagance . . . instead, what was waiting for me was a log cabin. Well, not a cabin exactly, but if there was such a thing as a log mansion, then that's what greeted me as I swung my legs out of the car.

It was sprawling, rustic, and blended into the forested setting perfectly. "Nassir does not live in a log house, Chuck." Disbelief was thick in my voice.

He chuckled and started up the front steps.

"Seriously, a guy that only wears Armani and Prada does not live in the middle of the forest like a lumberjack. What is going on here?"

"Sanctuary can look different for everyone, hon. It can look like a seedy strip club or a cabin in the woods. As long as that place feels safe to the people inside that's all that matters."

I followed him to the front door and waited while he rang the bell. I felt like someone had dropped me in the middle of a horror movie and any second now a psycho killer was going to jump out of the woods and hack me to bits. This couldn't be real life. My incredulity grew even larger when a woman that looked to be in her early twenties opened the door and smiled at Chuck.

She was dressed in all black and her gaze sharpened when it landed on me. She was really pretty, very petite, with long chocolate-colored hair and eyes. Her figure was killer and I knew from experience the shoes she had on her dainty little feet cost well over a grand. I couldn't help but stare at them as she ushered us into the house. I didn't know who she was but she seemed friendly enough toward Chuck even if she dismissed me as soon as I stepped over the threshold.

"Nassir is in the kitchen. He told me to expect a guest. I have a room made up for you in the guest wing of the house."

She didn't introduce herself, didn't spare me another look, just turned on those spectacular heels and disappeared somewhere into the belly of the house.

I looked at Chuck out of the corner of my eye. "She seems nice."

He grinned at me and guided me toward where I assumed the kitchen was. "Bayla used to work for the boss in a different capacity." He lifted his eyebrows up and I nodded that I understood. She was one of his escorts. Figured. Girls that looked like that really only had a few options when it came to making a living in the Point and most of them involved selling themselves in one way or another.

"When the house was completed he offered her a job looking after it. I think they come from similar backgrounds, and contrary to popular belief, the boss can be empathetic."

I wanted to ask exactly where it was they had come from.

I really knew so little about the man that been such a huge factor in my life for so long. The words never made it out, though, because we rounded the corner and I suddenly found myself in a sprawling, totally modern kitchen that had all the glass and stainless steel the outside of the house was missing. I was impressed, but it was the sight of Nassir, shirtless, with his back to me as he scrubbed his hands in the massive farm sink, that made me go numb.

He was muttering softly in a foreign language that didn't sound foreign to him at all and beneath the black ink that covered his pretty gold skin I could see mottled bruises along his ribs and across his shoulders. The tattoo was startling in its detail and size, but it was the man under it that made my mouth dry and my hands start to shake. I must have made a noise because he turned around from the sink and let his molten gaze drift over me as I stared at him dumbly.

His collarbone had a fist-size black-and-blue mark on it and there was a really ugly splotch of purple that sat right above his pants on one side. Underneath his fancy clothes he looked just as rough and beaten as the rest of us did. I moved forward when I noticed that his hands weren't only wet with water but also pink with blood.

"Were you fighting?" I knew he had been since Reeve told me so, but I couldn't imagine he had gone and found a fight in the few hours we had been separated.

I didn't even notice Chuck had made a silent exit as I grabbed Nassir's damp hands in my own. The skin was abraded and rubbed raw. It looked like he had taken a tumble off a bicycle and caught himself on asphalt.

As I was standing this close to him, with him being half dressed, the heat that popped off of him and hit me was almost enough to make my knees buckle. My devil was hot and he knew it. I could see the way my reaction to such a simple touch pleased him.

"These aren't from a fight. One of the shelves fell over in the cooler. I had to dive out of the way." His long fingers curled over so that he was holding my hands on top of his own. "The bruises, though . . . they *are* from a fight here or there."

My pulse kicked and I was sure he could feel it because his fingers tightened fractionally. I could tell how badly he wanted to curl his fingers around mine and pull me closer to him.

"Why were you fighting?" I wanted to hear him say he was sorry, that he felt bad for sending that homeless man to scare me. I wanted him to admit he was wrong and that he had purposely let himself take those bursting blows, hurting himself on the outside because he wasn't the kind of man that would ever admit he hurt on the inside for the mistakes he had made.

One of his raven-colored brows arched up and the corner of his lush mouth tilted up in a grin that actually hurt me to look at.

"Because you weren't here." That was as much of an apology and an explanation as I would ever get from him. So simple yet so unbelievably complicated. Everything with this man always was.

I pulled my hands off of his and took a step closer to him. When I was almost nose to nose with him, I reached out and touched the nasty spot right above his waist. I saw his abs constrict at the featherlight touch and it made me grin. His injured hands curled into fists at his sides.

"Well, I'm here now, so no more fighting to go along with the no touching."

I watched his jaw clench and his eyes light up at the center like a hot ember.

"We've been fighting against each other for years, Key. Are you going to stop? Are you ever going to let one of us win?" I pressed so close to him that he had to suck in a breath and lean against the counter to stay upright and support my weight without putting his hands on me.

"It hasn't been fighting, Nassir. It's been foreplay."

He wouldn't touch me, but I sure as hell was going to touch him. My lips touched his and I felt him suck in a breath so hard that it stole the air from my lungs. I felt his muscles tense up and in my head I added a check box next to my name for this small victory . . . that is, until he somehow maneuvered me around so that my back was to the counter, our bodies pressed together and perfectly aligned, my hands in his too long hair and his tongue in my mouth, all without laying a finger on me.

CHAPTER 6

Nassir

The second her lips touched mine I knew the years of waiting, of wanting, had been worth it.

I could die a happy man, a fulfilled man, a man that accomplished all he had ever set out to do. This tiny kiss, that little taste of her, was more of a victory than surviving anything in my youth or adulthood had been. She was my endgame. She was what had given my life meaning, and now she was breathing that very essence back into me and it felt perfect. She was everything.

My hands ached to touch her. My fingers twitched so hard they hurt as I latched them on to the edge of the marble counter behind her. I settled my hips into hers so that there was no mistaking what was happening between us. My dick throbbed, my heart pounded, and all I could do was brush my lips over hers and beg her to let me inside.

She wanted to control me. She wanted to call the shots and

make the moves so this game was hers to win, but I stopped playing with her the instant she took a bullet and nearly bled out in my arms. I wanted her forever, on my terms, and I knew the only way to make that happen was to make her want to surrender. She had to give herself up to me and to the kind of life I could offer her. I knew she didn't want to belong to me, but she did. I could tell by the way her hands shook when she plowed them into my hair and by the way she whimpered when she opened up to let me inside the warm cavern of her mouth. I felt her nipples peak against my bare chest and the tremor in her long legs as I forced a knee between them. I might not be able to touch but I sure as fuck could feel her. Taking away one sense had heightened the others to the point of almost painful sharpness.

It was more than a kiss. It was so much bigger than her challenging me. It was the start of something that had been simmering under the surface for years. The seeds had always existed in the ground, tiny and immature, and this kiss, this simple touch of the tip of my tongue to hers, was the rain they needed in order to grow. The way she pulled at me, the way she moved her hips restlessly against the insistent bulge in my pants as it pressed into her, was the sun that those tiny bits of nothing needed to flourish. It was the best goddamn foreplay that had ever existed.

I twisted my tongue around hers. I tasted every part of her I could, and as I leaned in closer, my hands began hurting with the effort it was taking to keep them off of her skin. It had been a long time coming, this first volley between us, and it was everything I had ever hoped for where this tricky, stubborn woman was concerned. She didn't stand still and let me kiss her, she kissed me back with everything she had, and soon our lips and tongues were engaged in an aroused battle and I swallowed down a moan as her teeth roughly abraded my bottom lip. I could have her but she was going to make me fight for it.

The kiss lasted for what felt like an eternity, and I only pulled back when my lungs started to scream that they needed air. I felt hot. I was beyond turned on, and as much as I wanted to drag her off to bed or hoist her up on the counter and make a space for myself between her legs, I knew that I couldn't do that. I wanted all the parts of her that made her match me in so many ways, not just her body.

I pushed off the counter and shoved my hands through my hair as I struggled to catch my breath. I watched her as she rubbed her thumb across her damp and swollen lips and smirked up at me in seductive victory.

"How bad do you want to put your hands on me right now, Nassir?" The taunt had no heat behind it because she knew I wanted it more than I wanted to live.

I blew out a breath and took a second to shift my focus off of her heaving chest and onto her light-colored eyes. The tempest that was always raging in the center of those gray depths had calmed and instead was sharpened and honed on me like a weapon. She knew just how easy it was to get to me and she was going to exploit this knowledge every chance she got. She wanted something, wanted me to understand why she was here now, why she was letting this happen between us finally. I considered myself a man of above-average intelligence. I wasn't a genius like my business partner but there wasn't much that slipped by me. Whatever was behind her change of heart and return home was as much a mystery to me as how my mother had been able to sell her only child out to the highest bidder.

"I've wanted to put my hands on you since the very beginning, but once they're there they're never coming off. You're going to have to ask me, Key. You're going to have to make me believe that you understand what it means when you ask me to touch you."

She scoffed at me but I could see my words made her uneasy. "What does it mean?"

I narrowed my eyes the slightest bit and exhaled slowly. She made it hard to breathe in the best way. "It means forever."

Something that looked like fear flashed across her gaze and the angry storm was back swirling at the center. "Forever doesn't seem to last very long in the Point."

"Forever is what you make of it." Forever could be a lifetime trying to right a wrong and wasting a life because you were filled with vengeance and hate, or it could be a youth wasted because of other people's ideals and beliefs. It could be a single second with the right person or an eternity lost chasing the wrong one.

She rolled her eyes at me and scooted around to where I was standing in the center of the kitchen. "This is going to end so badly between us, Nassir. You're going to have to share everything you've pillaged and plundered over the years and you're going to hate me for it. I want to get my hands on all of your shiny toys."

I lifted an eyebrow at her.

"Thinking about it ending in any way, shape, or form means you're admitting something finally started, and that's all I care about. I can learn to share, Key." It might take some time. I was used to be being greedy and selfish with my things and with my time.

She tucked the longer part of her hair back behind her ear and muttered, "I'll believe it when I see it, Gates." Her eyes darted around the kitchen and landed on the massive double doors that led to the back deck that virtually hung off the side of the mountain we were perched on. "Why do you live in a cabin out in the middle of the woods? I mean it's obviously more than a cabin, but seriously? A log house in the sticks? What's up with that?"

I turned my back on her and walked to the fridge to get a bottle of water. "It's the last place on earth anyone would ever look for me. Kind of like you in that diner." And that was the God's honest truth. "I have a suite built into the back of my office in the club so I can stay in the city if I need to, but this is home."

"It's beautiful, but not what I expected."

I thought the same thing about her time and time again. "Make yourself at home. Bayla keeps the pantry stocked, and the rest of your stuff including your car will be here in a few days. If you need anything in the meantime, just ask."

Her eyes snapped back to mine and I saw a pink stain start to spread across her high cheekbones.

"She lives here with you?"

It took me a second to understand who the "she" was that Key was talking about.

"Bayla? No. I live alone, but I work a lot and keep odd hours. This is a big house, so someone needs to look after it. She comes and goes as she pleases." I wondered if the heat I had seen on her face could be attributed to jealousy. That idea made my dick even harder than it already was. "Why?"

I would rather have all my teeth yanked out of my face with rusty pliers than tell her that Bayla had indeed been in my bed more often than not. Key was no fool, so she knew I had spent lots and lots of time with beautiful women over the years, but having the evidence of that right in front of her while I was trying to tie her to me with unbreakable chains wasn't in my best interests.

"Don't be ridiculous. I have watched you fuck your way through every pretty girl that happened across your path for years. You might've had your attention on them from time to time, but you were always looking at me." It was arrogant and made her sound so sure of herself, but she wasn't wrong, so I didn't argue.

"I not only looked at you, I always saw you." And I had. I saw the young girl scared but determined to take her clothes off so she could have something more later on down the line. I saw the young woman coming into her own as she realized she could use her looks and her body to rule her world and to control the people around her. I watched the woman she was now, back where she belonged and ready to usher her broken city into something new, something fierce and formidable.

She cocked her head to the side and regarded me solemnly for a long, quiet minute. "I've always seen you too, Nassir. I know who you really are."

I wanted to laugh. No, she didn't. No one did, not even Chuck, and he had almost all the gory details of my past festering and seething somewhere in his memory bank.

"Who am I, Key? Who do you really think I am?" The words sounded harsh and rumbled out from a place deep inside of my soul. Maybe if she could answer that question, I could finally have some peace. Maybe I could forget the horrible things I had done and the horrible things I was bound to keep on doing to keep my throne.

Calmly and totally serious she told me, "You're the opposite of a good man, Nassir, but that doesn't mean you aren't *my* man." Her stormy eyes flashed at me. "You're my man, and my devil . . . it depends on the day."

I didn't get a chance to respond because she turned on her heel and glided out of the kitchen. Even if I had had time to fire something back at her, I wasn't sure there was anything to say. She was right. I was the devil. I made bargains for souls that weren't mine and I played with fire every single time I stepped foot in the Point. Sins and vices were my playthings and punishment was second nature to me. Suffering felt like old hat and I was pretty sure any soul I might still have left after the life I had led before was now tainted with so much soot and blackness that there was no way it could ever come clean. She saw that part of me and she was still here.

She also saw the part of me that was reserved for her and her alone. The part of me that wanted to protect the innocent, that wanted to give the untouched and the unforgiven a fighting chance. She saw the part of me that still managed to care even though it had never known kindness or softness. It was the part of me she awakened when she looked up at me from the stage when she was just a kid.

I tossed the empty bottle in the recycle bin, scooped up my dirty shirt, and headed out toward the main part of the house. The guest rooms were upstairs on one side of the expansive sprawl and the master was on the other. I had some numbers to run before opening day and I was still waiting on a call from Chuck about whoever had been careless in the cooler earlier, but I was tired. Going head-to-head with Key and the sexual tension still humming in my blood made me feel lethargic.

I was surprised to see Bayla sitting on my white leather couch when I entered the living room. She was quiet and very discreet, which is why I kept her around. She was also very nice to look at and sucked cock like a champ, which had just been a side benefit of bringing her on before I knew Keelyn was going to be under the same roof. She typically knew when to make herself scarce, so I figured her appearance had to do with the woman that was back and determined to turn my entire world end over end.

"Why are you still here?"

The younger woman lifted her dark eyebrows and rose in an elegant motion off the couch. She walked toward me and took the shirt I was still holding out of my hands. I had sacrificed more than one really nice garment to the blood and grime that infiltrated my day-to-day, but this one was still salvageable.

"I'll drop this off at the cleaners for you on my way back into town. How long should I expect your guest to be staying?"

My jaw clenched, and I almost tugged the shirt back out of

her hands. I didn't like being questioned about anything, and as far as Keelyn was concerned, I wasn't going to try to explain that situation to anyone.

"For as long as she wants. Her stuff will be here tomorrow, and she better feel welcome. Do you hear what I am saying to you, Bayla?"

She had never struck me as jealous or proprietary before. Other women had come and gone on her watch, but Key was the first who was allowed to stay.

"I understand perfectly, Nassir. You like to pretend to be made of stone and ice, but you cannot stop yourself from trying to save tragic women. I have seen that firsthand."

They weren't tragic, they were innocent. When I had the means to offer someone the chance to save themselves, I never let it pass. I knew all about being on someone else's leash and coming to heel for a master I never wanted to serve, so I couldn't stop myself from offering the innocent a way out whenever I could. All of the people that worked for me knew there was a way out, there was no contract or intimidation, and I held that up as especially important for the women that worked for me. If they didn't want to dance, if they tired of selling sex, I made sure they had an escape route, and I always did my very best to make sure I had a spot for them in one of the less "objectifying" areas of my business. Few took me up on it. Selling sex was easy, and with me to keep them safe and vet their clients, the women that worked for me often did so without much thought to the future. I'd offered Key more than one exit strategy over the years, but the woman was determined to save herself. She was as far from tragic as they came, and that was one of the primary reasons I could never get her out of my system.

"I'm not trying to save anyone." In fact, whenever I looked into those cloudy gray eyes, it felt like she was the one trying to save me.

Bayla's dark eyes shifted away from my probing gaze and I saw her hands twisting in the expensive fabric of the shirt she had commandeered.

"She must be very special." Her voice was quiet as she turned on her heel and headed toward the front door. "I'll see you sometime tomorrow. Let me know if you have any specific instructions now that you have a permanent guest."

The front door clicked closed behind her and I sighed. Bayla's possessiveness was not a complication or headache I needed to deal with on top of getting the club opened up, and getting Key into my bed. It would be bothersome and time-consuming to find someone else to take care of the house, and I had no doubt that if I kicked her out of her current role, Bayla would end up back on the streets selling herself for money. I didn't want that to be the outcome because she was a good housekeeper and a decent woman, but I wasn't going to let anyone or anything stand in the way of getting what I had wanted for so long.

She'd come to me too young and too broken. I don't know if she found me because I was the lesser of two evils or because I felt familiar. There were a lot of different ethnicities and cultures at work in the Point. A lot of different voices and accents, a lot of variations of skin color, but we were all hiding and looking for something more than we had, wherever it was we originated from, so I always wondered if Bayla sought me out because I felt like a piece of home.

Prostitution was technically legal where I was from, as legal as the sex trade can ever be. However, vices and carnal desire always make man more monster than anything else, and in a place that was always in need of more money to fund a war and feed more terror, something as simple as selling sex legally turns ugly really fast. Bad men buy young girls and force them to work. That money then ends up in the hands of extremists, and girls too young to know what is happening to them are ruined forever.

Bayla suffered in silence as she was sold to a human trafficker and eventually landed on the streets of the Point. She was still in the hands of bad men and still having to do horrible things at an age when most girls are just learning to drive, but she survived. She made it, and when Novak finally went down and I moved in to take over all of his girls, she came to me first. My plan was to let them all go out on their own and be able to handle their money, but much to my surprise, they needed me. They needed the threat of my name and reputation to keep them safe out there on the streets, and Bayla was the first young woman to sign herself up for the partnership.

I never wanted to be responsible for the well-being of anyone else, never wanted that kind of responsibility, but the old adage that sex sells is very true, and ultimately I couldn't walk away from that kind of money. It was shocking how much it mattered to me that girls got taken care of, that they got paid for services rendered, that they had the final say in what they would or wouldn't do. I wanted them safe regardless of where their paychecks came from, so when any of them came to me after being knocked around or with a complaint about an uncooperative client, it made me furious. Far more furious than any of the men that tried to screw me over or take me down on any given day.

Grumbling under my breath about how complicated every single situation I got myself into always seemed to be, whether it was by my own making or someone else's, I pulled my phone out of my pocket as it started to vibrate.

Chuck's number flashed across the screen and I swiped to answer it while climbing up the stairs in the opposite direction of where everything inside me wanted to go. She was here. She was in my home. I had finally tasted her, inhaled her, and welcomed her. I felt like I could breathe again after suffocating for months without her.

"You have a name for me?" Forgetting to put champagne on the shelf might seem like such a simple, insignificant screw-up to most. To me it was almost unforgivable.

When someone was offered a chance, given the opportunity to be part of my business, they needed to shine. I was not a second-chance kind of man.

"Yeah. I looked at the tapes. It was a kid. One of the new barbacks. Took the cases in the cooler and got distracted by a pretty girl. You have a bunch of them wandering around that club and they aren't wearing very much."

"That's no excuse." I pushed my hand through my hair and headed off toward the bathroom attached to the master.

Chuck laughed drily. "I kind of figured you would say that, boss."

"Have him in my office in the morning."

"He's really just a kid, Nassir. The punishment needs to fit the crime."

I popped the button on my pants and reached in to crank the shower on as hot as it would go. Sometimes I thought if the water was hot enough, it would finally make me clean. So far there had never been enough heat. I was still just as dirty and tainted as I had always been.

"You suddenly questioning my methods?"

It was really, really quiet for a long time. So long I thought that maybe Chuck had hung up on me. I knew sometimes what I did was too extreme for him, that sometimes I reminded him of Novak, and it turned his stomach. To stay on top in a place like the Point, you had to leave an impression, even if it was just on a silly kid that got distracted by a nice ass in a short skirt. That was the next generation coming up to run these streets, and I would be damned if they weren't molded by my own hand and my experience.

I wouldn't force my vision on them. I would never ask them to fight my fight. I would never ask them to believe in anything that didn't matter to them, but I would teach them to be careful. I would teach them to watch themselves. I would teach them to identify a threat and to react accordingly. I would teach them how to survive the same way I had learned to survive.

"I might've questioned you before your girl came back, but now that she's here, I doubt you'll be as fucking unhinged as you've been. I had no idea Key was your own personal Jiminy Cricket."

I had no clue what he was talking about and I told him as much. He laughed again and filled me in over his chuckling.

"It's an old cartoon about a boy that isn't real but is given life because his creator loves him. He has a magical cricket that is his conscience and tries to show the boy right from wrong, guides him into making good choices. I had no idea that all these years Keelyn was the thing that was keeping you tethered to being a real boy. Without her around, you became something else, wooden and inhuman."

Even *with* her around I was something else. I had never been given a chance at being a real anything other than a killer, but with Key in my life, I could at least fake it, temper it down and pretend to be more man than monster wearing a muzzle and a leash.

"It's good for everyone that she's back, but I still want the kid in my office in the morning."

"I'll have him there. By the way, I went into the cooler because I know those shelves were installed right."

I shucked my pants off as the room got steamy and flattened my hand across the bruise that Key had touched. I could feel that touch like it was branded into my skin. That was what happened when I had to earn something instead of just taking it and possessing it: the reward lingered. The payoff was so much bigger. The victory hard won and ultimately that much more satisfying.

"What was wrong with them?"

"The top braces were unscrewed from the front section. They have these rubber stoppers on them to keep them from sliding across the metal of the walk-in, and those were missing. When you set the second case on the shelf, the weight was too much and it tipped the entire rack forward. You're really lucky you didn't get crushed. Those bitches are heavy."

I frowned into the mirror. "How does something like that happen?"

Chuck cleared his throat. "I don't know, but it doesn't happen by accident but there were too many people in and out of that cooler to tell if one person was in there longer than another."

I frowned, not liking the implication he was laying out for me. "You think someone deliberately took the stoppers and wanted the shelves to fall?"

"Yeah. I do."

"But how would they know I was the one that would walk into the cooler to move the champagne from the floor?"

"What if it wasn't meant for you, boss?"

"Someone messing with the club?" I swore and let my head fall forward so that I could rub the suddenly tense muscles at the back of my neck.

"It wouldn't be the first time, now, would it?" Chuck's voice was laced with sarcasm. My last club had been burned to a crisp, taking several customers with it, because a madman was hell-bent on destroying the Point and had known exactly where to hit. My clubs were the heartbeat of this city and the way I gave the masses the ability to chase all their dirty dragons was the lifeblood.

"Have your security guys keep an eye out. Let them know everyone is to be on high alert as we head into opening day."

"You got it. How did things go with having your girl home?"

"Fine, but I don't think Bayla is a fan of the current situation. She questioned me and she knows better."

He let out a low whistle. "That might get interesting."

I grunted. "It will not. Bayla works for me, nothing more. Keelyn is everything, so there will be no reason for anything to get interesting."

"We'll see about that. I'll see ya in the A.M., boss."

I hung up the phone and tossed it on the vanity so I could climb under the blistering spray of the shower. Since I was going to bed alone, I figured I might as well take care of the still-throbbing erection I had courtesy of that frantic make-out session in the kitchen. The only thing that was going to get interesting was all the different ways I was going to take Key when she finally came around.

He really was just a kid. Probably no older than twenty or twenty-one, but he walked into my office with enough swagger and self-assurance to choke a horse. He was chatting with Chuck about some game that had been on TV last night and didn't seem to pick up on the tension wafting off the big man or the irritation that I was sure was leaking from me.

He caught sight of me watching him from behind my desk and his friendly grin kicked up a notch as he moved toward me like an eager puppy. This was a kid that was used to getting by in life on his looks and his affable personality, and if he had been smarter he would've reminded me of Race. As it was, he had no clue what he was doing in my office or why I had summoned him.

He reached out a hand as he approached, his words coming out too fast as he moved.

"Hey, it's nice to finally meet you, man, I'm Tyler. I'm so stoked that I passed the background check and got the job. This club is so dope and the girls!" His eyes got huge as I reached for his outstretched hand. "The talent is off the charts."

I leaned forward and pulled on his hand a little so that he had to come closer to the edge of the desk. He gasped out a shocked little noise as I started to squeeze the palm clasped in my own.

"Tyler, is it?" He nodded jerkily as I continued to squeeze. He tried to subtly pull away from me, but I just hauled him closer, making him hit the edge of the desk until he grunted in pain. He put his free hand on the glass surface and tried to tug backward, but I had him and I wasn't letting go. "Did you leave two cases of very expensive champagne on the cooler floor yesterday during your shift?"

His eyes got even wider in his now flushed face and he was panting in earnest. He shook his head back and forth in the negative almost comically. He was panicking for real and I couldn't blame him.

I knew if I applied just a little bit more pressure, bones would start to snap. I squeezed just a fraction tighter until I heard a distinct pop as bone dislocated.

"Funny because I have video footage of you doing exactly that because you were distracted by—what did you call it, the talent? Do you think I keep people around that don't respect my business or my money, Tyler?"

I squeezed again and another knuckle slid out of place. The kid was straight up crying and turning purple. If it was up to me I would keep going. I would break all his fingers and kick his sloppy, snotty ass out to the curb, but Chuck was watching me carefully, so I stopped. I let go of the kid's hand and sat back in my chair while he fell to his knees on the other side of my desk.

"I should fire you, but my associate seems to think you can learn from your mistake. What do you say, Tyler, are you ever going to be so careless with my product again?"

The kid cradled his hand against his chest and behind his watery gaze I saw a flash of something that looked oddly familiar. Hatred.

He was humiliated and furious about it.

"No. No, I won't make that kind of mistake again, sir."

I nodded and indicated his hand with a wave of my own. "I don't have to tell you that a handshake is merely the tip of the iceberg when it comes to how I handle disappointment with my employees."

The kid gulped. "No, sir."

"Good. Now get out of my office." He clambered to his feet and rushed away from me, toward Chuck, and disappeared into the elevator.

Chuck shook his head at me and turned to follow the kid out. "You'll never be a real boy."

I rolled my eyes at him. Of course I wouldn't.

CHAPTER 7

Keelyn

Y*ou need to give it life."*
      I had no idea what Nassir meant by those words until the club opened its doors a day after I returned to the Point. I thought I was going to throw on something outrageously sexy, slick down my newly unmistakable hair, gloss on some ruby-red lipstick, wear the highest heels I could find, and mingle with the crowd. I was sadly mistaken.

I was used to selling sex to customers that knew they were going home alone. It was an entirely different ball game when the customers knew that every fantasy, every desire they had, was within reach. The air vibrated with anticipation and the waves of excitement that poured off the eager men and women as they entered the club were enough to drown in. I still had my doubts about Nassir's system of locks and keys, but he had a small army of security staff mingling unobtrusively among the clubgoers and the hired help. It was an anything-goes atmosphere, but the men in black suits wired up with headsets and sporting sharp-eyed stares reminded even the most outrageous customer that there were still rules that needed to be obeyed.

For the first hour I was unsure what to do with myself. I was stunned by how normal and how average most of the people that had forked over so much money to be a member of this exclusive club appeared to be. I was equally stunned by the number of couples that were milling about in the crowd. I threaded my way around the bodies, some dressed like they had just come from the office and some dressed a hundred times more scandalously than I was. I stopped to talk to a few young men that recognized me from my stripping days, told them no when they asked if I would be available for any "extra services" the club offered, and said a quick hello to a couple of girls I recognized from Spanky's that were now working here. I stopped to ask them how it all came about and was surprised when they told me Nassir made it happen. They didn't want to strip anymore, didn't want to be naked onstage, so he set them up in the lavish bar and told them they had a place in his juggernaut of sex and industry as long as they wanted one.

Pondering this new insight into the man who was forever surprising me, I made my way to the bar and asked the very cute bartender to pour me a shot of tequila. Drinking at the old Spanky's had been a terrible idea. The customers there were already handsy and grabby, so keeping your wits about you was a must. Here everyone seemed relatively well behaved and so excited to finally be inside the doors that no one was even really paying attention to me, so I figured a little liquid fortification wouldn't hurt anybody. I tossed the liquor back and hissed out a breath around the burn. I caught the eye of a pretty young woman standing next to me at the bar who was watching me closely. I lifted an eyebrow at her and signaled for another shot.

"Can I help you?"

She was attractive in a really unassuming way. Her blond hair was pulled back in a low ponytail, her eyes covered in chic and stylish eyeglass frames, and her outfit was obviously expensive, though it looked like it would be more appropriate in a five-star restaurant than a sex club, but her shoes—oh, I'd recognize those shiny black stilettos with their unmistakable red soles anywhere. The lady had excellent taste in footwear.

She lowered her eyes behind her glasses and I saw her blush. She lifted her fingers and fidgeted with the gold key that was hanging from her neck. She looked about as uncomfortable as any woman alone in this kind of establishment could look.

"No. I don't think anyone can help me. I'm not even really sure what I'm doing here." She lifted her gaze back up to me and shrugged.

I frowned a little and pushed the shot that was in front of me down to her. "Try that. It might help."

She looked at the shot glass then up to me. A half grin pulled at her lips. "Thanks, but I would choke on it and look ridiculous. That's why I was watching you. I was in awe of how effortlessly sexy you seem to be. You look like you were made to be part of this place. I feel so out of my element."

I wasn't sure if that was a compliment, but considering I stood to make a lot of money off of this club, money that I was determined to put back into the community in some way, I was going to choose to take it as one.

"What are you doing here, then? I know how much it costs to get your hand on that little key hanging around your neck, so obviously you want to be here."

She picked up the shot and tossed it back. It did make her cough and turn red. I bit back a laugh as I reached out to pat her on the back. Once she got some air back in her lungs, she looked at me through watery eyes and explained, "I have a very high-stress job and I work a million hours a week. I'm not really looking for a relationship or anything serious. I just wanted to go somewhere I could have fun, let go of the control a little. I thought this place was the perfect fit, but once I got here, the idea of forking over hard-earned cash for someone to put me over their knee and spank me seemed so cheap and silly." She sighed. "It's just ridiculous."

I let my gaze slide down from the top of her head to the tips of those fabulous shoes. If ever there was a lesson to be learned about not judging a book by its cover, this was it. I clicked my tongue at her and leaned a little closer so that I could lower my voice when I talked into her ear.

"You should never feel cheap or guilty for wanting what you want. You should be proud and not afraid to ask for it. Look around you." I indicated the packed club. "All these people are here for the same reason as you. And who says you have to pay for it? You're cute, you have great taste in shoes, and I bet we can find you a guy that would be more than happy to give you what you need at no extra cost."

She blinked at me again and I saw a warm flush work

into her cheeks. She looked so sweet and so proper that the idea that she wanted someone to spank her made me want to laugh, but I liked how unassuming she came across, so if that's what she was after, I would help her get it.

"I'm not very good with men. I'm shy and I have a hard time carrying on a conversation around someone I find attractive. I usually end up looking like an idiot."

I leaned back away from her and started scoping out the men circulating in the bar area. Many of them were already with women, many had that lock clicked shut where it dangled around their necks, and a few were obviously the hired help working the crowd to make a buck, but there were a few that appeared to be single and looked like they would be an all-right fit for the blonde.

"You don't need to have a conversation. All you need to do is find out if he's into what you're into, and if he is and you think he'll flip your switch, you give him the green light."

She gulped a little and fidgeted with the empty shot glass in front of her. "Doesn't that make me easy?"

I lifted both my eyebrows at her and indicated the tight, black leather pants I had on and the deep red bustier that was barely containing my chest. "Do I look like the type to judge? And what's easy? You had to buy a membership, work up the courage to come in here, and find the right guy. That all sounds like work to me. Besides, what happens in this club stays here. That's part of the fantasy. No one else should ever get a say in the kind of sex you choose to have as long as it's between consenting adults."

She considered me thoughtfully for a few seconds and then moved away from the bar. "You'll help me?"

I nodded. "Sure, and if I can't deliver, then you always have the option of taking one of Nassir's guys for a spin." I pointed to a beefy-looking young man that was obviously checking her out. She put a hand up to her neck again and turned wide eyes to me.

"Holy shit."

I laughed a little and took her elbow to guide her toward a table of guys that were just a few feet away. "He has good taste."

"Who? Nassir or that guy?" She had some sass. That made me like her even more.

"Both. Now let's go get you what you want."

The first table of guys was a bust. They were too young, and as soon as we approached they couldn't tear their eyes away from my boobs long enough to pay attention to my new friend. A guy at a second table had more potential, but when he tried to talk to the blonde, she really did clam up and the situation got awkward fast. I struck out with guy three as well. Turned out he was much more interested in the handsome bartender than he was in what we were offering, and I could feel the woman's confidence and enthusiasm starting to waver with each failure. I told her not to give up even though I was starting to wonder if I was going to be successful in my plans when an older gentleman caught my eye. He was standing off to the side of the crowd watching the circus with amused eyes. He had dark hair with a liberal sprinkling of silver woven into it and a strong jaw with a bit of dark scruff along the edge. He was very, very good-looking in a mature kind of way, and as I started to make my way toward him his gaze skimmed over me and landed solidly on my charge.

"Hi." I smiled up at him and was floored by the blinding-white smile I got back. Oh, this guy was good and he didn't even have to try.

"Hello." I noticed that the lock around his neck was very much open and signaling that he was unattached as I grabbed the blonde and wheeled her around in front of me.

"This is my friend . . ." I trailed off, realizing I hadn't even bothered to ask the other woman her name.

I nudged her until she offered up, "Clare."

"This is my friend Clare and she's looking for someone special."

His dark eyebrows shot up and that smile kicked up a notch. I thought I heard Clare whimper next to me.

"Is that so? What kind of someone special is Clare looking for?" Direct and charming, he was the perfect guy to give the little blonde what she needed for the night.

"Tell him, Clare."

She couldn't have been any redder if she tried. Her mouth opened and closed like a guppy and I thought she was going to blow it again when the man reached out and touched a finger to her lips.

"If you can't tell me, can you show me?" She shot wide eyes to me and then back to him. I took a step back as she nodded slowly. "Good girl. You want to give me that key?"

Without a word, she unhooked the necklace and handed it over to the silver fox. He put the end in the lock that dangled around his own neck and clicked the lock shut. Watching this, I realized how symbolic the action was. Her key into his lock: it was so sensual and a metaphor for so much more than sex.

She owned him for the night, and that had to make her feel like a million bucks.

She mouthed "thank you" over her shoulder as the man led her away and I wanted to give myself a pat on the back. I had always been solidly secure in my own sexuality and it looked like instead of projecting that out and getting others to lust after me, it was time I helped others find their inner stripper and comfort in their own wants and needs.

I mingled some more. Gave Chuck a quick hug when I passed him, did another shot at the bar, which somehow led to me having the bottle of tequila in my hand and encouraging a rather dowdy-looking woman to do body shots off the bar, and generally worked the crowd like a pro. I was totally getting into my groove, finally starting to understand what Nassir meant about giving the club life, when I found a man standing in the shadows off the dance floor while he watched a pretty boy dressed in nothing but a leather G-string gyrate to the EDM blasting through the club's sound system.

He was shifting uneasily from foot to foot, his eyes locked on the show the other man was putting on. I put a hand on his shoulder and smiled.

"Go talk to him. What could it hurt?" Only I should have paid closer attention because the man had his lock around his neck firmly clicked closed and it wasn't the designated color that indicated he was there for some same-sex action.

He puffed up and sputtered at me, "I'm here with my wife!"

I lifted up my hands in a gesture of surrender. "Sorry, friend. I just thought . . ."

"You thought what? Who are you? Get away from me."

The man stormed off in a huff and some of my good cheer dissipated. I wondered what he was doing here with his wife if he wasn't in search of an opportunity to explore his obvious desire to be with another man. Sad for him and really sad for his wife. I decided I needed a little break. I could only play sexual-fantasy fairy godmother for so long.

There was a break room on one of the floors, but the person I wanted was in his office on the top floor. I hadn't seen much of Nassir since I walked away from him after that kiss. My stuff had shown up at the house and the housekeeper that obviously hated me had made sure it all got delivered up to my borrowed room, but Nassir wasn't around. He hadn't even come back to the house last night, and when I asked the chilly woman in charge of his home about it, she just muttered that he often stayed in the city when he had business.

He came back to the mountain house to grab me for opening night, but we'd spent the ride mostly in silence. When I asked him what he expected me to do, he just looked at me out of those eyes that seemed to glow and told me to do whatever felt comfortable. He wanted me on the floor. He wanted me to mingle. He wanted me to make people comfortable and stick around. He wanted the club to be about more than sex, and I think I finally figured out how to do that.

Once we got to the massive building, he guided me inside, looked at me like he wanted to push me up against the wall and ravish me, and then disappeared without another word.

Well, now I had plenty to say to him. I wanted to ask him if I was doing all right, if the club was doing all right. I wanted him to tell me I was doing a good job and I really, really wanted him to kiss me again. The whole hands-to-himself thing was getting old really fast and he showed no sign of bending—let alone breaking—to give me what I wanted.

I pushed the button for the elevator that led to his office and put in the little card that would allow me access to his private space. The only people that could get up to the top floor besides Nassir were me and Chuck. Nassir was lording over his domain from relative security and I loved and hated that I was one of the few allowed inside the gates. I didn't want his keys to the kingdom; I wanted my own set.

When the doors whooshed open I was greeted with the sight of him behind his big desk in the center of the room. On the wall behind him, a collection of monitors with video feeds from the private client rooms blasted some of the most pornographic images I had ever seen in my life, along with shots of the parking lot, the dance floor, and the bar. I blinked in shock as I watched a man get guided around a room on a leash. I couldn't comprehend the image of a woman chained up spread eagle above the ground while two men moved sexually and aggressively in front and behind her. I couldn't look away as another image showed what had to be no less than six people engaged in a tangle of limbs as they took part in an orgy right before my eyes.

Nassir seemed oblivious to it all. He had two laptops open and was focused on something on his phone. He looked up when I started to move across the room toward him, but I couldn't meet his gaze. I was transfixed by what was happening behind him and couldn't look away.

"You have the private rooms wired?" It was a stupid question but it was all I could manage.

"Just the rooms that people pay for. The private rooms like the one you sent the blonde off into are not." He lifted an eyebrow at me. "By the way, that was nice what you did with her. That's exactly why I wanted you on board with this club. You understand human sexuality and the innate fear people have of it better than anyone I have ever met."

I lifted an eyebrow at him. "You do realize that a king without people to lord over is nothing more than a lonely man on a fancy chair, right? You can't have power if there isn't someone to exert it over. People and prestige go hand in hand, Nassir." I ignored the way my words made his face darken, and asked, "Why have cameras only in the rooms people pay for?"

He snorted and waved a hand behind his head. "Because people pay for outrageous stuff they can't get on their own. A little spanking, some light bondage, a submissive to practice basic S&M on, that's stuff any average Joe can usually scare up if they look hard enough." He hooked a thumb over his shoulder. "The kind of stuff going on in those rooms is easier to pay for."

"How can you work with all of that . . . sex"—I wasn't sure that was the right word for all the crazy I was witnessing behind him but it would have to do— "going on behind you? Isn't it distracting?"

He touched the screen of his phone and the video feed went black. "That is work. The guy on the end of the leash is a federal judge. The woman chained up is a district attorney and the couple that paid for the orgy own one of the biggest import and export companies in the state."

I pushed some of my hair off my face and moved to prop

myself up on the edge of his desk. "You set them up. They can't know you are filming them. They would never agree to that."

He leaned back in his chair and his dark eyebrows shot up. He always looked like he was up to no good—probably because he typically was.

"Sometimes people ignore all the risks associated with going after something they want. If I promise to make fantasy a reality, then all bets are off."

I sighed and let my gaze rove over him. He had on a dark gray shirt that was unbuttoned at the collar and his typical suit jacket and neatly pressed slacks. If I could see below the desk, I bet the shoes he had on cost more than mine. My devil dressed to the nines and always looked sharp. That was his disguise, but it never fooled me. I should be used to the impact he had on me but I wasn't, and my pulse jumped when his gaze settled on me.

"Do you even see human beings or just opportunities and dollar signs?" He'd told me that he saw me, but I wondered if I was an anomaly in his world.

"Depends on what I need them for. All of the people in those rooms knew what they were getting into when they plunked their cash down to indulge their proclivities. They know I'll give them anonymity, a place to do their thing, and in return, when I need a favor, they will provide it. It's an even exchange."

I crossed my arms over my chest, which pushed my breasts up and almost over the top of the fabric. Nassir noticed and my body reacted without thought. Being around him always made me feel like I was moving through a fog of sexual tension and repressed desire. He made the air thick and I could feel his eyes on me like a physical touch. It was getting tougher to convince myself that I couldn't do forever with a man like him.

"Nothing with you is an even exchange. They think you'll ask for one favor, but you won't. You'll ask for as many as you need, and if they don't comply, you'll remind them that you can air their dirty laundry anytime you want to. The second they stepped foot into your trap, you owned them."

He laced his fingers together and laid them across his flat stomach. I watched the movement and decided he was too far away. Before he could argue with me or tell me I was right about his tricks of the trade, I walked the rest of the way around his desk and planted myself squarely in his lap. He let out a surprised grunt and lifted his hands like he was going to pull me closer. At the last second he swore and put them on the arms of his chair, curling his fingers around the leather like it was a lifeline.

I used the tip of my index finger to trace the way his Adam's apple bobbed up and down as I breathed against his throat. I wanted to lick him, so I did. He tasted tangy and salty, just like I knew he would. He said my name in a low voice as I trailed the tip of my tongue along the thick vein that ran up the side of his neck until I reached his ear. His too-long hair tickled the end of my nose as I nuzzled into him and his body went stone still when I traced the outer shell of his ear before whispering, "How far do I have to push until you fall for me?"

He chuckled and it shifted me on his lap so that there was no missing the bulge hidden behind his expertly tailored trousers.

"I like it when you push at me, Key, even when you're

pushing me away. I mean, you're here and you're fighting, me or yourself. It doesn't matter." He smirked at me and my heart flipped over. "But I fell for you long ago, so there's nowhere else for me to go."

That made the iron grip I had on my heart slip just a fraction. It would be so very easy to hand it over to him.

I dipped my finger into the open collar of his shirt and traced a line down his sternum, popping his shirt buttons open as I went. His smooth, coppery skin was hot to the touch and my fingers wanted to brush across all of it. Being closer to him than I had ever allowed myself to be, I could see that Nassir's tailored suits hid far more than that massive tattoo that covered his back. He had puckered burn marks along his collarbone. There was a wicked scar that looked like someone had tried to cut him in half across his entire belly. He had more than one circular scar that was raised up and smooth. I knew exactly what they were from since I had the exact same kind of scar from where the bullet had torn through my shoulder. His torso was a road map of violent, ugly things, and as much as I wanted to hear the story behind each and every mark, the gory details chronicling his survival and victory, I knew that once I had them, once I knew him inside and out, I would never be able to escape. I didn't want the devil to be able to justify his actions. I knew his story was going to be tragic and full of suffering. I wasn't sure my heart was ready to hear it just yet, not when it was getting used to being in his hands and under his control.

"Why me, Nassir? You don't have patience for anything that isn't perfect and I am far from that. Why would you wait for me all this time, especially when you have beautiful women dying to take my place?" His gorgeous housekeeper immediately came to mind.

I reached the top of his pants and stopped so I could brush the back of my hands across the chiseled divots and lines that cut across his abdomen. The man was built. There wasn't an ounce of anything extra on him and every place I was pressed up against was hard and unyielding. Those pricy suits hid the body of a warrior, but the things that were darker, scarier, and fierce enough to control this city shone bright and clear out of those molten eyes.

"If not you, then who, Keelyn? Who else has the fight and the strength to stand with me in this city? You own a part of it just like I do. You earned your place here while I took mine, and you might not want to be Honor but you have it in spades. You care about this place and the people in it. You care about me even though you know you shouldn't. You're the only one in my life who has ever been worth waiting for."

I knew he was just stating the facts as he saw them, but to me it was the most romantic, most heartfelt thing any man, any person, had ever said to me, and as a result, more of my resolve slipped away. I wanted to be his equal, his perfect match, and it sounded like he had considered me that from the very start, even though I'd needed him to save me.

I kissed him on the cheek. It was silly and too tame for a man like Nassir Gates, but from the way his chest rumbled in reaction and the way his legs tensed under my backside, I knew it got to him as effectively as if I had sunk to my knees in front of him.

"When you're sweet like that, it makes it harder to remember why I want to hate you." I started tugging on his belt and his tight stomach pulled in even tighter as I got the leather open and slipped the button out of the hole.

I was expecting silk or maybe silky-smooth bare skin, but I was surprised when my questing fingers encountered only regular old cotton boxer briefs encasing an erection that flexed and throbbed as I reached for it. I heard him suck in a loud breath and his hand let go of the arm of the chair like he was going to try to stop me from pulling him free of the clothing that was separating me from my destination, but his iron will kicked in at the last second and his hands balled into fists as he narrowed his eyes at me.

"You can't hate me, Key. I wouldn't survive it."

I got my hand around him and couldn't hold back a whispery sigh of satisfaction as he pulsed hot and hard in my hand. He stretched and filled my grasp. He was even pretty and coppery where he stretched and grew to fill my palm. My hand looked so pale and delicate as it started to work him up and down. His body went rigid and his eyes burned at me. I wanted to get closer but he refused to move his hands off the arms of the chair and I couldn't shift my weight without falling off of his lap or letting go of his cock. His discipline was annoying if admittedly impressive, but I had a lot to lose if I didn't get him to give in . . . like my heart and soul.

I put my mouth over his and gave him a biting kiss. I wasn't surprised when he growled at me in frustration instead of kissing me back. I felt his breathing start to get erratic and grinned at him victoriously when I felt moisture start to leak out of the tip of his cock. I swirled the pearly drop around with the pad of my thumb and watched as it made him shiver. I was manhandling him like he was a piece of meat and his body couldn't help but react, and I knew that had to drive him crazy. Nassir liked to be in charge of everything and everyone.

I laughed lightly against his lips, twisted my wrist, and added a little more pressure as I continued to work him over. This time he kissed me back and it stole all the air from my lungs and all the sense from my head. He kissed like he did everything else, with finesse, with skill, with demand and force. My lips tingled and my tongue couldn't wait to chase his around as he invaded the damp cavern in my mouth. My center clenched and that place that ached for him between my legs went liquid and soft. If I was straddling him instead of sitting across him, I would be grinding myself against that turgid staff that was burning in my palm.

His head snapped back and his eyes popped with bronze embers as he bit out my name.

"Key." I knew he was close to coming and knew that I should calmly get up off his lap, leave him hanging rock hard and unsatisfied to show him I had the upper hand in this game, and show him I could be just as ruthless as he was when it came to getting what I wanted.

I couldn't do it, though. I wanted to watch him go over. I wanted to see him come apart for me. I wanted to see this man that manipulated everything and everyone around him fall because he couldn't control me and his reaction to me. There was a power in that, an intoxication that had me stroking my thumb under the sensitive rim of the head and pumping my fist up and down even faster. I lost myself kissing and licking on the side of his neck until his entire frame coiled up and then shuddered under me as hot liquid burst forth and slicked over both of us. It was a different kind of burn but it felt so good.

A long sigh escaped him as I lifted my head and looked down at him in satisfaction. He didn't look happy about the situation, but there was no mistaking the heated desire churning inside his eyes. He didn't touch me, but he wanted to, and the battle was almost a losing one. It was stamped on every line of his face. I leaned forward to kiss him on the cheek again and whispered softly in his ear, "I can't hate you, Nassir, but I don't know if I can love you the way you want me to either. They both feel impossible and scary."

He didn't say anything, but he did shift so he could pull open a drawer of his desk and grab some Kleenex so I could clean myself up after I climbed off of him. He was rumpled and disheveled. It was a good look for him and I had to admire my handiwork. He situated himself back into his pants and stood so that he was looming over me. The fire in his eyes had banked but it didn't make him look any less dangerous or fierce.

"The only guarantee in life is that we only have a limited amount of time on this planet, so we better make the most of it. We've already wasted a lot of that time skirting around the inevitable, Key. I'm not interested in giving any more of it, or you, up."

We both turned as the elevator made a whooshing sound, signaling that Chuck was on his way up to the office.

"I'm not giving you my heart." I said it the exact same way

that I had told him I was never coming home. Solidifying the fact that I was a terrible liar.

He reached out a hand like he was going to move some of the bright red hair off my face but then pulled it back at the last minute as if touching me would singe him.

"You don't have to give it to me, because I'm going to take it one way or the other. I've been stealing bits and pieces for years; you were just too busy struggling against me, determined to do things on your own and without me, to notice."

Had he been?

Was all his silent protection and wordless offering without getting a thing from me in return the way he had been making off with what I was so sure I wasn't willing to give? When he showed that he could care, that he had the capacity for kindness and compassion, it undid all the warnings he aroused in me. I was going to tell him to stop being sweet so I could think straight, but Chuck barreled through the doors looking stressed and annoyed.

"Why aren't you answering the phone and did you not just see what went down in the bar?"

His eyes shot to the black monitors behind the desk and then over our rumpled appearances. He shook his head and put his hands on his hips.

"You two are going to be the death of me—or each other. Quit fooling around and get back to business. We have a problem and I need to know how you want to handle it."

Nassir shot me a look out of the corner of his eye and I flushed.

Business-only arrangement, my ass.

CHAPTER 8

Nassir

The elevator ride down to the club was silent and the tension popping and snapping between me and Key was electric enough that it could power the entire building. Chuck kept giving me a look out of the corner of his eye that I purposely ignored. My nerves were already taut. Every last bit of self-control had already been used up while I wrestled with every instinct I had in order to keep my hands off of her while she played with me, tormented me. The veneer of civility that I wore was thin at best, and with Key poking at it, battering against it in order to get her own way, there wasn't much left to hold me in check.

"So some doughy guy and his wife got into it in the bar. Security was just getting ready to intervene when the wife took a beer bottle and smashed it against the edge of the table. She went after him with it, but security got to them before any damage could actually be done." Chuck shook his head. "Caused business in the bar to shut down for about thirty minutes or so. Security wants to know if you want to call the cops or not."

I pushed my hands through my hair and smoothed down the thoroughly wrinkled front of my shirt. I heard Key snicker at the motion, and cut her a hard look.

"I don't want the cops anywhere near this place. King will use any excuse he can find to shut us down and we haven't even been open for a day. I'll handle it." I sighed. "I knew jealous spouses were going to be part of the equation when we opened the doors. One person's wish list often leaves the other out in the cold."

Key gave a delicate little snort and was the first to step off the elevator when it hit the ground floor.

"They shouldn't be together if their wish list isn't the same. It'll never work out." She glided away like she was a queen leaving her peasants to do her bidding, and I watched her until I couldn't see her anymore.

"You're in trouble with that one, boss." Humor liberally laced Chuck's tone as we turned and went the opposite way from the bar.

"I know, but it's trouble that will be worth it in the end." I just had to convince Key of that.

We headed down a long hallway and to another elevator that went to the lower level of the building. Back when it had been offices the lower floor was used mostly to keep files and store information. I had turned it into a mini-jail of sorts. I knew there were going to be problems. Whenever you mixed sex, booze, and no limits, people tended to lose all their inhibitions and basic rationality. I knew that there were going to be club members that didn't want to follow the rules or respect the club, so I made sure I had a place to deal with them in my own way. All the rooms were made of concrete walls, sound-proof and escape-proof; whatever happened down here would never be heard anywhere else in the building. It was a scary place to be and I could see that the couple sequestered in this very unforgiving place knew that.

They were sitting in metal chairs on opposite sides of a small metal table. One of the security guys was standing between them just staring at the door, waiting for my arrival. When I pushed the metal door open he nodded at me silently and slipped out of the room, leaving me and Chuck alone with the obviously nervous couple. The wife was fidgeting with her fingernails and the husband was looking anywhere but at me.

"You signed a contract when you applied to be members of this club. In that contract it specifically states that you will leave at home any and all bullshit you wade in every day. I'm not a marriage counselor and this isn't therapy."

The man finally looked at me and then away as soon as our eyes met. I heard him gulp from across the room. The woman decided her best shot at getting out of here was to throw him under the bus.

"I shouldn't even be here!" She pointed at her husband with a shaking hand. "This is all his fault."

I lifted an eyebrow and walked over to take up the spot between them that the security guard had abandoned. I put my hands on the edge of the table and leaned down slightly. The woman reared back and the husband just let his head hang forward.

"The only law inside these doors is mine."

That brought the man's head up and he shot a pleading look in my direction. "I'm so sorry we disrupted your grand opening. Just let us go and we'll never come back." It was obvious he was familiar with the tales of how I handled disruptions in my business. Some of those tales were grossly exaggerated, but most were fairly accurate. I didn't let anyone mess with my money.

"Oh, you won't be coming back, that's a given. I'm just trying to decide if you'll be going anywhere from here on out without a permanent limp."

The woman let out an earsplitting shriek and shoved her chair back, knocking it over and making it bang loudly against the cement floor.

"This is all your fault, you pervert! If you could keep your sick perversions in check, we wouldn't even be here!"

The husband opened his mouth to argue, but then just gave up and hung his head. The wife was loud and obnoxious; no wonder he didn't try to fight back when she went after him. I would wager that his life was nothing more than pacifying her and being berated by her. "If I'm a pervert, what does that make you?" These were two people on very different pages.

I pushed up off the table and pinned the woman with a look. "Why did you come here in the first place if you weren't going to support his 'perversions'?"

She opened her mouth and then snapped it shut. She shook her head and looked at her husband for help. He sighed and let his head fall forward so that his forehead banged heavily on the metal table.

"She wanted to have a threesome . . . with another woman. It was supposed to put the spark back in our marriage." It was a common enough fantasy, especially in a union that was as obviously unhappy as this one.

"And . . . ?" Clearly I was missing part of the story.

The wife tossed her hair over her shoulder and waved her hand at her defeated spouse. "Kind of hard to have a threesome with another woman when your husband is too busy shoving his dick down a man's throat."

The husband groaned and I barked out a laugh. The woman scowled at me and I narrowed my eyes at her. "You're mad at him because he wants to be with a man and yet you're obviously the only one interested in being with another woman? You're both ridiculous and this isn't the place for either of you."

"We paid a fortune to be a part of this club and then waited forever for it to open." I couldn't believe she was going to argue with me.

To remind her exactly where she was and whose rules she was playing by, I moved around to her side of the table and kept walking toward her until she was backed into the concrete wall. I bent my head so that my mouth was right by her ear and asked her, "So what?"

She gulped and I could see that she was starting to sweat. The knowledge that I could literally make her and her spouse disappear was finally starting to sink in and she began to shake and get teary-eyed.

I backed off and gave them both a disgusted look. "I think the worst thing I can do to either one of you is send you home with each other. You can torture each other by staying together and not admitting you want other people. I'm keeping your deposit and the fees for membership." The wife opened her mouth to argue but I held up a hand to shut her down. "And if you think of calling the cops or trying to come after me for the money, I'll be more than happy to let your boss at the bank know about the nifty little embezzling scam you have going on." Knowledge was the ultimate power and I could see that she knew she was defeated.

Her eyes nearly popped out of her head and she started to sputter. I reached up and grabbed the key dangling around her neck and gave it a light tug. The chain holding it snapped and I motioned for Chuck to get the man's lock from around his neck. He clapped the man on the shoulder and helped him to his feet.

"Good luck with that one, son. You're gonna need it, and maybe stay away from anything sharp and pointy when you get home." The husband looked at Chuck, then at his wife.

"I'm leaving. When we get home I'm packing my shit up and I'm gone."

Chuck nodded as the irate woman's jaw dropped open. "What! You can't leave me!"

The husband snorted. "Sure I can. You aren't worth any of this aggravation, and tonight, with that guy, is the first time in years that I've had an actual erection without having to pop a Viagra. If I stay with you I will kill you or myself, so before it gets to that point, I'm gone." His gaze shifted to me and a half grin quirked up the corner of his mouth. "You might not think you're a marriage counselor, but you fixed this decades-long nightmare in twenty minutes. Thanks for setting me free."

Chuck walked to the door and put two fingers in his mouth to whistle for one of the security guards to escort the couple out of my dungeon. Once they were gone, we shared a look and burst out laughing. It was too ridiculous for words. Chuck clapped me on the back as we walked toward the elevator to head back up to the main level of the club.

"There's hope for you yet, boss."

I grunted. "Glad you think so."

Hope wasn't something I was very familiar with, so I would just have to take his word for it.

AFTER THE TINY hiccup on the first day, the rest of the week went smoothly. Key really settled into her role as hostess and caretaker of the patrons. She seemed to have an innate knack for finding the lost, the confused, and the timid and making them comfortable, helping them open up and really explore the adult playground I had built for them. She was also a wiz at livening up the bar on the slower weeknights, so even if I wasn't making money on the private rooms, I was still raking in a small fortune in liquor sales. She had no trouble getting on the bar and doing a little shimmy and shake or even putting her old job skills to use and offering up a much tamer peep show to get the crowd going. She was a perfect fit for the club and the perfect business partner. After a few days of watching some of the shyer female patrons, she suggested we do a ladies-only night. It was brilliant and something I doubt would've ever occurred to me. And after the debacle with the married couple on opening night, she also suggested we do a couples-only night. I liked the way her mind worked. She saw past the dollar signs to the people attached to the money, and that's what this place needed. That was something I could never do.

Along with all the good things that were happening, there were also some really annoying setbacks that seemed to keep popping up, which solidified the idea that someone was trying to mess with the club from the inside. It was also a major headache that I was spending most of my time trying to do damage control rather than persuading Key to give in to me, which is what I really wanted to be focused on. After she worked me over up in my office, she hadn't put her hands on me again, mostly because she didn't have an opportunity to do so. We were both working hard and I think she was a little gun-shy. We'd been sitting on a powder keg of repressed desire and untouched emotion for years. She lit the match and the fuse was burning. I think we both knew the explosion waiting for us when we ignited was going to be life-altering.

One of the annoyances that was taking up my time and making me ready to bang heads together was a missed liquor delivery that caused the bar to run dry one night and cost a fortune to rush-deliver over the weekend. Apparently someone had called in claiming to work for me and canceled the order right before it was supposed to be delivered. Someone went into the women's restrooms and shoved cotton T-shirts in all of the toilets and then flushed them all, causing a flood of epic proportions and a plumbing bill that was outrageous. They did it on two floors of the building, shutting down operations for half a night until I could get it fixed. The biggest clusterfuck happened on a Friday night. It was a packed house, people were getting their weekend groove on, the bar was full, all the rooms upstairs were full of people doing their thing, and I was finally thinking I was going to catch a break when all hell broke loose on the monitors I was watching behind the desk.

I saw one of the bartenders scream and jump up on the bar. Soon the other two followed suit and everyone in the packed bar looked like they were losing their damn minds and jumping up on whatever piece of furniture they could find. Key was in the center of the chaos looking as confused as I felt. People started pouring out of all the private rooms in various stages of undress, all with the same panicked look on their faces. I was climbing to my feet to head down to the floor to see what the hell was going on when I saw Key scream as a gigantic black rat ran across her foot. She hopped to her other foot and shot a look up to the camera she knew was watching her.

"There's hundreds of them!" I couldn't hear her, but I could see what she was saying plain as day.

I pulled my cell phone out of my pocket and dialed Chuck. "Rats?"

"Son of a bitch! It's like a goddamn plague in here!"

I swore and rushed to the elevator. "Start clearing everybody out."

"Already on it. Key is moving everyone in the bar to the front doors. This isn't good for business, boss."

"No shit. How in the hell did someone get hundreds of rats past our security?" I hated when anyone messed with my money, but I hated when someone outsmarted me even more.

"Don't know, but I'm not happy about it. I hate rats."

"I hate losing money. We're gonna be shut down for at least two days getting all those little creatures out of here."

"If not longer. I'll go pull up the video feed, but if it's like the last two incidents, there won't be anything."

I swore again as the elevator deposited me in the back hallway. I moved toward the bar area, ushering people toward the exit as I did so. They all looked kind of frantic and disgruntled that all their fun had been ruined for the weekend. I didn't apologize, but I did tell anyone that asked that they would of course be given a credit. It was a pain in the ass, and when a particularly fat and ugly rodent scurried across my foot, it was all I could do not to kick it into a wall. It was disgusting and had perfectly succeeded in shutting me down. Fury lashed hot and bright inside of me.

When I reached the bar I saw that Key had done a pretty good job of clearing out most of the patrons. The floor looked like it was alive as furry bodies climbed all over it and each other. I could see she was grossed out but keeping it together as she helped one of the bartenders off the bar and told them laughingly to take the rest of the night off. Our eyes met across the space and I motioned for her to go on and head outside as well. She nodded back and carefully picked her way across the vermin-covered floor. The noise of the rodents had my skin crawling as I went to follow her. The smell was enough to have me biting back bile, and the rage at all my hard work and careful planning being disrupted was enough to choke me.

I called Chuck and told him to make sure the building was clear of people and also to see if he could find a twenty-four-hour exterminator. He already had his guys doing a floor-by-floor sweep for any remaining clubgoers. He told me to take the night off and that we could tackle the mess and whoever was behind it in the morning.

I begrudgingly agreed and made my way over to where Keelyn was standing by her car.

"I need to burn everything I have on right now. You owe me a new pair of Jimmy Choos." She stuck out her foot and scowled at the strappy, nude-colored high heel her foot was encased in.

"I'll buy you whatever you want. Let's get out of here. I'll follow you up to the house." I had been spending so much time at the club I hadn't been to the mountain house in almost a full week. I was ready for a night in my own bed. Preferably with her under me . . . or over me . . . I wasn't too picky.

"Are we seriously going to just pretend like the entire club wasn't overrun with rats like some kind of plague and pestilence out of the Bible? What's going on, Nassir?"

I sighed and rubbed a hand roughly over my face. "I'm not sure. Can we talk about this later? I want a shower and five minutes to calm down so I don't put my fist through a wall."

She must have seen the barely contained violence that was boiling in my gaze because she took a step back without arguing and nodded. "Okay. I'll see you at the house."

She got into her little car, and I walked over to my much more expensive one. I loved the Bentley. It screamed king of the fucking mountain, but it was also fast and handled like a dream. I appreciated the opulence of it. I pulled out of the parking lot behind Key, making sure to keep her in sight as we tooled through the city. My mind was a million miles away, wondering how someone could be circumventing my security system and what they gained by messing with my new club.

I made enemies like it was the one job in life I was born to do, but most people with a grudge against me wanted to put my head on a pike not a dent in my fat pocketbook. I didn't understand it and that annoyed me even more. Revenge and retribution were the things I'd been weaned on, so I should be able to figure out why someone was toying with my new club. It all felt very random and woefully immature.

I rested my wrist on the steering wheel and forced myself to concentrate on the twin red taillights in front of me. Desire, sharp and jagged, poked at the anger that was flooding my veins. I would have Keelyn in my house, alone for the next few days, while the infestation at the club was taken care of. If there was ever an opportunity to show her that this thing between us was inevitable, this was it. She could push and push at me until she tired herself out and then I would pick her up and take her to bed because by then she would be begging me to. A grin pulled at the corner of my mouth at the idea of Keelyn Foster begging for anything, ever. It was a nice fantasy, but I knew she was going to fight me every step of the way. That's why no one else but her would do.

I squinted as bright lights suddenly illuminated the interior of the car. I glanced into the rearview mirror and frowned when all I could see was headlights because the car behind me was so close to my bumper. The hair on the back of my neck stood up a little as I eased my foot off the gas and slowed way down. I heard an engine rev up as the car behind me sped up instead of slowing down to match my new pace. I frowned and tightened my hands so that I was actually holding the steering wheel in a tight grip. I saw Key's taillights pull farther and farther away, which was what I wanted. I wasn't sure why the person behind me was riding my ass, but after the week I had had, I wasn't leaving anything to chance.

I let the Bentley pick up a little bit of speed and switched lanes to see if the person behind me would pass. They didn't. They switched lanes as well and I wasn't surprised in the slightest when I heard metal screech against metal as their bumper made contact with mine. The Bentley wobbled a little, but Bentleys were luxury cars made for rich people with a lot to lose, so the love tap barely sent me off course. I slammed the gas pedal down to the floor and the car leaped forward smoothly. I shot my gaze to the rearview to see if I could get a license plate or tell what kind of car it was, but the brights shining in my eyes made that impossible.

I knew I had the driving skills and the horsepower to outrun pretty much anyone on the road. But I didn't have that luxury, because as soon as I sped up I ended up catching up to the Honda and to Key, who had obviously slowed down to see where I had gone. I swore and tried to flash my lights at her to get her to move, but that just made her slow down even more, forcing me to slam on the brakes to avoid rear-ending her and pushing her off the road. I didn't have any choice but to let the other car that had been chasing me catch up. I didn't want to run the risk of speeding past Key and having the other driver pursue her instead. When the other car reached me it was still going top speed since the driver was trying to catch up to me, and the impact when our vehicles collided was brutal and violent enough that it sent the Bentley careening off the shoulder of the road.

I probably would've been able to regain control. The Bentley was made to take a hit; what it wasn't made to do was fly. The shoulder had enough of a lip on it that once the wheels caught it at the speed I was going, the car lifted up into the air. I watched everything go upside down, and I knew the impact was going to be harsh and violent. All I could think about was Key telling me my forever was never going to be as long as someone else's and how this just served to prove her point.

When the car came back down, it landed on the roof and everything crunched down around me like I was on the inside of a trash compactor. The noise was deafening and the impact was enough to rattle all of my bones. The top of my head collided with the concave metal—hard—and everything instantly went foggy and out of focus. I felt shards of glass shatter around me and pierce my skin. I had to blink blood out of my eyes as my vision started to get blurry. My head really hurt and everything was the wrong way, but I could smell gasoline and the copper scent of my own blood, so I knew I was still alive . . . at least for now. I tried to move so that I could release the seat belt, but the car had crunched so far down that this was impossible. I groaned and lifted a hand to the blood liberally flowing over my face.

I couldn't move. I was stuck upside down in the mangled mess of my car because someone had run me off the road. I groaned as my vision started to fade to black.

I heard someone call my name in a frantic voice and realized it had to be Key. I wanted to yell at her to stay in her car and just head to my house in the woods where it was safe, but I couldn't make words work. My tongue felt too thick in my mouth and my thoughts were fighting through a bunch of darkness and haze in the effort to become speech.

"Nassir! Are you okay? Oh my God, that SUV ran you off the road!"

Suddenly her face was in the window and I had to squint to see her clearly. Her gray eyes were taking up most of her face and her usual sexy sneer was replaced by pinched concern. "You're bleeding. Bad."

I couldn't reply, so I just closed my eyes and then startled when I felt her fingers tap against my cheek, at first softly, but when I refused to open my eyes she used more force.

"None of that. I called 911. They'll be here any second to get you out of there. Just hang in there." She sounded scared and really worried.

I sighed and turned into her touch. It felt really nice.

"Why didn't you just outrun that SUV, Nassir? As much as this car cost, I know it goes faster than that ordinary piece of junk."

She was stroking my cheek and I knew she was talking mostly to keep me awake and alert, but all I wanted to do was close my eyes. My head really hurt and it was starting to throb.

"Didn't want them to . . . hit . . . you . . . let them hit me." The words were slurred and I wasn't sure I got them out in the right order. I shuddered a little when she brushed her thumb along my bottom lip. I wished I could move my hands and that I wasn't hanging upside down.

"Jesus, Nassir. You can't do something that chivalrous and thoughtful and then die on me. Keep those eyes open."

I thought I heard sirens, but maybe it was just the ringing in my ears. I must have let my eyes drift all the way closed because my cheek stung as she full-on smacked me across it and barked my name in a panicked tone.

I peeled my lids open and tried to reassure her. "The devil doesn't die, Key. He just goes back home." Hell was always waiting.

Getting the words out took the last of my energy and I couldn't fight the darkness that was waiting to drag me under anymore.

CHAPTER 9

Keelyn

It took two paramedics and a uniformed police officer to pull me away from the car. I was freaking out and not thinking rationally because Nassir had blacked out, and I couldn't tell if his chest was still rising and falling. He was covered in blood and the car looked like a crushed soda can. He was too still, and if he wasn't giving me hell, then I knew something was really, really wrong with him. I decided if I took my eyes off him and couldn't touch him, he was going to be taken away from me forever, and that sent me into a full-fledged panic attack.

I was on my knees in the mud holding Nassir's pretty, bloodied face in my hands and saying his name over and over again when help arrived. He stopped responding to me and I didn't want to let him go, but the first responders thought I was in the way. The paramedics pulled me to my feet and handed me off to the cop as the fire department made their way down the hill carrying some kind of heavy-duty equipment that they were going to use to cut him out of the crumpled metal surrounding him.

"Is he breathing? I couldn't tell if he was breathing." I sounded frantic and kind of crazy, but the cop just kept hauling me away from the carnage up the embankment and toward where I had left the Honda parked askew on the side of the road. The lights from the sirens cast everything in an eerie light and I balked a little when I saw another cop putting a middle-aged woman in the back of a police car.

"Let the first responders get him out and then I'll make sure to get you an update on his condition. It's a shame. That's a really nice car."

I cut him a look and crossed my arms over my chest. The cop just lifted his eyebrows at me. "What? I've been on the streets since day one on patrol. I know all about Nassir Gates. Can't say I'm surprised a deranged lady tried to run him off the road. Lots of people want a piece of him for one reason or another."

I looked over at the hobbled SUV with the smashed-in front end and then over to the dejected woman in the back of the police car. I had no idea who she was, but she looked like the president of the PTA or a suburban mom. She definitely didn't look like the type of person that would have a grudge against Nassir or be crazed enough to try to kill him.

"Who is she? Why did she run him off the road?" I asked the question but it was almost drowned out by the screech of metal as they started pulling the car from around the injured man. I went to bolt back down the hill but the cop grabbed my elbow and held me in place.

"She said he ruined her life, that her husband left her because of him. She's a little wacky and not making much sense. She banged her head pretty good when she rammed into the Bentley, so she might not be operating on all cylinders."

I couldn't care less about how she was or if she was right in the head. I wanted to punch her in the face, and if Nassir was fatally injured no amount of police presence was going to keep me from ripping her apart. I was going to tell this to the cop, but voices started moving closer to the top of the hill, so I shook him off and rushed to the point where the road turned into grass. I almost collapsed back onto my already dirty knees. Not only was Nassir breathing and in one piece, he was standing wobbly on his feet and arguing with a paramedic that was trying to tell him that he needed to wait for the stretcher and backboard to be rolled down the hill.

I dashed back down the hill before the cop could snatch my arm again. I'd ditched my heels the first time I rushed down the embankment to see if he was okay, so the ground was cold under my bare feet, but all I felt was heat when Nassir's bronze gaze hit me. It wasn't as shiny and as lit up as it normally was, but I could see him in there, foggy with pain and dulled with confusion, but he was still my unbreakable, resilient devil.

I pushed a paramedic out of the way so that I could get to him, hearing myself sworn at and seeing myself glared at in the process. I put my hands on each of his cheeks and my fingers immediately got slick and red with the blood that was coating his face and running from the top of his head. He had multiple cuts on his face from the broken glass and a particularly nasty-looking slice right above the collar of his shirt that was leaking a steady trickle of crimson down the curve of his neck. But his chest was rising and falling with strong and steady breaths, and even though his skin was cold where I touched him, he was still vital and very much alive.

"You passed out and wouldn't wake up. You suck."

He lifted his hands and I could see them shaking. He was going to pull me to him, but at the last second he stopped himself and let them drop to his sides limply. Even as battered and barely holding himself upright as he was, his will to keep me, to challenge me, was stronger than the pain clearly stamped across his face.

"I was stuck upside down. All the blood rushed to my head. Let's get out of here." He grunted and lurched a few steps forward on wobbly legs.

"Hey, man, you need to head to the hospital. You're all kinds of messed up," one of the young paramedics called out to Nassir as he determinedly put one foot in front of the other. I slipped an arm around his waist and tugged on his arm until he wrapped it around my shoulder.

"I'm not going to the hospital." Nassir stumbled a little and almost pulled both of us to the ground. I squeezed him tighter as we took one slow step at a time.

"You need to get your head checked out, man. The roof of that car came right down on your head when you landed. You probably have a concussion, and you need stitches for sure." The paramedic sounded nervous as he followed behind our slow progress.

Nassir's muscles started to twitch as we hit the incline that led back up the road, but he didn't stop moving forward. He turned his head to look at the worried EMT and told him, "I'll be fine. I'm not going with you."

The guy obviously thought that was a bad idea, but as we finally crested the hill he just shook his head in defeat. "Okay, you can refuse further medical care, but you have to understand it isn't advisable. You need to see a doctor. You're going to have to sign a Refusal of Medical Assistance form before we can let you leave the scene."

Nassir listed really hard to the side and it took all my strength to keep him upright. I thought maybe I should just shove him in the back of the ambulance for his own good. His fingers curled around my own where I was clutching his hand and I abandoned that idea. I knew there was no forcing Nassir to do anything he didn't want to do.

"I'll sign whatever. I just want to go home."

"Okay, I'll get one, and we need one of the cops on the scene to witness it."

Nassir grunted and the EMT hurried off. I looked up at him from under my eyelashes and let him go as we reached the Honda so he could rest against the side of the car.

"You really are a mess, Nassir."

"Just banged up. This is nothing." He lifted an arm and rubbed the edge of his sleeve across his bloody face. I saw him wince when it came away redder than my hair. "They have any idea who ran me off the road?"

From anyone else, it would come across as simple curiosity, but I knew that coming from him, it was the beginning of his mind working toward payback and revenge.

"Some lady. She looked like a kindergarten teacher. She

told the cops you ruined her life and that her husband left her because of you. You have any idea who that is?"

He bit out a word in a language I didn't understand and then let his head fall forward on his neck. I thought maybe he was going to pass out again, so I pressed myself up against the front of him and put my hands on the roof of the car behind him, making a cage out of my body. He looked down at me and the corner of his mouth quirked up.

"She's the wife that went after her husband with the beer bottle. She's a piece of work, but I didn't think she'd be stupid enough to come after me."

"You do tend to bring out the worst in people." His chest rattled with something that was a rough and broken version of a laugh. Slowly his head fell forward until our foreheads were touching. I couldn't stop the sigh that fluttered out of me. For some reason, this moment felt more intimate than when I kissed him or when I had my hand around his dick.

"I want to go home."

I gulped a little because I had witnessed Nassir act a lot of different ways, but vulnerable and exposed was a new one. I'd seen him like that once before, as he held me as I bled all over the floor of the strip club when my city bit me hard. It was the look that sent me running and it was that same look that brought me back to him. It seemed to reach deep down inside of me and shake loose the last of the reserves I had stored up to fight him and resist him. Blood, injury, hurt, violence, disappointment, and risk were the things that made the Point what it was. They were a constant. That bad things would happen was certain and inevitable; what wasn't guaranteed, what wasn't common, was finding someone in this place that made you feel special and safe. It was almost unheard of to stumble across someone that made you feel worthwhile and told you time and time again they would fight for you. Coming across a powerful man that was willing to wait until you were ready for him was like coming upon a treasure hidden in a pile of garbage.

He was going to get taken away from me, or I was going to get taken away from him, but we had right now, and I understood that finally. I had spent so much time running from an inevitable disaster that I never stopped to allow the good things to flourish. I was strong on my own but even stronger with him by my side. I walked my own path but I never would have been able to take those steps if he hadn't been ahead of me clearing the way. I would rather have Nassir for a heartbeat than never have him at all, all the while spending however long either of us had left fighting an unseen future. I would rather fight with him and make up over and over again than keep fighting against the inevitable impact he was going to have on my life and the forever place he had in my heart.

"I'll take you home and take care of you, Nassir." I leaned forward so I could whisper the words against his neck. Finally, something shifted, something broke between us, and he wrapped his arms around me in a hug. When at last he put his hands on me, I felt his power more forcefully than I ever had before. I felt my heart slip down to my toes and then jump right back up and try to beat out of my chest to get to him. All of me wanted to make sure he was okay.

The paramedic and the cop that had hauled me up the hill earlier came over and Nassir and I broke apart long enough for him to sign the paperwork. The young EMT gave me a look and told me out of the corner of his mouth, "He really should be in the hospital. If you care about him, you should encourage him to go."

I shook my head. "I don't fight battles I can't win." Which was a lie because I had been fighting against Nassir for years and was about to lose everything I had to the man. "I'll keep an eye on him."

"If he starts to get nauseous or starts to black out again, bring him to the ER. That head wound isn't a joke. He could have serious brain trauma. That was a wicked crash."

I told the young first responder, "He has a really hard head." Nassir must have heard me because he gave me a dirty look and pushed off the car.

"Let's go."

He shuffled and limped to the passenger side of the car and got inside without any help or any more words. I shrugged at the cop and the paramedic and took the card the cop handed me, a card with his number printed on it and the number of the tow company that was hauling off the mangled car. He also said they might need to talk to Nassir when they decided exactly how they were going to charge the deranged female driver. I told them they could wait until he was feeling better and that they could get in touch with me if they needed anything in the meantime. Now that I'd realized that Nassir was as much mine as I was his, I was going to protect him the same way he was always protecting me. I was going to stop fighting him and start fighting anything that tried to get between us or tried to shorten the time we had together.

I got into the car and he immediately reached out and took my hand. It made my entire body shiver. At that moment I wanted him to take me, to put his hands on me and make me feel out of control; the feeling was so strong that all I could do was turn away from it. I never expected that Nassir's touching me with softness, with the need for comfort and care, would be what ruined me. That in the quiet and dark, his humanness would shine through and that would be what got to me. His violence and brutality had battered against the walls around my heart for years and only made a tiny bit of headway. But his vulnerability and weakness slipped right through like the barrier never even existed.

"How badly are you actually hurt?" I kept my voice low and his fingers twitched around mine, indicating he wasn't doing so hot.

"I have a concussion and the cut on my scalp needs to be sewn shut. The seat belt jacked my shoulder up and I think I have glass in my face, but I'll live. I've been through much worse."

I had never wanted to know about where he had been before coming here. I couldn't imagine any place uglier and more dangerous than this city, but Nassir never seemed to think the Point was that bad. I couldn't imagine worse and knew I should fear and not love the man that was able to survive it.

"You want to tell me about the worse?"

He turned his head to look at me and the edges of his mouth pulled down. "No, but one day I will. Do you think that woman had anything to do with the rats? Seems highly coincidental that the rats and the accident happened on the same night."

I drove into the hills and sighed when the ornate gate and the formidable guard came into view. He waved us in after giving Nassir a concerned once-over and I turned a little to answer my battered passenger. "I don't know. I got the cop's number, so I can call and ask him to question her about it, but that seems unlikely. Most women hate rodents and that was a lot of creepy-crawlies."

"True. And if she wanted after me, all she had to do was wait until I left work. No need to shut the business down. Son of a bitch, how many people are trying to fuck with me?" He sounded frustrated and pissed off.

I parked in front of the house and reached out to brush the back of my fingers across his cheek. "No more than usual. They've just been better at it lately."

He sighed and caught my wrist. "You're right. I've been focused on something else, so my guard has been down."

I realized he was talking about me, but he climbed out of the car with a groan before I could form a response. I scrambled after him and caught him as he got to the front door. He reached for the handle but the door opened before he made contact. Bayla stood on the other side and she gasped when she saw him.

He pushed past her without a word and headed right for the stairs that led up to his master suite. Her dark gaze landed on me, heavy and accusatory. "What happened to him?"

I had to physically move her out of my way to enter the house. She was a lot shorter than me but she was strong and she was sturdy. She grabbed my elbow and jerked me back around to face her once I crossed the threshold.

"I don't know what his deal with you is, but you're hurting him. He didn't fight until you left, and now that you're back, he's coming home damaged and bloody. You're ruining him."

I shook her off and put my hands on my hips. If Nassir hadn't been hurt and needing me, I would've thrown down with her. I wasn't scared to make a point with a well-placed fist in the face, but I had more pressing matters than a jealous housekeeper to attend to.

"He was ruined long before I entered the picture, lady. In fact, I'm the only thing that's ever had a shot at fixing him. Stay out of my way and mind your own business. When I decided to come home, it wasn't just returning to a place, it was me coming back to him. He's home to me, and that means I will destroy anyone or anything that messes with that."

The other woman stiffened and tossed back her long fall of dark hair. She was gearing up for a fight but I didn't give her the chance to start. I held up a hand and leaned closer so that we were almost nose to nose as I growled at her in a low tone, "If you want to keep your spot in his house, then learn your new place. The history between the two of us is heavy enough to crush anyone that gets under it. He made room for you in his house, but I'm the only one he's ever made room for in his life. Understand?"

It was proprietary and possessive. It felt really good to say. I'd been so worried about being his I never stopped to consider how amazing it would feel for him to be mine.

She arched a winged black brow and her mouth pulled

tight in a frown. "You're saying if it comes down to me or you that he will pick you."

"Damn straight. Now, excuse me, I have to go put him back together."

She watched me walk toward the stairs that led to Nassir, and said something in a foreign language as she slipped out the front door. One of these days I was going to have to ask Nassir what he was saying and what language he was saying it in. When I got up to his room I wasn't surprised to see that the entire space was decorated in black, and even in the wood-walled room it still managed to be modern and sleek. His bloody shirt was tossed carelessly on the bed next to his pants. I heard water running in the bathroom and followed the sound.

The room was steamy and I could see the golden silhouette of his powerful body behind the glass surround of the walk-in shower. I turned to look at myself in the mirror over the double sinks and cringed at the sight that greeted me. I looked like a wild woman. Streaks of dirt and blood ran across both my cheeks and my bright hair was standing up all over the place on the top of my head. Black eye makeup smeared under each eye made me look like a raccoon and I had twin splotches of hot pink on each cheek from adrenaline and stress. I looked like the Point had chewed on me and spit me out.

I turned around and propped myself against the chilly marble countertop of the vanity as the water shut off and Nassir stepped out. I never thought he could look more elegant than he did in one of his fancy suits, but totally naked, he was something to behold. The elegance was still there but it was buried under tawny skin stretched over hard muscle, and hidden behind various scars and marks. He looked powerful and strong even though he was obviously pale under his dark complexion.

He wrapped a black towel around his waist and nodded toward the shower. "You can clean up if you want. I need you to help me close this wound on my head."

I flinched and looked at his shiny wet locks. Heavy with water, his hair hit his shoulders and looked like black satin.

"Gross."

He chuckled drily. "You're filthy and need to clean up before I take you to bed."

I snorted at him and pushed off the counter. "You have a concussion and a head wound. You really think I'm going to have sex with you when you're all busted up?"

I gasped as he reached out and grabbed the front of my shirt to yank me toward him. He pulled me so that our chests were touching and then started tugging the shirt out of my pants so that he could wrestle the fabric up over my head.

"You think you have a choice? I told you once I got my hands on you, they weren't coming off."

I frowned and pulled back a bit as he expertly popped the clasp on my bra and moved his fingers to the button on my pants. "You're hurt, Nassir. I'm not going anywhere. Sex can wait until we both can enjoy it." I stepped out of my pants when they pooled around my ankles and his eyes got some of their usual fire back in them when he saw I hadn't been wearing anything underneath the skintight fabric.

"Get in the shower, Key." Deciding that was the best

course of action to avoid further argument, I climbed into the opulent glass enclosure and gave myself a quick scrub-down. When I got out he handed me a fluffy robe that was six sizes too big but immediately engulfed me in softness and comfort when I slid into it.

He had a black box open on the vanity and was digging through it. A pair of tweezers with blood on them were sitting next to the sink and he had a white bandage taped across the wound on the side of his neck. He had several little nicks on his cheeks and on his forehead that looked like he had gotten into a fight with the razor while he was shaving and the razor won.

"Jesus. You're doing your own triage."

"I had a few pieces of glass in my face I couldn't get out with my fingers. I can't see the top of my head, so I need you to put a stitch or two in to hold the gash closed."

I recoiled automatically at the brutality of it. "They have these people called doctors that go to school to learn how to do that."

"A doctor would want to shave my hair around the wound. No thank you. It's simple, like putting a button back onto a shirt."

I grimaced as he handed me a curved needle that looked like something out of a horror movie and some kind of shiny thread.

"You skipped the hospital because of your vanity? Give me a break, Nassir."

He moved to sit down on the toilet in front of me and bent his head down so I could see the three-inch gash that still looked really bloody and raw on the top of his head.

"I didn't go to the doctor because it's something I can take care of myself. I don't like other people's hands in anything I can take care of on my own."

"Not people, you stubborn man. A trained professional. You are taking being a control freak to an entirely new level. Do you have something to numb this up with or anything?"

He handed over a pair of latex gloves and put his elbows on his knees as he hunched over. "No. Just get it over with." He looked up at me from under his heavy brows and told me, "I never had control before I took it for myself. I almost died to get it, so now I'm protective about keeping it. Just like I never had a real reason to fight for something until you. I wanted you to stay innocent forever even though I knew you couldn't."

I bit my lip so hard that I thought I might break the skin. I threaded the needle and held it in my hand and just stared at the top of his head for another few minutes. I saw his shoulders rise and fall as he waited impatiently for me to begin.

"I need you to help me out here, Key. You know how hard it is for me to ask anyone for help?"

"I don't want to hurt you." I really didn't, but I couldn't deny his request for help either.

"You're here. I'm here. I'm going to take you to bed as soon as you get me all put back together. I'm feeling no pain."

I laughed a little and stepped between his knees and rested a hand on his silky hair. "You're a liar."

"I am . . . doesn't change the fact I'm feeling pretty good right nowww—" He broke off and hissed out the last of the word as I jabbed the end of the needle into one side of the slice and out the other. "Holy fuck, that burns." The sound the needle made sliding through his skin had my stomach tightening up and my hands shaking.

I didn't reply. I was using every ounce of concentration I had to put in a row of tiny, precise little black stitches. It was hard to see since the thread was the same color as his hair, but I somehow managed, and in just a few minutes the wound had four little knots holding it closed even though it still looked really angry and red.

"Done!" I snapped the gloves off and set the needle and thread down next to the sink. I squealed as his hands were suddenly under the bottom of the robe and skimming up the back of my legs.

"Thank you." His face moved forward and his lips hit me in the center of the chest where the robe draped open. His hands squeezed the globes of my ass and his tongue darted out to lick over the smooth surface of my bullet wound. "My head hurts." His voice was thin and strained. I rubbed my fingers under his wet hair at the base of his neck. He moved his face and used the tip of his nose to push the heavy fabric covering my breasts up out of his way. My spine went rigid when my nipple was suddenly sucked into the heat of his mouth.

"Nassir?" It was part question and part plea. I knew once his hands were on me there would never be a way I could live without his touch. It felt like he was creating something on my skin with every brush of his fingers and press of his damp mouth to my skin.

"I have to touch you, Key. I have to have you. Everything went black when I was hanging there trapped and the world was the wrong way around, and all I could think was 'I can't fucking die without touching her, without knowing how she feels.' All the horrible shit I've seen and done, and that would be my single regret."

He pulled on the belt of the robe and the heavy material fell away, leaving the front of me bared to his melted amber gaze. He sucked in an audible breath and pain flashed across his face, but only for a second because he moved to kiss me on the center of my chest then used his tongue to trail a damp path to my other nipple. Once he reached it, his teeth scraped across the pebbled tip and my eyes crossed.

"You can have me, but why don't we wait until you aren't hurting?"

He sighed jaggedly against the skin he'd left damp and aroused. "I've spent my entire life hurting. Hearing you say I can have you, that you are mine, is the first time that hurt has stopped. You have no idea the battles I've fought to be here waiting for you to be ready for me, Keelyn. The only thing that would keep me from you now is the end."

How was a girl supposed to say no to that?

A wry smile twisted my lips as I felt his cock stretch and twitch under the fabric of the towel keeping his erection from me.

"We just have to take it easy, okay?" I was forced to take a step back as he fluidly got to his feet in front of me, pushing my borrowed robe the rest of the way off of me as he went. His mouth hit mine and desire hit me like a punch in the gut, and his hands wrapped around my waist and pulled me flush against him so I could feel every hard, needy line of his body calling to mine.

"When has anything between us ever been easy?"

He had a point, but that didn't stop me from allowing him to back me into his bedroom and right toward the big bed right in the center of it.

CHAPTER 10

Nassir

My head felt like it was going to blow apart. The handful of Tylenol I had swallowed down before my shower wasn't doing anything to stop the throb and ache that was beating as steady as a drum behind my eyes and in my ears. The fact that my heart was thundering and my dick was so hard it hurt because I had a very naked Keelyn in front of me wasn't helping my comfort level at all. I forced myself to focus on all that soft skin, on those high and pert breasts with their perfectly pink nipples, on those long legs, toned and sleek from dancing, on that wild shock of red hair, and on the way her gray eyes softened and darkened like a storm cloud as she looked down at me.

I knew if she saw or sensed any of the discomfort that I was forcing back behind the years of desire I had for her, she would put a stop to all the things I wanted to do to her, and even if that was probably the smartest thing to do, it wasn't the least painful option. I had wanted her to be mine from the start. Now that she was here, now that she had surrendered, I couldn't waste any more time. Even if I felt a little like I was going to pass out if I moved too fast or turned my head the wrong way.

The back of her knees hit the bed and I kept moving until she was flat on her back and I could crawl up over her. I wanted to dominate. I wanted to own. I wanted to possess. But when I bent my head to claim that sassy mouth, the outside of my vision went fuzzy and something that felt like a hot poker sliced through my head. I groaned before I could make contact with her sweet lips and had to roll off her and onto my back in order to make the room stop spinning.

One of her tiny hands reached out and landed on my chest right over where my heart was trying to lunge out of my chest and eat her alive with all the hunger for her that had been gnashing inside of it for years.

"I told you I'm not going anywhere." She sounded so sure and so calm, while I felt like a wildfire of pain and desire was blazing uncontrollably inside of me.

Damn straight she wasn't going anywhere, and there was no way in hell a little headache and some cuts and bruises were going to stop me from finally getting what I always wanted from her. Everything.

On my back, the world seemed less fuzzy and some of the pressure inside my skull felt like it had let up. I grabbed her wrist and tugged on her until she got up onto her knees and straddled my supine body. I still had a towel wrapped around my hips, but it was doing little to keep my dick contained. The other part of me that had been longing for this woman for years was just as eager and ready to have its shot at her as my pounding heart was. Probably more so, if the way it pointed straight up like it was stretching up just to brush along her naked backside was any indication.

I glided my hand up over the curve of her ribs. I rubbed my palm over the surface of her full breasts and stopped to work her nipples into stiff little peaks. She whimpered a little and I reached up to grab her around the back of her neck so I could pull her down to me. Her lips touched mine lightly, and thankfully the room stayed put. My head still screamed at me and my shoulder wasn't happy with all the tugging and pulling, but her tongue darted between my lips and touched my own and any complaint I may have had drowned under the feel of her. Now that I could touch back, it felt like I didn't have enough hands to put on all the places I wanted to touch her.

I wanted to touch her cheek and wrap my fingers in her crazy red hair. I wanted to play with her breasts, test the weight of each of them, and make her nipples pucker and beg for me. I wanted to stroke the inside of her thigh and explore that sexy curve that led to the places on her body I most wanted at. I wanted to put my hands right against her wet center and pet her, tease her, fondle her, until she screamed my name and came all across my fingers like she had forced me to do in my office. It was like I had been given everything I ever asked for at one time and my head was whirling trying to figure out how to get ahold of all of that bounty at once.

"You kiss better than most men fuck." Her voice was husky and held a note of humor in it. I might not have been at my best but she was still turned on. I could feel where she was damp and hot between her legs where she was perched across my tight abdomen, and decided that while touching was nice, tasting would be even better. I kissed her again, this time with a bite, and moved my hands to the curve of her hips so that I could start moving her up my body.

She pulled away with wide eyes and didn't argue as I helped her scoot farther up the bed and closer to my face.

"I do everything better." I wasn't bragging. It was the simple truth. With her, there could never be anything better because this thing between us was the best there would ever be.

When she got her knees up by my head and had herself braced over my face, I turned and kissed her on the inside of her thigh. She flushed a pretty pink and I could see that her body was already getting slick and ready. Her blush traveled even into her most private places and it made me grin against her soft skin. I felt her thighs quiver and she looked down at me with a mixture of trepidation and anticipation. I grinned up at her as I curled my hands around her legs. "There is no way I can get at you the way I want without blacking out, so you're going to have to bring the goods to me." I was going to bury my face between her legs until we were both stupid with lust.

"I don't think that's such a great idea." Her words said one thing, but when I snaked a hand between us so that I could part her slippery folds to get at her clit, she shuddered over me and one of her hands landed on the top of my head. I winced because she nailed the gash she had just sewn shut and she immediately removed it. "See!" She hollered the word out, more because I was done talking and used my tongue to attack her than because she was actually upset or worried about my well-being.

She tasted like every dream I had ever had. She was warm and creamy. She was soft and pliant. She was spicy and sweet at the same time. She was greedy, but with every pull of her body around my tongue as I lapped at her, she muttered my name and tried to make sure she wasn't hurting me or putting too much of her weight on me as I devoured her.

I swirled my tongue around her opening, let it dance up inside of her, and let her flavor and excitement wash all over me. Her body started to move over me. Her back arched and her hands moved across her chest, so I switched tactics and trapped her little point of pleasure between my teeth and tugged—hard. She reared up almost all the way off me, but her change in position gave me the clearance I needed to finally get my hands on all her hot and needy parts.

I forced two fingers inside of her wet heat and her inner walls immediately started to grasp and pull at them. I continued to nibble on her clit and to flick it over and over again with the tip of my tongue while she really started to move and ride my face in earnest. Her eyes were squeezed shut. Her mouth was open just a tiny bit, and I could see her chest rising and falling in time to every twist and drag of my touch. She had her hands on her breasts and she had her nipples clasped between her fingers in a grip that looked almost painful. All her skin was a rosy pink, and when her eyes popped open and she looked down at me, I could see that she was there and going over right before she told me, "You aren't just better, you're the best."

That was nice to hear since I was basically an invalid trying to get her off with as little amount of effort as possible. Not how I pictured finally conquering this woman, but I would take her any way I could get her.

Her release rushed across my hand and into my mouth. Delicate flutters milked my fingers as they continued to play inside of her. She fell forward onto her hands over the top of my head and panted out choppy breaths as I wrung every last drop of pleasure I could from her perfect body. When she was done I pulled my hand from between her legs and lifted it to leave a stinging smack across her ass cheek. She reared up over me and moved herself back down to her original position, where she was sitting across my abs. I couldn't not touch her now that I had the opportunity, so I reached behind her and started to run my hands up and down either side of her spine. Her eyes were still foggy with desire and satisfaction as she gazed down at me.

I smirked up at her. "See. We both survived. No harm, no foul." Sometimes one had to lose a battle to ultimately win the war.

She narrowed her eyes at me and reached behind her to wrap her hand around the insistent erection that was all for her. It stretched and grew even harder in her soft palm and I thought my eyes were going to cross for a second. She rubbed the shaft up and down and spread the drop of moisture that leaked out of the tip around the tapered head. My stomach muscles went tight and my hands started to pull at her instead of soothing her.

"You say that, but I can see the lines of pain around your

eyes and you should be smiling because I just told you that you're the best I've ever had, and yet you look like you want to throw up." Her hand tightened around the base of my dick, which made my hips kick up and had me swearing because it made pain shoot hard and fast throughout my entire head. She clicked her tongue at me. "Just lie there. Be still and let me take care of you and then we can pick this up when you're feeling better."

Oh hell, no. I wasn't going to get this far, have her taste all inside my mouth and her hands on my dick, and not get inside of her. If she put her mouth anywhere near that aching erection it was going to be over in a second and I wasn't going to be able to claim her as mine. I wasn't going one more second without having her.

It took some effort and I really did have to fight back nausea and blackness as I jackknifed up and snatched her up around the waist. There was no more foreplay. There was none of my usual finesse. There was none of the skill I had just boasted about as I pulled her to me so that we were sitting on the edge of the bed pelvis to pelvis. She tried to protest. She told me to wait but I ignored it all, even the way her beautiful face blurred into two as I impaled her on my waiting erection.

She was so ready for it. She burned all around me, and my dick couldn't be happier to be caught in the suffocating prison of her body.

I needed to apologize for being so barbaric, but I couldn't talk, couldn't think, couldn't do anything but grab her ass and urge her to move. At first she was reluctant. She barely lifted herself up off of me, but it was enough to have her inner muscles loosen up around me and start to flutter. I groaned her name and clutched at her skin. She dropped her head forward into the curve of my neck and started to lick and suck on the tendon that was taut and straining there. If it was possible, her light touch had me growing even thicker and harder inside of her.

She started to move. Just a gentle rocking of her hips, a sexy little wiggle that shouldn't be enough for either of us, but I felt pleasure start to coil tight at the base of my spine. I had always figured when she came to me, when I got her, it would be explosive and volatile like the rest of our relationship always was. Never in a million years would I have imagined that she was going to make me as much hers as she was mine with gentle ministrations and sex so soft and sweet it felt like it wasn't even real. It was more than I deserved.

I urged her to move faster with greedy hands, but she resisted. She moved her mouth to my own and kissed me with everything she was feeling. There was desire in there but there was also fear and annoyance. There was softness, but more than that, there was the hardness she was going to have to possess in order to be with me. We kissed and kissed and kissed some more. We kissed until she started to grind on me a little harder and started to rub her chest against mine. We kissed until neither of us could breathe. We kissed until I knew I wasn't going to last any longer because I felt my balls tighten up and my heart start to miss beats.

Since I had taken her with zero delicacy, I knew she wasn't as close to the edge as I was, so to catch her up I got my fingers back between her legs where we were joined and pressed down on her clit with the flat of my thumb. She made a startled noise in her throat and definitely added a little speed to her bump and grind as I began to rub stiff little circles around that hot little button. One of her hands tangled in the ends of my hair and the other rested against my cheek. It was the most intimate connection I had ever had with another human being in my entire life, and when she smiled at me it was over. I pulled her down onto me and rolled over so that she was under me.

I thrust into her like a wild person. I rode her hard and fast until I felt her nails dig into my skin and my body started to break apart around me. The room was spinning. Things were starting to fade in and out around me, but she was coming in white-hot bursts and yelling my name as I collapsed on top of her and followed suit. My body felt wrung dry. My soul felt like it had been scrubbed clean with bleach. My heart felt like it had finally been rewarded for waiting and my mind was so full of rightness and contentment that for once, there was no place in it for all the things I had done, all the things I would do.

She wrapped her arms around my shoulders and whispered in my ear. "Are you alive?"

The truth was, I hadn't been alive until this very moment. "Yeah." I rolled off of her and onto my back with a groan. It felt good to shut my eyes. I felt her shift on the bed next to me. "How about you?"

She snorted and I pried open an eye to look at her as she climbed to her feet and looked down at me with censure.

"I'm great, other than the fact that we just had the world's greatest sex without talking about protection. That's an amateur move on both our parts, Nassir." I sighed and caught her arm, and pulled her down so that she was on the opposite side of the bed from where the obvious wet spot we left must have been.

"You're on the pill. I'm clean. You're clean. Everything is fine. Besides, when I said nothing was getting between us, that includes latex."

I shut my eyes again as she began to sputter indignantly next to me. "How do you know I'm on the pill and how do you know I'm clean?"

I sighed and clamped an arm around her as she tried to wiggle away from me. She should know better than that. I was never letting her go anywhere ever again.

"I know everything there is to know about you, Key. You are the only thing that has ever mattered to me, so I made sure that you were safe. *How* doesn't matter. *Why* does."

She didn't like my answer but she stopped fighting to get released. "I'm not property, Nassir."

I smoothed a hand over her hair and curled my fingers around the back of her neck. "You're worth everything, so that means I leave nothing to chance when it comes to you."

Her breath was warm and feathery on the side of my neck as she finally settled in next to me. "You can't do that anymore. We're in this together. I'm in your business, I'm in your home, and I'm in your bed. I'm right in the center of your world right now, Nassir. You have to talk to me and ask me what I want and what I think is best. What you can't do is control me. If you try to lock me up in a cage, this fragile thing we have between us will shatter when I beat it against the bars trying to get free."

I never could control her, and that's why she was perfect for me. I had spent too long being under the thumb of other people. Her fierce independence and thirst to be free of any constraints called to the part of me that had been smashed and destroyed while I was yanked around like a murderous puppet suspended from blood-soaked strings.

"You aren't *in* my world, Key, you *are* the center of it. You always have been. That means I want to care for you, not control you, but my methods in everything are extreme. I don't know how to do it any other way. Now, can we enjoy the fact that we waited years and years to fuck and it was everything it was supposed to be if not more? But right now I need to shut it down for a few minutes. My ears are ringing so loud I can hardly hear you."

The pain wasn't actually that bad, but my words got her to be quiet, and before I knew it, her rhythmic breathing and soft weight against my side had me struggling past all my aches and pains into slumber as well.

I WOKE UP the following morning with Key sprawled on top of me. I mean she was completely covering me and her hair was all up in my face. She had a knee between my legs and my morning erection couldn't be happier about the situation; unfortunately, my phone was vibrating somewhere on the hardwood floor in my pants, where they had been carelessly knocked off the bed during my haste to get inside of her last night.

I hated to disturb her but the rattle of the phone against the hard surface was driving me insane, so I rolled her off of me as gently as I could, and felt something inside my chest clench when she whimpered and reached for me in her sleep. A pout puckered her lips and a tiny little frown dipped between her eyebrows, and it made me grin. Even asleep, she was full of fight.

I scowled when I saw Race's information on the phone and pulled on a pair of loose cotton pants as I headed down to the living room.

"What?" We were business partners, but that didn't really mean we had the type of working relationship where we checked up on one another. At least we hadn't before now. I appreciated the guy's smarts and his willingness to get his hands dirty after Novak went down, but he was just a little too slick and far too clever for me to really trust him.

"Tell your guard dog to let me in the gate." He sounded as annoyed as I felt about receiving the early-morning call. I didn't bother to respond, but I did call down to the guard-house by the gate and tell them to let him in. Within minutes, the younger blond man was strolling through the front door without bothering to knock.

"You don't lock your front door? You have someone messing with your new club and someone trying to run you off the road, and you leave your fortress unsecured?"

My head still hurt but it was more of a dull throb than the sharp slashes of pain from yesterday. The stitches felt itchy and tight on my scalp and my shoulder and upper chest were a delightful shade of purple from where the seat belt had kept me in the car at the moment of impact. I ignored Race and made my way into the kitchen to scrounge up a bottle of water and maybe something for breakfast. He followed me still looking put out.

I chugged the entire bottle and put my hands on the island and stared at him.

"What are you doing here, Race?"

He adopted a similar pose on the opposite side of the island and met me glare for glare. "I want to know what you're going to do about someone messing with the club. It hasn't even been open for two weeks and you're already losing money."

"*We're* losing money."

Race nodded. "Exactly. As much as it galls me to admit it, we are in this together, Nassir. If things are going south I need to know, and maybe I can help stop the slide. If you fail, I fail, and if I fail, this city fails, and I won't let that happen."

I lifted a hand and rubbed it across the back of my neck to see if I could release some of the tension there.

"I'm sure Chuck told you about the stuff happening at the club, but how did you know about the car accident last night?"

He snorted and lifted his gold-colored eyebrows up to his hairline. "All the cops were talking about the Bentley getting totaled and how you looked like hammered dog shit but refused medical treatment. Titus overheard and mentioned it to Reeve. Reeve told Booker, and since I can't keep Karsen away from that guy no matter how hard I try, she overheard it and told me. Which pisses me off. I should've heard it from you, asshole."

Karsen was Race's girlfriend's little sister. She was seventeen going on thirty. He had taken them both in, built them an impenetrable castle right in the center of the Point, and was doing his damnedest to keep the teenager from getting her heart broken by the rough ex-con we had put in charge of security at the strip club. The pretty young thing had a crush on the scarred man that wouldn't seem to quit even though Race did everything in his power to squash it.

"I kicked a couple out of the club and the wife took exception. The Bentley is worse off than I am, and all I wanted to do after the crash was come home and clean myself up. I was asleep when you called, but I would've touched base with you when I got up and moving for the day."

He looked skeptical but relaxed some of the tension in his stance.

"I don't have the time or the patience to break in a new partner." He said it flippantly, but underneath his easy charm I could see that he was actually worried about me. I wasn't sure how I felt about that.

"I'm going over every inch of surveillance I can find on the club. I don't know how the person is getting away with all these little acts of sabotage, but I'll find out." I didn't share my feeling that it all felt like some kind of twisted juvenile retaliation for something.

"It has to be someone on the inside. One of the club members or one of the new staff."

I nodded a little bit in agreement. "Yeah. But I ran background checks on all of them and nothing popped up."

He cocked his head to the side. "Want me to have Stark dig a little deeper? His time isn't cheap, but if there's anything hiding anywhere, he'll find it."

I knew he would. The computer hacker was the one who

had tracked Key down in Denver for me after Titus refused to
help me pinpoint her exact location. Stark looked like a biker
or a professional cage fighter, but he really was just a bulked-
up and heavily tattooed computer nerd. He'd ended up on my
payroll more than once.

"Yeah. That might be a good place to start. Maybe he
can find some kind of connection I missed." I pushed off the
counter and turned to the fridge. My stomach growled at me,
letting me know that man could not live on water and mind-
blowing sex alone. "You want something to eat?"

Race shook his head. "No. I'm picking the girls up and
taking them to look at a couple of colleges out of town. Karsen
graduates at the end of the school year and I want her out of
this hellhole. I want her to have a shot at a normal life."

Now it was my turn to shake my head. "You really think
she's going to leave the Point? Her sister is here. Her life is
here . . ." I trailed off and he narrowed his eyes at me until they
were nothing more than green slits.

"Booker is here."

I shrugged. "She's had her sights on him for a long time."

"He's too old for her. He's too hard for her. He's too deep
into this life for her. He's too fucked up for her. He's too . . .
everything for her. She can go to college and meet a nice kid that
plays lacrosse or digs comic books or something. She deserves
better than what she can get here. She's young enough to have a
shot at something better than what's waiting for her here."

I pulled out a cast-iron skillet and some bacon and eggs and
set them next to the stove. Key's words about making choices
for her floated around in my head.

"You can force her to go, but you can't ever change her mind about who or what she wants. If you push her too hard you'll lose her altogether, and I bet you can figure out right where she'll run."

He swore under his breath. "She has a little while until she turns eighteen. Maybe I can change her mind before then."

"What does Booker have to say about it?" The big man wasn't exactly talkative, and since I let Reeve take over the reins at the strip club, I hardly saw either of them anymore except for brief moments when I stuck my head in to check on business.

"Booker wants to keep his job and wants to keep breathing, so he keeps his distance from her. But he knows she has a thing for him, and he went out of his way to risk his own neck to try to keep that creep Roark from hurting her. It's a nightmare is what it is."

He sounded so much like a disgruntled parent that it made me chuckle. "She's a sharp girl, and she got thrown into the deep end really young. Maybe she knows more about what's best for her than you give her credit for. I'm sure any responsible person out there would advise Brysen that you aren't exactly a knight in shining armor and yet you take care of her like she's some kind of precious jewel. No one is going to love her better than you, and you're a criminal, Race. We are no better or worse than Booker." That wasn't really true—I knew for a fact I was way worse than the scarred ex-con—but I didn't need to share that with the man I needed to run my enterprise with. He already didn't trust me. I didn't want him to be too scared of me and my past, just cautiously leery like he already was.

I thought maybe he needed a reminder that just because we were bad men and did business with bad men, it didn't mean we weren't capable of taking care of the good in our lives when we got our hands on it.

"Whatever. There is nothing wrong with wanting something more for those we care about. Isn't that why you let Keelyn run from you? You've always been twisted up about her, but you gave her a shot at something more."

I looked over his shoulder because I heard movement from the other side of the house. It was like he had summoned her from her slumber by saying her name. I tossed the bacon into the pan so I could feed her and take her back to bed when she finally decided to make an appearance.

"I knew there was nothing out there that was better for her than me. She just had to figure it out on her own."

He snorted. "You are such an arrogant bastard, Gates. I'm outta here. Keep me posted on what's happening with the club. I'll call Stark and have him swing by and grab all the files you have on the club members and the employees from Chuck. I'm just a little bit glad you aren't dead." He turned to leave the kitchen and called over his shoulder when I could no longer see him, "And I'm locking your goddamn door for you on my way out."

His spot across the island was taken up by a much prettier sight. She was wearing one of my shirts and nothing else, and even though her bright red hair was standing up all over her head like artificial flames, she was still the most beautiful thing in the world.

"You want to eat?"

She nodded sleepily and yawned. When she stretched her arms up above her head, I wanted to pull the island out of the ground with my bare hands to get a glimpse of how high the shirt rode up on her legs.

"How's your head?" Her voice was still thick with sleep and it made my dick twitch and my skin get tight.

"It was doing okay until Race started complaining about the trials and tribulations of raising a teenager."

She laughed a little and I felt it all the way in my gut. I decided maybe man could live on mind-blowing sex alone because I was far hungrier for her than I was for food. I moved the pan off the heat and prowled toward her.

"I thought we were gonna eat."

I grinned at her and made sure it showed all of my teeth. "Oh, we are." After all, I had been starving for her for years. Now it was time to have my fill.

CHAPTER 11

Keelyn

Every dirty thing we'd long denied each other was alive in his smile as he started toward me. Stripped of his armor of typically fancy duds and broken down to his most basic parts, Nassir was so much more dangerous. This was real. The man underneath the artifice—he was beautiful and ferocious. Raw, open, and completely unpolished.

Maybe it was the scars that liberally dotted every inch of his exposed chest. Maybe it was the sprawling canvas of black ink that covered his back from the base of his neck to the top of his perfectly sculpted ass. Maybe it was the ripple of muscle as he prowled toward me like a big, uncaged predator. Maybe it was the way his odd-colored eyes sparked and popped at me like hot embers. Maybe it was his too long hair and the way it contrasted with the stark white bandage still taped on the side of his neck. Really I knew it was all those things that made Nassir who he was, and they had my skin pebbling up and anxiety mixing with leftover and lazy desire in my blood. I sucked in a breath and did what I always did when I wasn't sure how to handle everything he was throwing my way.

I ran.

I pushed away from the kitchen counter and bolted toward the living room and the stairway that led up to the side of the house that was opposite his room. It was always fight or flight with him, not that it mattered which option I went with. Fight led to exhausting myself trying to wear him down while he stayed impenetrable, and flight led to him chasing after me until I was caught and had nowhere else to go. I wasn't sure I ever really wanted to win or get away from him in the first place, at least not anymore, but that didn't mean I was ever going to make him stop working to have any part of me.

I was almost to the top of the stairs when his hands landed on my hips and his hold sent me to my knees on the hard wooden surface. I put my hands out to catch myself from falling forward, which left me on my hands and knees in front of him as he leaned forward and coiled his hand in the fire-colored hair at the back of my head. He was gentle about it, and that had my tummy twisting up and my breath rushing out of my lungs.

His lips were soft when they landed near my cheek as he growled at me, "I'm always going to come after you, Key. It doesn't matter how fast you run or how far you go. I'm always going to be right behind you."

I wasn't sure if it was a threat or a promise, but hearing him say he would never stop coming after me was more of a turn-on than the fact that he worked his hands around to the shirt I had borrowed from his ridiculously massive closet and tore the front of it open, sending buttons bouncing all over the place and sailing down to the first floor.

I looked over my shoulder at him with a lifted eyebrow. "That's going to piss your bitchy housekeeper off."

He grunted a response, pulling the fabric off of me, leaving me naked and prone before him as he worked his hands around the front of me so that each of my breasts was trapped in his callused palms. The rough brush of his skin across my sensitive nipples had me drawing in a sharp breath and curling my hands around the edge of the step in front of me. It wasn't the most comfortable position to be in—the stairs were hard under my knees and I was arched at an awkward angle—but with him standing a few steps below me and looking at me like he was going to devour me in one gulp, I wasn't in any hurry to ask him to let me up.

He squeezed each breast and shifted his hands so that each nipple was trapped between his index and middle fingers. He pinched the puckered peaks with enough force that it had me sucking in air between my teeth in a mixture of pleasure and pain that was strong enough to make my head spin. His lips landed on the back of my neck and the scrape of his stubble across my skin had my spine bowing up in response. That was a hot spot for me and he was taking full advantage of the fact that I was immobile and pliant in front of him. His talented tongue dragged a wet path all the way to the center of my spine, which had me shivering in delight and mewling in almost protest as his hands got even more impatient on my breasts. It was a fine line between too much and just enough to make it hurt so good, and Nassir was walking it like a pro.

He bent forward again and I felt his heat envelop me. The shirt I had on was suddenly too much and I wanted it out of the way so I could feel all his smooth skin and hard physique pressed along me. "I like you like this." He let go of one of my nipples and the sudden blood flow into the previously trapped peak made my eyes slam shut. He brushed his thumb along the underside of my breast and let his fingers dance and skip across my quivering stomach toward my already slick and wanting center.

"On my hands and knees? Who doesn't want a girl in that position for them?" I meant to ask it sarcastically but he stopped to trace my belly button with his finger and my words came out sounding thin and breathy instead. Just that simple little caress had passion sparking white-hot inside me. I'd never experienced anything like it. My sexual experience was vast and varied. There wasn't much I hadn't tried or been interested in at one time or another, but nothing and no one came close to igniting the kind of response this man did. It was like my entire being had been waiting for him to come along and show me what it really meant to want, to need.

He kissed me on the shoulder and chuckled against my skin. "No not on your hands and knees. I don't care about the position, I care about the fact that you aren't trying to get away from me anymore. I like you caught, Key."

I whimpered a little as he stopped playing with my belly button and detoured to that part of my body that was anxiously waiting for him.

I was caught. I was trapped by his power and ensnared in his complex personality.

I gasped out his name and let my forehead fall forward to rest on the edge of the stair as he tapped my clit with his thumb and pumped his other digits in and out of the soaked opening of my sex. I couldn't stop my hips from moving back toward him, and over my shoulder I watched his eyes flare up like a wildfire at the motion. That golden caramel color was always so pretty and bright in his striking and harshly hewn face, but as he watched his fingers disappear inside me and the way I couldn't help but move on him, they bled fire and so much passion they looked almost too hot to be human.

His muscles were tense and his gaze was centered on where I was riding his hand; the raw desire etched on his features was enough to have me on the brink of an orgasm as he continued to circle that tight bundle of nerves at the heart of me with unrelenting pressure and unparalleled skill. He let go of the other breast, and when blood rushed back into that point, it hurt enough that I cried out and turned around to glare at him.

He just gave me a wicked grin and moved his unoccupied hand to stroke soothingly up and down my spine. I arched into the touch, let my eyes flutter closed at the dual stimulation, one naughty and one so sweet that it had my throat clogging with emotion. It was a lot to take in. I wondered if sex with him was always going to be something that felt like it was ripping my soul and heart apart and then putting them back together with him firmly in the places that had always been broken and torn.

He twisted his wrist and reached down to squeeze my ass as I bucked against him. I was so close to coming I could feel myself getting tighter around his playing fingers and moisture starting to slick around his motions. I groaned and forced my heavy head up off the stair so that I could look at him over my shoulder.

"I want you inside of me." There had been too much time wasted keeping him at an arm's length for self-preservation. Now that I was caught, I wanted every part of what caught meant. I wanted him to know I was willingly giving this to him and would give it to him any chance I got.

One of his dark eyebrows shot up and I thought he was going to argue or say something that would undoubtedly piss me off, but he just pulled my hips closer, yanking my knees closer to the edge of the step, and started to work his black sleep pants down around his lean hips. When his cock sprang free it made my mouth water. I had seen plenty of dick in my life and had intimate knowledge of enough of them to know that no cock should ever be considered beautiful, but Nassir's was. Like the rest of him, it sort of had a brutal elegance with its dusky color and eager head already leaking a drop of pre-come. It was long and just thick enough to make things interesting, and when he used his thumb to bend the rigid length down so that he could line himself up with my entrance, I couldn't hold back a sigh of satisfaction.

Unlike last night, he took his time as he slid inside my waiting folds. My body stretched, quaked, heated up, and wept for him as he slowly and achingly set himself all the way inside of me. It felt like being branded from the inside out. It felt like he was making a place for himself inside my body that no one else would ever be able to fill. It felt like he was showing me some hidden secret about sex and togetherness I had missed along the way. It felt deep and dangerous.

It felt like love.

His grip on my hips tightened as he pulled me tighter into his thrusting hips. He growled my name as my body pulled at him, clasped him hungrily and greedily. I couldn't do anything other than move with him, meet him thrust for thrust, and hold on as we pounded against one another.

It was hot. It was messy. It was animalistic. It was loud. It was a little rough. It was a lot dirty. It was better than anything had ever been before it. It was everything sex had been missing when I had it with someone that wasn't him. I wanted to scream. I wanted to cry. I wanted to tell him to never stop and beg him to just end it all at the same time. I didn't do any of that. I just chanted his name over and over again and tried to hold on to everything I was feeling so that I could remember this moment forever.

Suddenly he jerked me upright and wrapped an arm across my chest to pin me to his own sweaty torso. His arm landed across my breasts and his mouth bit down on the curve of my neck where it connected to my shoulder, and that was the last little bit of stimulation I could take. I let out a short gasp of surprise as my orgasm hit me like a train. I shattered into a thousand little pieces of pleasure and collapsed in his tight hold as he worked against me until he found his own release. He grumbled my name in my ear and rubbed his forearm across my already overly sensitized nipples, and I was stunned when that was enough to throw my body into another round of orgasmic aftershocks.

He held me like a doll while my body milked him dry and he panted his own pleasure into my hair. When it was all over I felt hollowed out and empty, like everything that I had just handed over to him. I didn't argue or even twitch when he pulled out of me, situated himself back into his pants, picked up the shirt he ruined pulling off of me, and bent to scoop me up in his arms. He took the last few steps at the top of the stairs and bypassed the room I had been staying in for the bathroom in the hallway. He didn't put me down when he reached in to crank on the water and I just let my head loll, useless against his chest. His heartbeat was steady and strong in my ear and it was almost enough to have me drifting back to sleep, until the shock of hot water hit my skin as he walked us both under the stream of the shower head. I didn't even notice him stripping down to get into the water.

I sputtered and glared at him as he chuckled and gently set me back on my feet. I narrowed my eyes at him and turned my back so he could scrub the sleepiness and sex off of my skin.

We didn't talk much as we both cleaned up, but I did notice he was taking extra care with his bruised shoulder and he avoided scrubbing the top of his head where I'd sewn the makeshift stitches. I rubbed flowery-smelling soap all over my skin and winced when I found the spots his scratchy face had rubbed raw. He just lifted an eyebrow at me when I smacked him in the belly with the back of my hand. It was like hitting a brick wall and he moved around me so that his broad back was facing me and hogging all the water. I was going to yell at him for being an inconsiderate jerk but my gaze landed on all that black ink that was now glistening and wet. It was such a big tattoo and so intricate and violent-looking. It was like an ancient tapestry inscribed on his flesh and I couldn't help but reach out and touch it with the tip of one finger.

"How did I never know you had this before that night I got shot? It seems so out of character for you."

He reached out and put his hands on the tiles in front of him and hung his head low as the water ran over him and I continued to trace the twisting lines that covered every single inch of his back.

"The Four Horsemen of the Apocalypse—Conquest, Famine, War, and Death. I've experienced all of the things that most religions believe will bring about the destruction of man. I lived all of it before I got my first kiss."

I recoiled in shock. He never talked about his past and the stark honesty he threw at me was overwhelming. I wasn't ready for the blunt way he dropped it on me.

"What do you mean?" I kept my voice low like I might startle him and went back to drawing over the tattoo with my finger.

"I was born outside Tel Aviv in a time when war was the most profitable thing for any government to be involved in. My mother was the daughter of an American diplomat and my father was an extremist." He snorted and looked at me from under his arm. "Today he would be called a terrorist, but then he was just considered a man deeply devoted to a cause."

I shivered a little at the bitterness in his tone. I had asked for the worst and it looked like I was about to get it. It looked like the devil was going to tell me how he came to be.

"My mom was young, lonely. Her parents were diplomats

and deeply invested in international relations. She knew a lot about war and strife in places all over the world at a very tender age. Her mother was killed on a humanitarian mission with Doctors Without Borders when she was sixteen. It was a huge blow to a young woman that was already mentally unstable. She saw people trying to do good and dying for it and that broke something inside of her. Something about people suffering and the endless struggle to save lives changed her. Her ideals got twisted and turned around. She blamed the government for both her unconventional childhood and her loss. She was suddenly very convinced that people had the right to their homeland and religious predilections without the interference of outside nations. I think the fact that her parents worked for the government and took her to so many fraught places was a huge part of why she picked the other side to fight for. She always told me she was snatched from outside an embassy school along with several of her classmates, but the reality was she set those other girls up to get abducted because she was working with the extremist group my father was leading. She called herself a rebel and a crusader but she was the same as my father, and when they met it was a disaster. Two people warped and fueled by violent ideology. He knew what kind of asset she would be because she was an American who just happened to think exactly like him. No one would ever suspect someone that looked like my mother, a woman that came from a life of privilege like she did, to be a terrorist. He died before I was born, so I have no idea if his ideologies fueled her or if hers made him even more of a threat. I do know that my mother used his death to manipulate and mold me into something that wasn't even close to human."

He shook his head from side to side, sending water droplets flying everywhere. "I existed to avenge my father's death and to carry on his fight for his beliefs . . . not mine, never mine. She was so twisted by hate and anger that I don't think she even remembered what she believed in at the end."

I sucked in a breath and frowned at him but he wouldn't look up at me or move even though the warm water was running out.

"Death and War shaped my life before I left the womb, and once I was old enough, all that mattered was Conquest. How many enemies could I kill? How many nonbelievers could I take out? How much damage could I do to a world that was full of sinners and enemies? I didn't understand any of it, but it was what sustained me. My mother starved me of love, of any kind of maternal care and kindness. To her I was just a tool, a weapon, and she used me as such. Famine doesn't just mean lack of food. I was hungry for any kind of human interaction. I was ravenous to make any kind of choice and decision that was my own."

I was crying. I could feel the hot tears tracking down my cheeks. I wrapped my arms around his waist and moved forward so I could press my damp face against his tattooed back. The devil existed because his life had been horrific and he wouldn't survive anywhere else but in hell. It was all he knew.

"You tell me I'm a control freak, and I am, but only because I have to be. I fought to be in control of my own life, to have a future away from anyone and everyone that only wanted to use me to kill. I feel like if I loosen my grip on that hard-won control, I might lose it. The things I've done . . ." He shook his head again. "I've seen the end of days, Key. I've been the man behind them. I can't afford to let any of that catch up to me here, so I keep my business and this city in an iron grasp to protect it. Do you understand what I'm trying to tell you?"

"I understand you do what you do because you think you have to, and that's good enough for me, Nassir."

He reached out and cranked the water off, and finally turned around to face me. His eyes were sharp points of amber in his face. His jaw was clenched tight and a muscle was twitching furiously in his cheek.

"Nassir Gates isn't even really my name. After my mom left me in the hands of an offshoot of one of my dad's terrorist groups, I got recruited by the Israeli Special Forces. They wanted me to kill too, only they wanted me to go after the people that had made me the way I was. Once again I was in a place with no control, no say in anything I did. I was unleashed and told to make it rain blood, so that's what I did." He reached out and put his hands on my shoulders and made sure that I was looking directly into his eyes. "I blew my cover to hell and got dragged into the desert and was left for dead. I killed everyone to get away. So many people." He blew out a long breath and his fingers curled into my skin. "When I got to the States I knew that man had to die, so I picked a name from each of the two nationalities that were responsible for making me who I was, and started over."

He leaned forward until our foreheads were touching, and when he breathed out again his breath feathered over my lips like a ghostly kiss.

"I was free but I had nothing to live for, no focus, no drive, and no reason for being. I had no skills beyond causing death and destruction and I was quickly falling into a place where I was sure all I was ever going to be was someone else's means to an end . . . but then I stumbled into the Point and I came across you."

I shivered in his hold and lifted up my arms to wrap them around his wide shoulders. I could feel that he was shaking just a little bit and I couldn't believe that this impossible, hard man was letting his armor break apart for me.

"You were too young, too soft, and too vulnerable and you knew it . . . but you were there on that stage anyway because you had a purpose. You wanted something and you were willing to do whatever it took to get it. That did something to me. In that split second of understanding, I found a reason, I found a cause of my own."

His arms wrapped around me and we were hugging while he shook and while I tried to process all the information he had just handed over to me. I always thought Nassir was the one with the upper hand, that he was the one moving the players across the game board in the way he wanted, but from what he just told me, it sounded like I had always been the one in the driver's seat. I wasn't sure what to do with that information. That kind of power over a man like him was intoxicating.

He broke the somber mood by dragging me back into the here and now. "I need to eat and find a bucket of Tylenol for my head. Come downstairs and I'll feed you."

I watched him rub himself down with a towel and pull his black pants back on. He shoved his dripping hair out of his face and winced when his hand brushed over the wound on the top of his head.

"Okay?"

I was far from okay but I stepped out of the shower and took the towel he offered me. I grabbed his hand when he turned to leave the bathroom and looked at him from under my lashes.

"I don't know who you were before you became Nassir Gates, but the man you are now . . ." I bit my lip and lifted both my eyebrows up at him. "He deserves every bit of the respect and control he's earned over the years. You also have parts inside of you that have always been worthy of kindness and care. Those parts are the ones that brought me back, Nassir. Those are the parts that make it impossible for me to hold on to my heart." He just stared at me for a long silent moment before dipping his chin down in a jerky nod and striding out of the bathroom.

Once he was gone I let out the breath I was holding and sat down heavily on the seat of the toilet. I winced a little as muscles that had been given a thorough workout both last night and on the stairs earlier let me know that they were there and pleasantly tender.

Nassir had always been a complicated man with layers and layers I was too afraid to dig into because I was sure I couldn't stand side by side with him when I got to the core of what made him the way he was. And I was right. His story about his family and what his youth had been like wasn't even something I could comprehend. Granted, my own childhood was a nightmare, but I didn't have bodies and war as my first memories like he did. I had no idea how he saw anything besides that. I had no idea how he had seen me all those years ago or why my inability to save myself from that grabby customer had been enough to make me his cause, but I was grateful that things had worked out that way.

When we first met I had been too immature and stubborn to understand what the attention of a man like Nassir meant. I wanted the same things he had been after. I wanted to be free and to control my own life. I wanted no man and no master in charge of the choices I made and the direction I traveled to make something of myself. Even back then, I knew if I tied myself to Nassir all of that would stop. It would just be him and that was the only thing that would matter to me, and that couldn't happen because I wanted to live.

Now I knew he was going to give just as much as he was going to take and I had to be deserving of all of it—good and bad—and I wasn't one hundred percent sure I was up to the task. His bad was scary, but I was used to it. His good was devastating, and every time he showed me a piece of it, I couldn't see anything else. I grumbled every bad word I could think of under my breath as I put myself back together to eat breakfast.

CHAPTER 12

Nassir

It took two days to clear out the vermin and clean up the club. That was a lot of money down the toilet and a lot of aggravation I had nowhere to put besides on Key. Luckily, she was made of strong stuff and could take everything, from my sullen and sharp mood to the less than delicate sex I kept throwing her way. She rolled her eyes at me a lot and told me to stop pouting about things I couldn't control. I grumbled at her until she got on her knees in front of me and wrapped that sassy mouth around my dick and I forgot what it ever felt like to be pissed off and stressed out. She made being trapped in my house for two days bearable, and shutting off business and the Point feel like second nature. Here in my mountain retreat, it was just me and her and that was all that I allowed to matter for a few quiet moments when she smiled at me or taunted me into going after her.

The reprieve was broken when the cop that had been on

the scene of the accident called and told Key they were releasing the woman who ran me off the road with nothing more than reckless-driving charges. He said they couldn't charge her with anything harsher since I had refused medical care on the scene. I thought Key was going to try to reach through the phone and choke the police officer as he relayed the information. When she hung up she ranted about how I could have died and about how unfair it was that the woman was getting away with just a slap on the wrist. She was convinced it was all some conspiracy because I was a less than upstanding member of society. She kept muttering about how justice was for everyone, not just for people that stayed on the straight and narrow.

I kissed her on the forehead and told her she didn't have to worry about me getting justice. That was one of those things I had no problem taking care of all by myself. I was way better at an eye for an eye than any kid in a police uniform was ever going to be. That revelation didn't make her very happy, but when I asked her to drive me into the city since I was currently carless, she didn't argue or pepper me with the million and one questions I could see clouding her eyes.

We got to the club and I could see her hesitancy when I went to pull open the back door. Luckily, nothing furry and disgusting rushed out at us and the cleaning crew had done a great job, leaving the place looking polished and back in its pristine condition. Key walked in front of me across the empty dance floor and to the back hall that led to my private elevator, dragging her fingers across the wall as we went. She looked at me over her shoulder with a soft grin pulling at her mouth.

"I never thought I would actually miss this place."

"The club or the Point?" I reached around her to push the button on the elevator and punched in the code to get it to go up to my office.

"Both." She walked in and leaned against the back wall and lifted her eyebrows at me as I followed her. I kept moving until my front was pressed up against hers and I could feel her nipples bead up against my chest. I put my hands on the mirrored wall next to her head.

"There's good stuff in both of those places if you know where to look for it."

She lifted her hand and put her fingers at the base of my throat where my black shirt was unbuttoned at the collar. She tapped her fingers in time to the beat of my pulse and stuck her tongue out to slick across her bottom lip. It made me growl at her and I saw satisfaction flare to life in her fog-colored gaze. She liked how easy I made it for her to handle me.

"I don't think I actually knew what good looked like until very recently. It can be hard to spot when it comes disguised as something else."

I lifted an eyebrow at her and bent my head just a little to replace her tongue with my own. I licked across the plump curve of her lip and then sank my teeth into it, making her groan quietly into my mouth.

"What was the good disguised as?" I pushed off the wall and stepped away from her as the doors whisked open and dumped us into my office. Chuck was standing in front of the bank of monitors watching surveillance video of the club and there was a thickly muscled man covered in tattoos sitting at my desk with three laptops open in front of him. They both looked up as we entered the room.

Key put a hand on my shoulder to stop me as she stood up on the tips of the glittery shoes she was wearing so she could whisper in my ear. "The good was disguised as the bad this entire time, but I can see it all so clearly now."

I put a hand on her waist and guided her into the room. Low enough so only she could hear, I told her truthfully, "The bad is only good for you, Key. You should remember that." Just because I let her inside of me, inside of everything I did, didn't mean I was going to be as transparent for anyone else as I was for her. In fact, now that she was inside, I was more apt to do whatever it took to keep her there no matter how ugly or extreme those actions might end up being. As always, the consequences be damned, just like I was.

The big guy with all the ink who was behind my desk stood up and cracked his spine. He looked like he should be breaking necks in my fight ring not working at a keyboard, but there was a sharpness in his slate-colored gaze as he peered at me from behind his heavy black eyeglass frames that let me know he wasn't the typical tech geek.

"Stark." I said his name in greeting and tilted my head in Key's direction for an introduction. "This is Keelyn. She's with me." I didn't know if I said this in order to stake my claim or in order to fend off any question as to why she was here. Either way she *was* with me from here on out.

I grunted as she dug an elbow in my side and strode forward to shake the other man's hand. "I bought into the business, so I'm just as anxious as Nassir is to see if you found anything that can help us put an end to all this nonsense. We can't afford to be shut down any longer."

I glowered at the back of her head as Stark suppressed a chuckle and returned her handshake. "Chuck filled me in when I got here and started digging into the files." He lifted his eyebrows at me and hooked a thumb over his shoulder at the monitors. "Plus, you're on the video feeds . . . a lot." He winked at me behind his glasses and Key shot me a horrified look over her shoulder.

I just shrugged at her and walked to the red leather chaise that was pushed up against the windows that overlooked the floor of the club. "You didn't ask if we were on camera before you shoved your hand down my pants and pulled my dick out; besides, I was the one with my junk on display. You were fully clothed."

She was a neon shade of pink and looked like she wanted to kill me. I thought it was kind of cute, so I just grinned at her. She narrowed her eyes at me and sank into one of the chairs on the opposite side of the desk.

"I hate you so much sometimes." Her growled words made both Chuck and Stark laugh.

I just nodded even though she was purposely not looking at me. "I know you do. So what do you guys have for me?"

I was changing the subject before she could really get worked up about the fact that both Stark and Chuck had probably gotten an eyeful. I wasn't embarrassed by much and the fact that I had a beautiful woman in my lap jerking me off certainly wouldn't ever make the list, but I doubted she felt the same way. I could tell she was furious by the stiff set of her shoulders and the way her sparkly shoe was tapping on the floor in front of her.

Chuck cleared his throat to break through some of the tension and pointed at one of the video feeds that looked like it was showing the loading dock in the back alley behind the club.

"Well, I think we figured out how the rats were brought into the club. This liquor delivery truck pulls up and unloads ten boxes on the back dock and then leaves without getting anything signed or without checking to see if anyone comes to bring the delivery inside. The truck stops, unloads, and then leaves. The boxes are fucking moving. I mean that shit is dancing like it's alive. The driver is obviously male but he has on a hat and overalls, so it's impossible to get a clear view of who he is. Stark has been working on it for over an hour."

A blurry image of what could be any young Caucasian male popped up in the center monitor. He was so nondescript it wasn't funny. The guy could literally be anyone.

"An hour later one of the barbacks goes outside to smoke, sees the boxes stacked up, and gets a dolly to haul them all inside the back door."

I swore and threw my head back against the back of the couch. "So he just brought in a bunch of wiggling boxes and didn't think to question what in the hell was going on? Does that make any sense at all?"

Chuck cleared his throat and rubbed his hands over his bald head. "It does when it's the same barback whose fingers you broke for leaving product lying on the floor, boss. Look at the way he has his hand all wrapped up. He was probably shitting his pants that you would do something much worse if another order got left unattended."

I stared up at the ceiling and let Chuck's gentle censure hit me.

Key's voice was confused when she asked, "So he brought the boxes full of rats inside, but did he let them all out? I mean if he opened the first box thinking it was alcohol and found a bunch of disgusting rodents inside, why wouldn't he alert someone? Why would he open all the boxes and cause such a mess?"

I sat up and narrowed my eyes at the monitor where the video of the kid pushing the stacks of moving boxes inside was rolling. "That's a good fucking question." Even if I had gone overboard in proving my point to the kid, something still wasn't adding up. "Was he the one that let the rats loose in the club?"

Chuck grunted. "He was. He brings all the boxes in and then opens them all. He even dumped them into the HVAC ducts. That's how they got into the private rooms. So I scrolled through the tape on the nights of the rest of the incidents and found this."

The video brought up the kid standing outside the ladies' room talking to one of the cocktail servers who was clearly on her way in to use the restroom. There were several minutes of flirting and then the girl nodded and took what looked like a bunch of wadded-up cotton from him before disappearing inside the restroom. Chuck fast-forwarded the tape to the bathroom on the second floor and the same thing happened with another one of the girls. The kid flashed a shit-eating grin at the camera and then disappeared back into the crowd of people in the club.

"Son of a bitch." I shoved my hands through my hair and started pacing back and forth. "He's messing with my business because I jacked his hand up?"

Chuck and Stark exchanged a look. It was Stark who spoke up. "I think it's more than that." He motioned to his bank of computers. "You hired a Tyler Finch and that's what his info says on his W-2 and driver's license, but the only Tyler Finch I can pull up with the same Social Security number is a middle-aged doctor in Akron, Ohio. He definitely isn't some kid from the Point."

"What are you trying to tell me? I have an impostor on the inside of my operation?"

"That's exactly what he's telling you, boss. We've been digging through everyone and everything we could find, and so far the kid is the only one that doesn't seem to check out, and he was the one in the cooler before those shelves fell. I think he took the job here just to get in on the inside and mess with the business."

"Why?" Key asked the question that was on the tip of my tongue. "What did you do to him?" She looked at me over her shoulder with her eyes narrowed.

I shrugged. "Nothing that I know of or can recall off the top of my head, but that doesn't mean anything. His dad could owe me and Race money, his mom could be one of the girls turning tricks on my watch, and I could've slept with his girlfriend or put her on the pole. Hell, maybe I just cut him off in traffic. The reasons for someone to have it in for me are endless and we won't know until we have a chat with him." I didn't even want to voice all the reasons why someone I knew before I found my way to the Point would want to tear my world apart from the inside out, but I could see the knowledge in both Chuck and Key's eyes as they watched me.

"He's good at being someone else. I've been trying to pull up anything on who he might really be but I can't find anything. He's a ghost."

I grunted. "All the stuff he did to the club was really juvenile, really immature. He didn't even avoid the cameras. He doesn't seem like any kind of criminal genius."

"Maybe he has someone helping him." Key's softly spoken words made sense. I figured it was the only way he could've obtained a fake ID and how he was able to digitally disappear.

Stark shrugged his massive shoulders, making the ink visible on his neck move. "Probably. I know a few underground tech kids that would be able to throw together this kind of smoke screen for the right price. They usually make money by getting the Hill kids fake IDs to sneak into your clubs, but a few of them could pull this off. I'll poke around."

I lifted my eyebrows. "I can do my own poking if you give me the names."

Key rolled her eyes. "You're scary to regular people, Gates. There's no way a bunch of awkward computer geeks are going to open up to you."

Stark crossed his arms over his chest and lowered his eyebrows over his dark gray eyes. "Not all computer guys are socially inept. Just like not all strippers are easy."

Key grinned at him and I saw him gulp a little bit. That smile of hers could really be the downfall of a man. It made you want to give her anything and everything you had.

"True, though I have been that far more often than I care to admit. So what do we do now?"

"You don't do anything. We find him and I'll handle it

from there." I made sure there was no room for argument in my tone but that didn't stop her from sputtering at me.

"This is my business too, Nassir. I need to be included in the things that affect it." Her tone told me I wasn't going to ever get away with simply telling her that I would take care of anything.

Chuck looked back and forth between us as I walked over behind her chair and bent to kiss her on the top of her head.

"This isn't about control or keeping you out of the club business, Key. This is about me handling what needs to be handled and you keeping your hands clean. I'll protect what's mine. I always have."

She tilted her head back so she could glare up at me. "So will I."

I adored her fierceness, but it was something that could get her into trouble. "This part of the business is on me. If things go south and someone ends up dead or behind bars, it will not be you—ever. I won't negotiate that with you." I inclined my head in Stark's direction. "Let me know as soon as you find anything. I don't care how much the information costs."

He gave me a lopsided grin. "That's a dangerous thing for a man with deep pockets to say."

I just grunted at him in response. "I have an errand to run. I'll be back before we open up for business tonight."

Chuck eyed me curiously as I asked to borrow the keys to his SUV. I needed to move getting a new car up on my priority list. "You need me?" He was a smart guy; he would know my request had to do with the address I'd asked him to pull up for me before Key and I got to the club.

"No. I just have a little something I need to take care of." I kissed Key on the top of the head again, but she surprised me by getting to her feet and walking toward the elevator with me. She practically dragged me into the little box with her once the doors swished open, and I was surprised how much force she had behind her shove when she forced me against the back wall and caged my head in between her hands as she loomed in front of me, striking and furious in equal measure.

"I can't believe you didn't stop me from pulling your cock out in front of a bunch of surveillance cameras. You're such an asshole. That's a total violation of privacy and consent, Nassir. No one gets to be a part of my sex life if they're going to play those kinds of games with me."

I put my hands on her hips and pulled her close so that our pelvises were lined up. I was hard. She was soft and quivering with rage. If I didn't have shit to do, I would be hiking up her short skirt and giving more cameras an even more graphic show, and I told her as much.

"Cameras aren't going to stop me from having you, Key. Neither is an audience." I decided not to mention that Chuck had seen her naked most of her adult life while she was on-stage at the old Spanky's.

She huffed out a heated breath and leaned forward so that our noses were almost touching. I could see not only anger but disappointment and embarrassment in her cloud-colored eyes.

"No, Nassir. You don't get to have your way and damn the consequences with me. You owe me an apology and you better make me believe that you will never violate me or my trust like that again or that video is the last memory you will have of me being anywhere near your dick. I'm mad at you *because* I'm mad at you. I know you're going off to do something that you might not make it back from and I don't want the last thing I feel toward you to be anger."

The doors opened and she followed me out into the hallway. I caught her wrist and pulled her to me so that I could give her a proper kiss. I nipped at her mouth and stroked her tongue with my own. I drew her in and teased her until she softened and wrapped her arms around my neck and kissed me back. I felt her soft little sigh all the way down into the deepest, darkest parts of me that had never seen the light of day.

I never apologized. Not for any of the things I had ever done, because to me an apology was as effective as slapping a Band-Aid on a bullet wound.

I rubbed my lips against hers and whispered, "I'm sorry." The words felt foreign and heavy on my tongue and I was shocked that I meant them. "I didn't stop to think that something like that would make you feel exposed and embarrassed. To be fair, I wasn't thinking about much beyond your hand on my cock."

She huffed out an annoyed sound and crossed her arms over her chest. Her gray eyes turned from fog to a full-on storm.

"It's not about being exposed exactly. It's about us being together and having that mean something special. I've been naked in front of more pairs of eyes than any one person can count. When I get naked with you or for you, I want it to mean more than that."

I swore. When she stopped fighting with me and showed me her soft underbelly, it made me see how really and truly awful I could be even with someone I so desperately wanted to be better for. I reached out and moved the hair that covered half of her face out of the way so that we were staring at each other.

"It means everything." I assumed she knew that.

She laughed a little and kissed me on the side of the neck, which made me shiver. "Then take better care of it. Be careful, okay? I'm just getting used to you being mine and I barely agreed to let myself be yours."

Those were her parting words as she walked away from me, and I headed out into the parking lot so I could go take care of one of the seemingly endless number of people that wanted to throw a wrench into my day-to-day operations.

I found the town-house complex where the woman that had run me off the road lived and found the specific unit number in the info Chuck had sent over to me. I sent him another message that I needed him to have Stark do a little creative banking for me before he went on his way. I also sent a text to the estranged husband letting him know I wanted him to meet me at her house and waited for a few minutes for him to show up. When a battered, old Jeep Cherokee parked in front of me, I got out of Chuck's SUV and waited for the man to make his way over to me.

He looked nervous but surprisingly better than the night I had had him in my dungeon at the club. Maybe being allowed to be who he really was had finally given him some peace.

"You aren't going to hurt her, are you?" He gulped as I told him I wanted him to get me into the woman's home.

"Do you care if I do?" I kept my voice even and took the key that he wrestled off his key ring and held out to me.

"Well, she's a royal bitch, but we were married for a long time. I mean, I don't want her dead or anything."

I just lifted my eyebrows at him, which made him gulp. "I guess the two of you should've thought about all of that before you decided to show up and force me into the middle of your marital troubles."

He held up his hands and backed away from me. "I don't want you in the middle of anything. Whatever business you have with my soon-to-be ex-wife is between the two of you. In fact, I was never even here."

He got in his car and roared away without looking back at me, so I crossed the street and made my way up to the front door. I put the key in the lock and pushed it open slowly so that if she was home I wouldn't alert her to my none-too-subtle home invasion. Once I had the door all the way open, I stepped into the house and listened for any sign of life. All the lights were out and I couldn't hear a TV or anything else that would indicate anyone was home, but I slipped through the rest of the two-bedroom layout just to make sure I was in fact alone. When my search for the homeowner came up empty, I returned to the living room and settled in to wait for my prey.

I sat on the couch, propped my Alden boots up on the coffee table, and took in the bric-a-brac that dotted the walls and shelves. It was a typical middle-income home. Comfortable with nice furnishings, but there wasn't a single family photo or picture of the once happy couple anywhere to be seen. Granted, maybe she had taken them down after her man left her and told her he preferred men, but still everything seemed cold and sterile.

I wondered if that was how my home felt to Key. I didn't have any kind of memories or things that I held on to. The place had been professionally decorated when I bought it and I never changed it much. It had no heart to speak of; at least it hadn't until she asked to stay there. Now I felt her in every wall, every piece of tile, and I saw her reflected back at me in every pane of glass. It had been a pretty shell before she showed up to fill it full with life. I don't think anyone would argue that she had filled me full with life too.

I don't know how long I sat there contemplating my life and the changes one fiery former stripper had brought into it when I suddenly heard the snick of a key in a lock. I didn't move but I did stretch my arms along the back of the couch and turn my face to the door so that she couldn't mistake who was waiting for her once she entered.

She was on the phone bemoaning having to spend the last couple days locked up and having to get bonded out. She had her hands full of shopping bags and was oblivious to the fact she wasn't alone until she was almost on top of me. When she had the door shut and locked behind her, she started to make her way into the living area of the town house. I saw the moment she realized something was wrong because she went still and her mouth quit moving . . . finally.

I smiled at her and her phone fell out of her hand as she turned to bolt for the door. I got to my feet and prowled toward her as she struggled with the lock. I even stopped to pick up her phone and disconnect the call she had been on. I slid the device into my pocket and put a hand on the door over her head as she finally got the lock twisted and tried to pull the door open.

"I'm calling the police! You better get out of here!"

She sounded nervous. She should.

"Don't be ridiculous. I've had my fill of you and your nonsense. I'm here to tell you exactly how things are going to go down from here on out, and you're going to listen to me or you're going to disappear and no one will ever find your body. Do you understand me?"

Her eyes got so big I didn't think they were going to stay in her face, but even with me looming over her and my very serious threat hanging in the air, she still didn't shut her mouth.

"You cannot break into my home and threaten me. You're going to go to jail."

If I was the type to roll my eyes, I would have. I towered over her, wanting her to feel caged in and trapped.

"I really liked that car you totaled. But more than that, if I hadn't been alone and you'd hurt someone I cared about with all your crazy, there would be no end to the lengths I would go to make you suffer. I don't think you understand who you're dealing with, so let me lay this out for you in terms you have to understand." I bent my head close to her ear and let my voice drop low and hints of my native language filter into it. "I have murdered guilty and innocent alike and never stopped to think about the difference. I am a man who has done and will do whatever it takes to stay on top and that makes me more dangerous than you can possibly imagine. I didn't earn my place, I took it." It was over-the-top but it was all also true.

"I do not take people who threaten me or my business lightly, so you have two choices. You can disappear or I can make you disappear. It's up to you."

I took a step away from her and smiled at her again. "Either option you pick, I'm taking all that money you've been skimming from your boss at the bank, after I let the oh-so-helpful boys in blue know about your sticky fingers."

She gasped and let her head thunk back against the door. "You can't do that! I need that money. I'm getting divorced thanks to you and now I have to pay all the fines for the accident. I won't make it. I'd be better off if you did just kill me."

I lifted an eyebrow at her dramatic wail. "Suffering the consequences of your own terrible decision making probably feels worse than death, but it isn't. For once, do something smart and just go."

She gave me an appraising look and sniffled a little. "Would you really make me disappear?"

I gave her a sharp nod. "I would. I know people in places where no one bothers to look. Where you ended up would feel like a death sentence and every single day you would wish you had made a different choice. You're annoying and dangerous. I don't want you around my city or the people in it."

Her bottom lip moved like she was about to cry, but I didn't buy the show for one second. I reached for the door and my hand grazed her hip. I saw another plan hatch in her eyes but pulled the door open behind her and moved her out of my way before she could even try to come on to me.

"You have until tomorrow to decide what to do. Don't bother looking for the stolen money. It's already gone." At least it should be if Chuck had passed my message along to Stark before he left the club. Having a computer hacker around was proving to be well worth the investment.

I shut the door behind me as she was sputtering about how there was no way she could leave without money or help. She was also calling me every nasty name in the book.

As I headed back to Chuck's SUV I thought he would be so proud of me. Sure, I had manipulated and threatened, maybe even used a little bit of force to make my point with the obnoxious woman, but I hadn't actually hurt her and I gave her an out. It was up to her to take it or leave it. If she didn't, I would do what had to be done.

That was something a real boy would do . . . well, a real boy who had to keep control of the underground empire that powered this cesspool of a city.

CHAPTER 13

Keelyn

Things went back to business as usual when Nassir came back from whatever mysterious errand he'd had to run. He returned looking unruffled and as polished as always. He also deflected any and all of my questions about where he'd been and what he'd been up to. He made it very clear where the lines in this fledgling togetherness were going to be drawn. He would give me all of what he had, but if he thought that any of his actions or practices would make me a person of interest to the authorities or put me in some kind of compromising situation, he wasn't going to utter a peep about them. It annoyed me and frustrated me, but then he reminded me that if I wanted to know about all the things he had done to get to where he was now, I would have to listen to all the stories filled with horror and death from his past.

He also told me that if something happened to him I was the one that was left in charge of the club. The club that provided so many jobs and so much income for the people of my city. I reeled a little that he said this so calmly, like I was the clear choice to take over for him. Me, not Race, not Chuck . . . but me. His partner in so much more than business. His equal in so many ways. I needed to keep my hands clean and head clear, so I agreed to stop pestering about his bad-guy stuff as long as he promised to let me know if shit was really going to hit the fan so I could grab a shovel and get ready to dig. He solemnly agreed and then dragged me out of the city and up into the Hill so he could buy a new car.

I asked him why he didn't just buy one from Bax. After all, the guy had the sweetest rides around in both the Point and the Hill. Nassir gave me a look out of the corner of his eye and chillingly reminded me that he had been responsible for getting Bax's girlfriend abducted by a bunch of thugs, even if he had done so at the behest of Bax's brother in order to set Novak up, and that he had also put Bax in the center of the fight ring with more than one dirty fighter. Bax was only as civil as he had to be and Nassir said he wouldn't put it past him to put him in a car that either exploded if it went over fifty miles an hour or one that would fall apart as soon as he drove it off the lot so Bax could shake him down for more money. He also tilted his narrow and perfectly sculpted nose in the air and told me when it came to his ride, he wanted refinement and handling more than noise and speed. He wanted something that looked good and made an impression over something that was powerful and annoyingly American. His words, not mine, but they made me laugh under my breath.

Sometimes I forgot he was from somewhere else. Sometimes I forgot that he had an entire history before the Point. Before me. But then he would say something like that or mutter things in a different language when he was distracted and I would remember he was exactly like the vehicles he preferred. Imported. Fast. Showstopping and extravagant. He wanted something that made an impression and I didn't bother to tell him he could be in a minivan and achieve that. In fact, as soon as he climbed out of the Honda he had a swarm of salesmen all over him, buzzing around like well-dressed bees.

Nassir grabbed my hand and pulled me past them. I could feel their eyes following us, trying to figure out the dynamic between the two of us. I would bet good money that even though my shoes cost a fortune and my outfit was chic and reasonably respectable for our errand, they all still thought I was one of his working girls. Everyone knew Nassir liked money and knew how he made it. While he radiated quiet dominance and authority, I knew that I radiated sex and all the things good girls didn't talk about when anyone else was around. I also knew that this constantly made people underestimate me.

He stopped in front of a low-slung Jaguar with a convertible top that was a pretty shade of dark green.

"What do you think?" His voice was low and the question was for my ears only. I shrugged.

"It's pretty but with people trying to run you off the road, maybe a soft top isn't the way to go." I looked at the window and the windshield for a price and couldn't find one. "How are you supposed to know how much it costs?"

He put his hand on my hip and splayed his fingers wide.

He brushed the tip of his nose around the shell of my ear and told me softly, "If you have to ask, then they assume you can't afford it."

I balked at that but had to scramble as he guided me over to an Audi that looked like something out of the future. No wonder Ana was up for all Christian's games. The car was hot and definitely a panty dropper. Nassir must have seen on my face my dislike of the weird bubble design because he just chuckled and moved on to a Mercedes that looked like something James Bond would drive. He shook his head when I told him my thoughts and told me Bond drove an Aston Martin and mentioned we could look at those too. I just rolled my eyes at him and continued to let him drag me around the showroom.

All the cars looked the same. Sleek, sexy, and very expensive. I couldn't believe he wasn't concerned about the cost, but as the hour wore on I realized he was waiting on me to find something that I actually liked. I had to pull him to a stop by the lapels of his suit jacket and tell him it didn't matter to me what he forked over his cash on. I finally shared with him my theory that he could drive a minivan and still be the most dangerously sexy man I had ever known.

That made his dark brows furrow over his candy-colored eyes and his mouth twist into a grimace of distaste. "I'm not driving a minivan—ever—but I do want something that's as sturdy as the Bentley, so how about we test-drive a Range Rover?"

I had no clue what a Range Rover was, but if it got me out of the car dealership and away from all the speculative looks

I could feel following us everywhere, then I was game. He crooked a finger and the swarm moved our way.

"I want to take the Range Rover for a test drive." He pointed to one that was a dark slate gray with a soft-looking dove-gray interior.

One of the salesmen adjusted his tie and put on his best buy-car-from-me grin. "Sure thing. I'll grab the keys and we'll head out."

Nassir tossed his arm across my shoulders and I wrapped my arm around his waist underneath his tailored jacket. By now the shock of how hard and tight his body was under that luxury fabric should've worn off, but it hadn't. The way his muscles tightened and coiled at my touch sent a shot of desire right between my legs. I leaned even more heavily into his side. The truth was I didn't care what anyone thought about me being there. It was like it was my own special reserved spot and I had earned my right to be in it.

"Just the keys. I don't need you to tag along." Nassir's tone left no room for argument, but the sales guy missed the memo.

"Uh . . . that vehicle costs over a hundred and fifty grand. It can't leave the showroom unattended." I smirked. I bet I could talk the guy down to a lower price. I was an excellent haggler.

Nassir's black eyebrows lifted and the corner of his mouth pulled down in a scowl that had sent many running in the other direction.

"If you want me to buy it, then it does." The guy looked over his shoulder at his cohorts and they were all suddenly really busy with their cell phones or other customers. He gulped and turned his attention back to us.

"Um . . . look. I could really use the sale, but that's against policy." He was starting to get antsy and, I think, was quickly realizing Nassir wasn't the average rich guy with disposable income to spread around.

"What's your commission if I buy it? Twenty-five percent on the front end?"

The guy gulped and nervously nodded. "So I'll give you your commission up front, you'll let me take the car."

The guy's eyes bugged in his face and he started to sweat. "That's like forty K?"

Nassir sighed. "Thanks. I can do math." I couldn't hold back the laugh that tripped over my lips at the dry sarcasm in his accented voice.

"Um . . . just let me . . . yeah . . . I'll be back." The salesman scampered away and I looked up at Nassir under my eyelashes.

"You just have that kind of cash on you?"

He looked down at me and I could see the humor burning in his melted gaze. "Sure. I'm paying cash for the car."

"Why won't you just let the poor guy do his job, then?"

When he smiled down at me all his teeth were showing and all the temptation that was this particular devil was flashed at me. "Because I'm not spending that kind of money on a car without seeing how we both fit in the backseat."

Obviously he wasn't talking about leg room, so I blushed but couldn't deny that his silky and seductive words had my pulse kicking.

The salesman came back over and said his manager agreed to take the forty grand as a deposit as long as Nassir agreed to fill out a waiver that had all his information on it, like car theft was really something Nassir wanted to add to his laundry list of criminal activity. He already had his hands full with extortion, racketeering, prostitution, money laundering, illegal gambling and fighting, and whatever else he had his fingers in that he wasn't telling me about.

We walked out to the front of the showroom and the still-anxious sales guy brought the fancy SUV around to the front of the building. He climbed out of the driver's side while Nassir guided me around to the passenger side and helped me climb into the seat. Nassir's fingers skated up my bare thigh and up under the hem of my skirt. I narrowed my eyes at him and crossed my legs, trapping his wandering hand before he could give the already overtaxed salesman something to really freak out over.

Nassir chuckled under his breath and leaned forward to kiss me as he wiggled his hand free. He shut the door and I saw the salesman frantically gesturing as he explained something to his manager. Nassir looked bored and exasperated but I was starting to think that was his default expression when he was dealing with anyone that wasn't me. He had a bunch of different ways of looking at me but none of them would ever be classified as bored, and that was just one more thing that made me feel more certain that I was supposed to be right next to him for as long as I could be.

He climbed into the driver's seat and pulled out of the lot. The leather interior was really nice and so were all the high-tech gadgets and knobs on the dash. I rubbed my fingers over the leather and looked at him out of the corner of my eye. "It's nice. Do you like it?"

He lifted his shoulder and let it fall as he guided the big vehicle out of the Hill and back toward the city. "It's fine. Bigger than I'm used to, but it handles fine. The leather is the same color as your eyes."

I jolted a little and turned all the way in my seat to look at him. "What?"

"The interior is the exact same color as your eyes. That gray looks like a rain cloud building in the sky."

I could only blink at him in surprise. It was when I least expected it that he always flashed me those parts of him that I wanted to snatch up and protect like they were a wounded bird not ready for flight yet.

I reached out a hand and put it on his thigh and squeezed. "You can find a spot to try out that backseat anytime now."

He put a hand over mine and laced our fingers together. "I would've pulled over on the street in front of the dealership if I wasn't worried about your aversion to having other people know what we're up to."

I bit my lip and unbuckled my seat belt so I could get to my knees in the seat. I put a hand on his shoulder for balance, took the hand he already had wrapped around mine, and put it between my legs, where I dragged our knuckles up my quivering thigh until I hit the sweet spot. I heard him groan softly when his hands encountered nothing but warm and willing flesh. I was already damp, and when he felt that, he untangled our hands and kept exploring on his own. I had no idea how he kept the SUV straight on the road as he used his fingers to spread my folds open and slip inside my opening.

"Nothing on underneath that short-ass skirt?" He asked the

obvious question as he continued to probe and spread wetness around while purposely avoiding that special spot he knew how to manipulate like a pro.

I was trying to stop myself from wantonly gyrating against his hand since we were still moving; while the windows might be tinted, they weren't dark enough to hide what we were doing in the front seat.

I gasped as he twisted his wrist and started to pump his fingers in and out of my now soaked opening.

"I pranced around in a G-string for most of my life. Having the option to go without is nice, and now that I never know when you're going to pounce, it seems silly to add that extra step when all I want is you, as deep as you can get, as fast as possible."

"Fuck." My words must have made his search for whatever spot he was looking for easier because the next thing I knew, the Range Rover was wheeling into a parking lot in front of what looked like an abandoned grocery store on the fringe of the city and there was no more talk of my underwear or lack thereof. There were a couple cars scattered around the lot but privacy suddenly didn't seem like such a big deal as Nassir wrenched his hand away from my needy center and pulled to a screeching stop.

Without a word he kicked open the door on his side of the car and climbed down to the asphalt. He shrugged out of his suit jacket and tossed it on the seat next to me. With his eyes hot on my own, I hiked up the edge of my skirt and used my own fingers to take up where he had left off. I rocked back at the first brush of my own fingers over flesh he had already worked up and sensitized with his rough caress. He growled at me and rolled up the sleeves of his linen shirt and continued to watch me as my eyes dipped to half-mast and my head fell back to thump against the window.

I knew how to touch myself, how to move my body to offer any man watching a show he wouldn't forget, but I couldn't remember a time where manipulating myself, touching myself with others' eyes on me, had ever felt this powerful, this dynamic and important. I wasn't even sure how much he could see since I was still dressed, and even though my skirt was short, it still kept the good stuff covered up and I hadn't pulled the material all the way to my waist . . . yet.

I stroked my fingers over my aching clit, which Nassir had purposely left abandoned and reaching for his touch. I hummed in satisfaction and panted when his eyes switched from that candied bronze color to straight golden fire. I whispered his name and imagined it was his thick fingers touching me, pretended it was his hands squeezing my breasts through the thin material of my tank top.

Suddenly he moved and slammed his door shut. I groaned but it turned into a squeal of surprise as his hands reached for me from the back of the car and hauled me from the front seat to the backseat through the slender opening between the driver and passenger seats. His impatience made me laugh but the feral look on his face and the heat in his eyes had the humor dying in my throat and turning into something heavier and thicker. He pushed me across the leather seat, and the friction was a sexy burn across my exposed skin. He had me so that I was half sitting, half lying against the door to the back of the vehicle. He crawled in across from me on his knees with his head ducked to keep it from hitting the ceiling as he pulled the door shut behind him.

We both fit.

There weren't going to be any crazy acrobatics or any inventive positions but we both definitely fit and his hands were harsh and impatient as he reached for my skirt and pushed the fabric up as high as it would go. Luckily, the material was stretchy; otherwise there was no way it would've been able to scrunch up over the curve of my ass where his hands landed. He lifted an eyebrow at me and gave me a grin that cut right into my heart like a sharpened blade.

"You can finish what you started in the front seat if you want. I can watch you find pleasure all day long."

As sexy as that sounded, I hadn't been kidding when I told him all I wanted was for him to get as deep inside of me as fast as he possibly could. I always felt like I was making up for lost time with him and trying to keep him as close as I possibly could for as long as I had him. I missed him when he wasn't inside of me, so I grabbed the front of his shirt with one hand and reached for his belt buckle, which had some designer name on it, with the other.

"Get inside of me, Nassir."

He just grunted as I worked his already straining erection free from his pants. It fell into my waiting hands already throbbing and ready. I pumped my fist up and down the shaft a few times but he wasn't in the mood to play around either because he pulled my hands away from his reaching flesh and pinned them to the door behind my head. I could see the windows already getting fogged over and it made me want to laugh a little.

He maneuvered himself on his knees between my legs, one of which was stretched out along the seats and the other was draped over the edge, my foot resting on the floor.

"What's that look for?" He grabbed the base of his cock and leaned forward, dragging the tip through my swollen and wet folds. Just the hint of him there had me bucking my hips up to get more contact but he pulled back and then moved forward again to hit my clit with the head of his erection. It sent pleasure zipping through every nerve ending I had and made it hard to think enough to answer his question. He watched my face and must've seen how much I liked what he was doing because he continued to rock against me and tease me without entering me.

"I was just thinking that I've never fooled around with a guy in the backseat of a car. So it's a first for me and I don't have many of those."

His hips picked up speed and I tugged at my hands. As good as it felt, I needed more. We were both still mostly dressed with just our most intimate and private parts connecting. It felt insanely good but I needed more of what he could give me and I could see he knew it.

He said something to me in that other language he slipped into and then pulled back just enough so that he could line himself up with the greedy opening of my body. His eyes sparked like a lit fuse and he bent his head down so that his mouth landed on mine. "I thought we talked about leaving all the *what* or *who* came before where it was?"

I tried to use my hips to make him drive himself into me since my hands were still locked up in his but he pulled away and just continued to hover right outside of where I needed him most. I frowned up at him and removed my leg that was hanging over the edge of the seat to wrap around his waist. It gave me enough leverage to push the tip of his engorged cock inside my waiting channel but he was too strong for anything more than that.

I sank my teeth into his bottom lip hard enough that he jerked his head back. I glowered up at him. "You own a lot of my firsts, Nassir. You were the first man that ever fought for me. You were the first man that ever made me feel safe. You were the first man never to judge me or give up on me when I was becoming who I was meant to be, and you have always been the first man that I was scared enough of to run from and obsessed with enough to run toward. All of those firsts matter and so does being the first guy to get me to fool around in the backseat of a car you don't even own yet. That should make you happy, not upset."

He lowered his head back down and kissed me with much more care than he had previously shown. He also let me draw him the rest of the way into my body and I groaned as he filled me up and as the strong muscles in his backside flexed under the pressure of my foot. Every time he was inside of me, the sense of completion that filled me up was almost too much to take.

I tugged at my hands until he let them go so I could weave my fingers into his long, silky hair.

He started to move with long, deep thrusts that pulled him

almost all the way out of my body and then pounded him back in. It made my head bounce against the car door but I didn't care.

"Not upset. Territorial. I waited for you and I'm not patient. I don't like to think about who was in my place while you were on the run from me." His hands gathered the material of my shirt along my sides until he had the fabric up over my breasts. He used his teeth to pull the cup of my bra down and then sucked my nipple into the hot cavern of his mouth. I jerked at the sensation and then tugged on his hair and started to wildly thrust back at his grinding hips when he scraped his teeth across the sensitive surface.

I tossed my head back and lifted myself up to rub against him so I could get as much friction between our bodies as the small space would allow. I had fistfuls of his hair in my hands and his saliva all over my breasts as he pulled the other side of my bra down and continued to bite and nibble on each puckered and excited peak. It was a lot. It was more than anyone that came before him had ever given me, but it wasn't quite enough, and Nassir, being so in tune to everything about me, knew it.

He pulled one of my hands out of his hair and tangled our fingers together like they had been when I started all of this moments ago. He rubbed the back of his knuckles across my breast bone and down the center of my body toward where we were joined. He rubbed circles on my belly with the back of my hand and then dragged our fingers to the spot where his much darker flesh was slick with wetness, shiny with desire, and moving rhythmically in and out of my body.

I couldn't look away, and when he dragged our combined fingers over the very top of my sex and used them to circle my straining clit, I started to vibrate and shake from the inside out. I don't know if it was the sight of this beautiful, powerful man owning me, giving me everything I ever asked for, or if it was the overload of stimulation, but I lasted about two more seconds before yelping his name and clamping down hard around his cock. My entire body bent up toward his so that my breasts were flattened against the fabric of his shirt and he let go of my hand so that he could hold on to me with one arm around my back as he braced the other one over my head and continued to rut into me.

His face was a dusky red color under his normally bronze complexion. His eyes were hot enough to burn through metal and his mouth was open as he panted out short little breaths and neared his own completion. I took my hand that was now lying useless on my lower stomach and lazily reached between his legs so I could fondle his tightly drawn-up sac. He was close and it only took the barest hint of my fingernails dragging along that paper-thin skin to have him erupting inside of me.

He collapsed in a heap on top of me and I was pretty sure he was going to have to buy the car even if he didn't like it because I could feel our combined juices leaking out between us. Sex was always kind of a mess, but with him there always seemed to be some kind of beauty and peace in the aftermath.

I plowed my fingers through the midnight hair at his temples and kissed him softly on the forehead.

"No one has ever been in your place, Gates." I took the

hand he still had propped up over my head and put it over where my heart was slowly beating to a sex-drunk beat. "Your place has always been the hardest to get into and you are the only one that ever came anywhere close to it." My heart was a fortress, and he was the only one that had ever had the keys to it.

He said something I didn't understand into my chest then kissed me right between the breasts as he got to his knees. When he pulled out of me we both groaned in disappointment at the lack of connection.

His shirt was now a wrinkled mess and he had a very obvious damp spot on the front of his slacks. The entire SUV smelled musky and there was no way anyone would miss that we had just been fucking like animals in the backseat. He grimaced and adjusted himself back into his clothes while I did the same thing. I didn't even have a Kleenex or anything to try to make myself less of a disaster.

We both made our way back into the front of the car and he pulled out of the parking lot and headed back toward the dealership. He reached out a hand without looking at me and brushed his thumb across the curve of my cheek.

"Don't ever doubt that I think you were worth the wait, Keelyn."

I didn't know what to say to that, so I just stayed silent as we pulled back into the luxury dealership. There were several guys gathered around obviously waiting to see if we were in fact going to bring the Range Rover back.

I took a deep breath and went to push open the door when Nassir reached out and stopped me with a hand on my shoulder.

"Just stay here. No one needs to know what you look like and smell like after I get you off. That's just for me."

I shook my head and grinned at him. "Let me talk to the salesman. I'm really good at negotiating with men." He lifted his dark eyebrows at me and I laughed. "Worst-case scenario, I can admit that we fucked in the back and that's going to seriously decrease the value, but trust me. I bet I can get you ten grand off the asking price."

"I can afford the asking price." He sounded arrogant and amused at the same time.

I clicked my tongue at him and shook my head. "We're business partners now, Nassir. That means there's no need to throw money around pointlessly." I gave him a pointed look. "Our future is tied together."

He watched me silently for a few minutes and then gave me a stiff nod. "Do your thing, puppet master."

It made me giddy. He wasn't going to try to control me or the situation. The man with his finger on the pulse of everything was giving me the reins, and nothing made me feel more powerful than that. He was bossy and manipulative, but he treated me like I demanded. He let me know I was his equal and that my thing was just as important as his thing. He trusted me to do "my thing," and my thing was people. It was why he'd brought me into the club. It was why I'd made a small fortune when I was stripping. I was why the Point would always be where my home and heart were because I understood the people that made it what it was.

I followed the salesman back to his office and started with a smile. He told me flatly that the sticker price was the final price and there was no room for negotiation. Plus, the guy already had his commission, so his interest in working out a deal was nil.

At least it was until I started asking him about his girlfriend. The one that was prominently displayed in a picture in a silver frame on his desk. His pretty blond girlfriend that he was going to ask to marry him. His pretty blond girlfriend that I was pretty sure I had seen in the Lock & Key on more than one occasion. When I mentioned she looked familiar, when I mentioned where I worked, his interest in talking and working out a deal for information perked right up. Maybe it was closer to bribery than negotiation, but at the end of the day it was all quid pro quo in my eyes.

It only took half an hour and I had the guy sweating and shaking for any kind of details about his precious lady love while I convinced him to knock twenty-five grand off the asking price of the car. I gave the salesman a card, told him to come see me at the club and I would set him straight about what he wasn't giving his girl at home and how he could make her happy. I got the deal, and fully planned on saving his relationship, and I didn't even have to take my boobs out to do it. It was all about people and understanding them.

I caught Nassir watching him from behind the window of the showroom, and when he smiled at me, everything he was to me was there in it. He was both my hero and my worst enemy. He had always been my savior and my captor. He was everything I ever wanted and everything I shouldn't allow in my life, and there was absolutely no one I loved to hate more than him.

I understood him better now than ever and I loved him, had always loved him, because he understood me.

CHAPTER 14

Nassir

I looked at the kid Stark shoved into the seat across from my desk with narrowed eyes. I couldn't tell if the body was a male or female with the grime coating his or her face and the ratty clothes that hung in loose layers on a slender and delicate-looking frame. Midnight eyes stared back at me, blazing with annoyance out of a face that was probably too refined and soft to belong to a man. Though there were hints of Asian ancestry in the features, it was as impossible to tell the ethnicity of the kid with certainty as it was to tell his/her gender.

Stark looked just as irritated as his charge. His heavily muscled and tattooed arms were crossed over his chest as he glared down at the top of the kid's head, which was covered in a filthy black beanie that further obstructed determining the gender of the street punk. There was a tic happening in Stark's jaw and I noticed he had a scrape across his forehead, while his glasses sat on his face crookedly.

"You wanted me to find who helped Tyler Finch get his new ID. You're looking at him." Obviously the kid hadn't wanted to cooperate and proved that by glaring sulkily at both of us and sinking farther down in the chair without saying a word. I still wasn't sold on the "him" part of that statement, but I didn't question Stark's assumption.

"You helped a young man pretend to be someone he is not so that he could get inside of my club. I don't care who you are or what laws you broke in helping him. I just want a real name and a location where I can find him. Mr. Finch and I are long overdue for a conversation."

Things at the club had been running like clockwork ever since the saboteur had been unveiled. There were no more incidents. No more sabotage, and even the patrons had all been on their best behavior. The cherry on my professional cake was when I purchased my new car with the money I had taken from the woman that tried to kill me. She had quietly left town, for once making the right choice. I also had all of Chuck's guys and the rest of my security at my other locations on high alert in case the impostor was stupid or brave enough to show his face now that he had to know we knew who was behind the destruction.

The dirty street kid crossed skinny arms over a thin chest and just stared at me balefully. The fact that those eyes didn't waver or even twitch had a little bit of admiration trickling in under my impatience to get this over with so I could find the impostor.

Stark swore and glowered at the kid, who seemed oblivious to all the heated anger being directed at him.

"I couldn't get him to talk to me either. I thought maybe you'd have more luck. I kill things with code not with weapons or my bare hands."

That made the kid stiffen. Tiny hands curled under the dirty fabric of the coat and that frail frame stiffened. Stark lifted his hands and scrubbed them over his face.

"A gamer buddy pointed me to a hipster coffee shop where a bunch of street kids that just happen to be really good with computers hang out and offer up stuff like new IDs for runaways and other kids that need to get off the grid. I asked a few of those kids, flashed around some of that cash you gave me, and they all told me to find Noe Lee."

I felt both my eyebrows shoot up. "'No'?"

The kid rolled dark eyes at me and finally spoke. "*N-O-E*. But it's pronounced like 'no.'"

The voice was clear and decidedly feminine, so I decided the kid had to be a young woman. That made the fact that Stark was sporting battle wounds even more impressive.

"So I go looking in every rathole hovel I can find, looking for Noe. I asked every hacker, hard-core gamer, programmer, and software engineer I could find who Noe is, and nobody had an answer." He shifted his weight and uncrossed his arms so that he could put his hands on the back of the girl's chair. "Imagine my surprise when I get home from a day of digging to find out that Noe decided to come find me. Every single thing of value I had in my town house is missing. My laptop. My desktop. Every hard drive, whether it was working or not, is gone. All my TVs are missing. If it was electronic, it's gone, and this little asshole was just sitting on my couch like he had every right to be there. You're footing the bill for all my shit, Gates."

"I don't like people digging into my business. I like to be left alone." The girl snapped the answer, apparently far more defiant than she should be in her current position.

"You also don't like showering if the way you smell is anything to go by." Stark's tone was petulant, and when the kid jerked her head back to glare up at him, the wool hat covering her head fell off and rivers of long black hair fell down around her dirty face. I saw surprise flash in the other man's face and soon a red flush was vying for the title of brightest color on his neck amid all the ink that swirled there. The man had been robbed and knocked around by a girl that probably weighed less than half of what he did.

"I don't like people in my business either and this kid you helped infiltrate my operation has cost me enough money and enough time. The only option you have here is to tell me who I'm after. I think you know that and I think that's why when you heard one of my people was looking for you, you made yourself easy to find."

"It's easy to disappear on the streets." Her tone was cold but I could see a sharp intelligence shining out of her dark gaze.

"It is. It's also easy to go missing from the streets and have no one realize you're gone."

The girl bit down on her lip and looked up at Stark like maybe he would be her lifeline. The tattooed hacker touched the mark on his forehead and muttered, "You're a goddamn girl" while shaking his head. Seeing that Stark wasn't going to be any help, she turned her attention back to me.

"Look, I've been living on the streets and on the run since I was just a kid. I know the rules in a place like this and the top one is look out for yourself first. When I heard Nassir Gates was looking for whoever helped someone get inside his new club, I knew enough money and big enough threats were going to get passed around that my name was going to come up. I just figured I would have some fun on my way here."

Stark grunted. "You stole all my shit."

She tilted her head back at him and grinned and I could see that she was probably a stunner under all that dirt and grime that covered her from head to toe. I could see that Stark saw it as well. Suddenly he took a step back from the chair like the girl occupying it was toxic.

"You had great stuff. There's nothing like a guy that knows his processors."

"If you were going to come in to see Nassir anyway, why did you jump me? Why did you punch me in the face and hit me with a lamp?" Now Stark sounded like a petulant kid.

She lifted up her shoulders and let them fall. I tried not to grimace at the cloud of dust that her move released. "You grabbed me. I don't like to be touched."

He barked out a swearword and his entire face flushed red. "You broke into my home and hijacked all my stuff. Of course I grabbed you." He sounded so exasperated that the entire thing would've been hilarious if I had more time and any kind of patience at all. "You don't need me anymore, do you, Gates? I need to get out of here."

I shook my head and told him to go, which left me alone with the girl. Her demeanor changed when we were alone but there was still a defiance about her that reminded me of my favorite ex-stripper. This girl was filthy. She smelled bad. She was obviously trying to downplay her gender, and yet she couldn't help but radiate confidence and her own kind of feminine power. It was the fight that always appealed to me.

"Tell me who the guy really is and I'll make it worth your while."

She snorted at me and scooted to the edge of the chair. "Are you kidding? The stuff I jacked from your tattooed friend will feed me and put a roof over my head for a few months. I just want you to leave me alone and forget what I look like and any part I played in Tyler messing with your club."

I leaned back in my chair and considered her for a moment. "Agreed . . . and you called him Tyler. Is that his real name?"

She threw herself back in the chair and I tried not to wince. I was going to have to hose the thing down when she was gone or maybe even burn it.

"Yeah. He's a friend of a friend. I know a few squatters and some gutter punks that like to come in and out of town on the trains, and one of them tracked me down saying he had a friend that needed help. I only mess around for people that really seem to need it. Kids on the run from shitty parents. Kids getting bounced from foster home to foster home because the dad had grabby hands. Occasionally I get a rich kid a fake ID, but that's only if I'm in dire straits. Anyway, my buddy says he knows Tyler from some shows and the kid has it really rough at home."

She was talking so fast it was almost hard to keep up with her, but I noticed she'd referred to my interloper as a kid, making me wonder how old she was. She looked like she couldn't be more than sixteen or seventeen.

"The dad's a bully and the mom's long gone. My buddy says Tyler has a couple sisters at home and the dad has been creeping on them in a totally unparental way, so he asks me to help the guy out. Says the kid just needs a decent job where he can earn some money and move himself and the sisters out of the house. So he brings the kid around so I can make him an ID. Only when he brings the kid around, I realize real quick that he isn't the sharpest tool in the shed. If I made him documents with a different name, he was gonna get busted in five seconds, so I found someone with a similar name and borrowed their identity for him."

"Tyler Finch is his real name?" I was a little confused by her story, mostly because she told it like the words couldn't get out of her mouth fast enough.

She shook her head and the stench of unwashed human and the sour smell that simply was the Point, which permeated anyone that survived on the streets here, hit me right in the nose. I must have made a face or indicated my distaste in some way because she grinned and it was all kinds of twisted and sharp.

"When you sleep under a bridge or behind a Dumpster, people treat you like the rest of the discarded trash that litters the ground. When you look like shit and smell even worse, the probability of anyone grabbing you and trying to make you do things you don't want to do goes way down." One of her feathery eyebrows winged up in a haughty look. "And no, his name was close, but I can't remember it exactly. It sounded like Finch. I can't tell you where he is because I don't know. I did my job, took the two hundred he paid me, and forgot about him until I heard you were looking for someone that manipulated an ID to get a job in your club. I knew it had to be Tyler." She held her hands up and shrugged at me. "I obviously don't own a computer, so it's not like I could have scanned his info in a file I can just e-mail to you."

"Your friend said he had a bad home life. He mention where the kid's family lived?"

She shook her head. "Just here in the city somewhere. Said the dad had been deep in the gutter for a long time. Apparently he was a user and liked to hit up all Novak's action."

I was racking my brain trying to find a link, any kind of connection that could have the kid desperate enough or angry enough to take on the devil in his own playground.

The girl cleared her throat and reached for her hat. "For what it's worth, he seemed like a nice enough kid. He just came across like he really wanted a job to help his family out. Your name didn't come up until after the fact because if he had mentioned wanting to get into business with you or any of your crew, I would've told him it was a bad idea. Men like you don't make things better. He didn't seem malicious or anything. He really didn't seem smart enough to put one over on you."

The slight dig was there but I let it go. The kid had messed with me using schoolyard tactics when I was used to outright warfare. We were fighting different kinds of battles, but if I had learned anything from the desert and my life there, it was that the most unassuming person could be the biggest threat.

Killers didn't come stamped with a big letter *K* in the center of their foreheads. They more often than not came with disarming grins and a friendly handshake right before they put a bullet between your eyes or a bomb under the front seat of your car. I wasn't going to underestimate the kid no matter how harmless or dumb he came across.

I needed to figure out what his deal was with me and I couldn't do that unless I tracked him down.

"The friend of yours who brought him to you in the first place, where can I find him?" She balked and started twisting her fingers together. She obviously didn't want to rat her buddy out to me. "You don't have to tell me, but then, when I send all my guys to rattle every squat and shake down every hostel they can find, I'll make sure they let all the street kids know you were the one that sent them."

Life was hard on the street. It was even harder when you were a woman. If I went and rattled enough cages and dropped her name when I did it, we both knew it would be a veritable death sentence for her unless she took the money she was gonna earn from the stuff she jacked from Stark and hit the road. The understanding of what I was telling her was clear in her gaze.

"His name is Squirrel. And that is seriously all I know him as. When he comes to town he likes to hang out at a bar down by the docks called the Blue Ribbon. They let a lot of metal and punk bands play there on the weekends, so the crust kids like to hang out there and drink cheap beer."

I had no idea what a crust kid was but it sounded like I was going to find out.

"How does one identify a young man named Squirrel?" I asked the question in complete seriousness, but she seemed to find it hilarious. She started laughing until she bent over and grabbed her stomach. When she looked back up at me, her cheeks had streaks where her tears had washed away the dirt.

"Kids get their names on the street for a reason. Look for a kid that looks like he could be smuggling food in his cheeks. He also has a tattoo on the back of his neck of something that looks like it could be a chipmunk or a squirrel. He's not going to want to talk to you. Those kids are going to scatter when they see you coming."

The cell phone lying on my desk started to ring and we both took that as a cue that our conversation had run its course. I picked it up and put it to my ear, and watched the girl slip silently out of my office. She was an interesting one, and I had a feeling even though I promised to forget she ever existed, I hadn't seen the last of her.

"Are you looking at the monitors?" Chuck's question was barked in my ear and I turned around in my chair, tapping the keys on my computer that turned the bank of security video feeds on behind my desk. Since it was the afternoon and nowhere near working hours yet, I had left them off while I talked to Noe.

When the screens fired back to life, it took every speck of self-control I had not to throw my cell phone at the monitors. At least twenty men wearing black tactical gear with the word "police" across the back were storming through the front doors of the club with weapons raised.

Luckily, there were no customers crowding the dance floor

or cluttering the bar area, but the employees that were milling about were all frantic as I watched the raid happen in front of me like it was a TV show.

"What?" I couldn't form any more words than that as I watched one of the cops approach Chuck, who still had his phone to his ear. The cop stopped in front of my head of security and I heard him ask where I was. On the video feed I saw Chuck hesitate for a second, but because I recognized the deep voice when the policeman spoke, I told Chuck to go ahead and bring him on up to my office while his cohorts continued to poke their noses and guns into every nook and cranny of my club.

I couldn't face the cop sitting down. Not when what I really wanted to do was take the automatic rifle he had in his hands, and turn it on him and demand he leave me and my business alone. He stripped off his protective face gear and glared at me just as hard as I was glaring at him.

I don't know how Titus King found himself on the right side of the law when he had every single characteristic that should have made him a man like me, terrible childhood and a parent that preferred death and brutality to loving nurture included.

"Why are you raiding my club, cop?" I put my hands on the edge of the desk to avoid pummeling him in the face.

Titus narrowed his eyes and I swore his hatred of me and what I did to keep this city alive blazed out of his gaze like the blue flame of a blowtorch.

"We got an anonymous tip that you received a delivery of cocaine and that you were sitting on it for one of your suppliers. The source sounded credible, so the lieutenant in charge of the drug unit decided a surprise takedown was in order."

"Why are *you* here, then?"

Titus grunted and I saw his black-gloved finger twitch where it was resting on the trigger guard of the gun he was holding.

"I'm here because it's no secret my very pregnant girlfriend works for you, and for some odd reason actually likes you and her job. I told the sergeant in charge of the tactical team that I wanted in just in case there was dope stashed here. I told him I would like nothing more than to lock you up and keep you away from my family." He glared at me even harder and a tic started working in his cheek. "I also told him that you're a sadistic bastard and if we did find anything illegal here, you wouldn't be above using innocent patrons as leverage in order to escape a drug bust." He snorted. "You're welcome."

If he thought I was going to thank him while my club was being ripped apart, he had another thing coming. I lifted my eyebrows at him and gave him a speculative smirk. "Does Reeve know you're here?"

He grunted his answer, which clearly meant he hadn't told her that he was coming to raid her boss's club. I bet that was going to go over really well when he got home from work. Reeve was a spitfire and she also carefully kept one foot on the right side of the law and the other hovering just enough over the edge of the wrong side to keep things interesting. She was an asset to me and my enterprise. She was also not going to like her man messing in my business, but more than that, she wasn't going to like that he kept her out of the loop because he knew she did have threads of loyalty attached to me even though Titus had tried to snip them time and time again.

"There are no drugs here. I don't have my hands in that stuff. The guys that move it and sell it answer to people in other countries, and I don't like the lack of control that gives an operation. I also let Keelyn and Race sink a ridiculous amount of money into this place to get it up and running. I wouldn't play around with their investment like that. I'm a businessman first and foremost, cop. I don't do things that endanger my money or my partners." I could get my hands on any illegal substance I wanted at any time, but that didn't mean I needed to have my fingers in the honeypot. Drugs were a hard line for me. When I first came to the States I'd dabbled here and there, testing the boundaries of my newly minted freedom. I realized very quickly how easy it would be to find myself tied to another kind of owner and I refused to risk it. I didn't want my business anywhere near people who so effortlessly corrupted and owned the weak and the desperate. I stayed away from the lure of narcotics, but the people I often found myself dealing with didn't. In order to keep my finger on the pulse, I had to know who dealt what, who imported what, and how they all managed their business, but I didn't consider them my colleagues.

"The source said that you keep the stash in a private room in the basement that is only accessible by private elevator."

The lightbulb went off and I swore in Arabic as I shoved my hands through my hair. "Was the source a woman?"

Titus's own dark eyebrows shot up until they almost touched the band of the black, knit cap covering his forehead.

"Why?"

I sighed and moved around my desk. I walked past him without saying anything but heard Chuck tell him to follow me.

"I had some problems with a woman and her husband. She didn't want to play by the rules, so I kicked her out." I punched the code in for the basement of the building once we were all in the elevator. I shook my head a little. "First I kicked her out of the club, then I kicked her out of the Point. She's mouthy and unstable. I should've known she would pull something like this."

I was regretting getting soft and letting her have an out. Being a real boy was bad for busniness.

"The basement is the security holding center for anyone that doesn't want to behave. Sex makes people crazy, makes them do things they would never ordinarily do in a million years." I leered at him and saw his jaw clench so hard I was surprised his teeth didn't break. "You know what I'm talking about, cop."

He didn't respond to the verbal jab but he did talk into the radio headset he was wearing to let the rest of his team know he was headed to the basement. Someone must've barked back that he needed to wait for backup because he coolly replied that he had the situation under control and would report back once the area was cleared.

Once the doors opened to my concrete prison, I saw Titus's eyes get wide and his irritation grow. He cut me a hard look as we stepped from the elevator into the barren hallway.

"You're a sociopath. You do know that, right? What kind of person builds their own jail under a nightclub?"

It was my turn not to respond. He did business his way, and I did it mine. I told Chuck to go ahead and let the cop wander through all the empty rooms, and stood back and watched his fruitless search. Even if I'd been inclined to keep a stash of dope on hand, I would never be stupid or simple enough to leave it in a place that would be so easy to find.

Titus was meticulous. He picked through each and every room, turned over tables and chairs, tinkered with light fixtures, and knocked his knuckles along the solid surface of the walls. If there had been drugs in my dungeon, the cop would've found them. He was at the last room, finishing up his thorough search, when all of a sudden ice-cold water started to rain down on us from the ceiling. All three of us barked out different swearwords and I looked at Chuck, who was on his phone screaming at his guys.

The water continued to cascade down from the ceiling, so there was no use in trying to wipe it out of my eyes or shake it off of my clothes. Titus was shooting every dirty word that existed at the ceiling and I knew we were going to have to hike out of the basement using the stairs because the elevator wouldn't work if there was a fire.

"What's going on?"

I asked Chuck the question when he was close enough that I could talk to him without having to shout over the roar of the sprinkler system.

"The cops upstairs were poking around in the ceiling looking for the supposed stash. One of them accidentally hit the valve for the fire prevention system. They can't figure out how to turn it off. It looks like our little rodent problem might have messed up some of our plumbing. Nasty little fuckers."

"Shut all the water down in the building before everything gets flooded."

Chuck shook his head as we reached the metal fire door and pushed through. "Can't. Fire systems run on a different source, so that even if something happens to the main water supply in the building, they still operate. We'll have to call out a professional to shut it down and we need the plumber to get his ass back in here."

I shook my dripping hair out of my eyes and glared at Titus, who was huffing along behind me, his gear making the climb out of the basement slightly more taxing for him than it was for me and Chuck.

"You and your boys cost me another day's worth of business, cop."

He whipped his soggy hat off of his head and blinked the onslaught of water out of his eyes.

"You can afford it, and I bet those private rooms you somehow managed to get around the antisolicitation laws are probably due for a good old-fashioned scrub-down."

His quip made Chuck laugh, but once we got to the main floor and hustled everyone outside, the laughter died in his throat. As the water continued to gush, the sight of half the police force and all of my staff shivering and cold shut down any humor he found in the situation.

I took my sodden suit jacket off and grimaced as rivers of water poured off of it and onto the ground around my feet.

"Expect a dry-cleaning bill." I muttered the words out of the corner of my mouth to Titus. "And good luck trying to get laid tonight. Your girl is going to be pissed that you kept the raid from her, but she's gonna be really pissed when she finds out you shut me down for no reason." I wiggled my eyebrows at him. "Like you said . . . she likes me."

I thought the big detective was going to lunge at me, but Chuck stepped between us and put a hand on the man's Kevlar-covered chest.

"Enough. There were no drugs, but you succeeded in ruining the boss's day, so let's all consider that a win and head to our separate corners of the city, shall we?"

Titus pointed a finger at me. "One of these days you're gonna give me a reason I can't ignore to lock you up, Gates."

I shrugged my shoulders and then cringed as the motion sent icy water right down the collar of my shirt and along my spine. "Probably." I mean I was already doing a shit ton of stuff that would mean a jail sentence if he knew about it, but I never had any intention of serving time. My entire life before the Point had been a long, horrific prison sentence, so I'd already done time as far as I was concerned.

I looked at Chuck. "Since we're dead in the water— literally—I have something else I need to take care of tonight." I made a face as water squished out of my shoes as I walked toward my new car.

The gold tooth flashed at me. "Do I even want to know?"

I smiled back at him. "I'm going Squirrel hunting."

His chuckle followed me as I sloshed my way to my SUV. I needed answers. I needed information and I needed a change of clothes. I was going to get my hands on all three and track down whoever this Tyler was and find out why exactly someone so young had it in for me. I wasn't an easy enemy to have and I couldn't figure out why the kid had decided to take on someone like me his first time out of the gate.

CHAPTER 15

Keelyn

I was really starting to hate the words "I have something to take care of." Whenever Nassir told me that, it meant he was dropping out of contact and was up to his neck in trouble. It was testing all my self-control not to bombard him with questions about what was on his agenda for the night as he changed into a very un-Nassir-looking outfit of black jeans, a black knit sweater, and heavy-looking black boots. There wasn't a logo or label to be seen, and when he twisted up his long hair into a perfectly coiled man-bun at the back of his head, I knew something was up. He never did anything with his hair, and once it was tied up and out of the way, all I wanted to do was pull it down and mess it up. He kissed me on his way out and told me not to wait up, which made me want to kick him. I believed he would keep me in the loop if it was something I needed to know, something that affected me or the club, but sending him off to do God knew what with God knew who was hard when we were so newly settled into sharing this life together.

I appreciated the fact that he wanted me to be able to claim ignorance about some of the more unsavory parts of his business, but I hated not knowing what exactly he was into and what the chances were of him making it back home in one piece. All that uncertainty and fear was why I had held him off for so long in the first place. The anxiety of what I was going to do if something really did happen to him while he was off doing whatever he did made my skin feel like it was a size too small for my entire body and I couldn't seem to stay still.

It sucked that the club was flooded because it left me with nothing to do and too much time on my hands. I started to wonder about the girls that had moved from the strip club to the new club. I wondered whether, if someone had offered them a way out, a way all the way out, they'd have taken it. So few people in this city, women especially, were ever offered an opportunity to experience life beyond the hard streets and crumbling economy that kept the Point what it was, and even though Nassir had his own type of escape route in place for the women he protected, he wasn't offering them anything outside of the city limits. Even after he'd cleaned up Spanky's and turned it into the Empire, it still amounted to little more than putting lipstick on a pig. There should be a way out for those who wanted it, and I started to wonder if the way I could help my community was by setting free those women that never really had a shot at surviving it.

I shouldn't have been surprised to see the gorgeous housekeeper making her way through Nassir's home, since I was stuck in for the night. She had been making herself scarce ever since our showdown the night Nassir got hurt. I assumed she was trying to be discreet and lay low so that I didn't tell Nassir to get rid of her. But as I watched her stroll through the house like she owned it, I started to wonder if I had been wrong. The other woman was entirely too comfortable in the space I had claimed as my own, and it rankled.

I moved to the top of the stairs and called down to her. "What are you doing here?"

She looked up at me without so much as a flinch or jolt of surprise. Her dark eyes took in my stance and the very obvious spill of belongings that I had left scattered all over behind me, things I hadn't found a spot for yet.

Something that was a bastardized version of a smile twisted her perfectly painted mouth. I hated that she was so stunning and just as mysterious as Nassir was. I didn't want her to be a better match for him than me. I didn't want anyone to understand my devil and why he existed the way I did.

"Working."

I felt my eyebrows shoot up at her snotty tone, but I cocked my head to the side and asked her, "If Nassir hadn't brought you here, if he had offered you a way out of the life and the city, would you have taken it?" I knew the woman had feelings for my devil but I was curious if that was all that kept her here. After all, those same kind of feelings were what brought me back.

She rolled her dark eyes and huffed at me. "You know nothing about me or my life. You have no idea what it's like to come from the kind of place where Nassir and I are from.

You know nothing of suffering and sacrifice. Here is so much better than there, so why would I go?" Her dark eyes tried to sear me with her obvious contempt and loathing. "I belong here, with him, but you . . . when he speaks to you in Arabic or Hebrew, can you even tell the difference? Would you even know if he told you he loved you in his native language? He deserves someone that knows what it's like to make it through hell and survive. He shouldn't ever be ashamed of who he is or how he got what he has. He should be proud he lived, that he was better than all the rest."

I walked down a few steps, dragging my fingers along the railing. I returned her twisted smile with one of my own as I got closer. She crossed her arms over her chest and continued to glare up at me.

"You think he *survived* hell?" I gave a bitter laugh. "He's the devil. He never left the inferno, he just jumped from one fire into the next. Does the Point have IEDs going off or RPGs taking out buildings? No, but it does have people fighting every single day for power and control. The Point is full of innocent people suffering, of men and women willing to sacrifice their lives for an unseen force that owns them. Where you're from, everything comes down to religion and belief; here addiction and greed control the masses. Nassir never stopped fighting. He just found another kind of battle. Now he's the general, not a foot soldier." I took another step down. "And the fact that he understands he won't ever be able to make up for all the things he did before getting to the Point is what keeps him human. His regret is what keeps him from going back to being nothing more than a weapon waiting to be aimed and used without thought as to who he might be pointed at. He cares about things here even if others don't see it. He has a cause here, his own kind of code, which might never make him a good man but does make him a better one than he was before. The Point gave Nassir his own kind of honor."

I finished walking down the stairs until I was just one above her and I could see the fury that my words had ignited inside of her. She was shaking just a little bit, and her cheeks were bright red.

I lifted an eyebrow at her and gave her a real smile, even though it was sharp and had a lot of teeth in it. "And I don't need to understand the words he says when he tells me every single day with his mouth, with his hands, with his cock, and the way he can't get enough of me tells me exactly how he feels about me. Not to mention he waited years for me to be ready for him. Not for sex, because he could have taken that anytime he wanted if he pushed; he waited for me to be strong enough and smart enough to stand at his side. I don't need a translator to understand that."

I knew it was going to annoy her. I was the only one Nassir had ever let all the way inside. I was the one he had been holding out for while he took Bayla to bed and then discarded her and everyone else as soon as I was ready for him. I didn't know her story but she had given me enough clues to let me know it was just as ugly as Nassir's, so of course she didn't want a Prince Charming. She wanted my prince of darkness. That he preferred me was a slap in her face especially since on paper, she was a better pick for him. She was arguably the better choice, but I was the one he had always wanted. I was the one he fought for.

I was anticipating her move before she made it. When you work with a bunch of cutthroat girls all out for the most money and the most attention from the customers, a throwdown every now and then is par for the course.

I caught her hand as it swung toward my face and grasped her thin wrist. I used the leverage I had to pull her closer to me and bent down so that I was right in her pretty face. She was flushed and breathing hard in her fury and her eyes were pits of hatred. If looks could kill, they would need more than one grave for me because she was murdering me over and over again with her gaze.

"I don't know where you're from or where you've been, but I'm from the Point, and I assure you that means I know how to fight for what I want. I'm anything but easy, honey. Don't let the high heels and the short skirts fool you."

She pulled her hand free and took a stumbling step back from me. I think the fact that I was ready to go toe-to-toe with her for the man we both wanted surprised her.

"He deserves more." To her it was that simple. Even though Nassir wasn't necessarily a good man, even though he had killed, had caused destruction and mayhem from the moment he came into the world, he deserved more because he had saved her and offered her a shot at a better life. To her I wasn't enough and I never would be.

"You shouldn't be here anyways. It's well past regular housekeeping hours and anything Nassir needs after dark I take care of." It was the last nail in the coffin to remind her that she was here to take care of the house and I was here to take care of the devil.

She flipped her fall of ebony hair over her shoulder and smirked at me. "He called me and told me to come pick up one of his suits. He said something happened at the club and it needs to go to the cleaners."

"And you couldn't wait until tomorrow to come get it? You had to come all the way up here tonight?" Her devotion and adoration was starting to seem a little more intense than that of a woman who was grateful to the man that had thrown her a lifeline. It made my already tight skin tense up even more and the hair on the back of my neck stand on end.

"When he asks me for something, I do it. I don't make him wait." The implication was crystal clear. I had made Nassir wait for years and years and in her eyes that was simply unacceptable. I didn't feel the need to tell her both of us needed that wait time for me to grow up. That I needed space to be able to understand that being with him wasn't a choice I could make with my brain. It was a decision my heart was going to be responsible for making, and until now my heart hadn't been in a place where it was strong enough to hold him.

I gave a little sniff and turned to head back up the stairs, calling to her over my shoulder, "Wait down there and I'll get it for you."

I was an idiot. I knew better than to turn my back on an enemy and this young woman was possibly the most dedicated enemy I had ever had in my life. I knew she hated me, hated that I had usurped her place and her role in this palatial mountain home. What I didn't know was that she must've had a death wish on top of it because when I felt her hands at my back, twisting in the fabric of my shirt, I knew she was going to pull me backward, which meant I was going to land right on top of her and neither one of us was going to bounce.

She screeched some kind of war cry into my ear as we both went pinwheeling through the air. I saw the ceiling sail by over my head as I started to go backward and I tried to make a desperate grab for the railing, but she was just too strong in her need to punish me for taking what she considered her own. I couldn't get a grip and I knew it was going to be hard landing when my feet kicked out in front of me and we both fell through the air.

I shouted in surprise and was cut short as we both hit the ground and I landed on top of the smaller woman. She didn't offer much of a cushion as both my elbows hit the hard wooden floor and the back of my head cracked solidly into her face. I heard her scream in pain and I rolled to the side so I could heft myself up to my hands and knees. I shook my head to try to clear the fuzz but her anger seemed to give her superhuman strength, because as she rolled in my direction she lifted her leg and slammed her foot into my ribs. The blow took me by surprise, and since I was already winded, it knocked me to the side, which had my head thudding heavily into the wall.

I was seeing stars and struggling to catch my breath. When I blinked so I could look at her I noticed she was staggering to her feet and that her face was covered in blood. Her nose looked a little bit askew but that didn't seem to be slowing her down at all. Her eyes were wild and she was focused on me.

I moved so that my back was against the wall and used the solid surface to lever myself into an upright position. Both of my arms burned all the way to my fingertips and I had a headache that was thundering and banging against my skull so hard it was almost impossible to find my balance. The other woman wiped her face with the back of her hand and I cringed when I saw blood smear from one side to the other. She looked crazed and ferocious.

"I will not stand by and let you ruin him." Her words were slurred and suddenly her accent got thicker. "I've had him. I've touched him in ways you and your ignorance will never understand. I came first." There was vehemence in her words that went beyond that of a lover scorned. Nassir, regardless of his intentions, had had an impact on this woman. This was more than a simple infatuation and it was going to blow up. Partly because there was no way I could resist slipping in one last snide comment.

"You may have come first, but I come last, and I keep coming last over and over again because we both know he can't keep his hands off of me. He's been reaching for me from the beginning, and now he won't let go. You he had no problem tossing away." Sure, I just called her trash, but she had called me worse. I figured it was a fair trade-off. Hanging out with a bunch of foulmouthed strippers meant I knew just how to come up with a dig guaranteed to hit where it hurt most.

I shook my head again and braced myself as she launched herself at me. She went right for my face and caught my hair in one of her hands. Someone needed to tell this chick that fighting like a girl wasn't going to get her anywhere. Hair pulling and face scratching were amateur hour, though my scalp did start to burn as handfuls of my hair got yanked in a bunch of different directions.

It was a dirty move, but I took the heel of my palm and

crammed it right into her already swollen and deformed nose. That sucker was sure as hell broken if the way she screamed was any indication. She was so loud I thought my eardrums were going to burst. While she was bent over clutching her face I pushed off the wall and walked over to her. It was my turn to grab a handful of hair so I could jerk her head up and have her looking at me through pain-filled eyes that were wet with a sheen of defeat and tears, but I could see that the battle was far from over on her end.

"He was ruined long before I got my hands on him. But he lets me see that there is more to him. He wants to be better than he was before and you can't stand that because it means *you* don't deserve him. You see him pushing himself to be a man that's too good for you because he's not a total monster . . . he's just a man with a little bit of the devil inside of him." It was more than a little bit but that was splitting hairs and I was done arguing with her about what was mine.

I claimed him.

I understood him.

I earned him.

I loved him.

There was no getting around the fact anymore. It wasn't fear or the magnetism that pulled us together that I couldn't escape. It was love, obsession, maybe even fate and purpose that tied us together. It was all around me, all inside of me, and it was all him. It had always been him.

"Get out of this house and don't come back. If you make me tell Nassir what happened here tonight, falling down the stairs and getting a broken nose will seem like child's play."

That was a threat that finally got through to her. The idea of him being the one to send her away, of him casting her aside for what had happened tonight, was what had her fleeing into the night. When Nassir got home I was going to have to ask him what the girl's backstory was because it must've been pretty bad for that to be what finally got through to her. Without another word, she spun on her heel and left without bothering to close the front door behind her.

I winced as my head continued to let me know it had taken a thorough pounding. I walked across the living room to shut the door, but as soon as I got there I was almost run over by yet another dark-haired beauty as she came flying through the entrance.

Reeve was already talking a mile a minute and her hands were waving in the air like she was conducting an invisible symphony. She was talking so fast I could only make out every other word. I heard "Titus," "asshole," "jerk face," and "I'll show him." She stomped into the house and looked like she was going to make her way to the kitchen when the blood smeared across the wall and floor brought her up short.

"What happened?"

I rubbed my forehead. "Reeve, how did you get up to the house? Nassir's guards don't let anyone through the gates."

"I'm pregnant and pissed off. I told the guy at the gate that if he didn't let me in I was going to call Nassir and tell him that he made me cry. He waffled for a minute but another car was coming out so he had to open the gate up anyways. I just drove through. Are you okay? What happened here?"

I followed her into the kitchen and took some ice out of the freezer to wrap up in a towel and put on the back of my head where my skull had smacked across the housekeeper's face.

"What are you doing here, Reeve? Does Titus know where you're at? If he comes looking for you and Nassir comes home and finds the cop here, it isn't going to be pretty for any of us after what went down at the club today." I didn't want to try to explain what had happneed with the housekeeper. It was going to be complicated enough telling Nassir the girl had to go without him resorting to drastic measures to get rid of her.

She walked around me, pulled open the fridge, and dug around until she found one of Nassir's bottles of water and an apple.

"That's why I'm here. I was so mad at Titus when he told me about the raid on the club. We got into a huge fight and we both said some pretty nasty things. I had to leave before it got worse. I told him I was coming to see you, but that doesn't mean he still won't show up. Overprotective idiot."

She did sound annoyed but her voice couldn't help but soften when she talked about her hot cop.

"Were you mad that he conducted the raid without telling you?"

She shook her head. "No, I mean he has to do his job. I don't always love it and sometimes I don't agree with how black and white he tends to be, but I love him, so that means I love everything about him. I don't get to pick and choose which parts I love. I was furious he didn't tell me because he thought I would tell Nassir. I love my job and I like working for him, but I'd never put him before the father of my child."

Her dark eyebrows knitted. "It hurt my feelings that Titus would question my loyalty like that."

Her teeth snapped into the apple and the crunch made me cringe. This headache felt like it was going to overrun my entire body. It was weird to be having this conversation with Reeve. Not too long ago I had been the girl flatly declaring that she wasn't good enough for the sexy detective. That had also resulted in a tussle, but Reeve was from the streets and actually knew how to throw a punch.

"Maybe he just wanted to keep you from having to make that choice. I mean he knows you love your job and he doesn't say much about the fact that you get your paycheck from a crime lord. Maybe he didn't want you to be caught between him and Nassir." Nassir liked having Reeve in charge of the club, but he didn't do anything without expecting something in return. He would've been annoyed to learn that she knew about Titus and the police raid without giving him some kind of heads-up. I wasn't sure he would take it as far as firing her or taking the strip club out of her hands, but I knew him well enough not to put anything past him.

She heaved a deep sigh and propped her chin on her hands. "He needs to give me the opportunity to show him I will always do right by him. I feel like he never even gives me an opportunity to screw up anymore."

I laughed but it turned into a groan. "Isn't that a good thing? Didn't you used to have screwing up down to an art form?"

Her dark blue eyes sparked with mischief. "But I know better now."

I put both of my hands on my temples and rubbed small circles. "How do you handle knowing your man is out there on the streets every day with a countless number of people trying to hurt him or worse? Every time he leaves the house, how do you not cling to him and try to make him stay? Especially now with a baby on the way. Don't you constantly worry about what you're going to do if something happens to him?" I was still so worried about letting Nassir have everything I was, and then being left alone when he was gone.

She blinked a little bit at my change of topic and tilted her head so that she was looking at me thoughtfully.

"You can't think that way. All you can do is love him the best you can while you've got him so that he has something extra important to come home to. Titus has always been pretty careful, but think about what Dovie goes through with Bax, or what Brysen has to go through wondering if Race is going to go up against someone determined not to pay their debt. All we can do is worry and waste time trying to control things that are out of our hands. These men we love . . ." She gave her head a little shake and a soft smile tilted up the edges of her mouth. "They should come with clear warning labels. Not that it would matter because our hearts wouldn't pay attention anyway."

I sighed and bent forward so I could rest my forehead on the cool marble surface of the island. "I've always worried about Nassir in a different way, but now that I'm letting myself love him, that worry feels like it might consume me."

"It's good to be scared. It keeps you careful, and with a guy like Nassir, being careful is the only way to be. It never gets easier because this place we all call home never gets easier."

"I guess if I wanted easy I would've just stayed in Denver." I lifted my head and gave her a wide-eyed look as my musings from earlier pushed their way back to the forefront of my mind. "Speaking of Denver, do you think that if there was a clear-cut way for people—I mean mostly the girls on the streets . . . if there was a way for them to get out of the Point and to experience life somewhere like Denver, they would take it? I mean it didn't work for me and it didn't work for you, but that's because too much of this place is inside of us."

She snorted a little and put her hand on her rounded belly. "Like an underground railroad for ex-strippers and hookers? You're going to help them find their way to freedom?"

I scowled at her because I didn't think the idea was a laughing matter. "Why not? No one was ever around to offer us a way out when we could've used one. Why can't I be the person there holding the door open to a better life?"

As Reeve realized that I was serious, some of the mirth dropped from her face and a genuine smile pulled at her lips. "There's no one those kind of girls would trust more than you. If you think you can make a difference, if you think this is your something more, then I say go for it. You can be like a fairy godmother, only instead of a wand, you come equipped with thousand-dollar heels."

That made me laugh, which in turn made my head throb. "I don't know about that, but I used to think that maybe just a better club for the dancers was enough, or a different way for them to make money. Now I'm thinking bigger and farther away from my own back door. I would have loved to make Denver work but it never felt like home. That opportunity should be given to someone that would appreciate it."

She hummed in agreement and pushed away from the

counter. "I can ask around and see what the girls at the club think. Some will never leave but I bet there are a few that would jump at the chance to live a different kind of life. I'm gonna go before Titus loses his patience and storms the castle. Thank you for making me see that his boneheaded actions were actually pretty sweet. Boys can be so dumb sometimes."

"No problem. Thank you for making me see that love has to be more powerful than fear. It's something I'll have to try to work on."

"It takes a brave woman to love the kind of men we love, Key, but they have to be just as brave to love us back. We're out on the same streets they are. We're fighting the same fight. It's just as scary for them to lose one of us because of this life. That's why they work to make it better as hard as they do. Remember that."

She gave me a hug good-bye, and it made me smile when her baby belly pressed into me. After she was gone I went to work cleaning up the mess the other brunette had caused in the living room. The task took longer than it should have since my ears were ringing and my head was still throbbing in time to my heartbeat, but I got everything looking all shiny and back to its original pristine condition.

I went back up to the master suite to find Nassir's stash of painkillers for my head and I was surprised that when I picked up my phone I had several missed messages from the man I was purposely trying not to worry myself sick over.

This music is awful.

Why don't these punk kids shower?

What are you doing and why aren't you answering me?
You better be in my bed thinking about me.
I see the kid I've been looking for. I'll be back soon. Be ready
    for me.

I bit my lip as a warm fuzzy feeling started to swirl around inside of me. The last message came only a few minutes ago but it made my heart flutter to know that I was on his mind while he was out in the big bad world doing big bad things. I *was* going to love him hard enough that he would always try his best to get back home in one piece.

I will always be ready for you.

It had taken a while to get there, but I was confident enough in myself and in him to know that this was true.

CHAPTER 16

Nassir

I was trying really hard not to touch anything or to brush up against any of the kids filling the dingy little club. I was used to dark and dank places. I was used to filth and grime, but there was something about all these kids milling about with unwashed bodies and spiked-up hair, when they all clearly originated from the suburbs, that somehow made the environment of the dive bar seem extra revolting. On top of the dirty bodies and the suspicious looks that kept getting cast my way, the blast of angry guitars and wailing from the emaciated-looking singer on the tiny stage were enough to have my ears bleeding. I distracted myself by texting Key and was annoyed even further by her lack of response. With the club closed so we could dry it out and repair the pipes, I knew she was at the house and couldn't figure out why she was ignoring me unless it was just to be contrary. She didn't love it that I refused to give her a play-by-play of my actions or that it had to be that way for her own good and my peace of mind.

I could think of a hundred and one places I would rather be, and just as I was about to give up thinking that maybe Noe's information had been dated and that maybe the elusive Squirrel had hopped a train out of town, I caught sight of a young man coming out of the bathroom at the back of the bar. He was rubbing the back of his hand across his face and the way his nose was twitching not only told me that he was probably high as a kite from doing rails in the bathroom, but made him look even more like the animal he was nicknamed after. The kid had dreadlocks and a vest covered in rivets and studs, making him look like a caricature of a punk rocker, and he was oblivious to my approach as I wound my way through thrashing bodies and tried to tune out the antiestablishment battle cry coming from the stage.

I was getting hard, side-eyed looks and I heard the words "cop" and "narc" whispered loudly by more than one clueless child. I don't know how anyone, even the young and innocent, could ever mistake me for one of the good guys, but as long as they moved out of my way and let me get at my target, I didn't bother to correct them.

When I reached Squirrel he was wildly bobbing his head up and down to a beat that had nothing to do with the noise coming from the band. His pupils were dilated so big that his eyes looked like shiny, black doll eyes and his mouth was twitching excitedly like he couldn't control it. He was waving his hands in the air over his head and I think maybe he was trying to sing along with the band, but really it just amounted to him screaming nonsense at the top of his lungs.

I fought down the urge to smack him across the face for his sheer silliness and instead put a hand in the center of his chest and pushed him backward. He was so messed up that he lost his balance and tipped over onto his backside on the dirty bar floor.

"Hey!" His outrage was given fuel by the drugs in his system and a couple of the other grungy, crazy-haired kids stopped their partying to take offense at the fact that one of their own was being pushed around.

I heard muttering and felt the attention shift to what was happening between me and the gutter punk, so I reached out a hand, which the kid took, to help him to his feet.

Stupid.

Once I had his wrist clasped in my hand, I yanked it around the front of his body, spinning him around so that his back was to my front and my hand wrapped fully and firmly around his throat. I moved the kid toward the doors that led to the back alley off the side of the bar. I heard him wheezing and saw the edge of his very puffy cheeks already starting to turn bright red from a lack of oxygen.

"If you struggle it just makes things worse. I just want to talk to you." I had my fingers tight enough to feel the air trapped in his lungs. Fingers clawed at my hand but I just kept moving the kid through the doors, and once we were outside, I backed him into the brick wall and held him there. I narrowed my eyes and told him, "Listen Squirrel, I have questions and you have the answers. You tell me what I want to know and I go away and you can go back to doing blow and acting like an idiot. Sound like a plan?"

I released his throat, which had him folded over and coughing dramatically. I curled my lip up in distaste and crossed my arms over my chest. First a disgusting club and now a repugnant and grotesque back alley. I was really glad I had left the designer duds at home for this outing. As if to validate that thought, at that moment a big, well-fed rat ran right between me and the kid with a squeak of alarm.

"You a cop?" The kid gasped the word out and his chubby cheeks started to fill as he struggled to suck in air.

Impatient, I snapped, "Do I look like a fucking cop?"

The kid let his head roll against the wall behind him and lifted filthy fingers to stroke at the circle of red marks I left around his neck.

"What do you want, dude?"

Dude? Was this kid for real? No one called me dude. I took a step closer to him. "I'm looking for a friend of yours. A kid named Tyler, and I need to find him tonight."

Even as hyped up on drugs as he was, I saw the recognition flash in the kid's blown-out gaze. His mouth started twitching and he began trying to slide along the wall like I wouldn't notice him moving away from me. The metal studs on his vest scraped noisily as he shifted and I didn't even bother to negotiate or barter.

I pulled my fist back and clocked the young man right in the nose. With the wall of the building behind him, his head didn't have anywhere to go, so his skull bounced off the bricks as his eyes crossed and his nose started to bleed from the blow.

I didn't hit him hard enough to break anything, but if he didn't get it together in the next minute or so, that would change.

"You know the kid. I need to find him and I want to know his real last name. You helped him get a job in my club. I can hold you responsible for all the shit he fucked up."

The kid held up his hands in front of him and started to shake his head. "That was Noe! She got him the ID. I just introduced them. Tyler was in a tough spot. I wanted to help."

"What's his real name?" I shook my hand out and the kid watched my move warily.

"Tyler French."

I frowned because the name didn't immediately ring any bells. It was disappointing. I thought once I had a name, a clear line between who the kid was and whatever reason I had given him to mess with me would be clear, but I ended up with nothing.

"Why does he have it in for me?" I let my fingers clench into a loose fist and the kid gulped. He lifted his hand to wipe his bloody nose and cringed when he came away with blood on his arm.

"I don't know. He wanted a job at the club really bad and that was all he said. Tyler's life is shit. His dad is a freak, one of those people that can't get rid of anything—ever. So he grew up in a junky house that was the worst on the block in a bad neighborhood. The old man was rough on him, really rough, so I wasn't surprised when he said he needed money to get out."

The kid shifted again and his eyes looked away from me and then back at me.

"What else?"

The puffy-faced young man slowly started to slide down the wall until he was resting at my feet with his head in his hands. He fisted a bunch of dreadlocks between his fingers and pulled.

"He also asked me to hook him up with a gun. He's got a couple sisters and Child Welfare just pulled them from his dad's care. I think that was the final straw for him. Like he had nothing left to lose, ya know?"

My back teeth clicked together in aggravation. "Did you come through for him?"

The kid peeked at me over his bent knees. "Yeah. I had a buddy that wanted to buy a plane ticket back home to New York. He sold Tyler a piece for a few hundred bucks."

"When was this?" This was information that made the situation with the unpredictable Tyler even more dangerous. Messing with my club and my money was one thing. Having the means to permanently take away the one thing I had ever wanted for myself was another. I couldn't risk Key like that. I wouldn't risk her.

"A few days ago."

"So where can I find Tyler French now?"

The kid shook his head and he looked like maybe he was going to cry. "I don't know, man. We run the streets. We hop trains. We sleep in squats and under bridges. It's not like we have addresses."

I grunted. "Tyler didn't look homeless when he worked for me."

"I don't know, man. I don't know where he's been staying. Maybe he got a girl or something."

I considered the cowering kid in front of me as I tried to

decide if he was telling me the truth or if he was protecting his friend. Between the bruised and bloody nose, the watery eyes, and the generally defeated demeanor, I came to the conclusion that he knew I wasn't messing around and could bring a world of hurt down on him if he wasn't up front with me.

"The worst house on the worst block, where can I find it?"

The kid folded forward and let his forehead rest on his knees. "Dude, Tyler's already got kicked around by life. Can't you just cut him a break?"

"No. Tell me where the house is."

The punk muttered the address and I slipped out of the alley and made my way to what really was the worst part of the Point. It was block after block of run-down single-family homes covered in graffiti and with bars on the windows. It was a neighborhood with asphalt instead of grass in the yards and a place where your neighbor was more than likely selling drugs rather than Girl Scout cookies. It was a neighborhood where, if you saw a woman on the street corner, she wasn't waiting for her kid to get out of school, she was waiting for a john to pull up so she could offer him a twenty-dollar blow job.

I found the worst house on the block with no trouble. There were rusted bikes in the front yard leaning up against the warped and cracked siding . . . like seven of them. There was a collection of broken coolers and a menagerie of car tires making an obstacle course to the front door. I debated knocking to see if the person in charge of this mess would come to the door, but decided against it. I didn't have time to waste and getting a rusted door slammed in my face just to have to force my way inside anyway seemed pointless, so I just put my shoulder against the flimsy wooden door and shoved. I heard the lock creak and the handle break away from the frame, but the whole thing barely moved.

I swore under my breath and put more of my weight into the motion. I heard something fall and a male voice bellow from somewhere inside. Once there was enough space to squeeze through, I entered the house and almost instantly regretted my decision. When the kid said the dad was the kind that never got rid of anything, maybe I had been so worried about finding the kid that I failed to read between the lines and realize that the dad was a hoarder. No wonder the kids had been pulled from the home. I hadn't ever been anywhere as horribly putrid or vile as the inside of this home.

It was alive with bugs and rodents. The smell was so pungent that I could practically see it hanging in the air in front of me. It smelled like trash, bodily fluids, and a general waste of life, with boxes, piles of trash, dirty clothing, and random junk that blocked me everywhere I turned.

I heard the voice calling out the name "Tyler" and then a litany of swearwords as I carefully picked my way through the maze of refuse and rubbish. The voice was slurred and sounded mean, so I couldn't blame the kid for wanting to get out of this hellhole. I just didn't know how all this came to have anything to do with me.

I knocked into a hidden shelf that was covered from top to bottom with empty beer cans and the ensuing noise made my skin crawl. I kept expecting the guy attached to the screaming voice to show up, but there was no sound of movement as I continued to navigate my way through the mess. It made me tense and had me on high alert, but once I picked my way through the junk and entered what I assumed was the main living area of the house, everything became clear.

The guy was sitting on a sagging couch. I could barely pick him out among the empty food containers and empty bottles and cans. He was listing to one side and it was pretty clear that he only had full function and total mobility on one side of his body. One arm hung listlessly at his side and one side of his face didn't react at all when he caught sight of me. The half of his face that did have mobility twitched and pulled tight in anger. It took a second but recognition slipped in, and all the bits and pieces that were missing from the puzzle started to click into place.

I lifted an eyebrow at the man as he continued to glare at me from the couch.

"You already destroyed my entire life, you foreign piece of shit. What are you doing here, Gates?"

I looked around at the mounds of stuff piled on top of more stuff and then glanced down at the floor, which literally seemed to move under my feet.

"If you had kept your hands to yourself, neither one of us would be here." Sitting across from me, forever altered and forever trapped in a prison of his own making, was the man that I had pulled off of Key and beaten within an inch of his life all those years ago.

"Fuck you. Get out of my house."

I could see how badly he wanted to get to his feet and confront me, but he lacked the strength to accomplish this.

"Where is your son?"

The man's face pinched in a furious frown and his good hand curled into a fist.

"I don't know. The little bastard took off weeks ago and I haven't seen him."

"You mean he didn't want to stay here in these luxurious accommodations?" I let the sarcasm drip from my voice.

The man growled and finally clawed and lumbered his way to his feet. One arm was useless by his side and one leg was slower and limped more than the other as he shuffled toward me.

"My old lady bailed when I ended up in the hospital after you were done with me. Couldn't really explain why I had my ass handed to me at a strip club, so the bitch got all uppity and took off, sticking me with the brats. I can't hardly fucking move thanks to you and yet I'm supposed to raise kids and take care of this shithole?"

"From what I hear, the state took your kids, and apparently the things you were doing to them mean this pigsty is exactly what you deserve."

One side of the man's face twitched and his eyes narrowed. "We all get what we deserve in the end, so where does that leave you, Gates?"

It was a good question. The answer was: probably where I started—in hell.

"I need to find your boy. You messed him up good and he's going to get himself in the same kind of trouble you found yourself in."

"I don't know where he is and I don't care. He's the one that called the state and had the girls yanked outta here. Now I don't got anyone to help me out around here. I might as well die."

The smell of the hovel was starting to get to me, and I could see the guy wouldn't be of any help even if he did know where his kid was at. This was a broken, twisted human being, and I could understand why his son held me personally responsible for his awful home life. Before I had given the old man a beatdown, he had no doubt been a terrible man, but some of that evil had been taken out of the home and spread around the Point. When I crippled him, made him homebound, undoubtedly all that awfulness had been trapped in these walls and buried the poor kids here right along with the hoard. He couldn't victimize the outside world so he kept all his deviant and violent tendencies right at home.

I met the man glare for glare. This was a time when the consequences of my actions were staring me right in the face and I had to be accountable for the things I had done. I was the one who put all this squalor in motion all those years ago by letting the monster I was trained to be off the leash. Showing my true colors had pushed Key away and had sent this man's son on a path of vengeance I couldn't blame him for choosing.

"Your family deserves better than you."

He grunted and took another tottering step toward me. "Get out of my house, Gates. I'll see you in hell."

That made me grin at him as I kicked my foot back so that it connected with a cluttered entertainment center piled high with garbage and other junk. The TV was the old tube kind that weighed a good couple of hundred pounds. I stepped out of the way just as the unit fell forward and landed right on the other man.

He screamed and went down to the grotesquely dirty floor

with a thud, his entire lower half caught under the weight of the unit and the old television. He gazed up at me with unfiltered hatred as I bent over and put my hands on my knees to look at him with disgust.

"I bring perdition with me wherever I go, so you won't have to look far. Maybe while you lie there, hungry, scared, worried if someone will find you in your own filth before you die, you can think about the fact that maybe if you had taken care of your own instead of perverting it, corrupting it, you would have had someone here to save you. You would have had someone around who cares if you live or die. Our actions define us and every move you've made from the start has been the wrong one."

With his good arm he was shoving at the furniture trapping him to the floor. He was huffing and puffing in exertion but that didn't stop him from telling me he wanted to kill me, and swearing vengeance and revenge with every other breath.

"What about your actions, Gates? What do they make you?" He indicated where I was going, leaving him pinned to the floor. "A pimp? A murderer? A fucking psychopath?"

Yeah, my actions definitely made me all of those things at one point or another, but they also made me a man that was taking care of his city, his business, and his woman. I wouldn't apologize for that. My methods didn't always lead to a perfect outcome but I had learned early on in life that the only way to get anywhere was to fight for what you wanted. So I would be accountable for the things I had screwed up and I would always fight and hopefully win. Even if that victory took years and years to earn.

I left the man on the floor, stuck and screaming after me. I sincerely hoped none of his neighbors got curious and went in and freed him. He deserved to die in the piles of his own filth. It was a fitting way for the bastard to go out.

It had been a waste of a night, considering that I now had a motive but still no location for Tyler, and I was annoyed that Key never texted me back. When I got back to my house in the woods, all I wanted to do was strip naked and scrub off everywhere I had been tonight. I felt like I was covered head to toe in the Point and the filthy atmosphere was suffocating me. I kicked off my boots before going inside and calling Keelyn's name.

I scowled when she didn't answer and worked my shirt off over my head as I headed up the stairs toward my room. My bed was obviously empty even though the lights in the room were on, and there was still no sign of Key. The suit I had asked Bayla to grab and take to the cleaners was in a heap in front of the closet, which was unusual. I added my shirt and the rest of my clothes from tonight to the pile and padded naked to the bathroom. I pushed the door open and came up short because Key was standing in front of the massive vanity meticulously placing all her different tubes and jars of makeup on the countertop.

She was humming under her breath and had earbuds dangling off either side of her face. She was dressed in nothing more than a tiny little tank top and a pair of stretchy yoga pants that were molded to her like a second skin while she wiggled and shook to the music only she could hear. I blinked at her like an idiot. Men used to pay hundreds of dollars a minute to get her to do that kind of show and here she was performing it in my bathroom for free.

I reached out a finger, hooked one of the buds, and yanked. "What are you doing?"

She whirled around and gaped at me. I wasn't sure if it was because I surprised her or because I was totally naked, but either way her jaw dropped and her gaze skipped over my stomach and went right to my dick, which, as always, was really happy to see her.

"I'm moving in. Where are your clothes? You're very naked."

I grunted and moved around her so I could crank on the shower. "They need to be burned. Even in the Point there are some places that are worse than others. I swear I saw all of them tonight. What do you mean you're moving in? Weren't you already here?"

I looked at her over my shoulder as steam started to billow out of the glass enclosure. Her eyes were locked on my backside, and if I wasn't mistaken she was licking her lips. I cleared my throat and grinned at her as she jerked her head up to look at me with a faint blush on her cheeks.

"I mean I moved in. My stuff is now with your stuff and you don't get to kick me out when we fight . . . which we will."

I scoffed at her and reached up to pull my hair down. "It took me too long to get you here. I would never kick you out." I let out an "oof" as she slammed into the front of me and I had to put my hands on her waist to keep us both from falling back into the open shower. "And you told me it isn't fighting . . . it's foreplay."

Her hands went up to my hair and started playing around with the tie that kept it trapped on the top of my head.

"I was dying to take it down as soon as you put it up." Her words were laced with humor and her breath was hot on my throat. My cock reacted predictably but so did my heart, which started to bang and slide all around the inside of my chest, trying to find enough room to fit now that she had meticulously put all the pieces of it back together.

"I'm really dirty. You might want to wait until I clean up before you put your hands on me."

She was combing her fingers through my now freed hair and gently working them through the parts that were tangled up from being tied up all night. She gave a delicate little snort and lifted up on her toes so that her lips could press into mine.

"A shower isn't going to make you clean, Nassir. I'll put my hands on you no matter what shape you come to me in, as long you get back to me in one piece. That's all I care about anymore."

It was a sweet sentiment, one that made my heart thud even harder for her and her alone, but it didn't change the fact that I was actually physically dirty and could feel the city sitting heavy in all my pores. Without warning, I took a big step backward and pulled her with me into the shower. She swore at me as the water drenched her and immediately plastered her clothes down her body. She used two hands to push her hair out of her face but begrudgingly took the body wash I handed her and started to work the liquid over my shoulders and chest while I scrubbed my hair within an inch of its life. She'd helped me pull those haphazard stitches out a few days ago, so it felt good to scrub my scalp.

"I like coming back to you." I meant coming back to her in my space, in my life, so deep there was no way she could ever leave.

"Good. Wanna tell me how your night went?" Her hands skated over my abs and her index finger dipped in my belly button, which had me sucking in a breath. I frowned when I noticed a dark shadow around her eye and what looked like a raw scrape mark at her hairline.

"After you tell me why you look like you ran face first into a wall."

She lifted a finger to her tender eye and winced. She raised a sleek eyebrow at me and pinched one of my nipples, twisting hard enough to make me grunt in pain.

"Let's just say you leave a lasting impression on the women in your life. We can talk about it later. It makes me kind of mad at you even though it's not really your fault. I want you to tell me about your night."

I scowled but could see by the stubborn tilt of her damp mouth that she wasn't going to budge on the subject, so I told her, "I found the kid's real name. Tried to track him down at his family's house. Nothing panned out, but now I understand why the kid has it in for me."

"Oh yeah?" Her hands got a little lower and I saw her smirk as my breathing faltered when she wrapped a soapy fist around the erection bobbing up and down in front of her.

"Yeah. Like you always tell me, my actions have consequences. The kid is one of them. I messed up and it in turn messed him up. I made him what he is, so I can't really fault him for wanting a piece of me. I've been there myself."

I grunted a little bit as she pushed me back under the spray of water so that all the suds sluiced down over my skin and onto the tile under our feet. Her gray eyes were luminous as she gazed up at me and it was a fog I never wanted to escape from.

"That makes me want to kiss you."

"What? Taking responsibility for the role I played in my own misery?"

"No." She leaned forward and pressed her lips to the center of my chest, where my heart did its very best to kiss her back. "You seeing someone as a person, as a human being that is a product of their environment. You being able to recognize his motives and their validity. That's new."

I threaded my fingers in the back of her neon-colored hair and bent my head to kiss her on the crown of her head. "You've made me soft. You always did."

She squeezed the very not-soft part of me that she still held in her hand. "Soft things can be harder to break than rigid things. They have more give in them and more bounce-back."

I hummed in agreement. "Didn't you say something about a kiss?" I wanted to change the subject to something a little lighter. I'd had enough of introspection and soul baring for the night. Plus, we were both wet and aroused. There were much more interesting things we could be doing with our mouths than talking.

She pulled back and smiled at me. She was spending too much time with the devil because temptation and promise dripped off every inch of her as she told me, "I sure did." It was pure wickedness that gleamed out of her eyes as she dropped to her knees in front of me and leaned forward to press the softest, sweetest kiss to the underside of my dick where it jutted up toward my belly. I groaned and she moved to press butterfly-light kisses all along one side and then down the other before pulling the entire length into the enveloping heat of her mouth. It made my eyes roll back in my head and I was pretty sure it was the best kiss I had ever received in my life.

I already had my hand on the back of her head, so I let her set a pace that worked for her and leaned back so that my back was against the shower wall. It was hot, slippery, and so goddamn sexy I felt my legs shake. She curled one hand around my hip for leverage as she bobbed up and down, going deeper and taking more of me inside with each pass. It made my abs tense up and my balls tighten. It made my spine lock and my skin pebble up in desire. She swirled her tongue around the plump head and I think there was even a gentle scrape of teeth involved at one point. All I knew was that it felt like being worshipped. Like being honored. Like she wanted to be exactly where she was, and when her free hand got creative and disappeared between my legs so that she could caresses and stroke my sensitive sac, I was pretty sure it was the first time this particular devil saw heaven.

I didn't last much longer after that. I groaned her name and it echoed off the tiled walls as I emptied myself into the back of her throat. As I leaned limply against the wall, feeling spent, shaky, and determined to be worth all the things this woman gave to me, I pulled her up to her feet and held her as she kissed me under the chin with a sassy grin on her pretty face.

"Not so soft."

That made me bark out a laugh as I wrapped an arm around her and picked her up off her feet. It would only take me a minute to recharge so I could kiss her back.

"Just enough hard and enough soft to make me the perfect man." I said it sarcastically because it was no secret that I was as far from perfect as any one man could be. I think that was why I pushed everyone else around me so hard.

She laughed uncontrollably as I started to tug and pull her wet clothes off of her. It was like pulling a wet suit off of a deep-sea diver. Her eyes darkened to slate and her smile softened as I kissed her and brushed her hair off her face. I wanted inside of her more than I wanted my next breath. There was no wait left in me when it came to her.

"Perfect for me."

Those words had my dick getting hard again and zeroing in on her soft center. I smoothed her wet and tangled hair off of her face and lowered my mouth to hers. When we were in bed together, or really whenever I took her, it felt frantic and rushed, like I was afraid she was going to change her mind on me at any time and disappear out of my life for good. With all her stuff mingled with mine, with her pliant and waiting under me, some of that rush took a backseat for once. I wanted to savor her. I wanted to breathe every sigh, feel every quiver, own every pull of her body as I pushed inside of her. I wanted to simply be with her and appreciate that we both got the opportunity to have each other.

Her tongue twisted around mine and her fingers dug into my shoulders as she lifted one long leg up to curl around my waist. I felt her heel on my ass urging me to move, but I resisted, content to feel her shift and flutter all along my buried erection.

I trailed a hand across her chest and cupped her breast in my hand. She arched into my touch and I felt her grinding against where we were joined. Her sharp little teeth nipped at the tip of my tongue and her eyes were all kinds of stormy as she got a fist in my hair and pulled my head up to look at her.

"Move your ass, Gates."

I chuckled and rubbed my chin across her shoulder while tracing the pulse that throbbed in the side of her neck with my tongue.

"I'm feeling you."

"Yeah, I feel you too, but it's not enough. Put that pretty dick to use."

That had me rearing back to loom over her. "You think my dick is pretty?"

She pushed her hips up against mine and groaned as our pubic bones mashed together, finally giving her the friction she was after.

"All of you is pretty and all of you feels really good, but I need you to move." Her other leg joined the first, and all I could do was let her pull me in. Not like I wanted to be anywhere else anyway. I liked that she wanted to take what she needed from me, that she had just as much impatience to be together as I did.

I braced my hands on the bed above her head and started to really move. I thrust into her hard enough to have her moving up the bed. She gasped in pleasure and her eyes drifted to half-mast as poignant pleasure overtook her pretty face. She clutched at my shoulders and held on as the ride got rougher and fiercer the wetter and hotter she became under me. It was like sinking into fire and heaven at the same time. It was the closest thing to love I had ever felt, and I wanted to be inside that feeling forever.

I reached for a pillow and shoved it under her already elevated hips as she fucked me back. The added lift let me get deeper, sink in farther, and she mewled at the sensation, which had my balls drawing up tight in pleasure.

I nibbled on her collarbone. She pulled on my hair and in an instant we broke apart together. She called me her devil and I called her my everything. We clung to each other, sweaty, spent, and forever entwined. My starved heart and soul were gorged to the point of overflowing and every battle I'd ever fought felt like it had been nothing if this was my victory, being here with her.

CHAPTER 17

Keelyn

Don't forget I have to drop all that stuff off at the cleaners sometime this afternoon."

I was sipping on some fancy coffee drink from a café that was most definitely not located in the Point and enjoying not having to navigate the streets as Nassir drove us into town. It had been a battle royal getting him to agree to let me ride along as he went into town to check on the club. He was worried about me being a target now that Tyler had a gun, but I shut him down with the simple statement that I was just as worried about something happening to him. In fact, I reminded him that the safest place for me had always been right by his side and that I had most of my life savings invested in the Lock & Key, so it was just as important to me to see how much damage had been done to the building as it was to him.

I hadn't told him about my newly formed idea for creating some kind of system to get people, those who were drowning and flailing, off the streets of our city, but after he unloaded everything he had found out about Tyler and his home life, I was more certain than ever it was something I wanted to make a reality. A kid like that needed a way out so that he didn't feel like his only option was to pull on the devil's tail. I wanted to make that kind of difference and I knew Nassir would support me even if his heart wasn't quite as lenient as mine. People were my thing, after all, and he was all about letting me do my thing.

I had to ask what he had done to the man that not only attacked me all those years ago but had also tortured his own family. Nassir had looked at me out of the corner of his eye and asked me if I really wanted to know. To my surprise I did.

I really did.

I wanted to know what he thought was a fitting punishment for a man that destroyed his children and ruined three young lives. I was expecting to be disgusted, to have my tummy turn and to have to force myself to sit still and not squirm while he recounted his actions. To my relief and surprise, when he explained that he simply knocked over the entertainment center and let the man stay pinned to the floor with very little hope for help coming along to save him, I thought it sounded almost too lenient.

I was expecting blood and guts. I was expecting horror stories and visions of punishment that would give me nightmares. What I got was a story about retribution for a man that deserved much worse. I wasn't sure if this leniency was a result of my influence on him but I liked to think so. He would always be something sharp and deadly on the inside, something that could be used to destroy, but every blade needs a sheath and every gun needs a holster to protect it. I had no problem offering myself up as the thing that kept this particular weapon secure.

"Why didn't Bayla come get that stuff and take it to the cleaners? I called her and told her there was stuff at the house she needed to pick up."

I flinched and absently lifted my fingers to touch the lump at the back of my head. If he had felt it when we were messing around, he hadn't mentioned it, and I wasn't really sure how to have this conversation with him and not get the jealous housekeeper into trouble.

I just wanted her gone, not punished. Loving a man like Nassir was already enough of a penance and a wound that would never heal. "I told her I would take care of it. We need to have a conversation about her and what exactly she does for you now that I'm staying with you indefinitely."

He made a noise in his throat and cut me a sharp look out of those burning eyes. "You aren't staying with me. You're *living* with me. Big difference, Key. Our lives are wrapped up together in a giant knot and you can't untie it without both of us unraveling."

He was so prickly about things like that. It was actually kind of cute . . . well, as cute as a man that was everything about sex and danger personified could be.

"You've always had me in knots, Nassir. I learned to stop struggling against them all the time because that only made them tighten."

One of his dark eyebrows winged upward and the corner

of his mouth kicked up in a sexy smirk that had me clenching my thighs.

"I'll put you in real knots one day and see how much you enjoy it."

Of course that brought to mind all the debauchery and experimentation that played out live and in color on the monitors in his office. Before working at the club, I would've told him to go to hell. Giving up that kind of control, especially to him, would've sent me into a panic and caused me to flee. Now it seemed intriguing and titillating. I blew out a low breath and reached out to put my hand on his hard thigh.

"Maybe. You'll have to work for it, though."

He chuckled and turned the SUV into the parking lot in front of the club. He parked next to a nondescript van that looked like it belonged to one of the work crews that were taking care of the drippy mess in the building.

"What happened with Bayla?" He shut the engine off and turned in his seat so that he was facing me. The look on his face was intense, so I was thinking really hard about the words I wanted to use to explain that I wanted the girl gone without ratting her out. To avoid that probing gaze, I shifted my eyes to the van and frowned a little when I saw the side door begin to open. I hadn't seen anyone working when we pulled up, so I thought it was weird that someone would be exiting the vehicle as soon as we rolled to a stop next to it. Only the door just rolled open a few inches. There definitely wasn't enough room for any kind of grown person to come in or out.

"That's odd." I was lifting my hand to point over Nassir's shoulder at the van when I saw the back end of the gun poke out of the opening. I didn't have to utter any more words. I frantically reached out and grabbed a fistful of Nassir's long hair to jerk his head down at the same time as I folded myself over. As soon as both of our heads were dash level, there was a deafening bang followed by the driver's window of the SUV shattering and covering both of us in a blanket of glass shards. I heard Nassir swear over my own startled scream as I lifted my hands to cover my head. Another blast rang out and I cowered into the smallest ball possible as the window on the passenger side of the car exploded and rained glass down on us.

Nassir was saying something to me and his eyes were huge in his face, and for the first time ever I could see fear twisting and turning in the molten depths. He leaned over my back, popping the lock on the seat belt and lifting up just enough to push my door open.

"Go!" He had his hands on my shoulder and was trying to push me out of the car, but I was too busy pulling on the front of his shirt to get him to come with me. I couldn't let him go. "Get out of here! Go find Chuck!"

Even if I didn't want to cooperate, there was no way Nassir was going to let me remain in the line of fire. In fact, as soon as I slid out of the car, with the help of a mighty shove from him, another shot rang out and I heard it thump into the metal on the opposite side of the Range Rover. I was gasping for air and trying to reach back into the car and blindly grab for Nassir so I could pull him out with me but my hands came up empty. It took every iota of courage I possessed to get on my knees and peek back inside the car. I was terrified I was going to find Nassir bloody and filled with holes, but instead he was sitting up straight behind the wheel of the SUV and looking directly into the barrel of the gun that was pointed at him.

I whispered his name and his eyes shifted to me, but they were wrong. The fire that usually lit them up was gone and in its place was a cool bronze that looked like it had been molded and crafted into some ancient weapon. He waved a hand at me and told me to get myself safe and then he pushed open the door of the car and stepped right into the line of fire. The barrel of the gun couldn't have been more than two feet away from the center of his chest. I screamed his name but he wouldn't look back at me. I frantically scrambled for my phone so I could call 911 and Chuck.

"I know why you want to hurt me, I understand why you think you want me dead, and I can't say I blame you."

Nassir's voice was calm. Too calm.

"I recognize that I made you into what you are, and that you think the only way to change your circumstances and to have a better life is to kill your creator. I grew up thinking the same thing."

I watched through the opening of the doors as the van door slid open a fraction more to show the entire pistol and the shaky arm of the kid holding it. It was obvious he wasn't familiar with the weapon and one of his hands was still all messed up, and that made me think Nassir might end up taking a bullet even if the kid didn't mean to fire one.

"The thing is, it doesn't matter where you go or who you punish or what kind of life you make for yourself, you'll always be that thing that was molded, crafted, formed. You will always be the product of the things you have done and the things that were done to you, but if you want a chance at any kind of life, if you want to be worthy of anything, you have to be more than what you were made to be. You have to break that creation apart and make something new."

The gun dipped down for a second and I saw the kid poke his head out. He looked so young, so untried, that I couldn't imagine him being the one that was behind all the things that had been happening at the club. I couldn't fathom that he was the one that might very well give my devil hell. I couldn't sit there and do nothing while the man I loved had a gun pointed at him. All this time I was determined to be by his side and that included when he was facing something that might end it all for both of us.

"You have no idea what he put us through." The kid sounded like he was going to cry.

I saw Nassir nod his head and looked down at the buzzing phone in my lap. I knew that Chuck was making his way around the back of the club and the cops were on their way. Chuck had heard the gunshots from inside. I crept around the fender and poked my head around the side. Both Nassir and the kid turned to look at me, and before I could say anything, Nassir took a step closer to the end of the gun so that now, if the kid did pull the trigger, there was nowhere for the bullet to go but right into the center of his chest.

"I do know and it isn't right. You didn't deserve it."

The kid snarled something low and furious as Nassir lifted his hands up and away from his chest. The kid slowly moved to exit the van, the gun only inches from the center of Nassir's chest. It was almost touching him. The kid wiped his free hand over his mouth and his eyes started to dart around the parking lot.

"He was always an asshole. He liked to use his fists on all of us. He drank too much, cheated on my mom, and there was never any money, but he was gone most of the time, so we just sort of weathered the storm when he was home."

I heard Nassir heave a sigh and I rose to my feet so that I was standing behind him. "Please don't do this." There was a quiver in my voice but my heart made me sound stronger than I was feeling. I touched my face, surprised to find a steady stream of silent tears running across my cheeks.

Nassir spared me a hard glance over his shoulder and turned back around to focus all his attention on the armed teenager. "Until I got my hands on the old man and you were trapped in a house with him." Nassir sounded resigned and regretful. His words were heavy and his posture was repentant. He was actually sorry for what had happened to the kid because of his actions, even if they had been done to save me.

"I could take the beatings because eventually I got big enough to fight back. The filth, and the abuse, meant nothing because all along the worst thing he was doing was touching my sisters. He couldn't go out after you crippled him, wouldn't leave the house because of his fucked-up face, so instead of being his kids, my sisters became his new targets. Their childhood, their innocence, was stolen because of you. At first I thought I could just ruin your business, make you mad, and force you to spend all your precious money, but then I realized it wasn't enough. You had to pay like we did. You should have your life, your future, taken away just like my sisters did."

Nassir made another noise low in his throat and I saw him wave his hand. A slight movement caught my eye and I saw Chuck and a couple of the other security staff creeping around the side of the building with their own guns drawn.

"I understand why you feel that way, I really do, but if you kill me, if you pull that trigger, you are making a choice that you can't unmake. You are doing exactly what your old man set you up to do. You are acting like nothing more than the monster I started to build all those years ago."

He reached out his hand to grab the kid's shoulder, and when the young man jerked away, I wasn't the only witness to the scene that gasped. Nassir was playing a dangerous game and he was going to lose everything if the kid didn't choose to play along. I was scared of losing him and my heart broke as he tried so desperately to make this troubled young man see that even in hell there were options. No matter where you were or what your future looked like, your life was a product of the choices you made. That was why I needed to be able to give the people here in the Point the chance to make better lives for themelves. Every action had a consequence and sometimes it was the consequences that could kill you.

"You have the opportunity to make your shitty life into something better. Go get your sisters out of the system and give them a better life, the life they always deserved. Worry about saving them and yourself instead of ruining something that's already been broken and repaired too many times to count. Put the gun down and make the choice to be something better than I am, to be better than what your old man tried to beat into you."

The gun wobbled a little and I thought my devil did his thing and bargained with his greatest asset—his life—and won. I tried to exhale a breath that felt like it was stuck in my throat, and I saw Chuck creeping closer and closer. His gaze was shifting between where I was still crouched behind the SUV and where Nassir stood with the young man on the other side.

"How am I supposed to be anything other than this?!" The kid's voice rose and I heard panic and something wild in it. "I didn't finish high school. I have no money, no job, and my family is in pieces. In this place, being a man makes you weak, but being a monster makes you a legend."

He was going to pull the trigger. I saw it at the same time Chuck did because I screamed Nassir's name and scrambled to my feet so I could launch myself across the front seats of the SUV to try to grab ahold of him. There was no way I was going to make it in time. The gun was too close to his chest and the kid had already made up his mind.

The first blast made me deaf and had Nassir wilting to the ground as soon as it sounded. I wasn't fast enough to get him before he hit the asphalt. The rapid blasts that followed had the kid's body jerking in a morbid dance in front of my eyes as bullets tore into him, making the gun fall out of his hand. He collapsed on the ground across from his victim.

I got out of the driver's side of the car and fell onto my knees next to Nassir's side. I couldn't tell where the bullet had entered him because there was so much blood seeping onto his chest. The white fabric of his shirt was turning entirely crimson and he wasn't moving at all. I pushed the sides of his suit jacket out of the way while I searched for a place to put pressure. I was watching him die right in front of me. Suddenly all those years of fighting to be independent, of struggling to make it on my own, felt wasted and foolish. I was more myself with him than I had ever been and now I felt like I was losing one of the best parts of me.

Chuck dropped down on the other side of him and tapped him on the cheek. Tarnished bronze eyes peeled open with great difficulty to peer up at us. "Already called the law. They got the medics with them, boss, so you hang in there."

"I can't see where he's hit, can you?" I felt like I needed to put pressure on the wound, to stem the flow of blood rushing out of the man I loved, but I was useless and all I could do was grab his lifeless hand and hold on. His fingers didn't even slightly twitch and I could see how hard it was for him to breathe.

"I think he got hit more than once. Idiot. Trying to negotiate with a gun pointed right at his heart. What were you thinking?"

Chuck seemed as worried and at as much of a loss as to what to do as I was. I leaned forward and pressed my lips to Nassir's. They were so cold and all I could taste was my own salty tears and the tang of blood. There was no life in there to kiss me back.

He was thinking he would offer the kid a break he had never been offered. He was thinking he would show the young man that when you had a reason, had a purpose, you could make choices that mattered. He was trying to tell him that even when you were broken and twisted deep down inside, there was always a way to get in there and shape all those mangled pieces into a better man. Maybe not a good man, definitely not a law-abiding and upstanding man, never an easy or agreeable man, but a man that was better than what he had been created to be.

"If you die on me I'm going to be so mad at you."

I whispered the words against his unresponsive mouth and started crying in earnest when a warm puff of air escaped to touch my lips.

He groaned low and deep but it meant he was alive still, so I would take it. Off in the distance, finally, the sounds of sirens could be heard. It wasn't like attending to two victims of a gunfight was anything new or worthy of extra haste in the Point.

"Theee . . . kiddd?" They weren't words so much as they were expulsions of air huffed and puffed out.

I looked over my shoulder at where the other body was sprawled, Chuck's guys keeping a close eye on him, but I could see multiple places where blood was pooling and leaking out of the young man and staining the parking lot underneath him.

I squeezed Nassir's fingers and cried even harder into him when I felt his struggle to curl around mine. "He didn't make the right choice."

I felt him shudder at my words but I couldn't explain anything further because the cops and the paramedics were suddenly all over us. I was pulled one way and Chuck was pulled the other, both of us complaining loudly, as uniformed professionals moved around Nassir's prone form. There was so much blood and so much noise I thought I was going to have a breakdown. When a cop tried to pull me aside to ask me what was going on, I swung at him without even thinking. Luckily, Chuck was there and wrapped me up in a huge bear hug while I collapsed in a sobbing mess into his arms.

"She just watched two people get shot not even ten feet in front of her and one of them is her man. Can you cut her some slack?"

The cop grumbled something but I couldn't focus on what he was saying because they were strapping Nassir to some hard-looking plastic board and hefting him onto the stretcher. They weren't taking him anywhere without me. I shoved at Chuck's arms until he set me free, and bolted to the back of the ambulance, only to be brought up short by one of the paramedics.

"Lady, he's in bad shape. You need to meet us at the hospital."

I would have taken a swing at him too if I couldn't see the other medic in the back of the ambulance swearing and rushing around trying to hook up Nassir to as many IVs and machines as the back of the emergency vehicle could hold.

"I'm going with him." I wasn't about to give the guy a chance to argue, so I just pushed past him and took a seat on the hard little bench so I could keep my eyes glued to what was happening to my now dying devil. Nassir must have been in really bad shape because even though there were two medics and they were a lot bigger than me, neither one wanted to waste time arguing with me. Instead they pulled the doors shut and began frantically working on him.

They had ripped his shirt open and I could see that Chuck

was right. The kid had managed to get off more than one shot. There was a perfectly round hole up high in his shoulder almost in the exact same spot where I had taken a bullet, but there was also one lower and more toward the center of his chest. From where I was sitting, it looked like it was exactly where his heart would be.

I started chanting "no, no, no, no" over and over again while the two men rushed around and muttered things to each other that didn't sound encouraging.

"His BP is crashing. Not good." One of the guys grabbed a syringe filled with something and started pumping it into one of the clear plastic tubes going into Nassir's arm. All I wanted to do was reach out and hold his hand, but we were moving too fast and I didn't want to get in the way of the men trying to save his life.

"Any word on the other GSW victim?" The guy that had tried to keep me from getting on the ambulance shook his head.

"He was DOA on the scene." His gaze skipped over to me. "Seems like you were pretty lucky to make it out of there un-scathed."

Oh, I was very much scathed. The one person in the world I knew that I would ever love and ever give myself completely to was struggling to stay alive and I could see him losing the battle with every minute that ticked by. It was grossly unsettling that Nassir could survive war, his own warped beginnings at the hands of a zealot, the corrupt manipulations of government and political power, and the streets of the Point only to be taken down by a kid that had been crafted in his mirror image.

I dropped my head into my hands and pulled on the front of my hair so hard that it hurt. "I'm not feeling so lucky at the moment."

"You should've just met us at the hospital. It's never easy to watch someone you care about hover on the verge of death."

I snapped my head up and glared at the insensitive ass. I didn't need to know how close Nassir was to not pulling through. I could see it for myself. His normally golden skin was waxy and tinged gray. His lips looked blue and there was still blood oozing out of him in more than one spot.

"I'm going to appreciate any time I have with him, even if that time is running out right in front of me."

Deciding I didn't care if I was in their way anymore, I reached out and found Nassir's hand so I could hold on to some part of him as we raced the rest of the way to the hospital. Once we got there, the doors to the ambulance swung open and an army of doctors and nurses rushed to attend to him. They were saying things like "shock," words like "blood transfusion" and "nonresponsive" hit me like bullets. I didn't want to let them take him out of my sight but I knew making the medical staff deal with a hysterical woman wouldn't help him, so I bit my lip and continued to cry as I stepped out of the boxy vehicle and watched them take my man away.

I don't know how long I stood there in front of the hospital covered in Nassir's blood, silently weeping and at a loss as to what to do with myself, but it was long enough for Chuck to eventually find me. When his arms wrapped around me and I was pulled to that barrel chest, the numbness that had been holding all my bits and pieces together evaporated and

I became a wailing, noisy, sloppy mess. I started screaming about the unfairness of it all, about how I would never forgive Nassir for pulling me so far in that I couldn't get out. I cursed a million different ways for his making me love him when he knew it was going to lead to this kind of heartache.

I ranted.

I raved.

I raged.

Chuck just held me and continued to pet my hair while I acted like a crazy person, and told me everything would be all right. When I finally calmed down, he pressed his cheek to the top of my head and gave a soft little chuckle.

Indignant that he could find anything funny about this dire situation, I dug my elbow into his ribs until he grunted and took a step back.

"How can you laugh at a time like this?" He reached out a hand and rubbed a finger over the frown lines that were dug in deep on my forehead.

"I'm laughing because I had almost this exact same conversation with Nassir when you got shot."

That made my heart dip and Reeve's words about our men being just as scared that something bad was going to happen to us drifted like smoke through my tumultuous thoughts.

I rubbed my chafed and raw cheeks furiously and tried to suck in enough air to calm myself down.

"Why would he take that kind of risk, Chuck? Why would he sacrifice himself like that?"

That gold tooth winked at me as he offered me a tiny little smile. He reached out and hooked an arm around my neck so we could go inside and see if Nassir did indeed have the luck of the devil.

Chuck pressed a kiss to my temple and whispered in my ear. "He did it because all the love you showed him proved that he could have turned into a real boy."

I gulped and felt a fresh wave of tears well up. I loved that Nassir was a real boy but I hated that being one meant he was just as vulnerable and fragile as the rest of us, and I couldn't help but have the fleeting thought that robots and puppets didn't bleed.

Nassir had to pull through. The Point hadn't seen the kind of hell on earth that would follow if he didn't.

CHAPTER 18

Nassir

I had been on the slippery edge of death more than one time in my twenty-seven years of life. I'd been shot, stabbed, blown up, starved, beaten, and even had my own hands in the mix by giving in to weakness and overdosing just to stop seeing the bodies drop and the blood flow. All the times when I knocked on death's door, the reception was exactly what one might have expected. I saw the fields of lost souls I had cultivated. I saw my mother, and even in her incorporeal state, felt the disappointment that still hung around her because I hadn't lived up to all of my potential as a killer and avenger. I finally had a face-to-face with my father, and in my limbo state he condemned me for not being a man of faith or conviction. Before, when I'd hovered between life and death, every action and its subsequent consequences played out before me, taunting me with the knowledge of how all the things I set in motion would eventually come around full circle. Violence and vengeance did not occur in a vacuum, and as everything inside of me struggled to fight for life, the loss I was feeling mingled with the pain was a constant reminder that there was no escaping from a lifetime of misdeeds.

This time, as I chased death down, it was distinctly different. I knocked on the door, probably harder than I ever had before, but for some reason death wasn't answering. No one was. So I was just there waiting to be let in or sent back.

I was caught in a void. No memories. No regrets. No family. No accomplishments. No demons. And maybe the most noticeable absence was that of love. I had never experienced love before, most assuredly not from my mother and definitely not from any of the other people that had filtered in and out of my life since I set myself free of the shackles of the man I was supposed to always be, but ever since Keelyn, there had been something different, and now that it was gone, I knew what it was.

Even when she wasn't mine, there was still love. It was prickly and sometimes uncomfortable. It was too big to fit anywhere. It was complex and often hidden behind things that were easier to identify, like lust, anger, and frustration, but regardless of all of that, I could see now that it was love and I missed it dearly while I was lost here in this nothingness.

I missed the bite of it and the softness that followed. I missed the way it was the only thing that filled me up when I had spent my life being so empty of everything. I missed the way it challenged me and forced me to do more, to be more. I missed the way that love made me think and consider my actions and their effect on others. I was not a *thing* anymore. I was a man . . . a man that loved a woman, had loved a woman with every broken part of me that the past had left me with, and now that it was gone, I really and truly understood what *my* hell was supposed to be like.

This . . .

This emptiness.

This nothing.

This void.

This hollowness.

This was actually hell, and sure, maybe I deserved it for all the bad things I had done in the past, but that didn't make the knowledge any easier to accept or the struggle against the constant blackness any less arduous.

I don't know how long I floated lost and alone. It felt like forever, and every single second that passed that I spent without the one thing I felt like I needed if I were to have even a slight chance at survival, I could feel myself sinking deeper and more fully into the abyss. It was pulling me under and I was helpless to stop it.

Just when I thought it was time to give up, time to surrender to the darkness and let the pit of nothing take me, I felt something . . . something sharp and awful.

Pain like a raging wildfire lit up all over me from the inside out. All that nothing was replaced with agony and ache like I had never experienced before. I was hollowed out, so empty of anything else that the pain ate me up like a meal. There was so much room inside of me for it to crawl into and settle down. It was a whole new kind of suffering and torture, but I welcomed it. I knew that as long as I was feeling something, even if it was something that would make most men wish for the quiet and enveloping blackness of death, I was alive and that thing I needed to live was out there somewhere, I just needed to find it.

I burned for days. Hotter than any fire, brighter than any star, more furious than any kind of hungry flame. The pain fed on me and then, somehow, some way, it took all I had to give and burned itself out and all that was left of me was ash. Light and fluffy ash that floated on soft breath, breath that whispered across my barren soul. I heard a voice call my name over and over again and the remnants of who I was picked up speed and tried to chase the noise down.

I tripped in the air. I free-fell from the nothing and the pain back into love.

It was there waiting with open arms to catch me. I heard it calling to me, guiding me in the only direction I could go when death didn't answer my knock. It was a journey that felt like it took forever. Every time I thought I was making my way to where I needed to be, to where I heard love calling me, something would get in my way. I would lose the sounds, the fire and pain would flare back up, and the darkness would again sneak up on me and try to pull me under. I didn't let it. Nothing mattered but getting to where love was waiting. Nothing could stand in the way of me getting to where I was always supposed to be.

I felt it all around me. Love wasn't just guiding me, it was pulling me, prodding me, filling me up, and pushing everything else out. Love was going to win and I simply had to let it happen, so I surrendered the fight and let love take me by the hand to lead me the rest of the way out of the darkness.

I was really uncomfortable, but when I finally managed to pull my eyes open, I was looking up at the prettiest cloudy day I had ever seen. The sky was stormy and there was rain falling from the clouds and landing on my face, but it was still the most welcome thing I had ever locked my eyes on.

She was blurry. In fact, I was seeing triplets that looked just like my Key with different hair, but there was no missing that my feisty fighter of a woman was hovering over me, pulling me from the threshold. Love wanted me more than death did. I tried to blink so that I could bring her into focus but that didn't work, and every time my eyes closed it felt like it took a monumental effort to get them back open.

I opened my mouth to ask her what happened, to ask her where I was and why her hair was now a deep, rich chocolate brown instead of Crayola red, but nothing came out. I wheezed like I was a thousand-year-old man, and suddenly Key's pretty, concerned face was replaced by a much sterner one. The guy had a stethoscope around his neck and was barking orders across me, and I vaguely felt my arm being picked up and the sheet that was covering me get shifted off my body.

I'm sure they had all kinds of important medical mumbo jumbo to take care of, but all I wanted was Key. I tried to shake the doctor off as he leaned over me, only to find that I was down to one working appendage. It seemed like my right arm was strapped pretty effectively to my chest, meaning I couldn't reach for my girl. That made me agitated, but I was pinned down and so very weak. I tried to call her name and realized the reason I couldn't was because I had something hard and plastic shoved between my teeth. I went to move my head to dislodge it only to have the doctor put his hand heavily on my forehead. I growled and went to jerk my head away, but that made black spots dance in front of my eyes and pain slice across my brain.

"You're upsetting him. Move out of my way." Key sounded annoyed and assertive. Yeah, everyone get out of her way so I can see my girl . . . my love.

The doctor's face was replaced with the one that had saved me, the one that meant everything.

"Nassir, you got hurt really, really bad. You need to let them check you out, okay? I promise I'm not going anywhere." Her hand reached out and brushed over my forehead. It felt really nice, so I closed my eyes and relaxed against her touch. It soothed me. It settled me, and before I knew it, pain and sleepiness sucked me back under.

It went on like that for days. I would wake up and Key would be there, touching me, talking to me, holding me, and then the doctors and nurses would get their hands in the mix and aggravate me until they had to pump sedatives into my system to get me to calm down. Eventually the ventilator was pulled out and she could touch her lips to mine. When she did she told me how close I had come to dying before her very eyes. One of the bullets had broken my clavicle and the one fired into the center of my chest had shattered when it hit my sternum and a few tiny pieces had gotten dangerously close to my heart. I'd needed immediate surgery and had barely pulled through. To make matters worse, I'd apparently had an allergic reaction to one of the heavy painkillers they were pumping into me and had almost kicked it again. It hadn't been an easy few weeks for her but she rarely left my side and she did more to calm me down and get me to cooperate with the hospital staff than the sedatives did.

When I could finally speak without coughing or feeling like my throat was a river of fiery pain and that my words were made of razor blades, I asked her about her hair.

She raised her hands to her head and started crying. Before I could hold a hand out to her, she climbed onto the side of the bed that didn't have my broken wing on it and put her head on my shoulder. She was delicate about it but it still hurt, not that I would ever complain. She put her hand over the obnoxiously thick dressing that was covering the center of my chest.

"I never want to see the color of blood again. Every time I looked in the mirror . . . all that red. All I could see was all of that blood flowing out of you. I couldn't take it anymore."

Now her hair was the color of mink. It looked sophisticated, still sexy and flirty in that uneven cut that hung longer on one side than the other, but it made her seem more refined than she had been before. Maybe a tad more grown up and mature, and after everything she had witnessed, how could she not be?

I told her about dying. I explained how I was there, ready to cross the threshold, but this time no one was there to answer the door. I told her about how there was nothing. How I was stuck and empty. I told her that the only thing that made any sense in all of it was her. I told her that in the nothing there was still the memory of how I felt about her. I told her that when I burned on the pyre of pain and agony, I remembered that her love was worth it and then I told her that she was what I needed to live for. She was what I had always lived for.

She was crying silent tears. I could feel them hitting my skin where the hospital gown was twisted between us. I found her hand with mine and squeezed.

"I probably have never done it right, but I have always loved you, Keelyn Foster."

"Neither one of us got it right from the start, but that doesn't mean we can't try harder from here on out. I love you too, Nassir Gates. We're bound to figure it out eventually."

Maybe that was the point. There wasn't a right or wrong way to love, there was just understanding that it was there and trying your best to treat it like the fragile, valuable, precious thing that it was.

I rubbed my thumb along the inside of her wrist and told her I wanted to talk to Dovie when I was released from the hospital.

Of course, she didn't want me anywhere near the redhead. She told me that Bax would freak out if I so much as looked sideways at his shy and sweet girlfriend. She was right, so I asked her to do me a favor. I told her that she needed to let Dovie know about the situation with Tyler French's little sisters. Those poor girls were really the biggest victims in all this tragedy. I told her that I wanted to make sure the girls got in with a good family, and I wasn't above dropping some cash around if that's what it took. Dovie worked with Social Services and the foster families in the Point, so I knew she could get me the information I needed to make sure those kids didn't have to suffer any more consequences of actions that weren't their own.

She nodded and told me she would take care of it. She was

already a few steps ahead of me in fact, and it wasn't just those girls she was interested in making sure had a better shot at a good life. She was so fucking impressive. I wanted her because she was my equal in so many ways, but I loved her fully and completely because she was always going to be better than me in so many other ways.

Key also told me that the cops had gone to the older French's house to check on the dad when she explained why the kid wanted to shoot me in the first place. They found him where I left him, trapped and angry as hell, and still ranting about how I needed to be arrested and thrown in jail for breaking and entering. But the cops were on their game and the reasons why his kids had been taken away were no secret to them, so once they pulled him free it was the deranged and crippled man who found himself in cuffs and hauled away.

When she was done talking about justice and fairness, we stayed there on the hospital bed until we both fell asleep.

I was stuck in the hospital for another week and I think the staff was onto the fact that I was running a criminal enterprise while under their care. It wasn't like I bothered to hide it. Chuck came by once a day to fill me in on what was going on at the club and with the other businesses, and Race kept popping in and out to check on me. Seemed like once I was out of commission he had done what any good partner would and stepped up to the plate to juggle all my ventures, even the ones he didn't want anything to do with. Maybe that whole partners-not-friends line was starting to get a little fuzzy. I'd never really had a friend before, but if Race wanted to be the first, I knew I could do a whole lot worse. Also, according to

Chuck, my lady had switched from sexpot to cutthroat busi-
nesswoman in my absence. I told him there was no switching.
She had always been savvy and smart; it was just that these
qualities were often overlooked because of the length of her
skirt. I picked her as my partner, in business and in life, for a
reason.

She was the one Race went to with questions about the
club and the girls. She was the one writing checks and pushing money around while I was laid up. She was taking care
of my empire while I was unable to, and according to Chuck,
she was damn good at it. With my future so precarious and
unknowable, Key had become the person to fear in my place,
and he laughingly told me she was much better at it than I
was. People were too dumbfounded by her bombshell looks
and megawatt smile to be threatened by her. She robbed them
blind and manipulated them and they didn't even know what
was happening. He told me that in the kind of negotiations in
which I usually left people peeing themselves or swearing to
take me down, she was instead leaving them thanking her.
That made me love her even more. If she lost me she would
have something I built, something I brought to life to hold on
to. My legacy would take care of her, and she would take care
of it, long after I was gone.

The day I got sprung from the doctor's care I don't know
who was more excited, me or them. Chuck rolled me down
the long hallway as the nurses and several of the other hospital
staff we passed looked visibly relieved to be rid of me. Key was
also really ready to have me back at home and eager to be my
one and only nurse. I still wasn't very mobile and I was doped

up on some pretty serious pain meds for the broken collar-bone and the cracked sternum. I was the walking wounded, but I couldn't complain because I was alive, and even though the kid who shot me hadn't made it, I knew I had done as right by him as I could. Taking responsibility stung but the pain was worth the salve it offered to my tattered soul.

Chuck actually had to drive us up to the house in the mountains because I couldn't bend down to get into Key's little Honda and the Range Rover was still missing all the glass and riddled with bullet holes. He also had to help maneuver me up the stairs and onto the couch in the living room because there was no way I was making it up the stairs into my bedroom. I uncomfortably shifted against the pillows and closed my eyes on a sigh as Key appeared with a bottle of water and a handful of pills for me to swallow down.

"You look really pale." She leaned over and pushed her fingers through my hair. I turned my face into her touch and kissed her palm. "If I can see how white you are under all that golden skin, there's a problem."

"I'm fine. You need to go back into town with Chuck and grab your car. We can't be trapped up here without a vehicle."

She scowled down at me. "No way. You just got home. I'm not leaving you here alone. I need to be close by if you need anything."

Chuck nodded. "Yeah, boss. You're a mess. Let your lady take care of you. I'll have a couple of my guys grab her ride and get it up here."

I didn't have the strength to argue, so I just held out my good arm and she sat down next to me and curled herself into my side. We sat in silence like that for a long time. Appreciating the time and the fact that we both had more of it, and that we could spend it together.

"You had to know he was going to pull the trigger. He felt like he had nothing to lose." Her voice was soft and her heart was in it.

"I've been him. I had to offer him the choice. A choice was something I never got, and now, after you, I'd like to think I would make the right one if I was in that place again."

"I would've never forgiven you if you died on me, Gates." I turned my head so I could kiss her on her temple.

"Yes, you would. You love me, so you forgive me everything as long as I'm properly apologetic." Something I'd never been before her. Being able to actually be sorry was the same as finding salvation.

She sighed. "Maybe, but you need to know if you go anywhere you're going to have to take me right along with you, Nassir."

I nodded just a little. "Same."

I couldn't hold back a yawn that was big enough to have my jaw cracking uncomfortably. I curled my arm around her tighter and asked, "Wanna take a nap with me on the couch?"

She put her hand over the bandage on my chest and traced a finger over the sling that held my injured side trapped down. "No. You rest, you need it."

I groaned in frustration but didn't argue with her when she bent down to pull my shoes off and then lifted my legs up so I was sprawled on my back as comfortably as I was going to get on the sofa. She leaned over me and gave me a quick kiss. It wasn't nearly enough but I obviously wasn't up for any more when just shifting my legs had pain shooting all along my spine. Plus, the pain meds were starting to kick in and everything was starting to feel heavy and hazy around me.

She pushed some of my hair back off my forehead and kissed me again. "I'm gonna go upstairs and work on a few things Race asked me to look over. Something is off with the girls at the massage parlor. He told me they've seen a slight drop in business lately and he wanted me to poke around and find out why. Just yell if you need me, okay?"

I didn't even have enough juice left to answer her before drugged sleep pulled me under.

I had no idea how much time had passed when I felt soft lips pressing on mine. It made me smile, especially when I felt light fingers drifting under the collar of my shirt to skim along all the gauze and tape covering me up. It was a nice way to wake up—at least I thought it was until I realized the lips were wrong, the touch was off, and there was also something cold and sharp pressed up against the side of my neck.

My eyes snapped open and locked with a midnight pair that had equal parts insanity and love floating around in their dark depths. Bayla was a small woman but the knife she had in her hand was anything but, and in my current condition, tossing her off of me without getting my throat sliced open might prove easier said than done.

"Bayla. What are you doing?" I tried to keep my voice low and level. Key was still somewhere in the house and I didn't want her to appear suddenly and have Bayla get agitated and crazy with that blade or, even worse, turn her homicidal attention on my lady.

"I've been waiting forever for you to come so I could see you. I missed you so much. I knew she was going to ruin you. Look at this mess. This never happened before her. You were the one making men bleed not the man bleeding." She climbed up on top of me and I tried not to scream in pain as her knee dug into the side with the shattered clavicle. That hurt like a son of a bitch. "She broke you." She sounded furious and sad at the same time.

The knife skipped right over my jugular and I swallowed at the scrape of it across my skin.

"This was my fault. I did this. The choices I made, the things I did, all led me to right here, Bayla. Key has nothing to do with it. I was always damaged. I was born that way."

She bent forward and I forced myself to stay absolutely still as she licked the side of my face. The edge of the knife dug into the skin below my jaw and I felt the warm trickle of blood start to run down my neck and into the fabric of my shirt.

"We aren't born broken, Nassir. Bad people get their hands on us and do things to us and that's what breaks us."

I gulped as my mind raced to figure out a way to disarm her and get her off of me with minimal damage to either of us.

"You're right; we were born into the hands of bad people, but I made the choice to be like them, Bayla. I made the choice to make my home and build my life in a place with just as much discord and suffering as where we come from."

That had her jerking upright so she was sitting on my waist with her hand right over the still raw and healing center of my chest. Between the painkillers and the pain of her weight on me, I was about to black out. I groaned before I could stop myself and I heard noise from upstairs as Key called my name.

"Are you up? Do you need anything?"

I saw Bayla's eyes widen in shock at the sound of Key's voice and she immediately scrambled off of me.

"Her car wasn't here. I thought we were alone."

"Wait!" I bellowed the word out as the dark-haired woman scrambled off me and headed in the direction of the stairs. The knife looked huge in her hand and she looked deranged as she looked over her shoulder and smiled at me while I struggled with everything I had in me to get to my feet and go after her to keep Key safe.

"You should love me. I was made for you, Nassir. We're the same."

I rolled off the couch with a thud and heard Key call my name again. This time her voice was closer and filled with concern.

I swore and fought to get to my feet. It wasn't easy with the room spinning and only having one working side, not to mention that I felt like I was going to throw up from the pain.

"Bayla!" I barked her name as I finally got my feet under me. I had to reach out and grab on to the couch for balance, but she stopped her movement toward the stairs when I said her name.

"I've never loved myself and I hate everything about where I'm from, so how on earth do you think I could love anyone even remotely like me?"

That made her waver but she obviously thought the obstacle to our eternal happiness together was the woman I had moved in right under her nose and proceeded to hand over everything I had to. She was going to go after Key and there was nothing I could do to stop her.

I bellowed Key's name and started the slow shuffle toward the stairs after the armed woman. "Bayla has a knife! You need to get out of here!" I wasn't sure any of it was making sense. I sounded and felt crazy. My body was my own enemy and it was making me more frustrated than I had ever been in my life.

Bayla was silent as a shadow as she hit the stairs. All I could see was that lethal blade in her hand and it made everything inside of me panic. I couldn't let anything happen to Key. She couldn't be one of those consequences I had just started to give a shit about.

"Didn't I fire you?" Key's voice was hard but didn't sound at all surprised. I shuffled across the floor but only got close enough that I could see the bottom part of her legs before I had to take a second to catch my breath. The firing was news to me, but then again, I had been preoccupied trying not to die.

"I'm going to kill you." Bayla said it with such conviction and certainty that it made my injured heart kick hard in my chest.

Key laughed and I was stunned. She didn't sound scared or worried at all. She sounded genuinely amused and slightly annoyed, nothing more.

"You already tried that once before. Remember how well it worked out for you? You need to leave, Bayla. Nassir's new thing is giving people choices, so I'm letting you have one. Go away or take me up on my offer to go somewhere else and start over. He's mine. This life is mine and there is no room for you in it. There never will be."

I saw the blade flash and Bayla's tawny skin flush an angry

beet red. She wasn't going to listen to reason. Much like Tyler French, Bayla had gone too far to return from the edge of insanity.

She gave a war cry and started to rush up the steps. I swore and screamed Key's name while limping forward, but all of that got drowned out as a gun fired and filled the interior of my home with noise and the pungent smell of gunpowder. I saw the knife fall and clatter down the steps and Bayla grab her shoulder and fold into a little ball as blood pushed out through her fingers. Key's bare feet and long legs padded down the rest of the steps and my eyes widened when I saw the black pistol she held in her hand. She squatted down in front of the other woman and reached out to pull her face up by her chin.

"I have really good aim, so I purposely didn't hit anything vital. You can disappear or I can make you disappear." She was even using the threats and promises that I laid down with my prey. It was ridiculously sexy and arousing. "That deck off the back of the house drops into a gorge that seems endless. I can toss you over the railing and no one will ever find your body. Do we have to have this conversation again? Because frankly I'm sick of trying to explain to you that he loves me, has always loved me, and you never stood a chance." Holy shit, was she ever *my* girl. Who knew that watching her toss threats and promising mayhem would be such a turn-on even if it wasn't the time or the place?

Bayla was sniffling and, unbelievably, looked at me for help. I snorted, mostly because Key had just delivered the exact same ultimatum I had used against the last woman that had been causing a headache in my life. Key had more than a little devil inside of her. "I'll help her toss you into the canyon," I put in. All I wanted to do was lie back down and hold on to my badass girl. Who needed Chuck to watch my back when I had her?

"I love you." She whispered the words and I thought Key was going to shoot her again.

"Maybe you do, but that's your mistake."

Hearing me tell her that her feelings were a mistake must have finally broken through to her. She levered herself to her feet, cast a longing look at me, and then rushed past me and out the door. I didn't know what kind of offer Key had made the woman before tonight, and when I stopped feeling like my entire body was turned inside out, I was going to make her tell me all about it. I wasn't surprised that Key had plans of her own for our city.

Once Bayla was gone, I collapsed onto the floor. Pain radiated along every nerve in my body and I couldn't stop the ceiling from dipping in and out of focus. I heard Key make her way over to me. She sat down by my hip and reached out to trace her fingers over my eyebrows.

"What else did Race teach you while I was in the hospital?"

She laughed softly. "It was actually Booker. Race said he didn't want any part of putting a weapon in my hands. He said I was dangerous enough as it was. I asked Chuck and he said it was something you would want to show me how to do—handle a weapon and protect myself. I figured I better be prepared since someone is always trying to knock my devil off his throne, so Reeve suggested Booker and he hooked me up. Apparently I'm a natural, which is a good thing when all of heaven and earth is trying to take the man I love from me. I'm not ever going to watch someone hold a weapon on you or on me and not be able to do something about it again."

I should be annoyed but I wasn't. I was proud of her. She knew what it was going to take to stand by my side and protect what was ours.

"So, that talk you wanted to have about Bayla before all hell broke loose . . . maybe you want to fill me in on that now."

She breathed out a little laugh and shifted around so she was lying on her back in the middle of the living room next to me. "Later. We have time."

Yes, we did. Time we had fought for, died for, bargained for, and ultimately earned in order to be together. Even spending time with this woman couldn't come easy and that made me appreciate every second of it . . . and of her, more.

"You think that's the last of the people trying to kill you we'll see for a while?" She sounded like she was kidding.

"Not even close."

That was what it was like to be a dishonorable man with a horrific past in a wrecked city. The consequences never seemed to end and I had a lifetime of them gunning for me.

CHAPTER 19

Keelyn

Four months later . . .

The two men across from me in the elevator were talking in a language I didn't understand. That happened a lot with the kinds of people Nassir did business with. These particular men were Eastern European, and I knew enough and could tell by the way they were looking at me that they weren't talking about the fabulous, purple Michael Kors heels decorating my feet.

One of the guys kept looking at the substantial rock that was sitting on my left hand and nudging his buddy. I think the gist of their conversation was that Nassir obviously had a weakness if he was going to put that kind of jewel on my hand and let me be involved in their business, but since I didn't speak what I assumed was Albanian, I couldn't be sure. I just kept my eyes on them as the elevator rose up to Nassir's office, and refused to show any emotion as they continued to chatter away. One of the guys leered at me and licked his lips in a really graphic way and I considered telling him the elevator was wired for both video and sound but figured he would find that out the hard way soon enough. I smirked back at him as the doors whooshed open and revealed the plush office, Nassir on his proverbial throne, and Chuck and several of his men flanking his sides.

Everyone in the room was glaring at the two guests and I felt the level of their confidence and bluster plummet as they walked ahead of me into the office. They were immediately surrounded and checked for weapons. Of course they were armed. It didn't seem to matter if it was the good guys or the bad guys coming to see Nassir, whoever was knocking on his door came equipped with guns and an agenda. The two guests shot nervous glances at each other as they were disarmed and shoved into the chairs on the opposite side of that massive desk. I maneuvered my way around them and went to lean against the side of Nassir's leather chair. I put my arm across the top of it and he reached out a hand and placed it on my knee. Together we stared at the men, who were both now sweating profusely and nervously shifting their weight from side to side.

Nassir's thumb moved in a lazy circle on the inside of my knee and I saw one of the men gulp as he realized maybe I was more than just the hostess showing them to their meeting or a trophy that sat prettily on Nassir's shelf. That had been my biggest fear, but every single day he put something else in my hands, some part of the business, some part of his life to make sure I knew how equally invested he was in our future. We weren't simply partners; we were a team, and sometimes that made me feel like we were unstoppable.

"You come into my town without asking. You bring girls that are too young and have no say in whether or not they want to work for you. You make money off of them and then don't pay them a dime. You even had the nerve to try to recruit Point girls to work in your flophouses, and you think I'm going to let any of that slide?"

Really, the new skin peddlers had been quiet about what they were doing. If it hadn't been for one of the young girls they trafficked in escaping and running into Noe and asking her for help, there was a chance we would've never known. The young street hooligan had brought the battered and damaged girl to Nassir and I could see that he decided on the spot that hell was going to rain down on everyone involved in the operation. He took over the responsibility of vengeance and I took over making sure the girls got out of the city and somewhere safe. I was finding that for every one girl I managed to get somewhere safe and settled into a new life, three new ones popped up on the streets or on the stage to take her place. As long as there were choices for them to make, I felt like I was doing the right thing, and when I thought I couldn't love Nassir any more than I already did, he offered to help me fund the project with some of the legal money he made from the strip club.

I turned him down because it was my baby and it was my heart. And honestly I think him and the life he offered were sometimes too tempting for the girls to say no to. I used his contacts and his name when the doors I wanted to open wouldn't do so, but now that I had his ring on my finger, my own name had almost as much sway as his did, and that did more for the part of me that was worried about my losing my sense of freedom and self than any of the gestures Nassir made to keep me feeling included. I had my own power, and even if a good chunk of it came from being the one and only woman to tame the devil, then so be it.

The first step in Nassir's revenge plot was making the new operation think he wanted to go into business with them; that's why these two were here.

These were the moneymen. The men who decided where to set up shop and how much to spend on getting an operation going. They were the ones that paid human traffickers for warm bodies and made the johns pay up when they were done. These were the guys that couldn't turn down an opportunity to meet with the man in charge of the underground parts of the city when word got out that he might have an offer to make them. Greed made people stupid.

One of the men cleared his throat and in very broken English told Nassir, "We do what you do."

I felt Nassir tense, and if I could see his face I knew his golden eyes would be narrowed. "No. You force women to have sex and then profit off their suffering. You hold them captive and torture them. I'm simply a man that offers the people in this city a choice."

The hand that wasn't resting on my bent leg started tapping on the top of his desk. I knew he was really annoyed if he was allowing himself to express emotion like that. He was usually so calm and still when he faced down an opponent.

"I'm shutting you down and running you out of my city."

One of the guys threw up his hands. "You cannot!"

The hand that was on my knee lifted and reached for the laptop in front of him. He pushed a button and the monitors behind us lit up. I didn't have to look over my shoulder to know they would show not one but two of the brothels run by these thugs' bosses being raided by police and immigration officers. As much as Nassir didn't trust Titus, having a tenuous working relationship with the cop was proving to be beneficial. Titus hadn't batted an eye when Nassir called and asked him to help get the girls free and the competition out of town; neither did he jump on board without hesitation. It was a well-choreographed dance between the right side of the law and wrong. It all depended on the situation who was going to lead and who was going to follow, but so far both men had managed to navigate the dance floor without stepping on each other's toes.

"The police, immigration people, and the federal authorities are stripping everything you have down to the bones as we speak. There will be no more girls, no more johns, and no more ways for you to make money off of someone else's suffering."

The two foreign gangsters were baffled, and I could see that they literally had no clue what to do. They started to talk to each other in their native language, but the tone was frantic and the pace quick. There were a lot of hand movements and glances flying around the room in panic.

Nassir heaved a sigh and leaned forward in his chair. I reached out a hand and threaded it through his long hair so I could rest my fingers on the back of his neck. It was like petting a panther right before it pounced.

"Enough." The word wasn't in English and I saw even more panic and fear start to build in their expressions. "I understand every single word you are saying and understood every syllable when you told your partner that you were going to wait to get my wife alone and show her what a real man can do."

I knew they hadn't been talking about my shoes. I shook my head at them and clicked my tongue. That's right, suckers. WIFE. That big-ass diamond on my finger wasn't just for show and Nassir didn't have a weakness, he had a wife that he would kill for without a second thought.

"P-p-lease . . ." Of course they would ask for leniency for themselves when they had no intention of showing those poor girls they trafficked and traded any such thing.

"You're on a boat back to your homeland in the morning." I saw both the men sag in relief, thinking they were getting off easy, but I knew my devil wasn't done playing with them just yet. "But before you go, you'll be spending the night in our special holding facility under the club."

If they weren't deplorable men, I could almost feel sorry for them. Nothing good ever happened when you had to spend the night in the dungeon under the club.

Nassir inclined his head in Chuck's direction and the security team moved forward to secure the men who were now babbling incoherently and struggling to get free. Nassir pointed to the one that had made the lewd comments about me and told Chuck, "The one with the big mouth . . . give him a reminder that it's wise to think before you speak."

Chuck's gold tooth flashed as his grin lit up his dark face. He muttered, "Gladly," and hauled the struggling men out of the office. I watched them until the elevator swallowed them up and whisked them away.

I dug my fingers into the tense muscles at the back of Nassir's neck and asked, "Really? All he said was that he could show me what a real man is like?"

Nassir snorted and reached out to turn the screens off behind us and to shut down his computer.

"No. He said really disgusting, crude things that you don't need to hear and that I sure as hell don't need to picture anyone doing to my wife."

"Are they going to make it on the boat in one piece or more likely in pieces?"

He snorted. "Depends on how much of a hassle they want to give the boys. Either way they won't be in the Point after tomorrow."

He tugged on my hand and pulled me around so that I was in front of him with my rear end resting against the edge of his desk. His candy-colored eyes gleamed up at me. They always did when he called me his wife.

When he first asked me if I wanted to get married, I had laughed it off, thinking it was the painkillers and too many close calls in such a short amount of time. But then he asked me the next day and the next. He asked me every single day for a month if today was the day I wanted to be his wife, and on the last day I finally told him yes. It took me a minute to get used to the idea of settling into something so traditional and steeped in custom. That didn't feel like us but it was obviously something that mattered deeply to him, and when he showed me his soft side, his vulnerable side, I couldn't keep saying no.

He wasted no time. I had a ring by lunchtime and an officiant—along with Chuck and Reeve, because I couldn't think of anyone else to act as a witness for me—there by dinner for the ceremony. It was fast. It was simple. It was quiet and solemn. There was no flare or show to it. It was so unlike everything in the rest of our relationship that it made me cry because it felt so perfect and special.

It was such a weird and ever-evolving thing, this relationship of ours. Some days we seemed like a typical married couple, sitting on the couch watching movies together—the first one I made him sit through was *Pinocchio;* obviously— arguing about whose turn it was to do the dishes, making love softly and sweetly while we told each other how happy we were together. Other days we dealt with people trying to kill us, trying to arrest us, trying to get between us and make us weaker because as a unit we were invincible. The city had no idea what would happen when Hades handed over half of the underworld to Persephone. She came into her own and was unstoppable. Those were the days we fucked, tore at each other, couldn't get enough as we tried to cram as much life and time as we had together into every second of every day. We were equally appreciative and greedy. It was never the same and it was never boring. Each day left a mark, a memory that I was happy to hold on to, and I could tell that the number of good memories was overtaking the number of poisonous ones from the past. Every single day, no matter what kind of day it was going to be, I faced it being proud to have a place by Nassir's side, and I never regretted making that ultimate commitment to him.

My ring sparkled as I brushed my fingers across his high cheekbone. "How about you picture all the things *you* want to do to your wife instead." Sitting in front of him on this desk was not a new position for me. In fact, it was one of my favorites. I had a lot of new favorites because of him. There wasn't a boundary he didn't try to cross, a sexual fantasy he didn't fulfill, and yes, being tied up in actual rope as long as he was the one doing it was a lot of fun, and I now had a better understanding of why all the people in this club paid him so much money to chase down their needs.

His eyebrows lifted up and his teeth flashed as a wicked grin spread across his handsome-as-sin face.

"My office always turns you on." His fingers brushed up along my thighs, taking the hem of my tight dress with them. Seeing him behind that big desk playing lord and master over all he surveyed turned me on, and now that I knew he would make sure no one was watching what went on between us in here anymore, I never denied myself having a piece of him.

"No. You doing your thing always turns me on. Power is sexy and it has always looked so effortless and easy on you."

"Hmm . . ." He got to his feet, which forced me to actually sit up on the desk as he made room for himself between my spread legs. "It looks good on you too, Keelyn."

I got ahold of the buttons on the front of his shirt and started meticulously pulling each one free of its hole. Usually I would rip the thing open to get to all that smooth, bronze skin lying underneath, but we had to be somewhere in a little bit and that didn't leave time for a wardrobe change.

"Not as good as you look on me, Gates." I purred the words as he maneuvered the bottom of my dress all the way up to my hips. The glass top of the desk was cold underneath my backside but he was so hot and hard in front of me that I didn't even notice. When the sides of his shirt fell open, my eyes landed not only on that massive scar that now ran all the way down his breastbone but on the new black-and-gray ink that covered his pectoral muscle right over his heart. An old lock was firmly snapped closed and attached to a thick chain that wound its way in ink all across his chest, over his shoulder, and down to his wrist. He didn't wear a ring like I did, but that tattoo was his way of telling the world he was taken, locked up and bound, and I was the Key. I had the symbolic key as well. I liked his tattoo so much, was so moved by the gesture, that I had gotten a dainty little skeleton key tattooed on the inside of my wrist. We matched and I loved it.

He used his finger to push some of my hair out of my face and bent forward to kiss me. I ended up leaning back on my elbows and almost knocking his laptop to the floor. He didn't seem to notice, so I let him make love to my mouth while his impatient hand tugged at the top of my dress, trying to get at my breasts. The material was too tight for that, so he gave a frustrated groan and bit down on my lip. These were my favorite times with him, when it was half making love and half fucking like wild beings. It fit the two parts of the man he was and I felt it in every touch and every swipe of his tongue along mine.

Since he couldn't get at my breasts or the nipples that were pushing against the fabric, all but taunting him, he took a step back and sat back in his chair. I fell all the way back so that my head thunked against the glass when he grabbed each of my ankles in his hard hands and lifted them up so that my fancy purple shoes were next to my bare ass and I was wide open and exposed to his heated gaze. It made me shiver even though I felt like it was a thousand degrees inside the office.

He started off by kissing the inside of my knee, then trailed his tongue in a searing path up my thigh. It made my skin quiver and my tummy dip. I couldn't imagine a more wanton and vulnerable position to be in, and that's what made it so sexy. One of my hands curled into a tight fist of anticipation on my stomach and the other buried itself in the midnight locks at the top of his head. I knew exactly where this was going and knew from experience I needed something to hold on to.

He blew a hot breath across my slick center and then I felt his teeth nip at the most sensitive part of me. It was a stinging touch that had my back arching and my hand yanking on his soft hair. He just chuckled into my folds and repeated the motion, only to follow it with a penetrating lick of his tongue. The stinging and soothing went on like that until I couldn't see straight. The tiny burn of pain so quickly followed by the assault of pleasure was making me crazy. I could feel my body shaking, my muscles quivering, everything inside of me getting loose and wet. I was muttering his name over and over like some kind of incantation, and that just drove him on further.

I felt his fingers slide inside of me. Felt my body drag and pull at him as it begged for release. He curled those talented digits into me and stroked and wiggled until I was sure the top of my head was going to blow off at the double stimulation. I gasped in outrage when all of it was suddenly taken away right on the brink of an orgasm that I was sure would turn me inside out. I was going to scream at him that he better finish what he started when I looked down to see him brushing his mouth and chin, which were shiny with my desire for him, against the inside of my thigh before he climbed back to his feet and yanked his belt off and his pants open.

I loved when his eyes looked like melted gold and flowed like a river of want and need all over me. I adored when he got impatient and ruffled in his need to be inside of me.

He grabbed my ankle again and this time maneuvered my leg up so that my foot was resting on his shoulder as he leaned forward and aligned his straining erection with my opening. His hands hit the desk above my shoulders, and as he pressed into me a glint of humor sparked in his eyes.

"Have I ever told you how happy I am that your years of dancing made you so flexible?"

If I hadn't been full of hard cock and on the verge of exploding, I would've rolled my eyes at him or maybe smacked him. Instead I grabbed either side of his shirt and pulled him down so I could kiss him as he started to move in and out of me at a frantic pace. The position he had me in let him go so deep that I felt like he was in places he had never been before. I groaned and held on to him even tighter as he began to pound into me hard enough to move us both across the top of the desk.

We panted into one another. Breathed one another in, and when he pushed himself up just enough to get a hand between where we were joined so he could rub firm circles across my clit with his thumb, that was all it took for me. I came on a breathless wail and in a wash of pleasure so hot and fierce I was surprised it didn't scald him.

He kissed me hard, put my other leg up on his shoulder, got better leverage for himself, and hammered into me a few more times until he found his own completion and filled me up in a rush of his desire.

When we were both replete and wasted, he pulled out of me and I knew he was watching as he did so. He was always watching the different ways we were connected to each other and it always made me feel so special and important when he did.

He flopped back in his big leather chair and pulled open his desk drawer. Like I said, it wasn't the first time this desk had been used for funny business instead of real business. We were prepared now. We both cleaned up and got situated back into our clothes. He kissed me hard on the mouth and pulled me down into his lap.

"We're going to be late to the party."

I rubbed my thumb along his jaw. "Worth it. Besides, the graduate will only have eyes for one person there anyways."

He grunted. "Booker. That little girl is almost legal, and once she is, shit's gonna hit the fan."

She laughed. "Yeah. Race keeps trying to encourage her to do a study abroad program, but she isn't biting."

He laughed a little. "Well, some things are worth waiting for. If it's supposed to happen, then it will when the time is right."

Or they were just going to have to make the time right for them like we had done. It would be interesting to see how it all played out once the stunning teenager was out from under Race's watchful eye.

WE WERE IN the Range Rover just pulling into the parking lot in front of the condos on the docks when a familiar face appeared and seemed to be anxiously awaiting our arrival.

Stark was pacing back and forth in front of the complex with his hands shoved deep into his pockets and a scowl marring his face behind his glasses.

"I've been waiting for you to get here." He spoke to Nassir but his gaze swept over me as well. "I need your help."

Nassir reached for my hand and tugged me to his side. "What's the problem?"

Stark was often called in for security upgrades and other fact-finding ventures Nassir needed him to undertake. I thought I knew the man fairly well but I had never seen him this agitated or upset before. Clearly, neither had Nassir. He looked as confused and wary as I felt.

"The girl that I brought to you, the street kid that had the info on the kid you were looking for, is missing."

I frowned and watched Nassir narrow his eyes at the other man as he asked, "What do you mean missing? She lives on the street. How can you tell?"

Stark growled and lifted his hands to pull at his hair. "Because she came to me for help and I turned her away. I felt like an ass about it afterward and went to find her to tell her I changed my mind, but she's nowhere. No one has seen hide nor hair of her. It's like she vanished off the face of the earth a few weeks ago."

I ran my hand up Nasir's tense arm and told Stark, "She just brought a girl to us. She's the reason Nassir was able to get the Eastern Europeans out of the Point."

His slate-gray eyes sharpened on me. "When was that?"

Nassir frowned "About two weeks ago."

Stark's pacing slowed down and he let out a deep breath. "Maybe she's all right, then. I would just like to know for sure. The stuff she was asking me to help her with . . ." He shook his head. "It sounded like pretty bad news."

Nassir shifted next to me. "What was she into?"

Stark cleared his throat and looked down at his feet. "She helps kids in bad situations get out. Her newest project wasn't some reject from the Point or even some lost rich kid from the Hill. It was Julia Grace."

I balked not because Noe was doing exactly the same thing I was doing with far less resources but because the name Stark dropped was very familiar. I felt Nassir go stone still next to me. "The mayor's teenage stepdaughter, Julia Grace?"

Stark nodded. "Yeah. Noe says the girl is in bad shape. I guess the mayor is one messed-up asshole and the girl needs out of the house and out of town. Noe wanted me to hack into a government database and pull a bunch of sealed military records on the guy. I told her no, mostly to be a dick since she hocked all my stuff. But like I said, I had a change of heart and now I can't find her. I think she might be in trouble, but if you just saw her maybe it's not as bad as I'm making it out to be."

I groaned. "This is the Point . . . it's probably worse than you think it is. Two weeks is a long time to be missing."

He nodded slowly. "That's what I'm afraid of."

Nassir swore and pulled me to him so that he could wrap his arm around me. Every time he heard about a woman in trouble or being hurt, he always wanted me as close as I could get.

"I'll put some of my guys on it, put the word out that I'm looking for her. I'll help you find her if she's still in town."

"And if she's in trouble?" Stark sounded desperate.

"Then I'll help you get her out of it." And he would. Stark seemed to know it too because he muttered a hasty "thank you" and disappeared back across the parking lot.

I squeezed Nassir around the waist and turned my face into his throat. "I love it when you're a real boy."

I felt his lips brush the top of my head. "You made me that way."

I sighed in contentment. I adored being his conscience and his better half. I loved that our love was his tether to his humanity and the small measure of morality that he managed to hold on to after everything that had happened to him. I would happily spend the rest of my days keeping my devil away from most forms of damnation but occasionally I wanted to run wild and be hedonistic with him on Pleasure Island. After all, it was only fitting that I gave the devil his due after the patience he showed while he waited for me to grow and mature into a woman that could stand by his side and give just as good as she got. I would spend every second of every day we had together giving it to him.

AUTHOR'S NOTE

I LOVE THIS BOOK SO MUCH!!!

That is all . . . I hope you enjoyed reading Nassir and Key as much as I enjoyed writing them.

This world of the Point holds a special and important place in my heart. Sometimes an author really does have to write the story in her head and in her heart and hope for the best because something else might be what her audience is after. In this case, I had a different book due and a different series I was supposed to be working on. I should have been able to walk away from the Point and to focus on something that didn't tie my guts in knots . . . but I couldn't.

I was compelled to write this book. Possessed by the story and the characters, so much so that I couldn't even remember the names of the characters in the other book I was supposed to be writing. Maybe it was because I was in a shaky place emotionally and creatively. The darkness and despair in the Point were oddly comforting, and writing a man and a woman that cared so little about anyone else's definition of success because they had such a singular vision of what that word meant to them actually helped propel me onward and upward. Writing this book made me a better writer, and as ridiculous as it sounds, I think writing it has made me a better person as well.

This story reminded me that I will always be the girl who goes her own way . . . even when that way is an uphill climb. Because the view at the end can be that much more rewarding for the effort it took to get to it.

ACKNOWLEDGMENTS

Oh, my brave and daring readers, the ones who stick with me through thick and thin, who never waver and never falter . . . this book is for you.

You inspire me, you encourage me, you impress me, you delight me, and if you are here at the end of this book with me . . . anticipating the next one, you fulfill me and give meaning not only to my life but to my career and words. If you are here at the end of this book with me, you mean more to me than words can ever express . . . Thank you for taking a chance on something new and letting me grow and flourish.

Reading a book might not seem like such a big thing . . . but when it's this book, in this series, it's HUGE . . . so huge, and it matters so much to me.

I wish there were better words than "thank you" because I would shower you all with them.

I have to give my bestie, Heather; my very magical story sensei, Denise; and the fantastic Vilma a special thank you for reading this book in its infancy (a long, long time ago), when it was an ugly, sloppy mess. There was a lot of carnage on the page and in my mind as I was trying to tell this story, and these ladies were a huge help to me in getting it hammered out. My rough drafts are always exactly that . . . this one was the worst of the bunch . . . fitting for the man painted on the pages, I guess.

I also owe Cora Carmack a few beers and a couple hugs for listening to me ramble on about plot points and backstory in between whining about how hard it was to get right. Not to mention endless texts and swearwords when I couldn't make it work.

Amanda (seriously, I can't believe that you're still here sometimes and that I haven't scared you away), Jessie, Caroline, Molly, Elle, KP, Stacey, and Melissa . . . thanks for never wavering, for staying the course, for navigating the waters no matter how choppy and treacherous they might get. Thanks for your faith and belief when I have none of my own. Thanks for reminding me this is a team sport when I often feel like I'm playing, winning, and losing solo. I push and you guys push harder. We got a good thing going, so let's see how long we can keep it up.

Thanks to the best folks a girl could have . . . if you see them at an event with me, give them a squeeze and tell them Jay loves them and tell my dad his mustache is cool . . . it really is the coolest.

Hey, Mike, you rock; I couldn't make it through most weeks without you, no joke. Thank you for always being rock solid, for being there, and for being my go-to guy for all things. Thanks for being the best movie date ever and for always sharing the popcorn.

To all the authors who are so disgustingly talented and so inordinately gracious with their time and gifts, thank you for being my inspirations and my friends. You are all brilliant and who you are as people as well as storytellers is unparalleled. This huge thanks and virtual hug goes out to Jennifer Armentrout, Jenn Foor, Jenn Cooksey, Jen McLaughlin, Tiffany King, Tina Gephart, Tillie Cole, Joanna Wylde, Kylie Scott, Cora Carmack, Emma Hart, Renee Carlino, Penelope Douglas, Kristen Proby, Amy Jackson, Nichole Chase, Tessa Bailey, J. Daniels, Rebecca Shea, Kristy Bromberg, Adriane Leigh, Laurelin Page, EK Blair, SC Stephens, Molly McAdams, Crystal Perkins, Tijan, Karina Halle, Christina Lauren, Chelsea M. Cameron, Sophie Jordan, Daisy Prescott, Michelle Valentine, Monica Murphy, Erin McCarthy, Liliana Hart, Laura Kaye, Heather Self, and Kathleen Tucker. Seriously, I admire every author on this list, and what they add to this business and to my writerly life. If you are looking for a solid book to read, I promise one of theirs won't disappoint.

Last but not least, thanks to my furry little entourage for being my heart and putting up with my office renovation, which made us all miserable during the revisions of this book. *Woof!*

If you would like to contact me, there are a bazillion places you can do so!

Check my website for updates, release dates, and all my events:

www.jaycrownover.com

I'm also all over the interwebs!

Please feel free to join my fan group on Facebook:

https://www.facebook.com/groups/crownoverscrowd/
https://www.facebook.com/jay.crownover
https://www.facebook.com/AuthorJayCrownover/
Follow me on Twitter: @jaycrownover
Follow me on InstaGram: @jay.crownover
https://www.goodreads.com/Crownover
http://www.donaghyliterary.com/jay-crownover.html
http://www.avonromance.com/author/jay-crownover

**STARK'S STORY COMING
SOON IN *DIGNITY* . . .**

Keep reading for an exclusive sneak peek at the next Saints
of Denver novel from *New York Times* bestselling author Jay
Crownover,

RIVETED

Everyone else in Dixie Carmichael's life has made falling in love look easy, and now she is ready for her own chance at some of that happily ever after. Which means she's done pining for the moody, silent former soldier who works with her at the bar that's become her home away from home. Nope. No more chasing the hot-as-heck thundercloud of a man and no more waiting for Mr. Right to find her; she's going hunting for him . . . even if she knows her heart is stuck on its stupid infatuation with Dash Churchill.

Denver has always been just a pit stop for Church on his way back to rural Mississippi. It was supposed to be simple, uneventful, but nothing could have prepared him for the bubbly, bouncy redhead with doe eyes and endless curves. Now he knows it's time to get out of Denver, fast. For a man used to living in the shadows, the idea of spending his days in the sun is nothing short of terrifying.

When Dixie and Church find themselves caught up in a homecoming overshadowed with lies and danger, Dixie realizes that while falling in love is easy, loving takes a whole lot more work . . . especially when Mr. Right thinks he's all wrong for you.

PROLOGUE

M y mom met her prince charming when she was a fresh-
man in college and my dad leaned over and asked to
borrow a pen so he could take notes. Rumpled, obviously
hungover but flashing a smile that promised a good time and
with a twinkle in his eyes, he was impossible to resist. She
always told me and my sister that it happened that fast. In a
split second she knew he was the one for her.

It was a sweet story. One that my parents shared with us
often, both still sharing private smiles and eyes still twinkling,
but neither one of us gave it much thought until my younger
sister met her very own prince before she was old enough to
drive. It was during a hard time in my family, hard for all of
us, but especially for her. She's always been the baby, been
spoiled and treated like a princess. When the attention was
yanked off of her in a really ugly way, she was lost and let the
family tragedy consume her. Lost in grief and confusion, she
somehow managed to sign herself up for auto shop instead of
an extracurricular that actually made sense for my very girly,
very feminine younger sibling. She spent five minutes in that

noisy, greasy garage, but she spent years and years leaning on and loving the quiet, enigmatic auburn-haired boy she met in those five minutes. He saved her and even though she was way too young to know anything about anything, she had the same story that my mother did . . . she just knew he was the one for her.

It happened fast in my family. We fell hard and we didn't get up once we fell. We stayed down and we loved hard and deep. I also learned as I watched all my friends, the men I worked with, the women that I considered sisters of the heart, that when it was right for anyone it happened fast and that they did indeed *just know*. They knew when it was right. They knew when it was going to last. They knew when it was worth fighting for. They knew they had found the person that might not necessarily be perfect, but they were without a doubt perfect for them. *They just knew.*

So I waited, admittedly impatiently and anxiously for my shot, for my turn to fall. I waited through my family healing, to come back with a love that was even stronger. I waited through my sister screwing up and desperately trying to repair her perfect. I waited through weddings and babies. I waited through danger and drama. I waited through one bad date and one failed relationship after another. I waited through nights alone and nights spent with the occasional someone I knew wasn't *the* one for me. I waited and waited as good men fell to even better women, all the while wondering when it was my turn. I waited and watched love that was easy and love that was hard, telling myself I was far more prepared for my fall than anyone else around me was. I wanted it so bad I could taste it . . . but the more I waited the more certain I was never going to fall.

I would be lying if I said that I didn't think Dash Churchill was something special the second he walked into the bar where I worked—all coiled tension, sexy swagger, and a black cloud of attitude hanging over him that seemed to dim even the brightest summer days. I had eyes and I had a vagina so all the things that I thought were special were the things those parts of my anatomy couldn't miss. Long-limbed, a body that looked like it was ripped from the cover of a *Men's Health* magazine, bronze skin, unforgettable eyes and mouth that even though it was constantly frowning brought to mind every single dirty, sexy thing a pair of lips like that was capable of doing. I liked the way he looked . . . a lot . . . but I couldn't say I much liked him. He was sullen, distant, uncommunicative, and there was an air about him that marked in no uncertain terms that he was dangerous. But more than that he was a very unhappy individual, and no amount of rest, relaxation, and good friends seemed to shake that dark storm that hung over him. It was a warning that I was smart enough to heed. I liked my days spent basking in the sun, not dancing in the rain.

I was friendly to Church because I was friendly to everyone. The first month or so we had an uneasy working relationship that involved me dancing around him while every other single and not-so-single woman that came into the bar where we worked did their best to catch his eye. It worked out well for me and seemingly for him so I went back to waiting for my perfect, my fairytale, my heroic knight, my unmatched hero. He had to be out there somewhere and I was starting to think if he wasn't looking for me I needed to start looking for him. My patience was wearing thin and my typically affable attitude was starting to get just as cloudy and gray as the one that hung over Church.

But then it happened and *I just knew*. I knew like I had never known anything as clearly and as unquestionably in my whole life. I knew with a rightness that shot through my soul and made my heart flip over in my chest.

I was trying to cash out a group of overly intoxicated and obviously difficult young men. It wasn't anything new. I'd been a cocktail waitress for a long time and knew how to handle myself and the customers. This group was no better or worse than any other one I'd had to deal with in all my years slinging drinks and working the floor, but they were loud and the things they were saying were easily heard throughout the bar. Some of it wasn't so bad. They liked my hair (curly and strawberry blond, who didn't like my damn hair?) and they liked the way my shirt fit tight and snug across my chest. I was a solid D cup, so again, who didn't like my tits? But they also had a lot to say about my ass, apparently it was too big for my small frame, and they didn't love my freckles. That red hair was authentic and as real as it could be so there wasn't much I could do about the colored specks that dotted the bridge of my nose and brushed the curve of my cheeks.

I had pretty thick skin; you had to when you worked in a bar, and liquor loosened tongues. I was ready to brush the entire conversation off and snatch the credit card off the table when I felt a hand on my lower back and a storm not just brewing, but collecting and gathering, ready to unleash hell at my back.

"You good, Dixie?" The question made me freeze and it wasn't just because it was asked into my ear with that slow southern drawl. It wasn't because he was so close I could feel every line of muscle in his massive body and both the heat of his skin and the chill of his icy anger pressing into my back.

No, I froze, riveted to the spot and stunned stupid because in twenty-six years no one had ever bothered to ask me if I was good. They always assumed I was.

I was the girl that could handle myself and everyone else around me.

I was the girl that never asked for help.

I was the girl that always smiled even when that smile hurt my face.

I was the girl that always had time for a friend even when I really didn't have that time.

I was the girl that everyone ran to with a problem because I would drop everything to help fix it even if it was unfixable.

I was the girl that never let anything or anyone drag me down and fought to keep everyone else up with me.

I was the girl that everyone always assumed was good . . . so they never asked . . . but he did and the world stopped. At least the world before I fell headfirst into the kind of love that was bound to hurt with Dash Churchill.

I gripped my pen and struggled to clear my throat. "I'm good, Church." My voice was barely a breath of sound and I felt his touch press even deeper into my lower back.

"You sure?" No I wasn't sure. I was as far from good as I had ever been and I had no clue what to do with it.

I gave a jerky nod and blew out a breath which had him

taking a step away from me. I looked at him over my shoulder and he returned the look. There was still no warmth in his fantastic eyes. There was no change in the harsh expression on his face. There was no knowledge that he had just fundamentally changed my life.

He was simply doing his job, making sure everything in the bar was okay and that the staff was safe, meanwhile I was shoved, arms falling, legs kicking, a scream ripped from my lungs in love with him because I might *know* he was it for me, but it was evident Church didn't have a clue.

No one had ever given me any idea how to handle it when the right one came along, but you weren't the right one for him.